A Blunt Grace

a novel

J. M. Unrue

Hardcover **ISBN:** 9798853413139

Paperback **ISBN:** 9798853415416

Other Fiction by the author—

The Loser Fandango and other tales of Americana

Van Boorean's Hill

Atlanta en Regalia

One

When all the votes were in and tallied, Eddie Lee Edwards was a lowlife. Crown to brow at a forty-five degree angle, bristled pate hostile to brush or comb, beak like the dorsal fin of a mud shark, sullen mouth so disproportionately small fit only for whistling and spitting—and he was a lousy whistler.

Scrunched shoulders bearing nothing, spindly arms averse to labor, skeletal fingers with nails gnawed midway to the quick, he moved inexorably slow on spider's legs and flat feet. A blind man would've thought he weighed three hundred pounds as he shuffled along.

Instead, he was a hundred-forty pound excrescence of Darwin's bane, a cartoon vulture-boy, hapless, feckless, pointless, and utterly devoid of introspection—misspelled graffiti on a bathroom wall, a crumbled dollar bill in a correct change only machine.

He had even been denied the benefit of the name Edward. Eddie Lee, legal and done, spawn of a mother bereft of decorum.

Traci, his *mater inopia*, had once been lovely though bore a dullard's mark from birth and beget two children a dozen years apart by two vaguely remembered men. Eddie Lee, of course, and Sharonia. She worked second shift at a trucker's plaza on I-69 northeast of Indianapolis and was in the habit of boarding and bedding vagabond truckers on a cyclical basis.

The trio lived in a mobile home park along a dirt-and-gravel road in boilerplate fashion as fixed in the cosmic construct as the lunar orbit, if not for some anomalous genetic mutations—some rare *cadeau inattendu.* The little girl, Sharonia, was a brilliant child.

Eddie Lee was a thief, and a prodigy.

By the time he was six years old he could palm a sugar packet without detection at his mother's workplace. When he was twelve, allowed to order coffee for a pre-puberty buzz, he could produce said packet as if from some parallel dimension without perceivable motion.

His artistic development was not without difficulty. Successful thievery required more than dexterity but stealth, audacity, and calmness of spirit. Copping a few bills from the teacher's lounge so deftly as to defy physical law meant nothing if his mere presence aroused suspicion.

Still, he had discovered his province and providence. Fingertips as thin as fried eggs made nimble and taught to grasp and hide within themselves a multitude of small treasures. Success bred confidence. Confidence bred purpose. Purpose bred necessity. Necessity bred success.

The artiste lacked only a milieu for his inspiration, a canvas worthy of his craft, a purpose fit for his embarkation. One serendipitous—if ironic—moment, an epiphany came upon him as if delivered by God Himself. Church.

He was sixteen years old and had never seen the interior high walls of a church. His original thought was to rob the place once he determined where the money was stashed between the offering collection and the deposit. Worse, he sat through an entire service before realizing Christians didn't trust anyone, either, and kept the funds under lock and key, usually guarded by at least one zealot until the bank run.

Then, as the offering plates were passed, Eddie had another epiphany, though creeping as slowly as polar dawn, with God patiently nodding until Eddie Lee finally grasped the divine intent of his atrophied feelers.

The following Sunday he reappeared bearing a few shabby dollar bills. During the hymn and hush of the offertory, as the brass-rimmed platen moved hand-to-hand in his direction, he neatly plopped the ones into the plate amid the smiles of his fellow worshippers...and plucked a twenty at the same time, cradling the bill in his palm until the prize could be placed in a pocket.

He was sixteen bucks to the good.

Thus began his calling, his ontogenesis, his holy mission.

He learned quickly. The louder the preacher, the greater the odds that congregants would use cash. He would sit at the end of a row nearest those who waved twenties like semaphore flags. Some folded multiple bills inside each other, simplifying his task. Services were held multiple times on Sundays. At a large community church he could move about unnoticed as the basket passed him three separate times.

By the time he was seventeen he was averaging six services a week, pledging his soiled currency and reaping about three hundred dollars. He was never greedy and came to be recognized, if unnamed, as a faithful disciple and proof positive that the ugly and malformed are yet established in God's enduring love.

At eighteen he had nearly twenty thousand dollars rolled, banded, and hidden in baking powder tins throughout his habitat. The small tribe remained poor though none the wiser. Eddie Lee began to probe the internet for greener pastures, seeking some enclave where mega-churches flourished along the fruited plain. He loved his job but wanted to cut back to four services a week. The preaching made him surly.

One Saturday night just after he turned nineteen, he returned home from the arcade to find his mother sitting in her robe on the arm of a chair while her paramour, who Eddie did not recognize, sat smiling and counting money. The Rumford tin sat open in the man's lap, the red label Eddie thought was an Indian but wasn't, gazing indifferently in his direction.

Eddie paled. "Where'd you get that?"

The trucker snickered and Traci beamed as if she'd found Jesus.

"It was right there in your dresser," she said innocently. "I was gonna lend Gene one of your sweaters and there it was. Where'd you get it?

"It's mine!" Eddie protested and reached as Gene slapped his hand away.

"Probably stole it," Gene grunted. "Finders keepers I say."

Eddie Lee was in a rage and this was as alien to him as clean underwear. His furnace fired, brought to a boil, and threatened to spew like a dog full of raw bacon. This was his promised land money, money he had suffered through hundreds of pestiferous sermons to earn. He stomped into the kitchen near tears, a shriek welling up in his throat.

The first item he found was a forty-ounce bottle of Big Bear malt liquor, empty except for a couple inches of backwash. He snatched the bottle by the neck and slammed Gene in the back of the head. The trucker slumped bleeding. Traci screeched and reached and Eddie backhanded her in the face, sending her cowering.

As his mother squalled and Gene groaned, Eddie Lee struggled to recall all his hiding places—between the slat under the bed, taped to the back of the mirror, stuck deep inside a pair of sneakers so old and rank a buzzard would recoil. He found them all, shoved them in a canvas bag with a few clothes and hurried to the door amid the chaos.

"Where ya going, Eddie Lee?"

He turned, his little sister at six stood wide-eyed, lip trembling. His expression softened.

"Gotta leave, baby. You be a good girl, okay?:

Then he was gone without a backward glance.

Eddie Lee had over twenty-five thousand dollars in cash when he landed in Union Hill, North Carolina, at the center of a triangle between the mountains of Asheville, the billows of Raleigh, and the red dirt of Charlotte. He had heard everyone thereabouts were high on church and a man couldn't walk five blocks in any direction and not find a ripe one. Easy pickin's so to say, and he set about to make his fortune.

He visited them all, honing his science, realizing the difficulty in sorting the indigent from the prosperous by the church's facade or the general aspect of the redeemed. A nicer edifice often meant checks. Some of the ready-cash ones catered to black people and no way could he fit in. He was a diligent student, however, and within two months he had his route and was making good money.

He also met Shorty and Sandy, Shorty's plus-sized plus one, though not at church. Shorty had approached Eddie Lee at the local pool hall and tried to sell him some pot that came all the way from Hawaii. Eddie Lee had never smoked pot before but grew to love it. A nice buzz was good for a comedown after the stresses of the job, not the least of which was wearing a tie and dress shoes.

Their friendship grew and soon Eddie Lee moved into the spare bedroom of their white-board old house. He didn't even have to tell them what he did for a living as Shorty likewise adhered to *omerta*. Shorty wasn't much of a dealer, had acquired only a small network and didn't seem troubled much by this. A substantial portion of profit went into research, anyway, and the house was always layered in fog.

Sandy worked the graveyard shift at the Laughing Willie bakery for ten bucks an hour. She never slept well in the daytime, grumbled a lot, and tried to nudge Shorty toward greener pastures, without much success. She also complained that breathing all that secondhand reefer smoke gave her bad dreams, but Shorty simply advised her to go with it.

Eddie Lee learned the warning signs of her distemper and kept to himself as much as possible. He bought a laptop and spent much of his day at a coffee shop clearing his head from the skunk weed and plotting his next move. He was always on the lookout for ecclesiastical utopia.

Despite its relative proximity to bustling populations, Union Hill was a small town. All of Davis County held only about a hundred thousand people. Still, his stash of cash was growing, he was earning four hundred dollars a week, and only had to pay three hundred dollars a month room and board. He had money in his pocket, a roof over his head, and all the powdered mini donuts he could eat.

Two

Arthur Bowman Carter III was neither the full disclosure of an acronym nor a CPA firm, but the name of the Davis County District Attorney. Called Bow by his friends, he was born with a silver teat in his mouth, or found one very soon thereafter.

His father, Arthur Jr., also a lawyer, had dipped his ringed pinkie into everything in the county and beyond. No road was paved, no building erected, no land zoned or rezoned without his embossed stationery somewhere in the file. He rarely practiced law in the adopted sense but was a friend to governors, senators, judges, and county commissioners.

Bow was predestined for the law, the freshest tooth on a durable, yet cranky, gear. Dynasties were asthmatic if not downright stertorous as the law of diminishing returns overwhelmed genetic evolution. He majored in poli-sci at Wake Forest and graduated from its law school on the four-year plan. As a legacy, he was admitted with prejudice and was given a pass on his protracted senior year when the old man died of an aneurism after missing a four-foot putt.

Bow was not a conventionally handsome man. His legs were too short for his torso and at five-nine should've been six-one. He was plain with brown everything, though was trim with good teeth and genuine smile.

He joined his father's firm and when the district attorney retired, ran as his father's son and won.

He married the first woman who slept with him, she, too, from another prominent family from Davis County, the Sparrows, who had made and maintained a fortune in budget furniture, even as more of this moved offshore to smaller, browner fingers.

Marie Sparrow Carter was also plain, but well-kept with an outer veneer of warmth and inner reserve. Aloof to outsiders, perhaps—but there were so few of these—she gave young Bow her body for the promise of an auspicious tomorrow, though without joy or delight and only vain satisfaction. They had a daughter, Ellen, now grown to womanhood with a daughter of her own, and had long since settled into a life of repose and small-town social calendars.

Oblivious to ordinary stresses lest generations of equilibrium be impeded, they lived in a balloon of stale air and were oblivious to this as well.

Bow was forty-eight, nearing forty-nine, and lived a life of good fortune as there were very few serious crimes in the district. He dispatched drunks, batterers, and those behind on their child support with the same staid conviction as his weekly sorties with his wife—dispensed just as quickly.

There was talk of a Congressional campaign the next year, though no one knew how to appeal to the Bohemians of Ashe County as these represented sixty percent of district voters. Bow secretly relished the fact. He had long-since abandoned ambition and never had much anyway. A purposeful, if unstimulating career, a good wife, a happy family, and the amity of his constituents were all that really mattered to him. That and a beautiful little granddaughter who called him Poppy.

Bow and Eddie Lee had crossed paths only once and that was seven years ago. This had been a watershed moment for them both, though Bow had been happy to return to scolding shirkers and low-enders. Shorty's murder was a vaporous memory and life was not built upon vaporous memories.

The rotund Sandy had been called out to work second shift, worked a double, and returned home the next morning smelling of honey bun glaze only to find Shorty dead on the floor, a gaping wound in his breadbasket, and a look of bewilderment on his immobile countenance. She found Eddie Lee sleeping the sleep of the unperturbed and called the police. The police found wide swaths of fresh blood on one of Eddie's T-shirts in the hamper and a bloody knife wrapped inside. Later, Sandy would testify that she was missing that very implement.

The trial of the decade (at least in those parts) lasted three weeks. Eddie had a public defender who railed against the unpolished nature of the evidence as indirect and incidental. Eddie did not hire an attorney because he did not want anyone to know he had money or its source. This became counterproductive and ultimately purposeless during cross-examination when he unwisely took the stand in his own defense.

"Isn't it true you have no visible means of support and were living off the good graces of Mr. Turner?"

"You mean Shorty?"

"I mean the *victim,* sir."

"I paid 'em three hundred dollars a month," he said proudly.

"Really. How did you manage this?"

Eddie pondered, his dull visage cycling through sludge until the dimmest of lights rose unobserved. "I stole that money fair and square. But I never killed nobody."

As titters rose among the court and the gavel fell, Bow smirked and faced the jury. "So, you're a murderer *and* a thief."

Sandy testified that Eddie had designs on her. This elicited a grunt-gag reflex from the defense table but was believable considering Eddie's sheer dearth of éclat, and despite the fact her stovepipe thighs echoed with the whish-whish of her hose upon her every step. She also testified that the night before the event she'd informed Eddie she'd decided to stay with Shorty and not abscond with the defendant as he'd proposed. Another groan from the defense and the gavel fell again.

Evidence notwithstanding, Bow's glorious closing argument, his *coup de maître*, brought all gathered into apostolic reverence for the honor of civilized men, which the defendant so obviously lacked.

"This was a crime of passion, yes, but more, a crime of desperation, of envy, a crime of desires no one should abide. This...this...man without conscience not only killed an innocent. He killed one of our own..."

Over the strident objections of Eddie's attorney, the fact that Shorty was a drug dealer and all-around reprobate was not allowed into evidence as he was never arrested. Eddie Lee was sentenced to life in prison with a minimum of twenty-five years. Thus began a corrective redirection of Eddie Lee Edwards sordid life.

Prison is no place for a thief, or at least one still practicing. Soon after he arrived, and determined to keep his skills finely attuned, Eddie Lee annexed two cookies, three cigarettes (though he did not smoke), a beaver-shot polaroid of Earl Ashby's lady love, and a guard's whistle—before he got caught with a silver dollar from the eighty year-old trusty who ran the library.

Earl was a genuine killer with little tolerance for the finer criminal arts. He broke all of Eddie's fingers. Not satisfied, he broke them all again when they healed. Others joined the alliance, even those who didn't even know Eddie Lee. This became an outré *cause celebre*, some mondo Neanderthal one-upmanship as to who could deliver the most damaging body shot upon the thief without discovery.

If not for the thrice-daily abuse, Eddie would have admired the stealth in which the inmates operated. By the end of the first year, Eddie Lee had been in the infirmary six times, the last when they had to remove his spleen. He was placed in solitary confinement after that.

There he went mad. As in owl-shit crazy, the mayor of bonkersville, in *sumamente loco*. As in whiplash ganglia and backfiring neurons and overloaded salivary glands. With no human contact for the bulk of the day, he blithely bounced a rubber ball against the wall of his cell. Other inmates on the row roared and gnashed and pled with the guard to take the damn ball away from him—and the guard complied to keep the peace.

Later, Eddie Lee was found trying to suffocate himself with his pillow. Unfortunately, he would pass out and his grip would automatically ease. He was given methaqualone in severe doses, and as he had no access to Grateful Dead recordings, could only sit and slobber in lude-nirvana.

During year four, and in that informal meeting time between shift changes in the guards' locker room, one told a newbie about the wack job in 8-C who had made a plate out of petrified watermelon rind and spent the day plucking rectangular pieces of paper from it. The story always evoked chortles and fraternity, and Eddie Lee passed into legend.

Destiny spat in Bow's direction and hit him square on the forehead. The long-term Democratic Congressman got his pecker caught in the wrong bush. While this was a faux pas in polite society, the transgression barely registered in the dulled theater of politics. What stirred the loins of the populace was that the damsel in question was the daughter of the Republican whip and only seventeen. Jailbait was gauche but with a right-winger? Nay.

Bow would run as a moderate Republican. The Judge, a white-haired lion who had been a co-conspirator of the elder Mr. Carter, and had recently retired, was leading the charge. Elise Harris had been Bow's right-hand woman for nearly a decade, and had also been instrumental in the Eddie Lee affair, and was considered an apt replacement as prosecutor.

Elise was death in black underwear. Raven-haired, pretty in a generic way, though perfectly formed, was never known to show her teeth when she smiled, though they were near-flawless. Fundamentally lazy at her craft, she managed to gain the confidence of all about her by long hours staring at files or the computer screen while scenes from a second-rate romance novel pirouetted through her head.

She was smart enough to remain unattached and celibate in Davis County. Through much trial-and-error, she maintained a triad of lovers sequestered in three different cities, Durham, Charlotte, and Columbia, South Carolina. She rotated each in sequence, unless an unforeseen scheduling conflict interfered, and from Friday evening until Sunday afternoon she thrashed and yipped her way through whatever energy her nervous system had stored during the week. Every fourth weekend was reserved for whichever of the three lotharios was the most libidinous at the time, gleaned from phone sex

Only her pug, Chuck, was on the receiving end of authentic affection, and he was the most neurotic creature in the solar system.

Three

Many of the current day anthropology weinerheads believe they have uncovered the whole of human ancestry. Not only that, they believe they have grasped most of how we once were, and how we came to be in such a sorry state.

Their indisputable thesis is this: we grew bigger brains and the other apes did not. This allowed us to become smarter. We developed more neurons and drew energy from our gut and muscles to keep the forge aglow. All other species simply lacked sufficient tools (or impetus) to become more like us.

Cetaceans lack hands and feet. No species wants a greater capacity for thought without the proper means to exploit it. What porpoise would choose to design a bicycle knowing the implement could neither be made nor utilized by its maker?

Experts advance the notion that current human intelligence began with one mutation, then other mutations as the first mutation made things crackle. This is why no other ape-kind evolved into genii, though there was once a chimp who could recite the alphabet in sign language while fondling itself with one foot and eating a banana with the other.

We are all prone to revisionism, especially when we run out of ideas. Perhaps this theory is overworked and overdone. Apes have it good and are content to remain delightfully off-center. There is little in the sagacious world that appeals to them. Too much responsibility. Too much wear-and-tear. Bad television.

In light of germane events, perhaps we should consider an alternate cause-and-effect.

What if the early ancestors of Homo Sapiens (us), began to cogitate first, and *then* the brain grew? One threw a sharp stick at a rat, and another realized the same method could be used to snag something larger—something that did not taste the way two-day-old B.O. smelled—the bumps and bruises attendant to such an escalation temporarily suspended. This would grow fifteen—twenty new brain cells. The real jolt came when a third person, probably a female, learned that the meat of any animal tasted *fantastico* when held over the lava pit for a time, with fewer post-repast dashes to the woods an added bonus.

The more the old tater is worked, the bigger it becomes, just like any other muscle. This doesn't happen in a year or even a century. Thinking is as much a long-term inherited trait as an overbite. Humankind may have taken certain pauses—such as remaining in the cold and freezing to death instead of migrating to fairer climes (then again, Canadians are still doing this)—but once a boulder begins to roll, it usually doesn't stop until an immoveable force gets in the way, oft times an entire village.

We think, therefore knowledge expands.

This is not physical growth in the sense of growing heads as big as pumpkins but in the exponential increase of brain cells and the connections between them. Additionally, as previously posited, this required less vacant space than new sources of energy. In order to accommodate such upgrades, pre-football man had to eat more, relax more, and sleep more. This was deemed as grandly copacetic until entire clans grew fat and lethargic and were eaten by very large cats with very large teeth.

So why does it matter? What difference could it make if a bigger brain initiated deeper thought, or deeper thought prompted a bigger brain?

Carelessness.

The human mind was not meant for such amplification. This is evident today in Washington, D. C., even after thousands of generations.

Had our brains ripened first, we would have been smart enough to stop thinking. Everything we needed was already available. Half a million years ago we could already hunt, farm, find shelter, hide, eat, drink fermented berries, and have sex. Basic language was sufficient. Having a few scribbles on the tree across from the poop pit supplied sufficient reading materials.

We wanted for nothing. Thus, we would have gotten smarter at our own pace, in our own way, and only as necessary—as in never showing your erection to the female in the next cave over when your mate is looking—or make faces at a dire wolf.

We would have been happy and not burdened by existential questions and contemplations of our potential, or our roles in the universe. We would have no doubt thrived, and eventually devised our own entertainments, i.e. Caveman Reality Theater, where the tribe's worst slackers would be tied to a tree outside a bear's den, daubed with honey, and watched as they struggled to escape before the bear got wind of them. The one not eaten could rejoin the group.

Instead, we thought. We were compelled to think, just as one with an empty stomach is compelled to eat, or a man with an itchy scrotum is compelled to scratch. We could not stop ourselves. Our brains grew, and we thought, even about why our brains were growing.

Couldn't we have simply stopped thinking and ended the process? No. Once a hunter speared the weird black cat with the white stripe down its back, there was no undoing it. He was ejected and shunned, and forced to live skinless for the duration.

We think because a stone was cast upon the universal pond and the ripples expanded. We even think about the content of the stone, and why there are ripples in the first place, and did so before we discovered hallucinogens.

We had it all and we blew it.

Now look at us. Everything leads to carelessness. We take unnecessary risks. We make extremely poor decisions. We talk too much. We mate with the wrong people. We watch cable news. We elect self-absorbed sociopaths. We floor it when we see a yellow light. We clean out our gutters with a ladder two feet too short. We leave our computers up at work with www.nakedweightlifters.com on the screen. We judge the efficacy of last Sunday's pizza by how long we can smell it before turning away.

Every thought beyond what is necessary to function creates carelessness.

Positive results prompt continuation. Negative results prompt cessation with less repetition as time passes. This was as much intelligence as we needed.

We do stupid things, not because we don't believe they are stupid, but because we believe we are too smart to get ourselves into a jam because of them.

We should have left well enough alone.

Then we wouldn't have hummus, soy milk, colonoscopies, daytime talk shows, hash tags, pleather, fanny packs, Tik Tok, or the banjo.

Intelligence led to suspicion. Suspicion led to curiosity—primarily as a palliative to ennui. Curiosity led to discovery. And discovery, as it so often does in the *faux pas* pantheon of human predilection, led to disaster—in this instance entangling the placid yet unwary Mr. Carter, Esquire, in its lubricious clutches.

Duke Law had a small group of third-year students who reviewed closed capital cases for sport, eschewing basketball or any other collegiate diversions in favor of the doctrine of juris prudence. One, Clara Barnwell, and pray God who among us would ever survive unscathed bearing the moniker Clara at twenty-five years of age, drew the dusty carton containing the slag of Eddie Lee Edwards.

Clara had a round featureless face where nose, cheek, mouth, and eyes seemed extemporaneously applied to a flat surface, except for thick Clark Kent glasses. She was fated for the ACLU in due course, whether her mien was a determining factor or not.

She was still stewed in the pain of idealism, at least for the miscreants of the world, and several things about the Eddie Lee case struck her as odd. Believing in ignorance but not gross stupidity, she could not believe Eddie Lee would stab a man, wipe the blood on one of his own shirts, put the knife and shirt in the most conspicuous place, then go to bed. (Of course she had never met Eddie Lee). She searched Eddie Lee's alibi—he was at church pursuing his trade when the crime occurred.

No proof existed, of course, no witnesses or friends who could attest to this. Even the people he sat beside in church could not remember him, much the same way amnesiacs blot out traumatic events. She Google-Mapped the area and got a feel for the geography. She laid out the route and all the streets between the ramshackle house and the church—a little less than a mile between the two and Eddie Lee did not have a vehicle.

Time of death had been placed at about eight p.m. Eddie Lee had said he left home at 6:30. She watched security camera footage from several businesses along the way. These had already been reviewed by the District Attorney's office. Nothing showed Eddie Lee in transit. The first image of him was at about 8:30 outside Disciple Baptist Church, caught in all his finery by an ATM camera across the street. Naturally, he could have murdered the victim and still have been a mile away in half an hour, though the image displayed no perspiration, no tension, no sense of hurry, no weariness from the trek.

She read Eddie Lee's original statement to the police.

"I go to different churches on Sunday night, whichever one feels right to me. Sometimes I don't know 'til I get there. I didn't go through town. I was thinking about Oak Avenue Baptist and took shortcuts through people's yards. Why didn't I stay? I got there and found out there was going to be, like, four people getting baptized and that was going to be at least two hours, so I moved on to Disciple."

When grilled about being in close proximity to such carnage as he arrived home, and not noticing the deceased, he said, "I went in through the back door and got in bed. I didn't see nothing."

Not a single usable camera shot could be found between the two churches. Clara, being a bright penny, played a hunch. She called Oak Avenue and discovered there had indeed been multiple baptisms that night because one of them had been the nephew of the church secretary who answered the phone, and who also lamented that the dunking hadn't stuck because the young man was presently AWOL from the Coast Guard.

Clara, sadly unskilled in duplicity, told the truth when asked about the nature of her inquiry, and the secretary sucked in her tongue and terminated the call. So, Clara played another hunch. She found the church bulletin online from that fateful week containing the names of the dunkees. She was able to run down two of them.

This time she told them she was from *Jesus Saves Magazine* and was doing an article on traditional baptism, and asked if they had taken any pictures or video from the sacred event. The first did, but these had long since been deleted. The other did as well, and had kept the disc (and over a hundred stills to boot), since the girl—who hadn't been a virgin since the age of fourteen, and had been called one-date Wanda since the ninth grade—had married an associate pastor and was now the mother of two holy babies.

A couple of weeks would pass until she received the disc. In the interim Clara played a third hunch. Laughing Willie had no security cameras because they kept no cash on the premises, and other than a few forklifts, didn't have anything that could be stolen for profit except knockoff twinkies. Half a block down the street, however, was an Elmo's convenience store that had every single pump, the entrance, and both exits monitored in all directions, no drive-offs tolerated. Feeling an upsurge in her loins previously unknown, she managed to secure copies of those as well.

Clara received Wanda's recordings while waiting for the others. The first images were pre-salvation, from an unsteady phone, and decidedly useless. The stills, too, showed a scrawny girl with big ears in a tent dress smiling as she prepared to deed her heart to the Lord. As the scene from the phone switched from outside shots to inside shots, the only editing being the on/off button, the phone camera, still unknowingly engaged, swung wildly in a noir vision of Hitchcockian reverie. Clara enlarged the five-second sequence, and slowed it to an even eerier crawl.

There was Eddie Lee, in harsh profile, staring at his feet in the background, just before he left for the second church. The video time read 7:52 p.m. This was not conclusive, of course, but significant. Between 7:52 and 8:30, Eddie Lee would have had to catch a ride to do the deed then catch a ride to the other church, or else sprint the impossible mile to the house, whack Shorty in hypersonic fashion, then sprint to the alternate venue. A good lawyer would've called this reasonable doubt.

The images from Elmo's were also illuminating. At about 7:45 p.m. twenty or so workers from Willies took to the air for a smoke. They were all shadowy and indiscernible. Within thirty seconds an old eggplant-colored Saturn bearing the corpulent Miss Sandy flashed by. At 8:07, she flashed back and was seen re-entering the plant.

At this point, an even greater, though equally unknown, wave of excitement, washed over Clara, and she took the results to her professor, Dr. Charles Drake. He told her to run with it. After assembling the evidence and writing a summary, she sent the package to the Davis County District Attorney's office, where the padded envelope landed on the desk of Elise Harris, and was immediately shoved into a drawer without being opened, presumed to be a solicitation for donations and neither she nor Bowman Carter attended Duke. What nerve!

Several weeks passed. Dr. Drake placed a call to Arthur Bowman Carter, III. This call was not returned. Nor were four or five others placed in succession. Bow was out amongst the citizenry, building goodwill to be the next neocon Representative to Washington.

So Dr. Drake, piqued in the erudite way of southern gentlemen, gave all the information to an acquaintance of his at the *Charlotte Observer*. The story broke eighty-two months into Eddie Lee's incarceration.

All regional news outlets were ablare before Bowman Carter was even aware.

A frantic call to his associate, Elise, revealed nothing. She had not seen any new evidence. She did, however, recall the package and finally opened it. She gulped and mustered a nanosecond of conscience, then hastily put the package at the bottom of the pile of growing mail on Carter's desk, running the lyrics to the Carpenters' *Close to You* through her head until she felt better.

When Bowman returned and reviewed the evidence, he was startled, stunned, shocked and aghast. He was also scared to his quaking knees. He had never faced such a remonstrance, had never been cornered by such overt dereliction. If the evidence wasn't damning, it was certainly purgatorial. He immediately issued a statement he would review all the findings. He also stated the police had thoroughly checked out Sandy's alibi, then lamely added the information from Duke Law had somehow escaped his attention.

He could have saved his breath. CNN was the first national news organization to air the story. More followed. The timeline and sequence of events were laid out end-to-end in precise detail. None could find a photo of Eddie Lee that didn't make him look like a serial killer, so they resorted to his high school yearbook picture, in which he was only sixteen, having dropped out at his earliest convenience.

Mr. Carter issued another statement he was reopening the case.

This, too, proved pointless.

Two weeks into the fray, growing by the day and expanding to include more players, the fair Sandy appeared on the courthouse steps with Bobby Childers, a former public defender in Winston-Salem who had risen to prominence as a defense attorney by gaining an innocent-by-reason-of-mental-defect verdict for a woman who had thrown her three preschool-aged children off a bridge.

Sandy had lost weight in the ensuing years, though her face remained beefy and as malleable as silly putty. She dressed in black like some grieving widow and addressed the throng of reporters in a small, plaintive voice while Bobby held fast to her elbow, as if giving her physical support.

"I was an abused woman," she began. "Not a week went by I was not abused in some way. I did not mean to kill Shorty Turner. He came at me and I grabbed the knife and stabbed him. Not long after that I found the Lord. I am truly sorry."

She answered no questions. Many were not even asked. If she had not intended to kill Shorty, why did she sneak in and out of work? If she had not intended to frame Eddie Lee, why did she wipe the knife on his shirt and place said same barely hidden? If she had been remorseful, why let Eddie Lee rot in prison for the past seven years?

The now apoplectic DA wanted to put her away for life. The circuit judge, who possessed a natural loathing for small-town politics, intervened and had her plead guilty to involuntary manslaughter. She was sentenced to eight years, one year more than Eddie Lee had already served, and could be released on good behavior in five.

Carter was to host a final press conference. The pandemonium had grown to a hundred media participants and multiples of onlookers. All he wanted was to lick his wounds and move on until the hubbub died down.

"Why didn't you challenge the police investigation?"

"I had no reason to doubt the evidence."

"Why did you ignore the information you received from Duke Law?"

"I didn't ignore it. I was unaware of it."

"How could that happen?"

"I don't know. I was unaware my office received it until sometime later."

"Do you have anything to say to Mr. Edwards?"

He paused. Long and noticeably and sighed low. "No. Justice ultimately prevailed."

"Not even an apology?"

He grew a scowl. "I did my job. No apologies necessary."

Eddie Lee was released, promised $74,000 in wrongful conviction compensation and billeted at Executive Suites until all the paperwork was concluded. He was interviewed many times but none ever ran. He was so stupefied and incoherent, not to mention camera-creepy, that all the reporters withdrew from him.

The story continued on without him, however, a universal montage featuring images of the original trial, when Eddie Lee was more presentable, the new evidence, press conferences—with the intermittent retreat to Eddie Lee as a sixteen-ear-old smiling awkwardly into an Olan Mills camera as he contemplated a perfect thieving future, save for having to work every weekend—and invariably closed with a somber correspondent waxing about the frailty of true justice in a voice much like James Earl Jones prepping to sing *Old Man Ribber.*

Bowman quietly left the congressional race and resumed his work. He was furious at Elise and sought her resignation. The Duke package had simply been misplaced, she contended. He was forced to relent, but he could never trust her again.

Within a week all the news organizations left, the final volley being a short clip of Eddie Lee emerging from the courthouse with his walking papers in one hand and his check in the other. His lawyer was smiling but Eddie Lee looked as pitiful and pathetic as Mother Teresa, his twice-broken hands arthritic and curled into claws, his skin as pale and gaunt as a bloodless corpse, his eyes as tiny and cold as a dead guinea pig—his entire mien mocking proof of life. No one could abide any more contact with him.

He was on his own.

His room had been paid for thirty days, so there he remained, watching television day-and-night, eating delivered food twice a day, hardly leaving or seeing sunlight except when the drapes were open. Even when the maid was there emptying his trash and changing his bed, he stood silently in the bathroom until she left.

His madness had become a cloak of torpidity. The only thing that held his attention, or even raised his pulse above malaise, was Carter's final press conference. He recorded it on TiVo, and between surfing forty-seven channels in rapid succession, alighting only to snippets of Family Feud or mixed martial arts, and then for no more than thirty seconds a whack, he would watch the stored clip fifteen or so times a day.

"I did my job. No apologies necessary."

Later, everyone discovered the gun had been lifted from a deputy sheriff's patrol car. This was a backup pistol hidden under the seat, not only against county policy but illegal besides. The deputy had not reported it missing for fear of losing his job.

Ellen Marie Larsen, nee Carter, was a lovely creature favored by the capriciousness of genetics. She had her mother's auburn hair and superlative build, and her father's round eyes and gentle demeanor. She was on her cell phone when she pulled into the semicircular driveway of the First United Methodist kindergarten. Her five-year-old daughter, Alyssa, had been lucky in the DNA lottery as well. She had her father's fair hair, complexion and relaxed disposition, and her mother's/grandfather's eyes and mouth.

Ellen was chatting with a friend. She looked up with the phone in her ear, bearing the same anticipatory smile she wore daily at this time, and froze. The phone dropped unceremoniously, bounced off the console and into the passenger seat.

Alyssa stood very still but crying, held in place by a gnarled paw and firm grip upon her tiny shoulder. The other paw held a pistol to her head. Alyssa quivered but remained petrified. The man looked distantly into the window of the black Escalade, unfocused, apparently seeing nothing. Ellen rolled down the window but did not speak, clutched in thudding fear, and could only look pleadingly in the pair's direction.

Strangely, the man wept as well, and shook even as he kept the barrel of the gun against the girl's temple. Finally, he forced himself to connect so his intention would not be doubted. Eddie Lee and Ellen's eyes met and held, as if something beyond desperation existed between them. As if in some other universe the disparate lives of such a pair could be mollified.

All was misery.

"No apology necessary," Eddie Lee said, and pulled the trigger. Ellen flinched at the sound even before she registered what had happened. Eddie

Lee then put the pistol to his own temple and pulled the trigger. He and the child collapsed into a heap. All in five seconds.

Ellen's body reacted before her brain. In her mind's eye there was nothing but a vacuum. Her hands tensed on the steering wheel and she vomited on her blouse. She shouldered open the car door and ran to the site. Her lungs were paralyzed and she did not breathe. She forced her hands to pull her daughter away from Eddie Lee. The top of the child's head flopped aside like a hinged lid, connected only by a slim isthmus of red bone and tissue, blonde pigtails still intact but not where they should be.

Ellen's voice shrieked, "No!" Her body slumped to the ground. She wailed pitifully, her arms clenched about her daughter's slack form as she held her to her breast and rocked.

With the contact, her mind woke and she was assaulted by images—by the terror in her little girl's eyes, by the lifelessness in the murderer's, by the smell of sulfur and the murmurs of the gathering crowd, and by the red-black hole of chaos.

Bowman wept and vomited, too, but this was not remedial. His bore the hot acid of scorn and self-loathing—conscience and culpability, and disbelief on a pathological scale. He was the first to rouse, however, and gathered them all together. All the cast were united in abject grief, though in ways as different as the means of expression.

Ellen and her husband, Jarod, sobbed ferociously. Marie moved about stiffly, her eyes constantly abrim, her lips continuously aquiver, though these were never given voice. Bowman had joined the land of the lost, a poor likeness of eternal emptiness.

These were souls torn apart so viciously had they been flesh none would have survived—and in truth, were little more than seething abscesses now.

Bowman bore the worst and exhibited the least. Ellen rejected all efforts of comfort from her father. She wouldn't even let him touch her. She clung to her husband and her mother, one or the other every waking minute.

Marie's indictment of Bowman was far less obvious but far more subversive. She spoke to him not at all. She slept on the sofa in her daughter's home from the first night through the funeral—then several weeks afterward. When Ellen's husband returned to work, Marie remained.

Bowman suffered his rejection and unspeakable sorrow alone. No one offered condolences directly to him, much less commiseration. These were reserved for the innocent. His wife and daughter offered no verbal condemnation, but neither did they offer forgiveness or any recognition of his suffering. He could not face anyone in the family without uttering "I'm so sorry," nascent with his every appearance among them—and they deafened themselves to it, and looked away.

He was allowed to ferment in his own infection, forsaken.

The Judge insisted Bowman take a leave of absence. This was neither a kindness nor an act of compassion. "We just can't have this," he said flatly. "We can't have you in the public eye, much less the courtroom, until this settles down."

Bowman accepted. Perhaps he shouldn't have. Idleness is toxic to anyone of duty, no matter how ill-fitting. He spent the hours watching old black-and-white movies to distract his ramping brain. He waited until nightfall to take long walks far from the neighborhood. These were not restorative. These were not even a kind of atonement. These were self-chastisement, self-prosecution, leading to the inevitable self-condemnation.

The walks failed to tire him enough to sleep.

How could things have gone so wrong? How could he have misinterpreted the facts of the case? How could he have known that confinement, albeit unmerited and untimely, could have transformed a lowlife into a monster, a fleck, a zero, into an—executioner. He was maddened by the truth. There had been a plot and a plan and no one had seen it coming. Why hadn't Eddie Lee been given his money and put on a plane to nowhere? Why had the life taken not been his? He would in his deepest yearning, desperately implore the miraculous to barter his life for the child's, even to the damning of his soul.

Who would call him Poppy now?

His wife had been absent for over a month following the catastrophe. Bowman rattled around the house like Jacob Marley seven years dead, exiled from those he needed so awfully.

On Sundays, he was allowed to sit with the family in church. His wife and son-in-law acknowledged him with a quick nod. His daughter would not make eye contact. As necessary as grief, proprieties must be upheld. The town lustfully watched the show within the show. Just before the service began, his wife leaned over and whispered.

"I want to come home after the service."

"Of course," Bowman replied.

He remembered nothing of the service. The entire hour was ethereal. At last his battered heart dared to beat a scant fraction faster, or if not faster, then an iota stronger, more resonant. Now, the true healing could begin. Now, whatever clemency was to be rendered would finally come. He was willing to proceed at a snail's pace, to have any modest semblance of his life back.

He was changing clothes when he heard the front door open. "I'll be right down," he called out.

He skipped down the stairs into the living room and stopped. Marie sat in the wing chair—the chair she had insisted on ordering in a fabric more expensive than the chair—a gold brocade with burgundy and green to tie into other colors in the room—colors she had changed long before the chair was even broken in.

She sat upright on the edge of the seat, her back stiff, her chin and eyes facing forward, her hands folded neatly in her lap, her legs crossed at the ankle in southern elegance. She did not look in his direction even as she spoke.

"I am not going to bear this shame with you," she said. "I know this is not all your fault, but we can no longer be a family...and I can no longer be a wife to you."

"You can't be serious."

Then she looked at him, her visage drawn and firm, unsympathetic and as cold as January. "I am completely serious. And if you care about us at all, you will leave this house without complaint and give us the chance to weather this indignity on our own."

Bowman grunted, even as the flimsy cords holding him aright sagged slip-knotted. "Indignity? What indignity? You think I don't feel as much pain as you and Ellie? You think I don't hurt every minute of the day?"

Marie blew a long, thin stream of air through her nose. "I do not doubt your pain. But we cannot help you and you cannot help us. You brought this upon us all. And now our granddaughter is dead." She paused, determined to stem the tears before they conveyed an unwanted invitation. "Will you leave us alone, or not?"

"I've already left you alone. You gave me no choice."

"Will you leave this house or not?"

Bowman's temper flashed red. What was this *we* shit? She wasn't the fucking queen of England. *We* was really Ellie, and eventually Ellie would need her father, too. He held his anger, however, and not because he respected her resolve.

He had seen that spoiled self-possession before. He had learned to give way, even as his wife made him an outcast. She had insinuated herself between him and his daughter, and no matter his contempt, his abject disdain for such self-centeredness in the guise of...family, he knew nothing good could come of objection or assertion.

"All right," he said finally. "I will leave."

Then, Marie rose and left. He reached out to her as she passed but she kept moving even as his hand brushed her shoulder a final time.

Four

Bowman moved into his father's old house. Some would have called it a mansion, a slight misnomer. The house was simply large—three stories of antebellum charm with Ionic columns. The house was used mainly for storage now and had been for many years. He'd considered selling many times but never consulted a realtor. He had grown up in that house, though was less a shrine than a mausoleum.

What furniture remained was draped in fatality. The whole place was as dusty as a ghost den. Appliances had been left in the kitchen, a refrigerator and stove. He carved out a nook for himself in the library, now empty of the desk and most of his father's books. He moved a simple twin bed there and used the closet for his clothes. He had left all personal effects behind. Marie would pack them eventually. An old file cabinet served as a dresser. An adjoining bathroom needed only a new shower curtain and a few toiletries to function.

The entire space he used was about eight hundred square feet, less than a fifth of what was available. He rarely moved beyond this area, except to an old rocker on the back veranda. The rest of the house remained eerie and untouched.

Since he could not return to work, and was loath to be seen out and about—though he initially believed any scorn directed at him was imagined and would pass—he needed an occupation. No matter what he thought, how he struggled to clear his head, how he knew he would hit the ya-ya express if he did not find something to do, he spent most of his time lying on the small bed torturing himself. As he could not forgive himself, he sought forgiveness from the only source that mattered.

One morning he drove by his former residence and saw his wife's car. So he went to his daughter's. Her husband had gone to work and she would be alone. He rapped gently on the door. After about fifteen seconds, she answered. The drama did not ensue as a play, where expressions were hazy, or as a film, with subtlety and a delicate air. The drama launched as a low-rated TV movie where the ads were for denture adhesive, incontinency, Publisher's Clearing House Sweepstakes, and the AARP.

She squinted immediately and pressed her lips into a disappearing line. "I can't see you right now, Daddy."

Bowman had never realized how many of her mother's mannerisms his daughter had inherited. "Can't we just talk?"

She began to cry. She put her hands over her ears and vigorously shook her head. "No, no, no, no, no."

At that moment Marie pulled into the driveway. She was set to charge even before she was out of the car. "What are you doing here?"

"I just wanted to talk," he said softly.

She stalked to the porch and through the doorway. She reached an arm around her daughter and turned, "If you do this again, I'll call the police."

She closed the door and the locks slammed into place.

The next morning the Judge appeared at the door of the old place. Bowman went to the door in a T-shirt and striped pajama bottoms. He looked out through the translucent glass at the shock of white fur, and opened the door.

The Judge looked sour, as if he had expected a good BM that morning and had produced only wind. “We need to talk,” he said, and entered without an invitation.

A pair of large tub chairs occupied the living room and the two sat opposite each other atop the sheets long employed. The Judge put his hands on his knees and looked straight ahead.

“I know you are going through a lot but you cannot harass your family,” the Judge began, “especially at a time like this.”

“Harass them?” Bowman protested. “I can’t even talk to my own daughter?”

“She doesn’t want you,” the Judge said. “Neither does Marie.”

“Marie is the cause of this. I’m not going to divorce my daughter.”

The Judge nodded imperceptibly and locked his fingers together. “The County Commission wants to remove you. I appealed for a leave-of-absence on your behalf. But I was denied.”

Bowman sneered. If the Judge said he wanted the County Commission to dye themselves orange and meet naked, they would have. He was rankled, injured, and felt betrayed. He anguished because he could feel nothing else.

“There has to be a recall election to remove me.”

The Judge shook his head. “Not happening, Bow. You put us through an election you know you cannot win and the whole district will turn against you.”

“Everyone has already turned against me. And for what? Doing my job with the evidence I had?”

The Judge ignored him. "How are you for money?"

"I can't believe this."

"Do you have enough money to get by for a year or two?"

"A year or two? Jesus Christ! You try to bounce me and I'll sue your ass off!"

"And you'll lose!" the Judge returned. He sighed, softening. "Look, I'm trying to help you. You aren't in any shape to do the job and we can't leave it open-ended. I think I can convince the District to pay you six month's severance. If—you step down without a ruckus. Do it for the sake of self-respect, man."

Bowman allowed the umbral cloak he had worn these weeks to completely enshroud him. He could not prevail without a fight and the will for battle was simpering and weak. He rubbed his eyes with the heels of his hands. "What am I supposed to do?"

"Practice law. Eventually. Probably not here. In a year or so when your head is on straight, you can start over somewhere else."

Tears gathered unbeckoned. "Without my family?"

The Judge opened his hands as if in contrition, though his mindset was at the far extreme. He prevailed in all business dealings and recognized the moment the scales tipped. "You'll be divorced anyway. I can't speak for Ellen, but it will take time. A very long time."

Whether it was a last gram of character, as the Judge had suggested, or simple pride, Bowman stood. "I'll resign. And I don't want your money."

When one becomes a party to death, one is truly dead in some fashion, the depth of which is reliant upon how strong the ties are to the deceased, and how much time remains in one's own lifespan. This death-by-proxy is as real as gravity and as tangible as iron. This surrogate demise possesses weight and materiality—a death of gnawing mites, and irrevocable.

This alternate death then becomes a nether world of longing. Bowman Carter's ties to the irretrievably dead were profound, and he was now horrified by the prospect of living to old age.

This *spectral dissolution* is a death of poverty, a complacent death. No amelioration may penetrate beyond the walls of this prison, taunting by its distance yet still alight.

This death clings so tightly to the flesh even the air falters. This death reeks unkind to undo the life garnered and held and spent in optimism. Only a sliver of any good thing rendered by heart and hand are met. The rest has burned away.

This death makes no sound, deluding the deceased to presume its departure, until the awakening and the blister of noise proves otherwise. This death hobbles the dead by its very nature, the way the nurturing sun can scorch the landscape.

This death can only be supplanted by life, speck by immaterial speck, and should the dead falter, can recast every stray particle to its most recent, ghastly self.

To again become a part of living is so arduous the dead do not even recognize progress when it rises, and then in mere motes of abatement. After all this, should some mean success shine visible, ugly, ragged scars remain and fester in the dark.

Once snared in the coils of doom, alcohol is a platitude—a simpering banality of weakness and resignation. Disgrace is the faint confirmation of sanction.

Bowman's justification was simpler. He did not know how to obtain any other form of anesthesia. He would have used morphine or ketamine had he a source. He had never been much of a drinker, either, so he hoped for a quick and successful resolution.

Sadly, he detested the taste of everything he tried.

Then, as if upon some divine spindle, *deus ex machina*.

Glancing at the back label of a vodka bottle he noticed a recipe for White Russian.

Vodka is mild, the good stuff flavorless, though still forty percent alcohol. Put vodka and coffee liqueur in a glass of ice, add real cream, stir gently, and you are on the Soporific Express.

Bowman became a master mixologist inside a week. He found a vodka he liked, Finlandia, and Kahlua, which was not only a coffee-flavored liqueur, but contained rum for spice, and used heavier whipping cream instead of the canonical..

He was a natural. He enjoyed watching the slurry as he added each component, blending them just to the point of foaming, then allowing the mixture to alloy.

As he became more proficient, the volume of vodka increased and the other ingredients decreased. He also began to eschew ice once he mastered the chilling process. Wet the outside of a glass and place it in the freezer for exactly nine minutes. He found eighty-ounce glass decanters—glass incapable of tainting the essence—with lids to ensnare every vapor, and plied his trade with relish.

He would make three decanters at a time, cover them with opaque bags to defeat even the most persistent light, and put the containers in the refrigerator. Each would be retrieved in the old FIFO (first-in, first-out) inventory system, though were so quickly consumed the order didn't matter. This process was precisely executed and afterward came the palliative of heavenly ingurgitation.

He never had less than two gallons on hand and soon consumed a liter a day. As he often forgot to eat, and became immune to hunger, if not thirst, his alchemy had more than the desired effect. After a few weeks, he had mastered a schedule.

He would wake around eight, though at times seven, and guzzle six ounces to clear the phlegm once relegated to OJ. This was not to savor but defibrillation, a waste of inventory, perhaps, yet effective.

Then began his workday. He would sit in the old rocker out back, especially in the mild morning sun, and the sun shone sharp. sparing none for the sake of one, and conjure images of his granddaughter as she had been and in exacting detail.

He would remember every curl and lash, every pink circle of skin, every smile with small, temporary teeth. He exerted himself in every fashion to resurrect the pain. This became slightly more difficult as the weeks passed and his wakening muffled by the previous night's toddy.

Soon, however, he wept.

At times he would weep so hard he would retch. His endurance was notable. He could weep for ten minutes straight, sobbing so vigorously he would lose his breath and begin to cough in wracking gulps. All the while some memory of the child would be fixed in his imagining as if glued to the post before him.

Brain sufficiently benumbed, he was usually fit until lunchtime. He would chug three or four ounces more ounces like CPR, and would take another hour or so to finish off an eight-ounce glass. Afterward he would read.

He had found boxes of his father's books. Anything he was not remotely interested in, yet would hold his attention sufficiently to forgo recollection—and his father had plenty of these—were deemed suitable. He read *The Iliad* and *The Odyssey*, *The Barchester Chronicles*, *Middlemarch*, and in a fit of desperation, a law book, *The Practice of the Court of Admiralty in England and Ireland*, by Richard Watts.

Then it was time for his nap. Most of the time he would sleep hard until five or six. When he woke, he downed another six ounces to clear the muci and settled in for the evening.

The evening consisted of supper and more reading, as he would nurse another dozen ounces while indulging his blighted and diminishing noggin with gems such as *The Portrait of a Lady*, *The Ballad of Peckham Rye, and The Time Machine.* The only occasion he cast a genuine smile was reading *1984*, by George Orwell.

Lest he indulge in any fantasy of recovery, he immediately moved on to *The Murders in the Rue Morgue.*

Finally, he would sleep again until the next day's routine recommenced.

He settled in for the long haul having achieved such earnest practice. He spoke to no one. Realizing his body craved more diverse nourishment, he risked an excursion to Costco at three a.m. and bought several cases of assorted snacks—Fritos, Funyuns, Doritos, Munchos, Ruffles, Tostitos, Cheetos, and plain old Lays potato chips.

He became forgetful. He found it increasingly difficult to conjure images of the child in life. So he remembered the last he had seen of her as she lay in a slim, white coffin, dressed in pink, her head resting on a fluffy pillow, her curls unfurled upon it.

The mortician had done an admirable job of reassembling her scalp, though her face was not quite right, appearing sullen and dispirited, and not quite like her at all—a waxen likeness by someone not yet expert. Only the family had been allowed to see her and Bowman had been the last before the lid was closed.

Also during this time, now approaching its third month, he did not often shower, shave, or brush his teeth, or change any article of clothing except for his T-shirt, which was the only type of shirt he wore, and every third one of these was crusted with puke. The world would soon stretch into June, and in the summer fever, he had ripened into fetor.

One muggy night he had a ponderous revelation. He was reading a narrative on Sherman's march to the sea. This was a dry rendering, as vapid as a dead twig, absent of motive, observation, sensation or revelation—merely an account of the who, where, and how many.

Yet here was the divination; he had always kept a certain affection for the Isle of Palms, a barrier island off Charleston, South Carolina. Bowman and his wife had taken their honeymoon there. He had vacationed there with his wife and daughter. He had taught Ellen how to make sandcastles with a plastic pail.

He would follow in Sherman's footsteps, more or less, as there would be a different route, different destination, and different modus operandi.

He would drink himself to the sea, and once there, drown himself in the Atlantic Ocean. Everything was all so perfectly clear now. Everyone would be satisfied. He would remember no more. He would irretrievably join the immortal in the land of telegnosis. He would exchange the living death for the permanent one, and without delay.

He *was* delayed, in fact, because he passed out. When he woke in the deep night, stars sewn against the still black sky, he left. He showered, changed into clean clothing, but packed nothing except a cooler with three decanters of libation, and set out.

He stuck to the back roads, as he did not intend to vary his drinking schedule, or at least as little as possible. Why trifle with success? He had not gone fifty miles before he pulled into a rest area, downed as much of his elixir as he could hold in one go, and fell asleep. Again, this was a coma-sleep, a deep, hollow, dreamless sleep.

He woke about five in the afternoon. He dragged himself into the restroom to use the facilities. He washed his face, glancing at himself in the mirror. His beard was uneven, peppered with gray, a thick, circular patch on each cheek, then a narrow, hairless divide, to a full, curly beard along the jaw line, the last of these resembling an Amishman.

He did not dwell on his pallor or the condition of his eyes. He already knew the sacrifices his new vocation demanded. His hair had grown to cover the tops of his ears, flipping up in the back, and he took a moment to play with it. He had never worn long hair before and it looked sharp against his thin face.

He stopped for a break at a bar near Spartanburg, South Carolina, called The Remedy. Fitting and apt. The bar was narrow and filled with ruffians and rogues—or at least roguish rednecks in cowboy boots with women to match. These were hard women with pitted faces, makeup as thick and oily as a coat of acrylic paint, and the odor of generic CVS perfume laced with eau de tobacco. Hank, Jr., was cranking on the sound system. The walls were lined with poker machines with a denimed caboose on every stool.

Not one to diversify, Bowman ordered a White Russian without reservation or embarrassment. The bartender was another redneck. The man had a big belly and a button near the hem of his shirt had come undone, revealing a cavernous navel which even in the poor light looked like a blimp's-eye-view of the old Turner Field.

Bowman drank. The Russian was watered down and flavorless. He should have specified the vodka by brand. The cream was as bland as skim milk.

"Try whipping cream next time," Bowman offered.

The bartender wriggled his lips. "Don't get much call for those."

Bowman suckled his drink and spun on his stool. Looking about, he did not see relaxation. He saw restlessness and constriction. Every person postured and moved in agitation, a hyper-aspect of allergic frustration born of misfortune too wily to overcome. Even the scattered laughter had a contentious edge, a thin combination of menace and defeat.

A man too drunk to pass as sentient sat on the stool next to him. Bowman politely nodded but the man simply gaped at him. After a moment he pointed, his finger hovering for a moment in amnesia.

"You're the guy who let that boy out of jail," he said. His tone was both sloppy and accusing.

Bowman raised his glass. "No, I'm that guy who put that boy in jail who turned out to be innocent," he said, taking a gulp.

This was a loser. A loser's loser, unkempt by ignorance, not design, unsavory by nature, not choice, ugly by genetics, not carelessness. He had a Clemson Tiger tattoo on his forearm. The closest he had ever gotten to college was the parking lot of the football stadium. He was also missing an incisor on his right side. He clenched his face, looking more pitiful than mean, all this doubtlessly resultant of too many Democrats in Congress.

"I got eighteen months just for holding. For holding, if you can believe that shit!"

A sane man would have moved away or at least ignored him. Bowman smiled large. "No, you got six months for holding. You got a year for being too stupid to live."

When Bowman came to, he first noticed the pain in his cheekbone and the persistent ache in his neck. He flexed his mouth several times. Painfully sore, but still worked. Unlike his cohort, his incisor was intact, though probably superfluous. He sat up.

He was in a jail cell. He was lying on the concrete floor, the empty cot protruding from the wall. His new profession inhibited him from ever being completely sober but he was vaguely functional. His mouth was so dry he couldn't work up a good spit. His back hurt from the hard surface. He stood to see if he could. He wobbled a bit but remained erect. He leaned against the wall to await his fate, or at least to get the blood circulating.

He was released. He couldn't be arrested for public drunkenness because he had never left the bar. He couldn't be arrested for assault because he had never thrown a punch. The jailer wore a crew cut and red face, and looked like an old drill sergeant too wide now for active duty. Bowman signed for his wallet and keys.

"I take it you'll be going home now," the jailer said.

Bowman knew few would comprehend the elegance of his plan, including the jailer. "I guess so."

The jailer put the paperwork aside. "I know who you are. I know what you been through. You need to pull it together before you get yourself killed."

Bowman grinned knowingly. "I know."

Five

Initially, he was as bewildered as a freshly neutered poodle. Then he realized his car was still at the bar. Barely nine a.m., the sun already full of haste and worry. He had not even begun to walk before the sweat broke out on his forehead. It was a two-mile hike to the bar. He wasn't concerned. He did a couple of miles on the treadmill every day or so. Of course that had been before his demise.

As he walked, the toxins rose and puddled and aspirated through his pores. After a mile sweat was free-flowing, oozing consistently to give every square of flesh a sheen. Then, disaster. All his beautiful voodoo failed. The purge doused the apathy and antipathy. Recall slithered upward, stuttered, then hummed like a cyclotron.

Images purified by fire slammed against his interior skull like buckshot. These strobed behind his unfocused eyes—his granddaughter's shiver when he blew on her neck—his daughter's laughter—his wife's look of approval—his life. His clean, simple life.

This was accompanied by the pain, the sharp sting of the sun in his eyes, but more, the addled muck of soreness in every cell, the gummy languor of stagnation, as he remembered the why of it all. He sought healing oblivion. He quickened his pace. Sobriety was an infection.

Through several near-empty parking lots he spotted his car. He left the sidewalk and cut across the asphalt. He gripped the handle with quivering hand. Locked. He clenched his fists, the weight of his beleaguered soul pulling him under. Then he remembered. The envelope from the jailer. He tore open the envelope and snatched the keys. He unlocked the door and tossed his wallet on the passenger seat.

The inside of the car was already sweltering, the air thick as fog. He opened the cooler. The ice had melted, the water tepid. He seized the container. The solution had lost its chill. No matter. He flipped the lid and guzzled what remained, tasting nothing as he drained a full cup-and-a-half to residual foam.

He started the car and turned the air conditioner to max, awaiting the stale thud of limbo. Bile rose hot and angry. He vomited. He held his head out the doorway and gushed ache and aid together onto the asphalt, so infused one could not be distinguished from the other. Then he sat back, lamenting the waste of so much ambrosia .

Once the car cooled, he felt better. He stopped at a convenience store and bought a bag of ice, filled the cooler mid-way, drove south to the next rest area, and parked in the shade to nap.

Darkness had fallen when he stirred. He looked at the clock. Barely noon. He started.

The apocalypse had come, the end of time. The entire world would join him in unmitigated despair. What if the Rapture had come and he had missed it? At least he would no longer be alone. He would join the rest of the unwashed, the wailing of a suspect population.

Then the rain came, and thunder exploded at the same time. A storm. A simple, summer thunderstorm.

He was down to his last decanter. Perhaps he should rent a motel room and resupply. He chewed on that bone for a minute. He took a single sip, then sat and waited. After fifteen minutes the rain subsided, though the storm remained in meaningful fury. He eased onto the highway. Disguised as he was by the mantle of the weather, he remained on the interstate all the way to Columbia.

He exited to find back roads. Some of these were heavily traveled. U.S. Highway 1 was the old route to Florida before the Interstate, all the way to Key West. He turned south twice again, and made his way onto a two-lane state highway with little traffic—the woodpecker trail—lined with pine trees and scattered habitats on both sides mile-after-mile. This was not the forest primeval. This was the ragged underbrush of the hinterland.

Darkness trudged on, though still afternoon, heavy clouds spoiling the day. The rain was persistent, the road like an endless black tunnel. He turned south once again on State Highway 64. The narrow trail was so close to the woods a fallen limb could have reached its shoulder.

The speed limit was fifty-five but this had to be for locals who knew the turns and straightaways. He cruised at fifty. Not a five-mile stretch passed where he didn't see roadkill. The wipers played a Scottish drone, Bowman, half in the bag, fought to stay on the lookout for every creature possessed of fatalism.

He slurped as he drove, replacing the container in the cooler each time. He was pissing against the wind. Cold cooler air scarcely had a chance to circulate before he pulled the bottle and took another hooter. This was also a one-armed juggle for him, requiring a mind ill-used and antagonistic toward any rational thought—though his next exercise was a simple computation with no philosophical connotations.

Here was the math of it; his final container held eighty ounces. He had already absorbed a dozen of these, albeit in small doses. He could synthesize another batch eventually but he did not know the when or where or if. He also had to imbibe enough to remain insensate—an edgeless, colorless paralysis—yet still operate the vehicle with relative aplomb.

This was like those equations on standardized tests. If a train left Chicago...If a man operated a vehicle at an average speed of—fifty miles an hour, had sixty-eight ounces of antidote, needed anywhere from four-to-seven ounces every forty-five to seventy minutes to incapacitate the mind to all but primary functions, could he transit the remaining hundred-fifty miles without refueling?

Unfortunately, this brain-bugger was real, and compounded by the fact Bowman had sucked at math even when he was sane. He would just have to wait and see. His resolve to self-submerge into abeyance was undeterred.

A couple hours later he had a stout buzz going. Ahead was a crossroads. Not a town. A wide spot in the road where an old-fashioned grocery store with two gas pumps sat, the entrance to an AME church across the road, and a used car lot with six bastardly vehicles in what was essentially someone's front yard.

The speed limit fell to forty-five. Bowman took his foot off the gas but was still going fifty when he cleared the zone. He had only gone a few hundred yards before flashing blue lights emerged from the woods near the store and headed in his direction. He had spent the night before in jail for the first time in his life. He had been inanimate then. Now he was conscious, if not completely *au courant*. Jail would be a dreaded and avoidable brand of stagnation.

Again he was required to think, now more difficult than math. First, he could pull over. He had his license and registration and believed he could function. He had nothing to ameliorate his breath. Dammit! Foiled by the lack of foresight to buy a buck's worth of Tic-Tacs.

Secondly, he could pull over, comply with a respectful smile, pretend he had laryngitis, and keep his fat trap shut. Yeah, that could work. Jesus fucking Christ! The cooler.

He grabbed the container and tried to shove it under the seat. The gap was too narrow. He opened the console. Too shallow. He could sit on it. Too awkward. Okay. Just hide the bottle. The lid fell off and he held tight to thwart the slosh. Shit! Shit! Shit!

As he entered a long, sweeping turn, he lost sight of the cop. He looked for a side road, even a driveway where he could pull in and feign abandonment. Nothing. Maybe he should just pull over and take his medicine. A DUI? In the bung of South Carolina? Nope. Drowning was preferable.

An idea fired like the rattle of an old lawnmower. Abandonment could still work. He could hide.

He hit the gas, pushing the pedal halfway to the floor. He was still able to hug the curve at seventy. He felt like a NASCAR driver, slipping into the high groove as the car hit eighty. He was still accelerating when he exited the curve into another long straightaway.

He floored it again, warping to ninety miles an hour, carving a wake in the flowing water like a speedboat. There was no oncoming traffic. He straddled the yellow line to give himself more room to maneuver, and a fraction more reaction time for any suicidal animals. When next he saw the patrol car he had at least a quarter-mile lead . Hah! Decent math after all.

He pulled off the road, extinguished the lights, grabbed the container, locked the car, and fled into the trees. No one had an advantage in the murky woods, law or not.

He was completely unaware the trooper was answering a call, had already stopped, and had no interest in him whatsoever.

The woods wore gloom like a cloak. His vision was better than he expected in the dusky dim but the rain cast a translucent sheet upon everything. He could tell openings from the trees, but little in the way of egress. He scooted with the Russian hugged against his chest as fast as his too-short legs would carry him. Small branches striped his arms and swatted his face, but still he ran. He could not read the topography, however, and tripped over a dip and tumbled. He managed to hold the decanter aside as he fell and slid.

He fell a second time over an exposed tree root, but without major damage to the container or its contents. He held the container aloft as if fording a swollen creek with the Olympic torch. His person, however, was thoroughly nicked and scraped. He thought it clever to vary from a straight line, so he moved left, right, northwest, northeast, like a linebacker with an intercepted pass. Finally, his lungs gave out and he had to stop.

His chest ballooned from lack of breath but he deferred his own recovery to remain quiet for a few seconds. He listened. He did not hear footsteps or any thrashing through the brush. He turned in a slow circle and did not see the faintest halo of blue light anywhere. He slugged down a gulp and leaned against a tree to suck in air. The sounds of the storm surrounded him, and then rose the ghostly screech of a bird of prey, which caused him to freeze.

Drenched hair to toe, he wore his soggy clothes like a second skin. In time, he headed in the general direction of the road. He walked ten minutes before realizing he wasn't sure the direction he moved was the true location of the road. He took another slug of jug juice and continued on.

He had deviated so much during his escape he realized he could not duplicate his movements. So he set a straight course back the way he guessed he had come. Eventually he would come to a road.

He walked forever, though in reality barely a half hour. He still sweat in the downpour and this provoked the sting on his arms, neck, and face, the pain sharp and nagging. He held the container up in an effort to gauge how much remained. He couldn't tell. He stuck a stick down to the bottom, pulled it out, and used his tongue to measure. He figured he had at least ten ounces left.

He was lost—as in Mojave Desert lost—but would not acknowledge this. By now he was good and lubricated, with no doubt or concern, except that he needed to continue, toward the Isle of Palms, toward harborage and asphyxiation.

He was thirsty with no water. Hungry with no food. Damn! He had left all his Cheetos behind. Up ahead was another clearing. He would stop and rest, try to get his bearings. He stepped onto a small incline. He climbed and stood at the top. Thunder rumbled and the storm raged. He couldn't see ten feet in front of him with any certainty.

He took a single step forward—and touched asphalt. This was a road. By all appearances, the road he had taken. He couldn't be sure. He had no idea which direction his car was. He would just have to walk a mile or so each way.

He was exhausted, body and soul.

He sat down beside the road. Soon, he whimpered. Mostly he wept for himself, how he had drawn such a sorry lot—how he had accepted there would be no reprieve. His sorrow was not for the events which led to the conclusion, but for the necessity of the conclusion in a world where he no longer had a place. He choked down the remainder of his brew, slopped liquid dripping down his chin and neck, then angrily cast the decanter aside.

He lost consciousness sobbing. Soon, he dreamt, vague, amorphous dreams—reminders of the Reaper's summons.

First, he dreamed he was standing alongside a road amid a storm. A car pulled up and stopped, wavering and unsubstantial. A window before him slowly sank to invisibility. He opened his mouth to speak, but belched wet, sour fumes instead, long like the low of a cow. The image sped away.

Deeper down—He was separated from his body, only his mind alive. A voice speaking in an alien tongue clacked about him. For a moment he recognized it—Spanish?—but it could have easily been some esoteric tongue.

The voice spoke. "Where are you going?"

Well, that's the question, isn't it? A distant voice that sounded familiar said "Ocean."

Then he felt movement. He was floating on air. After a few seconds, he lay flat upon a solid surface, and felt a rumble beneath him. There was a covering above him but he couldn't be sure what it was. The ceiling seemed to bulge and contract, breathing in and out like bellows, the harsh drumming overhead.

"Muy Borracho," the first voice said, followed by titters of mischievous laughter. He realized he must be Hellbound, surrounded by imps. Next

(and he did not know how long), everything stopped. He was frozen in place, still the rat-a-tat-tat above him.

More voices. Quick. Agitated. Again in the same pecking language.

"Quien es este hombre?"

"Esta perdido."

"Que vas a hacer con el?"

"Llevalo al Papa."

"Bien. Buena."

Bowman tumbled. Strangely, he stood again and hovered, his feet barely skirting the ground, oblivious. He was plopped onto another hard floor, this one with ridges digging into his back. Not painful but uncomfortable. For a moment he saw a face—a Mayan king. Perhaps he was to be sacrificed to Acan, the god of wine. He smiled in the dream, and as he did, the heavens once again began to move as a hum grew beneath him.

No more drumming. The rain had stopped. Above, a charcoal sky tumbled like smoke. Of course. He had reached the gates of Hell. Judgment would come soon and he was strangely relieved.

The hum. Continual. Constant. Soothing at times but baffling.

Inside the dream, he slept. Into eternity he ventured. Farther and farther. The Universe became still. An angel spoke from the void.

Perhaps not. The voice had an edge and sounded like someone doing a bad Scarlett O'Hara. A witch. An enchantress, sent to prepare him for sacrifice.

"Graw-see-yus. I'll take it from here."

Time passed. Sanity began to inch in on mouse feet. Now he sat slumped, his head resting against cool glass. The tumultuous gray gave way to harsh lights, cast in rime, and a buzz surrounded him like a hundred different chants from the proselytes. Perhaps they would grant him a final request and cast him into the sea before he woke. Only a dream.

He roused, not knowing if he was still dreaming. He lay on a soft bed. A gift before passing. He tried to focus. A wall curved steeply above his head. He reached a trembling finger but could not touch it. He panicked. He was in an enormous coffin. He had been buried alive! He flailed in every direction. He struck something solid behind him. Pain flared. Maybe this, too, was a part of his death, to feel the pain of every movement, to feel the pain of a million fractious thoughts—forever.

He tried to rise and tumbled off the bed onto a floor. He stood, woozy, but staggered against a sharp edge that punched his thigh. He winced and stumbled. Obstacles were everywhere. He was on a narrow path. He wobbled step-by-step, bumping against a small protrusion, clouting his shoulder on the edge of a shelf. Damnation was a passageway with traps lying in wait.

Through a veiled opening, a bright light haloed, spread in every direction. Bowman never lost sight as he plunged ahead. The Light of Life Eternal. If he could only escape this gauntlet. If only he could reach the gates. He saw the end of the burrow ahead and the light beyond. He despaired, finding the way blocked by a wall.

Then to his right he saw the outline of a door. He fell against it, fumbled for a handle. He found it. Turned it. The door opened and he took a step...only to pitch into empty air with nothing beneath his feet. He fell and landed on his hands and knees. The surface was dirty and stuck to him at every point of contact. He crawled forward toward the light.

He looked up into the luminance perched high upon a post that seemed to quaver. There he saw the faces of Fred Flintstone and Bambi's Aunt

Ena in smoke and shadow. Surrounding them was a thick, syrupy odor, sickeningly sweet like decomposition. He squeezed his eyes shut.

Suddenly, he crumbled, and gushed corruption from deep within his gut.

He heard the drawn out voice of the witch. "Yep. That's just how I found him."

Again, Bowman dreamt amid the sensation of being pulled along, then gently placed upon the soft bed. Other sounds and voices invaded his dreams but he was once again inanimate. How long this lasted, he did not know. In timelessness he woke. Darkness surrounded him and he lay still for a moment to make certain he was truly awake, though he was no longer so addled.

His head throbbed. His ribs ached. His stomach clenched into empty space. His mouth was a parched sewer tasting of rot. He struggled to sit up. On the wall across from him was a light switch. He lifted it. The light was vague and hollow but at least he could see.

His afterlife was an old Airstream trailer. He was in the back bedroom. Through the narrow door he saw a small kitchen area on the right—a dinette table and two chairs with miniature appliances and cabinets. On the left was a closet and a closet-sized bathroom. Beyond this was a built-in sofa with a table at one end. Across the narrow aisle stood a short counter and a pair of captain's style barstools. In front of these a wall reached about two-thirds the way to the ceiling. Past the wall was the entrance door on the right and a small sitting area on the left with two frayed side chairs in a green the color of snot.

He was alive, if not alert, and stood, immediately bracing himself. Into the open area, he became aware of the curved ceiling overhead, where a small fan moved noiselessly except for the pulse of circulating air.

He opened the refrigerator door. He found a carton of orange juice inside. He did not have the wherewithal to seek a glass. He downed several swallows, hoping the juice would stay put. He washed his face in the kitchen sink. He was barefooted, dressed in a pair of sweatpants many sizes too big, and a T-shirt hanging to his knees and billowing at his sides.

He retraced his steps but could not find his shoes. He did find a worn pair of thongs and slid his feet into them. Again, they were too large. He felt like the Incredible Shrinking Man, or at least a child playing in his father's clothes. He went outside.

True night had seized the sky, and hot, the air thick as a blanket, hovering in still, invisible clouds all around him. The trailer was near the edge of a parking lot beside a stand of trees. He thought he heard the distant sound of water, more lapping than flow, but did not investigate.

Fifty feet ahead, along the edge of the parking lot, was the back entrance to a single story, masonry block building. The heavy door stood open but the screen door was closed. The lot held a handful of cars. Beyond was a city street dotted with fast food places slow with inactivity. A large neon sign stood as sentinel in the front. It read: Jimmy's Bar-B-Q, with a dancing pig at the bottom.

He shuffled across to the screen door. Inside he could hear bustle and activity, though of what sort, he didn't know. He opened the door and entered a large kitchen area. He could see Ena through a window above a high counter picking up plates of ribs and slaw. She spun away and disappeared without acknowledging him.

A short, portly Latino man was emptying a rolling cart of dirty dishes and stacking them near a large, double sink. Then he disappeared through a swinging door. A middle-aged woman with coke-bottle glasses and a snood holding straight gray hair in place was working a griddle.

She was large from shoulder-to-waist, but her backside was disproportionately outsized, appearing at first to swallow her torso. Her pants were tight against her legs and even tighter against her rear. How the hell do they make britches to hold that shape? Her cheeks curled inward indicating the absence of teeth. Several long worktables dominated the center aisle with stainless steel appliances in the rear.

An old wall clock advertising Goody's Powders read eight forty-five.

The entire right-hand wall held a couple of wide grills and several cooktops. Fred Flintstone wore a white paper garrison cap that resembled what soda jerks used to wear when such things existed. Fred was about six-three, six-four. His apron reached from chest to knees.

His shirt and pants were loose and baggy, his bulk still implied. His head was too large for his neck and perched there like a ball on a tee. He was broad-shouldered, barrel-chested, thick-in-the-middle, but with too-thin hips and skinny legs. His white hospital pants were hiked up to the meatier part of his belly and tied with a sewn-in cord. Still, they bunched at the top and migrated downward with his movement.

Fred was the first to notice him. He was flipping ribs over an open-flame grill and did not stop or slow his motion. He did not smile or nod. His face showed nothing at all.

"Can you wash dishes?" he bellowed across the room. This caused the lady in the hairnet to look toward the sinks. She smiled slightly, keeping her mouth closed, then returned to the task-at-hand.

Bowman merely stood there, still in a state of asphyxia, tottering.

"See that pile of round things?" Fred boomed.

He looked. "You mean the plates?"

"Exactly. Wash in sink one. Rinse in sink two. Use the hose. Drain in the drainer. Wipe and put away later."

He gaped stupidly from Fred to the disordered stack of dishes back to Fred, but finally slid a few steps toward the sink.

"Okay," he said.

The soapy water was scalding and Bow jerked his hands back. He found a pair of yellow rubber gloves on an overhead shelf and slipped them on. He could still feel the rising heat from the water but tolerably now. He began in slow-motion. The dishes stank of the same thickly sweet smell permeating the air and he gagged again for a second as his stomach seized.

The gooey coating wiped off easily in the suds. He moved the dish to the rinse sink. Again, the water was scorching, and again an odor rose, faint, and smelling like some industrial solvent, but after a dunk, he rinsed the dish with the hose and set it in the rack.

The rinse water basin soon became tainted. Remnants of detergent floated on the surface. After several dishes he began to hose the dishes over the wash sink, and place them in clear hot water to sterilize. The water rose in the first sink but that was easy to remedy. Drain some of the water out, add a bit more detergent and refill.

He soon developed a rhythm. He would wash and rinse several dishes and place them in the disinfecting sink. After a good soaking, he would wipe them and set them in the tray. After every twenty dishes or so, he would change the rinsing water and add a few droplets of the disinfectant. He didn't ask how much. He judged by smell, and would start over if too strong, or add a bit more if too weak. Every time he reached the end, the short Latino man would replenish the pile. He smiled at Bow and Bow smiled back.

Bow was sweating and enveloped in a sour cloud of his own body odor. No one else complained and he kept going. He was beginning to detox, but without the tipsy trembles. He felt better as his pores began to unplug, though he craved a belt.

After a time, he looked at the clock. It was nine-twenty. He didn't know where he was, or even what day it was. Aunt Ena came and went. The next time she returned, the cook spoke to her over his shoulder without looking.

"What's going on out there?"

"Four drag-assers," she said in her Dogpatch voice. "Never trust a man who uses a toothpick in public."

"Then lock the door. Nobody else in."

"Yeah, yeah," she grumbled.

The woman in the hairnet brought pots and pans to the washing station. Some of these had baked-on crud as tight as liquid cement. The brush was useless. So was the plastic scouring pad. He had more success letting each piece soak in the suds then scraping with a large spoon.

Soon, all but the kitchen lights were extinguished. The rolling dish cart stood empty and its jockey was nowhere to be seen. No Ena, either. Fred and the magna-derriered lady were busy stashing bowls and implements.

Bow stood by the sink, ill-at-ease, not knowing what to do, like someone locked out of his car.

Fred gave him the eye. "That's it for tonight. Go get some rest. But take the pullout this time."

He nodded in reply. What was the pullout? He swung open the screen door.

"And take a shower, for Christ's sake!" Fred barked. "You reek like dead ass."

Six

As each soul flees beyond mortal constraints and is admitted to the continuum, the first welcome port is Perdition. This is not punishment nor a warning to repent. The time for warnings has passed. The time for punishment doesn't exist in the absolute except for the unchecked circumvolutions of a disorganized mind.

The place—as it will appear to be a physical reality—doesn't matter. In the beginning this may be a simple room. There, every traveler will be greeted by a guide, or given instructions, or urged beyond comprehension toward certain movement. This is no Dickensian *mea culpa*. This is to show the consequences and ultimate outcomes of paths not taken.

Since every action represents a course variation, no matter how slight, these create millions of possibilities. Nearly all can be ignored. These illuminations do not reveal how crossing an intersection, or entering a building, or walking among an ever-changing throng of people, ten minutes earlier or later, altered subsequent events.

These reflections reveal how major decisions or circumstances created an avenue, and what would have occurred had those steps moved us in a different direction.

Some major choices are well considered, though doubt may persist afterward. Perhaps these have been examined and assessed for many potential results, so at least there is a certain confidence going forward. Unpleasant surprises may arise, and a return to the manner and means of how choices were made can provide a reassurance that these are yet valid.

At times there is reckless presumption and major choices are made spontaneously. These may even seem necessary under dire circumstances, but are usually capricious under most.

As these results are more predictable in the adverse, there is a tendency to take the line of least resistance—to wit: blame someone else. In the interim, there may arise the realization that the time spent in recovery and reestablished forward momentum is greater than the time spent in both the original decision and resultant fallout.

(Shigetaka Kurita is forced to create an entirely new emoji).

Minor decisions usually cause minimal harm when they turn, just as they provide minimum pleasure when they prove successful.

Yet as these alternative endings are reviewed, a single proposition becomes clear.

No matter what choices are made, or how long the deliberation, or how neurotic or rational thought processes are analyzed, troubles lurk like karmic cooties.

One variation may be flawless, and the next is made with haste in confidence, only to yield an eruption. Sometimes rash decisions are made that evolve perfectly, then with inflated hubris the next bold choice ruptures and reeks like day-old sauerkraut.

Key to all understanding is patience. As decisions progress, hopefully with lessons learned, and outcomes emerge in haze or effulgent cast, only fruition informs the merits of choices.

All these things tend to find equilibrium, unless there is such foreboding no rational decisions can be made or such paralytic inertia none are made at all.

Happiness and hopelessness may arrive at separate times, at various levels, and with arbitrary results, but in the end the stacks tend to even out or else made bearable through experience.

Everything relevant to choice—thought, feeling, and act—in the inescapable duality of life, arrives according to its own conceit.

Aunt Ena, henceforth, Darlene, was something of a paradox, a nod to the sick wit of mitochondria, a structural throwback to bygone elegance, with Popeye's Olive Oyl in countermand.

From neck to ankle she was perfect, naturally tanned like Ava Gardner, soft-fleshed like Ingrid Bergman, buxom like Jane Russell—her breasts were flawless though they hung large like melons on the vine—narrow-waisted with firm and flaring hips like Elizabeth Taylor.

She was more than Venus de Milo. She was the muse through which all like virtuosity was realized.

As for the rest... her face was ovine—too long, too narrow, her forehead too broad, her chin too thin, her eyes a themeless sepia tone, her mouth so large a laugh could swallow her face to the eyelash. Her front teeth were square and equine and protruded from the opening to rest in worn grooves upon her lower lip. Her dark, recklessly dyed hair too brassy, unwieldy, and fell like loose cord to her shoulders,

Yet it was her nose that drew the most immediate attention. Beginning between her eyes and descending, thin, flat, and only slightly tapered, it cast a shadow upon the Cupid's bow. Her nares were disproportionately round and open, and left such a small space between the septa and upper lip she could wipe her nose with the tip of her tongue.

Her feet were enormous—man-sized. These were pontoons, designed by nature to be hidden or camouflaged, covered by the hem of a long skirt or wrapped in plain, flat shoes to fade into the background. Instead, they were brazen in flip flops, flashing bright red toenail polish, defying anonymity.

Worse, she had a most severe and exaggerated case of Morton's toe. This was not merely Greek foot, this was maximus peditum Greek. Her second toe extruded nearly two inches beyond her big toe. This toe was an obelisk, a flip off to everyone from Florida to Delaware, a theremin echoing cosmic pulses to every new-ager in the southeastern United States, the landmark every hiney-probing alien species used to locate planet Earth.

She also had the appearance of being taller than she was, at five-six, because she was blessed with perfect posture, no doubt birthed from such capable ballast feet-wise.

Bow stirred and sat up. The bottom of the built-in sofa pulled out and away from the wall and the back dropped flat like a futon. The dip in the center where the two met was a nuisance but he had slept without interruption. He felt better, more like terminal less like extinct. A pot of coffee and a glass of tomato juice sat on a TV tray. He tasted the tomato juice then took a long drink to clear his palate. There were lumps in the juice. He hesitated but bit down on one. Flavorless.

"There's garbanza beans in it. You need to get your stomach working again."

His reflexes were far too slow to hurry. He looked across the trailer at Darlene sitting at the dinette table reading *US Magazine*. She wore shorts, a halter and sandals. Her uniform hung from a window sash above her nurse's shoes. Bow poured a cup of coffee and sipped it.

"What time is it?" he asked.

"Nine. We don't open 'til eleven. Take your time."

He stood to go to the bathroom. He was wearing the same oversized clothes he had worn the previous night. He relieved himself and peered into the small mirror. His cheekbone was still bruised from his earlier altercation and now ringed purple. One brow ridge had a red knot protruding. His beard was uneven and unruly. After he emerged, he folded the sheet and blanket, and put them in the corner with the pillow on top. He retrieved his coffee cup and joined Darlene at the table.

Across from him, she unfolded the wormhole between her lips, smiled warmly and put out her hand. "I'm Darlene."

He shook hands. "Bow. Bow Carter."

"I know. Well, I didn't right away but the Pope knew who you were."

"Who?"

She spoke with no hint of levity. "The Pope. This is his trailer you're staying in."

Bow blinked to clear the cobwebs. "You mean the cook?"

"Yeah."

He slurped at his mug. He had landed at the city limits of Oddburg. "Where am I?"

"Port Royal," she answered. "South Carolina."

"Where?"

"Port Royal," she repeated. "Near Beaufort. On the coast."

He shook his head. "How did I get here?"

"A couple fellas found you beside the road up country. They thought you were dead at first. They brought you to Walterboro. They were going to leave you at the hospital or give you to the cops but one of them said you were headed for the ocean. So The Pope asked me if I was ready. I thought about it, figured I was, and came and got you."

"Why do you keep calling him the Pope?"

"Everyone calls him that," she said simply. "Where were you headed?"

"Charleston. Isle of Palms." He pushed from inside-out, trying to bring more sense to bear. "I had a car."

Darlene lifted her brows. "Don't know nothin' about that. It's probably hell and gone."

Bow took a deep breath. "Ready for what?"

"Huh?"

"You said he asked you if you were ready."

"Oh. To take you on as a project."

"In what way?"

She grinned a gaping pit. "Get your head outta your ass and back on your shoulders."

Bow scowled. "That's crazy. I'm a grown man."

"Who gives a Sally Suckwilder about that? You're in no shape to go anywhere or do much yet."

Bow fell silent. His head spun. "I just need time to get it together. Until I get my bearings."

Darlene rose. "Fine by me. And you're welcome. We're open eleven to eleven today. Eleven to nine during the week. Noon to six on Sunday. Closed Monday."

He nodded absently. "What day is it?"

"Saturday," she said. "Friday and Saturday are jammin'."

"I don't know what that means."

"You should."

He looked at her blankly. "Why's that?"

"You're the new dishwasher."

Then she approached and hugged him, awkwardly as he was still sitting, but she put her arms around his shoulders and pressed her cheek against his. "It'll be alright." Then she left.

Bow showered in the tiny cubicle. The shower head was attached to a short hose and after spraying himself from head-to-foot, he returned the nozzle to its hanger and held his head under the spray for several minutes. He shaved his face clean and cleaned his teeth as best he could with his finger. He gargled mouthwash and nearly puked. He tucked his hair behind his ears, and dressed in another oversized T-shirt and comfy pants left for him. At ten-fifty he walked across the lot to the rear entrance door.

The Pope, formerly Fred, was busy preparing the grill. He wore the same hat and apron, and exactly the same-type ensemble as the day before but they fit him better than they fit Bow. His bulk, or absence of bulk, lay hidden in folds of fabric. His arms seemed disproportionately thin but wiry.

The hairnet lady with the magnum posterior was making coleslaw in a vat the size of a wash tub. She looked up and smiled, again not showing teeth. Her teeth were in plain view, however, in a glass on her table, beaming unnaturally. She must have liked to work au naturel and air out her gums as she did not have to meet the public.

"Sorry I didn't introduce myself last night. I'm Debbie."

"Bow," he answered, with a weak wave.

The Pope looked at him without expression. "Back off on the disinfectant a bit. People smell it on the dishes they freak out. Think it's Clorox." Bow nodded in reply and filled the sink with hot water. "Let Darlene show you around before we open," he continued. "Darlene!"

Darlene appeared at the doorway and smiled broadly at Bow. "C'mon. I'll give you the one-finger tour."

As Bow soon discovered, this meant she led him a few steps into the dining areas and stopped, pointing at everything corner-to-corner with a crooked index finger. The restaurant was relatively small—maybe room for sixty or seventy if all the seats were full. Pairs sat at tables for four. Four sat at booths for six. The place was neat and clean but the furniture was old, the seats a faded red vinyl. Mounted fish adorned on the walls, curious for a place that didn't serve seafood.

"This's the dining room," she said, pointing, her finger extending and recoiling like a turn signal. "The bathrooms are around the back corner. There's the front door. We never use that one. Employees come and go through the kitchen. We have a full menu, but mainly serve pulled pork, brisket, and ribs. The Pope makes the best ribs in the state," she added. "It'll be busy all day."

The same short, stocky Latino man was wheeling his cart around wiping down tables.

"That's Bob," Darlene said. "He doesn't talk. We don't even know if his name is really Bob."

"Is he deaf?" Bow asked.

"I don't think so. Hey, Bob!" she called. The man turned and looked at her. "No, he ain't deaf."

A man in his late sixties, early seventies, sat on a stool behind a counter cash register. He was dark-complexioned with some kind of Mediterranean influence, bald except a charcoal strip above his ears that met in the back. He had a new unlit cigar between his teeth and was counting money for the till.

"That's Abe," Darlene said, though they didn't approach. "He's the owner."

"Who's Jimmy?"

"Ain't no Jimmy. Who wants to get ribs from a place called Abe's Bar-B-Q? Hey Abe!"

The man moved his eyes without moving his head.

"This is Bow! Bow, Abe."

Bow waved. Abe returned to his money without speaking.

"Abe's a good guy. Him and me tussle some. Other than that, it's a decent place."

Later Bow met Mickey, another waitress, a tall—very tall, at least six feet— black lady in her thirties. Her hair was snug against her head like a skull cap, she wore no makeup, was flat-chested, and instead of a skirt wore a white shirt and black trousers. Bow knew butch when he saw it.

"Where'd you play ball?" he asked innocently.

She frowned and squinted. "What makes you think I played ball? Because I'm tall and black?"

Bow retreated a foot. "No. Sorry. Meant no disrespect."

Mickey grinned like an Irish setter. "Just pullin' your pud. Just up the road a ways. South Carolina State."

Khrystile was a kid of nineteen who was virtually cadaverous, with short, poorly bleached blonde hair, too-thick green eyeliner, essence of spoilt fruit parfum, nails chewed to the nub, and who chain-smoked. She took a break every hour and huffed down two Marlboros in five minutes. She tried to be discreet. She washed her hands and lips afterward, and went through two packs of watermelon Trident every shift, but still smelled like the viewing room of a hillbilly mortuary. Her eyes were vacant and she had no grip at all as they shook hands.

Darlene led him back toward the kitchen. "That's it. You met Debbie. She does the prep."

"Why does she keep her teeth on the table?"

"So she doesn't lose them," Darlene said plainly.

"Why doesn't she wear them?"

"She huffed too much vinegar fumes one day and had a coughing fit. Slung her chompers right into a pot of chili. Weren't for the five second rule we'd a lost the whole five gallons."

Bow set up his station, mindful to curtail the disinfectant. He ran the hot water full-tilt and put on his gloves. As Darlene predicted, the day hummed. He did not dawdle but kept a steady pace and only fell behind twice.

At two Debbie brought him a bowl of chicken noodle soup and a half dozen Ritz crackers. He floated the crackers atop the soup, then crunched and drowned them with his spoon. The soup was excellent, with fork-sized chunks of chicken. He ate slowly to curb his stomach's rebellion but was back at the sinks in ten minutes. At seven he passed on a plate of barbecue and ate a house salad with raspberry vinaigrette instead. His stomach was still AWOL and growled like an old Studebaker.

He broke a heavy sweat early-on. He half-expected the perspiration to be deep brown or at least sickly yellow, but the blight was invisible, the droplets milky at worst. He realized the benefits of detoxing but the beads on his forehead dribbled into his eyes and burned. Finally, he snagged a clean dish towel and tied it around his head. This worked, but he looked like a Halloween Samurai.

Once, he stepped into the dining room to stretch his legs. The place was astir. Darlene moved in long, even strides, competent, organized. She was not much more than a kid herself—twenty-five, twenty-six? Mickey was steady and meticulous, the pleasure upon her face contrived and pasted there, and she stalked the floor like a man. Khrystile dashed around like a shih-tzu.

Bow listened for a moment. The overhead music was from a contemporary Christian station.

Who are you, Lord? I need to know you...

Darlene barked loudly on the fly. "Jesus Christ, Abe. Change the goddam station!"

Midnight peeked around the corner before the doors were finally locked. Bow stood outside in the back. He didn't know exactly what to do. Conscious now, at least in a rudimentary sense, he felt like a trespasser and did not enter the trailer. He was tired—good tired—but craved a drink. He downed a ten-ounce bottle of water filled from the sink. This quelled his thirst but not his hunger. He would have to make some White Russian soon.

A few minutes later the Pope exited and locked the door. Again, he looked at Bow impassively. Without his hat his head looked even more profound, square and ossified. His eyes were placid and intelligent. With hair buzzed close to his scalp, he looked less like Fred and more like Curly Howard as if fresh from a Mensa meeting.

"Let's have a smoke," he said, and walked toward the trees.

"I don't smoke," Bow replied.

The Pope did not look toward him. "Then you can watch."

Locals simply called it the river. This was actually Port Royal Sound and was fed by several rivers, the Broad, the Coosawhatchie, the Colleton, the Pocatoligo, the Chechessee, and others. Port Royal is an island, sharing its space with the town of Beaufort. The sound is part of the Intracoastal Waterway and is also a tidal straight, with much more seawater than fresh.

Dolphin and saltwater fish fed and frolicked in the river. All the barrier islands are separated by such straights, all eventually leading to the Atlantic Ocean. The tides create wide expanses of salt marsh completely submerged at least once a day.

Port Royal Sound has the highest tides along the eastern coastline and during high tide does most resemble a river, mimicking the sounds of a river, the subdued rush of flowing water, articulating north and south, licking the sandy banks arrhythmically, especially with the wakes of the legion of boats that disturb the calm—some for commerce, more for pleasure, many for good ol' boys to do devilry.

Once beyond reach of the tall lights in the parking lot, the night was gloomy-dark and only traces of distant sparkle could be seen across the sound. The clearing was small, a floor of pine needles, surrounded by brush, small palmettos, and guardian southern pines. Bow made out the outline of a couple of chairs with an upended wooden crate as a table between.

"Have a seat," the Pope said.

Bow moved toward the chair.

"Not that one," the Pope indicated.

Two ancient Adirondack chairs had been weathered by time and the elements. One, the off-limits chair, had so many pillows and cushions attached to appear tumorous. There were two cushions on the back and two on the lumbar. There were four for the seat, one large one beneath covering the entire seat, one above it covering three-quarters of the seat where butt-cheeks had worn depressions, and two smaller ones on the sides overlapping the arms. The other chair had the customary single back and seat cushions.

The chair was suspect but Bow sat comfortably. The Pope gradually slid into his, nudging his lower back and hips before the rest of him sank into foam. After a few seconds he took a cigarette out of a box and lit it, satisfied.

"Those things will kill you," Bow said in jest.

"What a lovely thought," the Pope answered. He inhaled deeply. "It takes me an hour or more to unwind. Short day tomorrow and we're off Monday, so it doesn't bother me to lose a little sleep tonight. Couldn't sleep without decompressing anyway."

Only the light over the rear door of the diner and the dregs of those in the parking lot penetrated the darkness. Bow worried about vermin and snakes and could not completely relax. The night was stagnant, hot and uncomfortable. If he remained still, he might loosen up but his mind worked constantly. He was also among strangers.

"Thanks for the bed," he offered.

"You're Darlene's project. I'm just along for the ride."

"Yeah, I don't get that. Sounds weird."

"Try not to be too sensitive about it. She needs to develop her sense of responsibility."

"It still sounds kind of juvenile to me."

The Pope exhaled smoke heavily into the still air. The cloud lingered and rolled for several seconds before dissipating. "Maybe. But consider the alternative."

"What alternative?"

"She could've left you where you were."

Bow weighed this for a moment. "I don't think I'll be here very long."

"Doesn't matter. Let her look out for you."

Bow extended his legs as far as they would go. They ached from standing so long but he felt purposeful. This was the most productive day he'd had in months.

"Why do they call you the Pope?" he asked. Even in the shadows, the Pope's eyes twinkled at that.

"It's just a nickname. I can't remember who started it."

"What's your real name?"

"How do you know Pope isn't my real name?"

"I don't."

The Pope flicked a roll of ash. "There you have it."

"Is Pope your real name?" Bow asked.

"No."

He didn't pursue further. This was just a side street to La-La Lane in Oddburg. Even so, in the quiet calm he felt less septic, less edgy, though still greatly out-of-place. Morbid thoughts nudged their way to the fore uninvited. He found comfort in the knowledge that the deep water at hand would serve his mission just as well as the straits off the Isle of Palms if so disposed.

"You know who I am."

"I know who you were. I know what happened to you. I don't know who you are now. I doubt you've changed much yet."

A wrinkled nose, as if defying malodor. "I don't know what that means."

"You're still you, for the most part."

"So?"

The Pope eyed him intently. "You're still smart in all the wrong ways. The G-O-P abandoned you to the fates and here you are. Obviously, that would prompt some alteration in anyone smart in all the right ways."A short huff. "Sorry. That makes no sense."

"Good. That's a start."

Anxiety reared anew. Perhaps he should gather himself and bail. Where would he go? The wind brushed through the pines, not a soothing sound. The needles whisked together like the tail of a rattler.

"Does my smoke bother you?" the Pope asked politely.

"No," Bow replied.

The Pope then chuckled to himself, prompting Bow to look. "You know the real difference between a Democrat and Republican?" he asked.

"What?"

"A Democrat will give you someone else's money to buy a car, whether you need one or not. A Republican is a car dealer who uses his own kids in commercials."

Later, he woke from a nightmare. He was tied to the gold brocaded chair in his living room. No matter how hard he tried, he couldn't free himself.

His wife and daughter stood before him, each armed with a pistol. They took turns shooting at him, missing by a breath each time. Both spit coarse laughter every time he flinched.

Seven

He woke at seven. He'd only slept six hours. The gap in the pullout had warped his spine. He gently twisted his neck until it popped. The Pope was nowhere to be found. Bow showered, shaved, and gargled. He combed his hair straight back.

When he re-entered the room, Darlene sat in the same chair reading the same *US Magazine*. Maybe the Pope had left the door unlocked. She had made coffee and Bow poured a half cup and grabbed skim milk from the refrigerator and hazelnut flavoring from the cabinet. He reheated the watered-down brew in the microwave.

"What's up?" he asked.

"Walmart. You need clothes."

"Walmart has clothes?"

"Yep. All I can afford." Her flip-flops were on the floor. Her flexed foot looked like a crowd doing the wave with Bill Walton in the middle.

Bow answered the ding of the microwave and retrieved his cup. "You don't have to buy me clothes."

"No?"

"Of course not. I've got money."

"Where?"

He searched the ledge above the sofa-bed for his wallet. A few personal items were there—a set of keys, sixty-seven cents in change, some lint and a Frito. He quickly searched the whole area, his grimace growing with each failure.

"Where the hell is my wallet?"

"Aha."

He looked at her. "What's that supposed to mean?"

"It ain't here. Probably where your car is."

"Shit! Can you take me out there? It can't be all that far. I've got six hundred dollars in cash."

"It's gone. I already had somebody check."

He spun in a slow circle before facing her again. "Damn. Damn, damn, damn, damn, damn."

"Amen, brother. Impounded I reckon. God only knows where. Maybe traced it back to where you came from. Anybody know where you are?"

"No." He snapped his fingers as if struck by the light. "I've got credit cards. I can call and get replacements."

"Any of those cards in just your name?"

He pondered. "My county-issued one— No. I guess not. You think my personal cards have been cancelled?

"You could try and see."

"The money in my bank account?"

"Joint account?"

"Yeah."

"You can check but my guess is you've been thrown off the bus unless you want to go back and fight about it. You up for that?"

His face drooped. "No. Not now. This isn't right."

Darlene raised her hand. “Well, who gives a Fanny Fartblossom about right?” She rose and put an arm around his shoulder, squeezing it in commiseration the way a mother would a child.

“I got it covered, Bow. It’s okay.”

Darlene drove a 2000 Kia Sephia with chipping paint. The muffler had a hole in it and the floorboard was full of empty coffee cups and fast food containers. He kicked enough aside to put his feet flat as they lumbered away.

At Walmart he bought a pack of fresh underwear and T-shirts. He bought four pullover shirts, two pairs of jeans, and two pairs of khakis. He bought a bundle of sweat socks and a pair of cheap tennis shoes. He also bought a toothbrush and toiletries. Darlene paid with seven twenties.

Bow was as contrite as a two-timing husband as he grabbed the bag. “I’ll pay you back.”

“You better believe it,” she answered.

Just south of the Pope’s riparian lounge area grew a cluster of ragged water oaks, limbs enmeshed as if fighting for air. Beyond this was another clearing, a larger one, surrounded by irregular pines like a redneck Stonehenge. A crowd of about twenty-five people mingled, and smoke rose from amidst them.

“What’s going on?” Bow asked.

“Church,” Darlene answered.

At first Bow thought these were homeless people but the parking lot was littered with decomposing cars, old trucks, and jury-rigged choppers. Pieces of cardboard substituted for windows in a couple, broken doors wired shut in another, lights or other parts held in place by duct tape on several.

Curiously, he also saw a trio of full-function vehicles, even a Cadillac and a Lexus.

Most of the congregants had bad skin, bad (or missing) teeth, unruly hair, nicotine-stained fingers and nails, and skewed faces, naturally or otherwise. These were the downtrodden, poor swimmers against the tide, *les grands perdants*, and if not presently, then in the recent past.

They gathered in small groups and smoked and chatted in brash tones, the accumulation of which offended not only the atmosphere about them but probably God Almighty himself.

Scattered among them, like pearls in a mud puddle, were several people of more suitable dress, good hygiene, and with a splash of élan. This was the oddest collection of humanity he had ever seen—or at least voluntarily affiliated.

Another spray of smoke lifted from a large grill where the Pope turned ribs al fresco. He looked up as the pair approached.

Bow leaned into Darlene and whispered, "Who are these people?"

Her whisper was airy but too loud, like a child just learning how it's done. "People the Pope has helped. There's a lot more but they've either moved on or just don't come regular."

She turned to the gathered and shouted, "Hey everybody. This is Bow!"

Bow waved sheepishly and everyone waved back before instantly resuming whatever had engaged them. He found a spot a few yards behind the grill, partially hidden by a twisted palmetto bush.

He surreptitiously surveyed the crowd. These were people who knew the dimensions of a jail cell, who lived in perpetual disaffection. These were the uglies of hereditary malefaction and probably couldn't say who the governor of their own state was, much less recognize a fallen-from-grace District Attorney a day's drive away. Even so, he felt passively exposed..

The Pope served up ribs and boiled corn-on-the-cob. A couple of large Igloos dispensed iced tea. Bow ate a whole ear of corn. He nibbled a small rib. He wasn't sure how his stomach would react. Barbecued ribs, if not entirely benign, were moderately more nutritious than taco flavored chips.

He had not tasted any of the Pope's pork. The meat was delectable, easily the most savory sauce to ever strafe his innards. He gnawed the meat in small bites and helped himself to another, more formidable pig bone. Occasionally he would get wind of the gristle and his gut would shimmy, but he managed. He walked up to The Pope.

"This is great Q."

The Pope whispered secretly. "You'd think people would realize it's only caramelized sugar."

After everyone had eaten and deposited their leavings in a rusted fifty-five gallon drum, they collected in a semi-circle before an oak stump a foot high. There were no chairs. There was nothing at all except adulterated nature. The Pope stepped up and everybody became still. Bow stood away and didn't make a sound.

The Pope began in a low, conversational voice.

"There are many mysteries in the Universe, some profound and others merely curious. Like why do they call it rolling the dice when cubes can't roll. They can't even tumble, as frequently suggested. The bounce, like a fat boy at a disco."

Chuckles stirred among the crowd and died.

"Why do women with big cabooses wear thongs at the beach? Why do hookers look so good on TV and so bad in real life? Why do celebrities wear revealing dresses at awards shows, then lose their shit when they flash a boob or air out the muffin?"

The Pope paused among the titters.

"As an irrelevant aside to this, one of my greatest fantasies is to have one of those interviewers on the red carpet walk up to some starlet with her high beams covered by band-aids and say, "Wow. Nice tits."

Laughter swarmed and ebbed. A truck from the road shifted gears as it gained speed. The wind rose and overhead the clouds swelled. As if in accompaniment, so did the Pope's voice.

"Why does Disney keep taking obstreperous little hams and turn them into stars? Why do people believe in Noah's Ark but not in climate change? Why do they call it a blow job when nobody actually blows? Why do little people have chubby thighs? Why do black people get tattoos?! And what the FUCK is a super model?"

Laughter rolled through the crowd. As the sound subsided, the Pope resumed, now *pianissimo*.

"Why has the American dream abandoned us?"

"What happened to *our* American dream?" he repeated.

The crowd fell silent as the smiles diminished, hollowing before fading.

"Now you may wonder, isn't America the land of opportunity? Sure it is. But America has never been the land of *equal* opportunity. America is the land of *legacy* opportunity. Everywhere you look you will see the sons and daughters of people who handed down opportunity through money or connections or birthright.

"Beyond any sense of fundamental unfairness, we who lack are still expected to give these people a howdy-doo and bended knee. Well, so be it. We can only wish they would at least be honest about it, maybe even a little modest about it.

"Rich people aren't special because they're rich. They're rich because someone else was special. And the only way to have *equal* opportunity is for everyone to start on a level playing field and that can't happen because these people would no longer be unique and that they cannot abide. They would be one of the many instead of one of the few.

"So here's what I say. Why not give everyone a million-dollar stake?"

A few whoops echoed around the clearing but Bow shrank a little uncomfortably, wondering what kind of mine field he'd wandered into, though no one gave him so much as a passing glance.

The Pope continued. "Now, it's true many would squander it. By looking at you, most of you could go through it in a weekend." A chorus of cackles rose. "Others would just laze about until the money ran out.

"Yet some would invest it and it would grow. And the growth would grow. And some would surpass those fortuitous few, being as smart, or smarter, as diligent, or more diligent, even lucky or more lucky, because it is only the seat at the table that separates us.

"And some would build empires beyond what anyone could envision. They would see what the few do not see. They would be energized far beyond what the few could muster, because the few have never had their backs to the wall.

"Those of newfound abundance might raise the bar . Some might naturally become arrogant, proud, flaming arseholes."

Again, snickers peppered the air.

"But no one would be denied this one chance to make it happen.

"What is the lesson to be learned from this? For us, maybe none. We may never have the wherewithal to be anything more than what we are right now. At the very least do everything you can to create a legacy for your children and grandchildren. Make them stay in school. Teach them to save money. Buy as much life insurance as you can afford. Do everything you can with the knowledge that anything is better than nothing.

"Next Sunday is the Fourth of July. We will not meet. Happy Independence Day!"

As Bow wandered away from the gathered, he did not feel enlightened in any way. He did, however, feel lighter, as if the air around him had calmed fractious nerves. If there was danger, this went unrecognized, nor was he callous or ungrateful. Such strange tidings seemed befitting in such a strange place.

He never expected to be in Port Royal. He wasn't convinced he should be there at all, though now with full stomach, and little sickness in his gut, he felt passably sane and adequately concealed from calamity.

He survived the week without disintegrating. Friday night had been brutal, while those who were not traveling the holiday weekend sated themselves as if for some imagined famine to come. Bow helped Bob wipe down the tables to prep for opening. Oddly, the last thing done before the door locked for the night, and the first thing done before the day's business was to wipe down the tables, as if mischievous elves had sprayed pee everywhere during the night.

Bob was an exceptionally pleasant fellow and not just because he was mute. He seemed to take immense joy in his work. Bow waited for him to break into a dance at any moment. He did smile, however, every time he and Bow made eye contact. Bow's abandoned and atrophied cheek muscles performed only in a perfunctory manner but grew more limber by the day.

He heard the odd sniffing before he saw anything. Some rheumy affliction of unknown source. The noise emanated from Mickey in her dark trousers and shoes, who seemed less ill than in mourning, as if she had run over a squirrel on the way to work and heard the crunch. She did not speak to anyone as she tied the apron around her waist and lit out for the rest room.

Darlene appeared at his shoulder. She looked worried, catching her bottom lip between her teeth. She sighed woefully.

"That poor guy. Must've run outta money for his shots."

Bow turned to face her. "Guy? What guy? What shots?"

Darlene lowered her voice. "Hormones. You know, for the big changeover."

He was baffled. "What?"

"Oh. Yeah. I guess nobody told you. Mickey's gonna be a man. For now, she's still at least half woman. She's had her boobs whacked and all but still has the old pecker trap, if you know what I mean. She ain't got no more insurance and has to pay for her hormone shots as she goes. Every time she runs short she gets this way."

Bow looked to the restroom door as if some freakish creature might suddenly appear. "No kidding."

"No kidding. Those shots are expensive, too." Darlene adopted a woeful cast. "Sorry thing. He ain't never gonna get a dick this way. And he's getting so close, too."

He continued to stare mortified. This state of humanity was as alien to him as his Walmart clothes. He did manage a supportive nod at least when Mickey exited the bathroom. Mickey's lips trembled as he/she induced a weak return.

"Is she—he—going to be able to work today?"

Darlene nodded the affirmative. "He's an ace when it comes to work. He'll get it done and then go in the can to cry every so often. He needs a big tip day. Think I'll hit everybody up for five."

Bow shook his head. "Sorry. I'm busted."

Darlene tenderly patted his back. "It ain't forever."

Then she set about rolling silverware sets in coarse napkins.

Saturday was even busier than Friday. Bow barely got in a couple of five-minute breaks. Even then he had to hurry to catch up. He wondered why Abe hadn't invested in a dish washing machine. After the diner closed that night the Pope came to him as he was stacking clean dishes and gave him three hundred twenty dollars cash.

"What's this?" Bow asked.

"Pay," the Pope answered. "Forty hours at eight dollars an hour. Tax-free. We're considering last Friday and Saturday as a tryout, if that's agreeable."

Bow stared at the bills, then folded them and shoved them into his pocket without counting. "Thanks."

"No thanks required. You earned it."

The Pope moved away. After a moment Bow said, "You know I won't be here long."

The big man turned again and shrugged. "As long as you wash dishes, you're going to get paid for it."

"What about rent?"

"First month is free. A hundred bucks a month after that."

Bow repaid Darlene the money for his clothes and supplies. She winked at him and shoved the bills into her bra. "Money's a wonderful thing, ain't it?"

Bow had never carried cash before. He absent-mindedly felt the lump in his pocket. "Yes. It is."

Jimmy's was only closed four days a year. Thanksgiving Day, though there was money to be made as some would prefer pulled pork to yard bird. Christmas Day, as most of the denizens of Port Royal were gentiles. New Year's Day, another potential boon flushed, perhaps as much due to the condition of the population—including the workers—than any other reason. And July 4th, hail to America, or at least what was left of her, though it seemed fitting and apt that the most widespread celebrations involved explosions.

Bow stepped in, then helped Darlene into a scarred, tri-hull boat that had to be at least forty years old. The boat rocked with their movement. The landing lay in the narrows, the narrows too much so to be called a river though the river itself was calm. The Pope sat in the driver's seat. Bow and Darlene sat in a pair of seats facing sternward, leaving the passenger seat in the front empty.

The Pope started the motor, sputtering and spitting blue smoke, coughing to life. The smell was oily and pungent. After several moments, the engine idled roughly. He put the boat into reverse and they were free.

They stayed close to shore as they moved north with the flow to avoid other, more formidable craft. The Pope turned to speak a couple of times, but scrubbed all effort when all he heard from Darlene was "What?" "What?" Except for the slope of the banks the surrounding land was flat. The highest points were the bridges to other islands at either end of the strait, like guardian keeps protecting the meager enclave.

They moved so slowly at first the wake sloshed into the boat. They gradually increased speed and the boat rose. The sun offered an early warning of the burn to come and the air smelled of fish. A dolphin swam nearby, matching them knot-for-knot then grew impatient and went on its way.

In the distance was the mouth of the river and the bay, where the watery plane of the Atlantic Ocean churned not too far beyond. Hidden among the pines he saw glimpses of houses in an upscale development. Most of these had steps leading down to small docks on the river. More often than not a shiny missile-shaped boat was secured nearby.

On the near side, along the main road past the restaurant, the backs of houses leaned over ample yards to the river. Most still had large lots, though the real land had been sold off eons ago. Some had been remodeled into B & Bs. Others were grand old places with columns, porticos, and wide porches.

As the boat surged, Bow recognized a thready tranquility in the old homes. Yet he was also aware of the ghosts contained within the walls of those relics, the memories of a more genteel era fraught with unrecognized lies.

He had never considered himself a southerner, though North Carolina thought otherwise, but was not ignorant of the land he inhabited. His had been a small-town upbringing, little different from the burgs of New York or New England. He was aware of his history, however, a passive understanding of cultural deceits.

Through the doorways of a forgotten past, perplexed phantoms wandered the hallways or stood bewildered by the back door, wondering where all the fields had gone. Sorrow was rooted here in blood and war and death-of-spirit . Even now the old ladies of the house, gray and tremulous with little authority left in their voices, mourned only the loss of standing with no contrition for the horrific violations of others. The ghosts of slaves sang only dirges while their masters self-piteously wept.

In a borrowed boat on the Fourth of July, Bow became sullen, far removed from life and the resoluteness of death. He stared down at the water parted by the wake. Sobriety had altered his perspective. His would not be a noble death should he proceed. Now he was an inconspicuous and ignominious creature cloistered in a tiny corner of a tiny room in a tiny building in a tiny town. More fitting, perhaps, more relevant.

How simple it would be to slip over the side. He would be noticed, of course, but too late. If he did not flail and submerged quickly, he would immediately be out-of-reach. The undercurrent here was strong. He would descend like a stone, discharging his last breath of free air.

Then, he would inhale that conclusive gulp of water. Moisture would burrow into the lining of his lungs and attack the red blood cells with haste and ferocity. His epiglottis would seal like the lair of a trap-door spider, blocking all breath in an effort to protect his already wounded pleura.

His instincts would have him gag, fly to the surface and cough himself to life. If he could manage the few seconds necessary to lose consciousness, he would succeed, and be embraced by the sovereigns of the drink. Quick to complete, an oath fulfilled. He would at last be free of every offense.

His reticence had to be more than just sobriety. He puzzled to himself—had the torment become as seemly as his own paltry breath—life itself little more than some trivial enterprise?

There was also a measure of fear, amplified by ongoing grief. What if beyond the façade of perfect light were dark arms, their reach interminable, their grip unbreakable, leaving his disposition, even in utter regret, untenable.

He was as afraid of death as he was of living. No, he knew he would not soon relent to his own end, though as a compromise, neither would he commit to fair and generous life. He would persist in his penance.

The boat began a slow arc for the return trip. Bow opened his eyes, knowing he would survive the day, and probably the next, but was no more relieved than he had been before.

A few days later Khrystile came to work in obvious pain. She had wrenched her back and twisted a knee. She walked with difficulty, stiffly, erecting herself as if a more upright posture softened a portion of her suffering. Her eyes were unlit, her lips tight. She managed to be cordial, however brief or strained, to every customer.

Darlene was lazy that day and it couldn't have come at a worse time. Even Bow noticed. The day was slow but steady, as was every weekday, causing Mickey and Khrystile to serve the majority of customers, each busy and bustling in their own ways. Khrystile struggled the most but suffered her injury without giving ground.

Bow followed Darlene out the back door during a break. Darlene lit a generic cigarette and sucked in the smoky air.

"I didn't know you smoked," he said.

"I don't. Not really."

"So I'm imagining that pack in your pocket and the cigarette in your hand."

"I mean I'm not hooked. I smoke maybe three cigs a week. Usually the pack goes stale before I can finish it. You should try it."

"I don't need any more bad habits."

"It settles the nerves. And if you don't turn into an addict it works pretty good."

"What are you nervous about?"

She watched the ash grow until gravity took over. "More worried, I reckon."

"About what?"

She tossed the stub of her cigarette on the ground. She smashed it beneath her heel as if smothering the life from it.

"Well, you know about Mickey. Whenever he needs money I let him take a few extra tables. Now, it's Khrystile again."

"What do you mean?"

"Her boyfriend's a psycho. He hurts her for the hell of it. He likes to put things up her happy hole. Her butt, too. Once I heard he put dildoes up the back and front.soaked with enough Pam to grease up every pink gladiola this side of Atlanta."

Bow winced. He had seen abused women, had tried the offending partners.

"That's awful."

"You bet your hairy ass it is."

"So why don't you take more customers so she can take it easier?"

"Nuh-uh. She told me once she was trying to save enough money in case she had to run away. Shit, I need the money, too. I ain't much better off than them two. But who else is gonna do anything?"

Bow felt guilty for doubting her. "That's very kind of you."

"Kind don't put grits in the pot."

"I can give you more money if you need—"

"No, no. It's okay." She grinned large. "I like to bitch is all."

"You can bitch at me any time."

"Thanks." She scratched under her nose. "That's how the Pope found her," she said.

"Khrystile?"

Darlene nodded. "In the emergency room. Something had gotten stuck up there. She was in awful shape. He gave her this job."

"How did he know about her?"

"How does he know about anything he knows? Maybe he's psychic."

Eight

Summer is always oppressive along the southern coast. Fiery blasts supplant trade winds. The night breeze is unbreathable. An invigorating splash in the ocean becomes a salty stew in eighty-five-degree water. The air is so sticky a shower mingles with sweat. Air conditioning is useless except within ten feet of a vent. Cars need to be cooled down (as opposed to warmed up), before driving. The interior is so hot microwave popcorn blooms on the dashboard. Some people won't even spit for fear of dehydrating.

Summer in Port Royal is a reminder that all the denizens of Beaufort County must suffer equally at times.

A peculiarity, though self-evident, is that once the temperature rises above ninety degrees, with accompanying humidity above eighty percent, the essence of man begins to deteriorate. Gone is the pleasant disposition and forbearance. Gone is any desire to advance equity and balance adverse forces. Common civility is abandoned and an undead collection of malcontents takes its place. People tend to avoid each other lest they commit homicide.

The dining room was air-conditioned but the kitchen was not. Two large fans created a Saharan wind that clashed together and was capable of producing twisters. Worse, poor Pope stood over heated surfaces all day.

Debbie managed by mopping her face every few minutes. Bow set a bucket of ice water on a table near his station, and every so often would dunk his head to the shoulder.

Again, equality reigned. Everyone was pissy.

Bow had created a territory for himself in a seven-by-seven space, and was so well organized he barely had to move. He had the intake table for the dirty dishes within arm's reach. He had the soapy water, which he changed out at least once every six or seven loads. His system to maintain the blistering rinse water worked to perfection—he kept the water trickling in and punched a small hole in the stopper to keep the water draining out at precisely the same rate—so the sink always had clean water. This was in addition to the rinse hose he used to obliterate thick clusters of froth. He had a soaking tub for the pots and pans.

He made his own scouring device for baked-on crud. He took a short brush handle and attached the blade-end of an unused ice scraper. Windshields remained happily aloof during Port Royal winters. The scrubber was flexible and didn't scratch the pans. He created a multi-tiered drying rack so that fresh dishes and silverware were always available to stack. There hadn't been a complaint about any dried food or spots on dishes, silverware, and glasses since the first week.

He had also found an old sleeping bag he bought at a garage sale and fixed it to a piece of plywood. This became the platform upon which he stood. This made being on his feet the entire shift tolerable.

He was always a bit scruffy, as he wore a T-shirt, jeans, and moccasins without socks as his uniform, and only shaved every-other-day. But he was always clean. He could no longer stand to have dried perspiration on his skin for any length of time. No matter what else may have changed, he hated being dirty—worse, feeling dirty.

Sundays may have only been a six-hour shift but they were the busiest six hours Bow had ever spent. He fell behind with the opening rush. He had gotten a proper headband and at least kept most of the salty sweat droplets out of his eyes. He had to drink a half-gallon of water a day just to break even.

After closing, the staff had limited free rein of the kitchen. Bob, Khrystile, Mickey, and Debbie took ribs, pulled pork, and macaroni salad to go. Darlene made a pulled pork sandwich, baptized with enough hot sauce to vaporize her bowels.

The Pope was still putting things away, looking like a man who got caught in the rain. Bow made a large salad and topped it with bits from two large pieces of bacon. He opened the swinging door into the main dining area with his back. The difference in atmosphere was immediate.

The Pope looked at him.

"I'll clean up after myself," Bow said. "I need to cool off while I eat."

The Pope said nothing and resumed his chore.

Bow sat at a center table directly beneath an air conditioning vent. Abe still sat on his stool at the cash register counting money, putting it into the deposit bag, and filling in the deposit slip lines. Bow offered a three-inch wave but Abe remained focused on his task. They did not speak to each other. Bow didn't know if Abe even remembered him. He didn't mind. There was something liberating about eating without conversation.

He had stopped making his libation completely. This was not a matter of new fortitude. His once-adored analgesic was simply no longer refreshing.

The potion was so thick that even half-frozen was too heavy and syrupy. He had not planned to quit. He did not fling a fist in the air to theme music. He just stopped. Perspiration had purged him, and busyness had allowed him to close the gates to insensibility—and the more he remained sober, the better he felt sober.

He bought a prepaid charge card and a prepaid cell phone. He loaded the phone with tunes and got a set of ear buds. Steady work with the music pounding was adequate misdirection, and afterward he was too tired to think much. He did not need drink to quash his guilt—a faulty and fickle companion, anyway. He had resigned himself to chastisement much like a condemned man.

Only in his dreams—cruel, gruesome dreams—was his culpability raised time and again. He would wake and feel his body to make sure he was among the living. He had not become braver or even more resilient in any real sense. He had not learned to control recurrent injury . He had no feelings at all beneath the flesh. He had been anesthetized against any sensitivity to anything.

All real and potential deserts were so ingrained as to grant him partial immunity, as resistance to poison could be boosted with frequent small doses of the same toxin. He did not collapse beneath the sharper jabs of remorse or regret. Neither did he feel joy, empathy, or pleasure. How he had accomplished this, he wasn't sure, but he assented to the exchange.

He enjoyed his music, filling the phone with progressive rock, the grand noise of his youth. Loud and proud. A pretense to badness. The heartbeat of rebellion he had relished but never displayed to another human being, nor lived. He hardly ever stood stock-still at the sinks anymore. He moved and grooved to the tunes.

After all this, he still craved the occasional alcohol jolt without fear of relapse. With Deep Purple's *Highway Star* racing from ear to cerebral cortex, he stepped up to one of the large commercial refrigerators. He peered in at the many varieties of beer. Most he knew, but some had odd names and odd labels. He called to the Pope over his shoulder. "Do you know beer?"

The Pope flinched. "Ye Gods, Henry. Don't shout at me."

Bow turned the music off and pulled the buds from his ears. "Sorry. Do you know beer?"

The Pope continued to mix his magic sauce, his recipe safe and secure, the savory aroma afloat in the blow of the mean interior wind.

"I know seven-thousand-year-old jars with beer residue have been discovered in ancient Mesopotamia," the Pope replied.

"Looking for something smooth, without that bitter beer taste."

"You mean A & W."

Bow kept searching the chilled shelves. "Never been a beer drinker. Don't know which tastes like what."

"You've never been a drinker at all. You could have hurt yourself."

"I think that was point."

"And now?"

"Now, I just want a beer."

"Amstel Light," The Pope said.

Later that evening, Bow sat in the old Adirondack chair he had taken as his own, nursing his second beer. The beer was smoother than he had anticipated. He didn't really like the taste, but held each sip in his cheeks until the alcohol bit into the sensitive flesh, was absorbed, and then swallowed. He could adapt.

The woods closest to the river were yellow pine. Non-southerners might rhapsodize about evergreens, evoking winter enchantments or vague Christmas feelings, but those were Northern and Western pines, firs and spruce. Yellow pines are not pretty trees. Though endowed with needles and cones a foot long or more, and growing to a height of eighty feet, the limbs do not grow evenly or proportionately or symmetrically. There may be long gaps between arms, and crooks and elbows abound. By day they are pitiful to tender eyes, or ignored, and by night they resemble misbegotten trolls with many twisted hands and malformed warts covering brown, patchy skin.

He still did not feel completely at ease in the trailer when the Pope was there. Such a small space, after all, and he was still a guest, albeit a quasi-renter. The Pope never made him feel unwelcome but Bow knew this was an unnatural arrangement, not to mention that when both were inside, the Pope treated him as little more than an obstacle to move around. Fortunately, the Pope was gone a lot, even through the night.

The Pope arrived and settled into his throne with a sound like an orgasm after a two-month drought.. "Damn," he muttered. "Forgot my cigs."

"I'll get them," Bow offered, already on his feet. "Where are they?"

"On the counter in the back."

He found them. A brand he had never heard of. Dunhill. Menthol. In an odd-shaped box. The lighter was a flip-top Zippo, with a logo on one side, featuring a book with crossed briar pipes like a coat of arms, bearing the name Pipe & Page.

"They're British," the Pope said, lighting one. "It's a vanity, I know, but it's one of my few luxuries."

"What's Pipe and Page?" Bow asked.

"A little shop I used to own. I sold books and tobacco. I would let people try different tobaccos and cigars. I had open packs of some of the more exotic cigarettes for people to try. I made a little patio out back in the alley for people to smoke. I served coffee free. Had books and magazines."

"What happened?"

One shoulder rose, almost imperceptibly. "All the stores sold tobacco. And the big book retailers were starting to take over." He brought the cigarette to his lips, then paused. "It was a long time ago."

There was more to the tale but Bow didn't want to pry. Even if he had, the Pope would not respond with the whole truth. He waited to see if the Pope would continue but he didn't.

"It bugs me that Darlene still thinks she's somehow responsible for me. She keeps interrogating me about how I feel. Like I've been exposed to nuclear fallout or something."

"Well, don't tell her that. She would be crushed."

Bow tried to settle. For now, he simply wanted to be left alone, to stew in his own gall if his only option.

"You want to talk about Eddie Lee?" The Pope asked suddenly.

Bow whipped his gaze around. "No."

The Pope bowed his back and rotated his shoulders in one subtle motion. "You'll have to eventually."

A rabid shake of the head. "No I won't. Why would you even say that?"

"You'll never be free of him if you don't."

"Look. I know you're trying to help, but you are way out of line here. Please. Please. Please. Leave it alone."

The Pope lightly scratched his chest through his shirt. "He was a loser." His tone was flat and dispassionate.

"Of course he was."

"So he had no choice."

"What the hell are you talking about? He had a choice!"

"And he made you into a loser."

Anger seized Bow and he reddened. "I said leave it the fuck alone!"

The Pope sighed deeply. "I mean no offense."

Bow slumped glumly and lowered his voice. "I can't talk about this."

"Will you listen then?" the Pope asked. The response was silence.

He continued in pleasant, comforting tones, even if the words left solace wanting.

"There are three types of losers. Losers by birth, losers by choice, and losers by circumstance. Losers by birth are so damaged maybe only one in a thousand can make it out alive. They don't know any other way. That's Eddie Lee.

"Losers by choice have dug such a deep hole they can only escape if they're motivated enough. Not many do. It's easier to adapt to being a loser."

He paused and took a long drag. "Then there are losers by circumstance. Something has happened and suddenly there is a dark hole that wasn't there before. And they are so shocked to see the hole they've fallen into, they don't know what to do. And it can take a long time before they realize they are actually able to dig out of it. That's you."

Bow shifted uncomfortably. As he was about to reply—something akin to 'You are so full of shit'—the Pope resumed.

"You can do this, you know. Whatever you were before is still in there somewhere. And eventually, if you decide it's worth it, you can find enough of it and crawl out. You aren't stuck there forever."

Bow flicked at a fly on the arm of his chair. "You have no idea how bad it was."

"I know. But until you really want out, you'll be a loser by choice," the Pope answered. "Like me."

He had always been an early riser. Bed by eleven, wake at six-thirty. This was a routine established by repetition, as well as the physical necessity of sitting in the quiet and injecting caffeine until the attic light came on. He had never suffered a loss of function because of this. Now he could not sleep soundly at all. He woke up tired, his brain in a fog. Caffeine was no longer as effective. Neither was a shower. This was doubly troublesome because the shower stall made him claustrophobic, as if he couldn't breathe.

So he decided to run. He had never been a runner. He had walked and biked, all indoors. His stumpy legs carried him only three-quarters the distance as a man with a normal stride. He wasn't afraid of exercise but had never pushed himself, not with weights, man-sized equipment, or testosterone-laced remonstrations.

He pretended to stretch, pointlessly pulling each foot up behind him, squatting with his hands on his hips (as if preparing for the kazachok), and twisting his head from side-to-side. A dirty red path lined the riverbank. This had not been constructed as it was uneven, narrowing in odd places with deep indentations in others. Probably eaten away over time. Perhaps some unnamed Native had dragged his feet too much, or a well-intentioned adventurer clomped along, traveling the path day-after-day, and riding a clumsy horse.

Regardless, Bow set out at an easy lope. He was fortunate in the beginning that the trail lay behind the backs of commercial buildings. He did not want to dodge traffic or alter his pace. In fact, he did not want to encounter anyone at all. He did not want to have to offer a greeting, gesture, or have his artless form on display.

After a hundred yards or so he already doubted his readiness. His thudding style crippled his shins. His lungs bellowed erratically. His breath lurched then failed, and he labored to breathe at all. After two hundred yards he stopped, choking like an asthmatic with a fetish for burning tires. He walked on, desperately trying to remember if he was supposed to breathe in through his mouth and out through his nose or vice-versa.

Finally, he turned and walked back the way he came, verily defeated, his mind still as vague and soupy as a pothead's, though not as civilized.

From the beginning, Bow fretted Mondays. His body needed the break but he had nothing to occupy himself as handily as work. Even awash in music so loud anyone could hear it through his earbuds and not miss a lyric, he was not pacified. He read old paperbacks he borrowed from the Pope. Most of them were science fiction and held his attention about as well as a campaign speech. He would consider and oppugn the need to move about in the same continuous thought

So he sat, and moped, and picked his mental nose.

Darlene appeared at eight-thirty that morning. Bow was happy to see her. Again, the Pope was in the ether somewhere.

“I need you to come with me,” she said.

“Where?”

“I’ll explain it on the way.”

Bow got in her car and held his feet aloft until he was able to clear a spot for them on the floorboard. When Darlene got in, he asked. “Why don’t we clean out your car first?”

“Sorry,” she said. “I never have nobody riding with me.”

“Just pull over by the dumpster.”

She did and Bowman tossed coffee cups, fountain soda cups, fast food bags, and a couple of unidentified little brown things he gripped with as little of the tips of his fingers as possible.

“Why do you eat fast food when you work at a restaurant?” he asked, reseating himself.

“Can’t eat barbecue every day.”

“There’s other stuff. Salad, soup, sandwiches.”

She started the car, shuddering and wheezing to life. “Reckon I never thought about it. When I get hungry I just stop at the first place I come to.”

“You could plan ahead.”

“I don’t know. I ain’t very smart.”

They pulled onto the road and headed north.

“I’m sure you’re plenty smart.”

“No, I ain’t.”

“What makes you think that?”

She paused thoughtfully. “Well, for one, what you just said.”

“All you have to do is plan. Think about what you want to eat the next day and get it from the restaurant.”

"See, that's another reason I ain't smart."

"What is?"

"I don't know what I want 'til I'm hungry and when I'm hungry I'm nowhere near this place."

Once out of Port Royal they turned onto a two-lane state road. The tree line was thin and the sun shone in indifferent beams, surrounded by dark gray cotton. A storm might be brewing. The road had recently gotten a new layer of blacktop but the lines down the center were a few inches off, making one lane narrower than the other. Maybe semis were expected to only move in one direction. Soon the road opened to large plots of land, farms and homesteads with thick circles of grass and patchy spots of dirt. A few sedate cows grazed on benign hills.

One moment the road would be a narrow gap leading through the woods, then just as quickly expand to open land, alternating as a tease to the senses. Some of the land was ugly with parched grass, scrub trees and bushes—and no houses to be seen. Some were lovely, green and dotted with old oaks. Most of the fields were vacant, like a country devoid of substance or life.

"Where are we going?" Bow asked.

"Estill," Darlene answered. She was edgy, her fingers anxiously rubbing the steering wheel.

"Estill a town?"

She made a face. "Sorta."

"What's in Estill?"

"My kid," she answered.

He was not surprised. "Boy or girl?"

"Little boy. Just turned three. He lives with Mama."

"Oh."

"I know. He should be with me."

"Why isn't he?"

"Because I suck at it."

"What makes you think that?"

"It's true. And the Pope told me. You know, my last name is Askew. The Pope says it's A-skew, like a little bit off."

"I'm not sure you should take everything he says so seriously."

She paused. Her eyes misted over but her voice did not crack. "I was working in a convenience store with a belly out to here. The Pope came in a few times and out of the blue one day asked me if we could talk. I knew he wasn't hitting on me because like I said, I was big as a house, so I said okay. He asked me if there was a man around to help with the baby and I said no. I know who the baby's daddy is but we was never really together. We would meet up at this club on Friday or Saturday night and dance. Then we would...you know. After a couple of months of that I got pregnant. Guess I shoulda taken precautions. I told him I was pregnant and he said sorry but he didn't want no part of it so that was that."

"You could take him to court. He'd still have to pay child support."

"I don't even know where he is. I'm not sure I could remember his last name. Anyway, I told the Pope wasn't no man around. Then he asked if I had any dreams. I wasn't sure what he meant. I said nope. Then he asked if there was anything I really wanted to be—like a secretary or a hair stylist or what not. I couldn't think of anything, so again I said nope. I didn't see him for a while, but just before I calved he come back and said he had a job for me that was better than what I was doing, and he would make sure I would get through all this baby stuff okay. But there was a catch."

"What was the catch?"

"That I let someone else raise the baby until I figured out something to do with my life. So Mama's had him all along. Funny thing, I like waitressing. I made over thirty thousand dollars last year and a lot of that was in cash. But rent's expensive and I give a lot to Mama."

"And being a waitress is not good enough to take him back?"

"Not according to the Pope, it ain't."

"A mother is crucial to a baby. I don't see that you owe him anything."

"He kept his word," she said simply. "He took care of me when I had the baby. He took care of the baby, too. He did that for three whole months. Then I started working for him and Abe and took the baby to Mama's. So I'm keeping my word. Maybe I'll figure something out I want to do more than waitressing. Maybe someday I'll find a dream."

"So that's what we're doing."

"Yep. I try to come up every Monday. Other times, too, like for a birthday or a holiday or just because I want to. But most every Monday for sure."

"Why would you want me along?"

She ruefully dipped her chin. "Sorry about that. It ain't that I think you owe me or nothing but Mama and I don't see eye-to-eye about anything. She disowned me when I got pregnant. I'm hoping she won't get on me so much in front of a stranger."

As they neared Estill shacks lined the road. These were little more than sheds, the corners propped up on blocks, a small porch with a sagging roof, a screen door. The wood was bowed and bare, never touched by paint, or if ever, so long ago the memory failed. A few had shingles on the outer walls, many of these dangling or missing altogether.

All the inhabitants were black. At every shack multi-generations were in residence. A granny sat on the porch, sometimes alone, sometimes with a son or daughter, sometimes with kids. Kids ran about outside, ducking beneath clothes on a line or racing out-of-sight around the back corner. The first and second generation would scold them without moving. Every place was a reproduction of the first and every yard contained some old behemoth of a car that had once been keen in its prime but now brandished the wear of twenty-plus years.

When they reached the town, known only as such by a water tower bearing the name, and blemished with a handful of nondescript buildings, Bow didn't see any white people, as if the plantation had folded, the owners off to a better world, the slaves remaining on the property to fend for themselves because they had nowhere else to go. Even after a hundred-and-sixty years, the bathos and bafflement were palpable.

The driveway was hardpan. So was the yard. A couple of anemic rose bushes empty of blossoms marked the entrance. A few landscaping blocks marked a walkway. The rest was bald with a scattered thatch of centipede grass every few feet. All roasted in the summer sun.

The house was red brick with a screened-in front porch. The window sashes and porch frames had once been painted white, now long neglected.

A tall, pale woman with bony limbs and large belly stood near the front door. She was younger than Bow but looked older. She wore pale green polyester shorts, a striped halter top, and flip-flops. Her hair was thin, dyed a harsh red-brown into small ringlets. The dye had turned her scalp pink.

Her face was long and thin, and Darlene's nose hung from the center of it. Her bare legs were veiny and resembled a street map of Myrtle Beach.

She held the boy on her hip with one hand and a cigarette in the other. Her nails were fake and done in a purple polka-dot pattern. The boy squirmed so she put him down. He ran to Darlene and she scooped him up and held him close.

"Juney June!"

"Don't squeeze him like that," the woman chided.

Darlene ignored her and swung the giggling boy in her arms.

The boy was a chunk with chubby legs and chubby cheeks, and a little, round Buddha belly. His hair was a light brown, also curled into tight ringlets, these more natural, and bushed out into a small Afro. His eyes were yellow and his skin was the same brown as his hair.

After a minute Mama looked at Bow through squints and cigarette smoke. "Who's this?"

"This is my friend, Bow," Darlene answered. "He works with me."

Bow stepped forward and offered his hand. Mama shook it limp-wristed, sizing him up. She took note of his congenital health and low-mileage face. "I know she don't know how to keep her knees together," she said, "but steer clear if you can."

He wondered if she was teasing or really had such a low opinion of her daughter. He was mortified regardless.

"Mama!" Darlene protested. "It ain't like that at all."

They went in and sat in old wicker rockers on the front porch. Mama went to fetch some iced tea.

"What's his name?" Bow asked.

"Randall Gene. Randall was my daddy's name and I just liked Gene. We call him Junior. Don't say Randall around Mama. She'll shit a brick."

"Well, if his father is named Randall, too..."

"He isn't."

"I thought he was a junior."

"Yeah. What's his father's name got to do with that?"

Mama returned with three glasses of iced tea. The tea was cold and minty. Bow took a long drink before putting his glass on a small side table. "Thank you."

"So what's your story?" Mama asked.

"Mama. Leave him alone."

"Actually, I was just passing through and thought I'd stay in Port Royal awhile."

"Uh-huh."

"I'm sorry. Is it Mrs. Askew?"

Mama hiccupped a grunt. "It ain't been Mrs. Askew in fifteen years. It's just plain Ruth."

He nodded. "Your daughter has helped me a great deal."

"I'll bet she has."

He ignored the gibe. "I was in pretty bad shape when I landed here."

"Where you from?"

"Small town near Hickory, North Carolina."

"What do you do up there?"

"Mama!"

"Shush it, girl. You ain't never brought nobody home. So I got a right to know something about him."

Bow dodged the original question. “I just came along for the ride,” he said. “Just to get out and about.”

“Well, answer me this, Bo. And I’ll know if you’re lyin.’ Are you here to help keep her out of trouble, or to get her back in?”

“Mama! Honest-to-God!”

“I’ve been...sick,” Bow said. “She’s helped me get back on my feet. That’s all there is to it.”

Ruth looked at her daughter. “I hope you’re taking measures this time. Can’t take any more babies.”

Darlene lowered her head, as chastened as when she’d been a child.

They drove back the first few miles in silence. Bow rested his head and watched the uninviting land move by.

“Sorry about that,” Darlene said with a sigh. “She acts like I’m twelve years old.”

“It’s okay,” he said gently. “She’s just...” He stopped.

“What?”

“Nothing.”

“Tell me.”

“I can’t. Who am I to say anything? Look at me. The shape I’m in.”

“I know you’re smart. You were a lawyer and all that. Finish. Please.”

The air was empty for a time. “She’s tired. Maybe she was born tired. She didn’t know how to be a wife. She didn’t know how to be a mother. And now she’s a grandmother with the responsibility for a small child. All the things she didn’t know how to do wore her out. She just wants to look after herself.”

"Oh my God," Darlene gasped. "You're right. She ran Daddy off. All she did when I was coming up was harp at me. She was glad when I left. Oh my God," she repeated. "You think she would hurt Junior?"

"No. Of course not. She's just going to struggle a little."

"Lord, lord. I need to find a dream, don't I? And quick."

"Darlene, you can get him any time you want. You have a place to live. You have a job."

"But I got nobody to keep him when I'm working."

He hadn't considered this. "You'll figure something out. You've got plenty of time. Didn't mean to upset you."

"Will you help me?" she asked.

He peeked at her. He should have kept his yapper sealed. Helping required a lot of energy. He wasn't sure he was capable of reaching much beyond narrowed walls.

Even when things had been gloriously pedantic, he had passed his time in a muted but ingrained routine. He had loved his wife and daughter. He had worshipped his granddaughter, but everything had been managed without him—as he had wanted. His wife had interests to satisfy herself without him. His daughter had married young, embraced marriage and motherhood. He had not been required to exert the least amount of horsepower to maintain the proper order and balance. All he had had to do was work and appear when summoned.

As he avoided her expectant gaze, he realized she didn't yet know how futility lay before her—how time crept undetected, and circumstance could wrap itself around the throat in the guise of reassurance, then squeeze. Survival often passes as life's most significant objective. Sometimes the only respite is surrender.

"Yeah," he said. "We'll work on it together. But you'll have to be patient."

Darlene beamed. "I will."

The trip was over an hour and monotonous. Bow tried to enjoy the environment, appreciate whatever charm there might be, no matter the expense to his imagination. Empty land—even when barren—made the world seem more tolerant.

"Your baby's father is black?" he asked. A stupid question and only to quell the blues, and he wondered why it was the first thing that came to mind.

"Yeah. That bother you?" she said seriously.

"No. Why would it? It's none of my business."

"But if it was your business, would it bother you?"

He thought for a moment. He had not inherited the prejudices of his culture. His life had narrowed the spectrum of contemplation, anyway. "No. It wouldn't bother me."

"It's not like I have a thing for black guys or anything. I just thought we hit it off."

"You didn't do anything wrong," he added. "I wasn't passing judgment. Life just hands us things sometimes we aren't prepared for."

"I get that. I don't get pregnant, everything is the same as it was. I get pregnant, everything goes to shit."

"Maybe. I don't know."

She puffed her cheeks. "But if I don't get pregnant, I don't meet the Pope and I don't get a new job, and I don't have the chance for a dream."

"You could do that on your own."

"No I couldn't."

“What makes you think you couldn’t?”

She pondered, one eye closed. “Slick sidewalks.”

“How’s that?”

“One time a couple winters ago we had a cold snap. It was raining with a little sleet mixed in. We never get much of that, you know, when it gets near freezing and then wet. I slipped on the sidewalk coming into work and busted my ass.”

“What does that have to do with anything?”

“Before, I wouldn’t a had nobody to pick me up. Now I did.”

Soon they turned onto familiar streets toward Port Royal.

Nine

"The giant squid has been the stuff of legend for ages. Everyone from Christopher Columbus to Jules Verne believed in this monster of the deep. And every so often, a dead one, or odd pieces of a dead one, would wash ashore somewhere. But since the squid is a deep-sea creature, living two-to-three thousand feet below the surface, they were hard to track—much less find in the wild.

"In September of 2004, a group of Japanese scientists set out to photograph a living giant squid. They do love their sushi."

The two men with nice cars cackled. Everyone else was silent.

"They dropped cameras to the depths. To attract the creature to the cameras, they also dropped a baited line.

"In 2005, they finally succeeded. But the squid got caught up in the bait line. It struggled to escape for over four hours, finally getting free but losing a tentacle in the process.

"A year later, in December 2006, a giant squid was finally caught alive and in one piece. But shortly after being brought to the surface, it died.

"So, of the first two giant squids ever found alive, one was maimed and the other dead. It's like finding a Sasquatch and shooting it to prove it was real.

"This is us in a nutshell, people," the Pope said. "Our species. Homo sapiens. We leave unspeakable messes in our wakes for others to clean up. Not only do the ends justify the means, we blame the means for poor results, as if we had no decision in the process. And we can't seem to succeed without destroying something along the way. All we seem to manage is, 'Shit, wish I coulda got that sucker alive.' We go out into the world as guests at the Y and piss in the pool..."

After closing, Bow and the Pope sat in a corner of the diner with the lights off. Only a security light over the door separated spirits from the material world. The area was lit enough for them to see each other. Both needed a break from the heat. An overhead vent rattled as cold air fell into the room.

Bow was overstrung, his muscles coiled into rods, his mind too weary to even roam the netherworld. The Pope sipped a glass of ice water and nibbled on saltine crackers. Ten p.m., but not yet the darkest dark. The night crept along to snuff out the day, though stealthily, as if to avoid attention.

Bow looked at the cigarette pack "Can I try one of those?"

The Pope's eyebrows rose in slow motion. "You ever smoke before?"

"Not as a habit."

"Sorry. You can't."

Bow was irked. "Good, Lord, I'm not a kid."

"No. I mean you can't smoke in here. It's against the law. We can go outside in a bit." Then, the Pope sighed and said, "I have a favor to ask."

"Shoot."

"Don't fill Darlene's head full of bullshit. She can't take care of herself much less a kid. Her old lady may not be the best choice but at least she's there most of the time."

He felt a pang of resentment. Apparently, nothing was private. "She keeps saying she can't keep her son until she finds her dream," he said finally. "I don't get that."

"She has no ambition, no desire to better herself. She won't stick with anything. She can't be a mother until she can do that. And if she had Junior with her—even if she could pull that part of it off—she would trip over her own big feet and fall. And then two lives would be fucked up."

"Seems you don't have any confidence in her."

"Not for something like this. Not until she's capable of commitment."

Bow bristled within. This guy wasn't her father and it wasn't his decision. He sat, still perturbed, now peppered with gloom. "Well, I think it's her choice to make."

"Fine. Just keep that to yourself."

Bow scowled but if the Pope noticed, he didn't react. He then offered an olive branch. "You know, you're the first thing she's ever committed to for more than a week."

Bow let the moment pass. "Except when she tricks me into running interference between her and her mother."

The Pope grinned. "That's my girl."

Time lapsed and stretched. The dining room was pacifying and calm. Neither seemed to mind the silence. This was a resting place for both. Maybe more alike than either realized. They reached a tacit understanding.

Bow said, "Well, I think she believes in it, anyway. Finding her place in the world and all that."

The Pope nodded. "That's new, too. Maybe I should thank you."

"Just trying to stay out of everybody's way. I won't be here long."

"You want to talk about Eddie Lee?"

"Nope."

"Okay." Then the Pope snickered to himself. "Once Darlene cleaned the big coffee urns with a ton of soap but did a piss-poor job of rinsing all the detergent out. People got the rowdy shits. Abe had to go into the bathrooms and spray and plunge after each person came out because you could smell it all the way to the front door."

Bow smiled despite himself.

"You sure you don't want to talk about Eddie Lee?"

"No! Not now. Not ever."

"No problem. Just wondering."

"I'm still trying to figure out a lot of things."

"The universal predicament in the cosmic consciousness?"

"No."

"Then what?"

He paused, bereft of all but a blunted grace. "Everything. Like this place. These people. You."

"Well, don't let us distract you." The Pope then closed his eyes and pinched the bridge of his nose with his first two fingers as if to placate a headache. "In the beginning, the only thing I had going for me was that I can make food people will pay to eat. I had tinkered with barbecue recipes for years.

"Abe had a small sweat shop in Brooklyn. He did contract sewing. When he retired he moved here. He wanted to own a little place somewhere warm most of the time. He bought Jimmy's. It was failing. He couldn't communicate with anyone and he went through a half dozen cooks because he kept asking for something *unique* and none of them had the slightest idea what he was talking about. He was going through money faster than an ex-con in a whorehouse. I had to beg him to give me a shot. It worked out. Everyone associated with this place has a story. You've heard some of them."

"Yeah."

He eyed Bow directly, as if to give weight to every word. "Mickey taught health and coached middle school basketball. Then she decided to—be someone else. They booted her. Debbie lost her husband a few years ago. She fell in with a guy who was taking her money. I gave her a job, helped her find a new place. Next time the guy showed, she wasn't there. No forwarding address. New phone number. Bob doesn't speak English. Hell, I'm not sure he can speak anything. He couldn't even get a job as a bus boy because he had no one to translate for him or fill out an application. I hired him about the same way I hired you. Just pointed at a tub and a cart and he took it the rest of the way. Khrystile...probably isn't going to make it. She's young and immature and stupid. She's just a leaf in the wind and when she falls, somebody is going to step on her and crunch she will go."

"You reach out to people."

The Pope shrugged. "Anybody can. It's the only other thing I'm good at."

"I don't believe that."

"You'd be surprised how easy it is, especially how little effort it takes."

"That's not all of it, is it?"

"Well, don't try too hard to figure things out. You'd be in over your head." Angry words, but not said angrily.

"Just trying to get a handle."

"Will it help you accomplish anything?"

"No. Probably not."

"If it makes you feel any better you don't have to call me the Pope. You can call me Calvin if you want."

"Is that your real name?"

"No. But I've always liked the sound of it."

With that, Bow's muscles unwound a bit.

He felt the shock when they went outside. The heat was cruel and smothering. He had gone from chilled pudding to mousse flambé. His shirt stuck to him immediately. He breathed shallowly, afraid to inhale.

The Pope shook a couple of cigarettes loose and lit his. He passed the other and the lighter to Bow. Bow didn't hesitate. He lipped it and lit up like a pro. He sucked in a puff. The

Pope waited for him to gag and wheeze but he didn't.

After a few puffs, Bow held the cigarette like a wand, the orange glow flitting like a firefly. His movement made trails against the night. Arcs and lines lived but an instant before vanishing.

"Stop that," the Pope said. "Smoke it or put it out but don't play with it."

Bow smiled to himself and puffed again.

The Pope flicked the fire off his cigarette, wadded the butt and tossed it in the dumpster.

"You know why it's so hard for these people you work with to get clear of all the crap?"

"They make the same mistakes over and over?"

"Good answer. But no. Luck."

"What do you mean?"

"Luck is the most powerful force in the universe. And frivolous. Luck of biology, luck of environment, luck of the draw. You can't overcome bad luck without resources. Money can overcome bad luck. Strength of character can overcome bad luck, but even then, it leaves a trace of itself behind. The first time their luck turns bad they are rattled. The second time, they expect it to happen. After that they spend all their time waiting for it, knowing something bad's coming just around the bend. They can't see anything else." He took a long breath. "You know why most lottery winners lose it all eventually?"

"They're careless and make bad decisions?"

"Yeah. But why are they so careless? They can't stand good luck. They don't know how to act. They have no frame of reference for it."

Bow arched his back to stretch the knots. "I grew up being taught faith could overcome bad luck. I was never really sure how it was supposed to work, but most of the people I knew believed some version of it."

"Faith is belief in the impossible. It only helps those who croak before something bad happens and they lose their faith. I believe in God. I just don't believe God does anything. That's why I believe in luck."

"Sometimes you can make your own luck."

"Yeah, but that's not really luck. Luck is something you don't earn. Maybe there's enough luck out there even for somebody like you."

The river may still be a passage to the eastern sea but is not used as much commercially as in the past, existing now mainly for play and display, and some transport, as it has few other functions and no pressing business to address. The river minded its own business and if possessed of an opinion about anything, never let on.

Bow had gotten stronger. He hadn't given up running after that first day. He grew increasingly dependent on his morning purge. He had gone a quarter mile and was already panting but he continued on, desperate to inure himself against psychic siege.

A new nightmare had invaded his sleep. In the dream he was moving toward the patch of grass adjacent to the drop-off area of his granddaughter's school. He was running, though moving no closer. Ahead was Eddie Lee holding a pistol to her head. Bow gasped and strained and felt a mighty surge of energy—yet remained fixed in place. He reached his hand toward them, still so far away. The gun fired, and he woke.

The image plagued him but was not reality. He had not seen his granddaughter until later that night, after the mortician had done his best, when it was too late to mitigate anything. He ran hard, racking sinew and lung, somehow believing if he were exhausted no strength could be stolen from him.

His dead granddaughter. What a pitiless picture to have in his head. An entire city could be exterminated and he wouldn't have kept it in memory as long or deep. An airline crash could cremate hundreds but in their anonymity, and without the mind's eye fixed upon that sickly sight, he would not spend more than a day in commiseration.

Even when his father died suddenly, the loss edged and pointy for a time, he did not spend so many hours in so many days and nights consumed by such endless and terrible imaginings as this.

At a half mile the path dissolved, and he slalomed between the trees, trying not to slow his pace. Civilization had begun. These were the homes of antiquity he had seen from the boat, yielding to grubby undergrowth as the new world arced west and north. Farther ahead, the beginnings of salt marshes guarded the land between the earth and brackish water, with dense carpets of tall grasses, small, circular copses of shrubs and scattered, runted trees, all veiling water beneath—water and plants that would snatch a leg and hold it firm.

Some parts of the marsh were impossible to traverse without knowing if the next step would sink in mud to the knees—or higher. Sparrows, gulls, and oyster catchers were nimble enough to trespass there, but not man. Closer to the shoreline were thickets of saltmarsh cordgrass that hid creatures who wanted to remain hidden. Any creature wanting to remain hidden would not receive visitors kindly.

Still he ran, then turned and headed home, now slowed by deprivation and lactic acid. He knew, of course, why the image was of Eddie Lee with the gun, though there were other horrors he had known in the calm and quiet of the funeral home, the church, the grave site. These, too, dug at him with barbed claws.

He had been the catalyst. He had made the decisions that toppled the first domino. Eddie Lee was not there to answer for his disgrace. He was. He was to bear the colors, to dash into the fray—the spray of bullets and the thunder of cannons. He was unutterably ignorant of how he might eventually put aside the self-indictment and despair. Maybe he never would.

So he ran with a single mission. To manage in consciousness what he was unable to do in narcoma. He would carry the terrible weight upon his back until he could more readily bear it without being crushed beneath it.

As he knelt breathless upon the ground at the end of the round-trip, his penance for the day was complete, except in the vagaries of wishful thinking, where Eddie Lee would turn the gun on him instead.

We are free because he shed his blood, purified by the holy flood...

"Jesus Christ, Abe. Change the goddam station!"

Sobs emanated from the ladies' room, sounding like a lost puppy, drawing the attention of all the tables near the door.

Darlene, arms full of steaming dishes, shook her head and muttered to herself. "We got to get that poor boy a wiener."

During the summer there was always a late crowd determined to reduce the porcine population. Bow stood behind the diner and lit a cigarette. He had begun to buy the Pope's brand so he didn't feel like a mooch and took pride in his ability to smoke no more than two on even the worst day. Darlene joined him on break.

Her face was wet with sweat at the hairline and she pushed it back and repaired her ponytail. Her ears were like French doors, bookending a mask of indeterminate species.

"So you took up the habit."

"I only smoke a couple day. I enjoy it. It helps me unwind a little."

"Told you so. I hear it's really good after sex, too." She said in a teasing voice.

"I think about sex less than I think about eating. Sometimes the smell of meat cooking still makes me queasy."

"See, I'm exactly the opposite. I think about sex all the time but don't have nobody to do it with.

He felt slightly emasculated. "I'm sure you can find somebody if you want to."

She met his eyes. "No. Not no more. Don't want any more tryouts. I'm gonna wait until I love somebody and he loves me."

"You want romance."

"Who gives a Tommy Tittweaker about romance?"

"I thought you said—"

"I want love. Ain't the same thing."

He spent a moment deciphering this. He smoothed his shirt and pants with his palms. He struggled to recall either love or romance.

He paid the next month's rent in advance. He even went out of his way to keep the trailer furnished with soap, cleaner, paper towels, napkins, trash bags, and bottled water. The Pope offered no appreciation for any of this except by using it all.

Bow bought a few more clothes and put the rest of his money in a coffee can in an airspace under his pull-out bed. Most weeks he could put aside two hundred dollars. Eddie Lee would have been impressed.

He bought Darlene a pair of Italian sandals that covered most of her toes, and he downloaded a slew of new music. His tastes remained the same—Aerosmith, the Eagles, Fleetwood Mac, A/C D/C, Van Halen, Paul McCartney (the Beatles and Wings), The Who, and an obscure British band called the Strawbs he had heard on the college radio station once and liked them.

Darlene fussed over her gift but soon complained that her toes needed the environs to breathe and would reserve the new sandals for special occasions. Bow tried not to show his disappointment. When she would sit and remove a sandal, and flex her toes like a one-armed referee signaling a touchdown, he would at times involuntarily draw back.

He had begun to buy the Sunday *Charlotte Observer* and read every word. Usually, he would go into the empty diner on Monday morning and sit in the back corner. The diner was stifling at first. Abe was notoriously cheap and turned the thermostat to ninety degrees when the diner was closed. Bow moved it to sixty and put on coffee while waiting for the room to cool.

He usually flipped on the lights, but today read by daylight as there had been an intermittent but steady parade of cars creeping by to see if the diner was open. One had actually stopped, and some round-headed git banged on the door just above the Closed sign.

Bow crouched down and sneaked into the kitchen, and hid for several minutes before the man finally got into his car and drove away. People were so fucking clueless.

The *Observer* was his only connection to the outer world. There was a tiny, 7-inch TV in the trailer but without cable or dish, only got two channels and was too small to watch anyway except within six inches.

He always saved the Lifestyle section for last, an alien treasure and source of much needed amusement—as is life among the vacuous.

Three or four entire pages were devoted to oblivious celebrities absent of any relationship to the common folk, and if not who was bopping who, or chronicling new forms of self-aggrandizement with no small portion of hyperbole, belched every ill manner of real-world events through their singular, and rabidly outlandish, perspectives; fires, floods, storms, tornados, hurricanes, and general distemper provided ample fuel for the shamelessly affected—

Reality star/model/singer Galaxa Miaxa commented, "My heart goes out to all those people recovering from that terrible fire. I burned myself on my pool float just last week so I know how they feel. I release part of my ch'i to them"—

...The sultry star of Beaver Tango is hosting a fondue brunch fund-raiser to send the troops samples of her new fragrance Randy Candy'— "I know you'll just love it. Smells like home."

..."God bless you, Kansas. Tornadoes are b-a-d news...oh, Arkansas. Sorry, they're spelled the same."

Hip hop star Buzz 2 Big bought a share of the struggling Ottawa Senators today to save the franchise. "I didn't know hockey was played on ice," he commented, "but I down witit."

Perhaps exploitation of the proletariat is a tradition handed down from first age entertainers. Maybe court jesters of old made merry during the Plague.

"Anyone see that guy whose nose fell off? At least he won't have to smell his neighbors anymore."

The following Sunday at church Bow left wondering if he and the Pope indeed shared some psychic connection.

"As quickly as you can think of three famous people. Now. Think how you know them. Now, think if you really should, if they are worth knowing at all or should shuffle off into obscurity. Do they contribute to the common good or simply add more shit to the pile? All we can do is pray God they don't breed."

Even so, Bow enjoyed his paper. Charlotte was close enough for him to realize North Carolina was still functioning without him. Besides, he needed contact with the outside world, however remote.

At noon he made a sandwich. In the afternoon he walked through old Port Royal, whose history predates the Revolutionary War and still has a few landmarks to prove it. Even then the population was split between those sympathetic to the Americans and those sympathetic to the Tories.

During the Civil War everyone had been on the same side. Port Royal had managed to avoid General Sherman, perhaps by being too far off the path.

The main streets were landscaped and perfectly clean and resembled parts of Main Street Disneyworld. No one wore an animal costume but there was a horse-drawn carriage filled with soggy tourists wishing they had stayed in Wisconsin.

Unknown to most people, Port Royal was the first settlement in the New World. It existed three years before St. Augustine and forty-five years before Jamestown. The deepest natural harbor on the Atlantic coast is nearby. Port Royal has also flown the flags of France,

Spain, England, Scotland, the Confederacy, and the USA.

During Reconstruction new entrepreneurs envisioned Port Royal as a major center of commerce as it already had the largest cotton compressor in the world. Shrimp, clams, and oysters flourished after that. No one can say for sure, but some have speculated the reason Port Royal never reached its full potential was the pervasive stink of dead sea creatures.

Bow returned through the woods and hiked down to a narrow creek to cool off. He waded from one slippery rock to another. He lit on one just wide enough for a pair of feet. He sat down for a moment and dug his toes into the sandy bottom. He could not deny that a flawless day encircled him and that death had taken a brief respite.

Just then a fat brown snake swam from beneath the same rock, brushing his leg before circling back toward him. He leapt backward in two fluid moves and fled, his second run of the day.

He sat in the air-conditioned comfort of the dining room and re-read the sports page, including every box score. He contemplated taking a nap but the only spot not roasting was the diner. The puny air conditioning in the trailer did little during the heat of the day. Why would anyone contrive a domicile, even a temporary one, wrapped in aluminum, baking like a Sunday pot roast.

Then he wondered about the contents of the padlocked footlocker at the end of the Pope's bed. What could the man possibly have worthy of being locked?

Despite the clever use of adjectives, metaphors, and idioms—and references to the punishing heat of June and July—there is little to adequately convey the pure worse-no-bullshit-inferno intensity of August without first-hand experience. People have been known to puddle and be washed away by the rain.

Rain comes every day in August but usually for a short duration, and successful only in generating steam off the pavement hot enough to scald. The locals are accustomed to the heat but not immune. Old women sit on their porches in their house dresses with the hem rolled up past their knees and their stockings rolled down to their ankles, working a handheld fan a hundred swipes a minute.

Dogs have been known to defect to a neighbor's yard if a sprinkler is running.

Workers at the diner took turns spending their breaks in the walk-in freezer, five minutes timed to the second, for safety as much as fairness. Debbie wore shorts and a thin, sleeveless top. The shorts made her legs and backside look like a Picasso when he was still trying to find his niche.

The Pope sweated violently and lost three pounds a day, but seemed less troubled except for frequent passes over his face with a wet cloth kept in icy water.

Mickey must have used a half-can of deodorant each broiling day because he smelled like a botanical garden much of the time, eventually beginning to molt like stinkweed as the day wore on, and would come back to Bow's sink, open his shirt—proudly revealing his newly contoured chest and reworked nipples--wash his pits from rib to elbow, then go outside to apply phase two of the fragrances of Holland.

Khrystile perspired from the top of her head down and wore a towel around her neck like a boa to stem the flow. Every couple of hours she would wash her face and pile her hair atop her head until it drooped like the belly of a New Jersey cop.

Poor Darlene became so aromatic, Bow felt sorry for her. She was aware of this, having learned to frequently sniff the air like a hound during some exceptional torridity, after gassing herself unconscious in the fifth grade. She would powder sanitary napkins in baking soda and tape them under her arms. For an ancillary location, she filled a sandwich bag with crushed ice and slipped this into her bosom. She could squeeze five pounds of dead weight between her breasts if needs be.

August in the Lowcountry is like the color red; seductive from a distance—a willowy figure in a dress or a flashy car. A cardinal or a basket of apples. A rose bush in full bloom or a bowl of raspberries.

Then, affronted by lingering examination, eyes move away as such spectra are readily abandoned, shunned, and ignored.

Simply because they are too damn...red.

Ten

The Pope and Bow moved their old chairs nearer the river's edge and into more shade. They rarely sat out in daylight, but on this Thursday they lounged before opening. This was the cool of the day and the heat was still ferocious, but the sun was hidden behind the trees.

In a narrow breach between the pines Bow saw the faint reaches of the Atlantic like a mirage. A cruise ship passed in the distance, moving in slow motion.

The river does not provoke the same longing as the sea. There is no desire to flee the calamity of the world and simply embrace the ebb and flow of time in its narrows. There is little attraction to seek immortality from its shore when every outward vision is limited by growth and clutter, natural or manmade.

The sea is its own god, its own universe, its own world in which humanity has no true part.

From the sea, storms gather and rise to destroy lives and property. If stranded, the sea provides nothing to slake the thirst. The sea engulfs completely, swallowing whole any unwary intruder. The sea is reckless, secure in its own might, its own piety, its own measure.

The sea is also faithful, its currents true if ever evolving.

Had the tilt of the earth been a mere few degrees aside, men may have evolved into denizens of the deep.

The sea is a reminder men are not in control of this world. The sea is a warning there is ever danger in the murky deep. The sea does not alter from tick-to-tock except at its own leisure, its movements never quite coherent. The sea is always a fickle stranger, yet still calls out its summons in the dearest of all voices.

Bow was trying iced coffee for the first time. Not the same. Didn't have the same bite as fresh hot, even after being reduced to a coffee-flavored beverage laden with hazelnut syrup.

The Pope was lost in thought. No, not lost. The Pope was never lost. He sorted as he internally viewed some impression known only to him.

There was a loud thrashing in the water near a sandbar a hundred yards offshore, far too rowdy to be fish.

"Dolphins," the Pope said.

"Fighting?"

"Gang bangs," he replied.

"You're kidding."

"Dolphins do gang bangs. Two males will hold a female against the sand and take turns going at her."

"That's bizarre."

"It's their rules. Dolphins are also one of the few species besides humans that have sex for non-procreative entertainment."

"Huh."

The Pope fired up a cigarette, the smoke hanging in stagnant clouds. "Dolphins also like to get stoned."

A staccato grunt. "How's that?"

"Pufferfish have a deadly toxin as a defense mechanism. Dolphins will harass them until they release the toxin. It has the same effect on them as marijuana on humans."

"You are a fountain of useless information."

"That I am. And don't be such a fud."

Bow chuckled to himself. Soon it would be time to work. Both seemed to recall this at the same moment. Neither was very excited. Subdued to the point of stupor. The kitchen was even less tolerable than the open air.

A car rumbled down the street and even across the breadth of the parking lot the thumping beat of the sound system echoed across the way.

"A tribesman, no doubt," the Pope said.

Bow grinned. "Was that a racist crack?"

"I don't know. Maybe."

"You should do one of your lectures on that."

"Can't do racism."

"Why not?"

"Haven't decided if I'm for it or against it."

"Ha ha."

The moment lapsed. After a moment, the Pope smiled. "You know why God invented orgasms?"

"Why?"

"So black people know when to stop."

"That's so rude."

"I know. Black people are extremely important to our culture. Young black men especially."

"Yeah?"

"Of course. How else would ugly white girls get prom dates?"

Bow laughed genuinely. "That's terrible."

"But you laughed. See, that's the thing about cultural bias. We still find it funny. Like rednecks or A-rabs or Moos-lims."

"Yeah, maybe."

"Well, black people will never be truly free until hip-hop dies."

Sunday morning had cooled a few degrees and they gathered for free ribs, corn, and slaw. Extra gallons of tea waited in reserve. Everyone knew the respite was fleeting.

"Labor Day celebrates us, the working men and women of America, though I know some of you have gone out of your way to avoid this honor."

The laughter was sparse and revelatory.

"I look at you and can't help but notice there are only a couple of black faces here. I do stop and wonder sometimes why I don't have more black people as friends. Truth is, I did not grow up with black people. There weren't a lot of black people where I used to live.

"If I am biased at all, it's because there are cultural elements within our fair land, and sad to say, a lot of these just don't interest me. It isn't personal. I'm not really interested in dance mixes, Oprah, romance novels, or the sons of Finland for that matter."

Titters welled and died.

"So, what's the difference between racism and cultural disregard? Well, the most obvious one is that we didn't chain up and drag guys with names like Lars and Ole over here to do our dirty work."

Laughter trickled through the crowd.

"Yeah, I know. All that was a long time ago and a lot of people think it's all over and done with.

"But let's face it. Racism of every sort is still with us, whether it's a white cop shooting an unarmed black man or giving a wider berth to a black woman in the grocery aisle than we would a white woman. Even more discouraging is that racism will remain with us as long as we don't fully understand what racism is at its heart.

"We are a people of intellectual sloth. We somehow believe that what we don't know can't hurt us."

"See, racism exists because white people still believe that black people *let* themselves become slaves. White people mistakenly believe they would have handled things differently if the roles had been reversed. That they would have *never* allowed themselves to be slaves, ignoring that if you're tied up with a gun to your head you'll do anything to survive.

"Ironically, the only way our very American version of racism could have been avoided is if the first slaves had crept into their masters' houses and slit the throats of everyone inside while they slept. Mercilessly and with finality."

All sound suddenly evaporated as if the whole world hitched for a moment.

"I know, I know, that's harsh. But stay with me.

"These slaves would have been killed, of course. And there were revolts and uprisings and runaways, but not enough to make a dent.

"Now I know this is a big ask, but if the first slaves had slaughtered the families that enslaved them, and had been willing to sacrifice themselves—how many would have died? Five thousand, ten thousand? Twenty thousand? A lot of lives, yes, but nothing like the four million who were ultimately enslaved.

"The traders, the sellers, the owners, everyone involved would have been forced to say, 'These people are fucked up-crazy and will never be tamed.' And by the end of the sixteen hundreds, say, slavery would not have existed here.

"And the saddest, most soul-wrenching part of all is that the only way black people could have earned the respect they were entitled to as human beings would have been to kill every white person they met. And that is a fucking tragedy.

"So consider this. There is no white person in this country who didn't gain something from black people somewhere along the line, especially here in good ol' Dixie.

"Not because of what they did for us, but because of what they were not allowed to do for themselves."

Labor Day weekend was more chaotic than mealtime at the dog pound. Everyone who worked at Jimmy's was on overload, except Abe, who sat on his stool, chewed on his unlit cigar, and took in and counted the money. In fact, the only time his mien changed was when he was counting money, and then there was a scarcely seen, slightly crazed glint in his eyes.

To many of the locals, Labor Day could have been called Liberation Weekend. The kids were back in school and the Yankees and other foreigners had gone home. The next batch—the snowbirds—would not arrive until December or January.

As Darlene would say, "It's either screamin' kids or grouchy old farts. Pick your poison."

For the next three months or so, locals would fill the tables. They were flush with optimism, even with the knowledge that autumn would bring a certain melancholy, and Labor Day weekend served as its genesis even though it was still eighty-five degrees.

Paradoxically, the diner would be closed on Labor Day, a Monday.

Saturday was intense, non-stop, but a good day for all, as each hostess had pockets pole-dancingly flush with singles.

Twenty bucks from each was kicked back to the kitchen workers and Bob. Khrystile only managed five, and stiffed poor Bob completely, who did not seem to notice or show concern.

Khrystile had a new Mister and upkeep on Harleys was expensive. Darlene had a pocket wad so big it looked as if she had a penis. Mickey might finally be able to afford a down payment on one.

The summer of heartbreak was over for Bow. Naturally, the heartbreak was not.

Labor Day became a lazy day, and one of the few where he expected to see no one.

Darlene went to see Junior. The Pope was gone, as usual.

After his run and reading the paper, Bow made himself restless by worrying about becoming restless. Somehow he made it all the way to five without any major upheaval. At six he warmed some spaghetti—the Pope's spaghetti was perfect, heavy on meat, low on sauce—and toasted a couple of pieces of thick-sliced bread. His appetite had completely rebounded and one of the benefits of being the dishwasher at Jimmy's was he never had to eat anything he didn't like. There was always—**always**—something near-orgasmic in the Pope's repertoire.

He hadn't gained much weight. Mainly he had regained the weight he had lost on the White Russian and potato chip diet. He was tanned with a coppery hue, and strong. Rare was the day when he did not run, and rarer still was the day he fully spent himself. He kept saving money, and his hair was finally long enough for a nub in the back, held with a rubber band.

He still could not sleep more than six hours a night but more often than not—perhaps more than half the time—he rested without such furious psychical disturbances. These subconscious plays were no less troubling when they appeared but more sanely tolerated.

He utilized anything and everything at his disposal to put down the beast—exercise or caffeine or guitar music loud enough to make one's testicles cramp in pain—work and the company of the Pope and Darlene, even when he could not get a word in sideways—and a routine steadfastly held.

If any effort were at all successful, he would maintain the course until failing. Perhaps this was not healing as much as the application of all his resources and the occupation of all his senses, but he had made progress.

He talked himself into drinking an Amstel Light but became warm before he was halfway through, and the rest watered a bush. At seven Darlene pulled up. He was surprised to see her. Whatever else, she never brought him down.

They went for a walk. Heading south, there was not a true path, mostly an area where little would grow, and what did grow had been stomped flat. The trail meandered through the trees, down to the bank, and then paralleled the river, as if whatever creatures had been the original trailblazers had eaten fermented berries and staggered along, or else lost their sense of direction.

They passed the site of the Proclamation Tree, where on Christmas, 1863, the first reading of the Emancipation Proclamation took place. Odds are, this was a lump of coal for most white people thereabouts.

Port Royal is muggy even when it's temperate. There is only less muggy and more muggy. Northerners would still shrivel and die but to the natives, September was the first month of relief. Bow was pacified by their slow pace. Ahead was the base of the island and the narrows of the Colleton River. Here there were clusters of docks and boats still in use.

"Whoever finds the first second-hand condom wins," Darlene said.

"Why would people come out here?" he asked. "There's no place to lie down."

"The Pope calls it the exuberance of youth," she answered. "I never did. I didn't have a place to put my big ass, I wouldn't do it."

Bow looked out at the bridge to Parris Island, where newbie Marines learned to kill and, hopefully, dodge bullets. Port Royal annexed Parris Island several years ago and doubled its population but the grunts rarely came into town. Charleston and Savannah offered more exotica, though time off during basic was scant at best.

He breathed deep. Salt air was thin and barely detectable, and most of the time was a figment created by proximity, not reality.

"God, I love the fall," Darlene muttered.

Bow made a faux snickering noise. "It's eighty degrees and the trees still have their leaves."

"I guess. But you can tell something's coming. The sun is cockeyed and daylight doesn't last as long."

"I used to love the fall, too," he said wistfully. He took a breath and forced his mood upward. "So how is Junior?"

She looked straight ahead. "I don't have a dream yet."

"You will."

"Think so?"

"I do."

"What about you?"

He did not answer right away. "My days of dreams are long gone."

"Did you ever?"

"Well, I did what I was supposed to do, I guess."

"I'm sure you were good at it."

"I was. Once I guess. Now I just want to be less...heartsick."

She looked at him. "Yeah."

"Anyway, I don't want you to feel I'm a project anymore."

Her disappointment showed in a gaping maw. "How come?"

"I'm getting better, for one. You've got yourself and Junior to look after."

"Who gives a Harry Hairpie about that?"

"I do. You have helped me pull it together and I appreciate it. You can still do that as a friend. But whatever happens, it's up to me to fix it, not you."

She took the crook of his arm. "The Pope warned me not to mention any of this straight out, so I haven't. But what happened to you was a tragedy—"

"Maybe, but—"

"Just listen to me. Please. If I get sidetracked, I won't remember what I was going to say and I'll just babble."

"Okay."

"I don't know how much you have hurt, and I don't know anything about your life back there, or how bad it fell apart. But I think you didn't really have nobody. If you did, I wouldn't a found you. So, maybe I won't understand everything, but you'll still have me if you need me. I won't give up and I won't go away."

Bow felt a sudden heat rise and fill his chest. Even before the tragedy, he'd always been subject to the fitfulness of others. He had been second-guessed in his job by the Judge and his cronies. His wife had a whole life apart from him, and he had forfeited all measure of intimacy for a sense of permanence and stability.

His daughter had grown away from him years before. She and her mother had been at odds much of the time but he had been excluded from all meaningful aspects of her growing up.

She had met a man in college and married. Bow had walked her down the aisle as his reward. Marie had planned everything and was there to take the accolades. Even when his granddaughter had been born, Bow had become progenitor in name only. He could not even hold the child without being corrected at every turn. He had sacrificed any aspirations of happiness for the mechanics of the perfunctory, and in the end, such sacrifice had purposed nothing.

And here was Darlene, this distorted and beautiful soul, this rogue eidolon from another planet.

"Thank you," he said finally.

She reached for and held him. Bow raised his arms but let them rest lightly on her hips, even as she drew him in. Finally, he slid his arms around her and held his breath, basking in the tenderness of foreign affection.

The Pope played with his lighter, flipping the lid open and closed.

"Either light it or put it away," Bow joked, "but don't play with it."

The corners of the Pope's mouth turned upward ever so slightly. He rarely revealed what he was really thinking but it was certain to be a distance removed from whatever he said.

"You want to talk about Eddie Lee?" He said this off-handedly, as if customary.

Bow answered in kind. "No. No. A thousand times no. Stop trying to be a buttinsky."

"You know the word quidnunc means busybody."

"So does yenta."

"Touche." The Pope tipped his head. "You ever considered that people like Eddie Lee just don't belong in this world."

Bow grunted, now agitated. "No. People do things. Sometimes they turn out bad. It doesn't have anything to do with anything else."

"You made my point. There is what someone *should* be and what someone *wants* to be. It happens to a lot of people—maybe most people. But it's an impossible condition for someone like Eddie Lee."

Bow became more irritated. "That's bullshit."

The Pope seemed to acquire more energy and sat up straight. His voice had returned as well. "He was doomed the first time he stole something and got away with it."

"You mean like Karma?"

"Not Karma. Plausibility. Eddie Lee should have been a welder or a carpenter. Something he was capable of being besides a thief. Instead, he became a thief. Even if everything else about him was the same—his IQ, his lack of scruples, his...unseemliness—had he been a welder or a carpenter, none of this would have ever happened."

"I'm tired of hearing about Eddie fucking Lee," Bow grumbled.

"You became what you should be."

"And look how that turned out."

"That's where you're wrong. You got blistered but it doesn't mean you shouldn't have been a lawyer."

"Well, I'm not a lawyer anymore."

The Pope paused, lit a cigarette, then yawned, inhaling as if short of breath. Bow noticed but said nothing. "You don't have to believe me. It doesn't change anything. People who aren't what they should be can't hack it in this world. Some work very hard to be something other than what they should be. But it's still a sad, sorry waste of humanity."

Bow waited. There was nothing more. "Are you what you should be?"

The Pope gazed outward as if his train-of-thought had leaked away. Perhaps the question was too unwieldy to bear. He blew out a slow, steady stream of smoke.

"No."

Eleven

The end-of-summer boom had brought a temporary prosperity to everyone at Jimmy's. There was pale euphoria all around. Bow had saved nearly a thousand dollars, not the least bit guilty he had paid no taxes. Darlene bought new work shoes, her old ones worn from the inside out.

Mickey had been able to afford a few more hormone treatments. Another three and he could drop to a maintenance dose and claim his manhood. He had sprouted a few fuzzy black ringlets of hair on his upper chest. He undid his top button to display them. The Pope told him to close the flap. He complied, but managed to leave a narrow opening between the first and second button, so that whenever he would draw a mighty breath, a couple strands would pop out to be seen by all.

By noon he had hyperventilated so much he nearly fainted and dropped a tray of chili fries. He remedied the gap, but was then seen rubbing his five o'clock shadow, which in this particular case was three days old.

Wednesday night after work Darlene approached Bow. She always held his arm in private. Bow had come to realize this was not a flirtation, nor even amelioration. This was a silent promise of genuine fondness—that these hands would never be so far removed as to be unfound if sought.

Her smile was always infectious, always mischievous, a chamber of wonder encompassing her overlong face.

"I need a date for Sunday night."

"For what?"

"It's a surprise."

Bow's nostrils widened. "What kind of surprise?"

"A good surprise."

"Will you promise to wear a bra?"

"And panties."

"Okay. What time?"

"Eight."

"I'll be ready."

Bow didn't have anything decent to wear. He bought a pair of dark gray slacks, a pale green long-sleeved shirt, a tan pullover sweater, and a pair of knock-off Rockports. He forgot about dress socks, but borrowed a pair from the Pope, who hadn't worn them in ten years. He thought without sentiment about how similar-looking togs had been part of his daily uniform for over twenty years. Odd, the recollections of so many once-noteworthy things not ruefully missed.

Darlene was beautiful, and not just from mandible to tarsus. She wore a red blouse with puffed shoulders and an A-line hem, ivory jeans with a slight flair at the bottom, and red, low-heeled pumps. Her hair had been set in thick curls and long waves, and minimal makeup expertly applied.

When she moved in for a hug, he caught the scent of slightly musky lilac.

"You smell nice," he whispered.

She leaned back and pulled her neckline down to reveal a black lacy bra. "And got all my undies on, too."

She took his elbow and led him to her car. When he opened the passenger door he saw that the interior had been cleaned, vacuumed, and smelled of Christmas.

"You cleaned your car."

"Hey, I know how to treat a man right."

As they drove, Bow felt light-heartened, unafraid. "I want to tell you something."

"You want my body and can't take it no more?"

"Close."

"Fire away."

"It probably won't make much sense."

"Who gives a Bucky Fuqua about that?"

He took a moment. "You're the best friend I ever had."

Darlene did not answer and the rankled engine was the only sound. Then she sniffed. Loud enough for him to hear. Loud enough for the entire population of Beaufort County to hear.

In the dark, he could only see her silhouette. She still said nothing. "I just wanted to thank you," he added.

She snorted again, and reached across the console and gripped his hand. They rode on in silence.

Much later, she said, "Have you said anything to The Pope about this?"

"About what?"

"That you want to heal up and get your life back."

"A different life."

"Yeah, but does he know?"

"I think so, why?"

She seemed uneasy. “Has he said anything about your coming out project?”

“My what?”

“Like a way to prove you’re serious about it. You know what needs to be done to move on, and all that, and you promise to keep at it. Kinda like the eighth grade.”

“This is the first I’ve heard of it.”

“Well, don’t be surprised.”

“What is it exactly? Like a contract?”

“No. Something you have to do. It’s like, as he would say, ‘getting out of your comfort zone’.”

“Good Lord. If I were any more out of my comfort zone, I’d be on a different planet.”

“Don’t worry. It won’t be anything dangerous. Just something you’d never do on your own. I’m sure he’ll come up with something good.”

Bow was suddenly apprehensive. “What did you have to do?”

Even in the dark he could see her nose wrinkle. “Volunteer at an old people’s home every Sunday night for two whole months. Clean up after them and such. It was awful. My sinuses still ain’t all the way healed up.”

Uh-oh was far too mild a reaction.

The Beaufort County Playhouse was an old theatre that had been glorious once, before movies were digital, too expensive, too loud, and too silly. Fortunately, the regal lady had been preserved, more or less. The brick front and overhead marquee remained unchanged. The lobby had ditched the confetti carpet and most of the snack stands. Now, only beverages were served, even wine if desired.

Inside, the ceiling formed a penumbra thirty feet above the seats, its face painted gold and covered in finely detailed relief. The seats had been reupholstered in a dark burgundy, the walls draped floor to ceiling in crimson velvet.

In the lobby, Bow had seen posters propped on easels offering a portent of the night's presentation. Lawrence Dilworth, recently of the Macon Arts Festival, was to perform a one-man show as General Robert E. Lee. Mr. Dilworth was too fat to be a plausible facsimile but possessed the white hair and beard, and the rebel uniform fit, without which he would have looked more like Santy.

Below in smaller pictures was the actor as George Washington, the Apostle Paul, and Dave Thomas of Wendy's.

Darlene leaned in with tangible excitement. "I saw him do Ben Franklin a few years ago and it was fantastic."

She had secured great seats in the perfect center, halfway in and halfway down, and likely to avoid the crunch of anyone squeezing in or out. Bow looked at her again, still seeing her organic energy and took her hand as the lights dimmed. Applause could wait until warranted.

Mr. Dilworth used a black cane to great effect, as the instrument was probably necessary, and sipped water from a plastic bottle every so often. Damn the anachronism, this was art.

"Ah was offered the command of the Union Army, but mah heart was in Virginia."

As there were no recordings of Lee's voice, great liberties could be taken, but Bow doubted the general had sounded so much like Yosemite Sam. His skepticism was not merely the product of current inclination.

This developed and ripened over many years as a prosecutor. Everyone had an alibi. Everyone had a *good* reason. Guilty or not, everyone was *blameless*.

As for Lee—historically—no matter the slaughter invoked to preserve free labor, the permeable corruption of the rebel leadership to eschew the inevitable, the wanton waste of resources, human and material, and the spiteful justification of every action even in defeat, Lee's legacy as a man of honor had outlived him to this day.

Bow knew honor by its absence. He had not been raised among honorable men. His father wasn't honorable. The Judge wasn't honorable. The closest he had ever come to a true man of honor was one of his first-year law professors, and he had the luxury of living in the cloister of academia, where even the most outlandish thought patterns were greeted with a yea, Lord.

The oratory was long and punctuated with frequent pauses, many unnecessary. The man's contrived stares into the ozone looked more like a search for forgotten lines than solemnity. Still, the evening allowed him to be among people in the most casual manner, where no questions were asked, no pointed stares, nothing more than smiles and nods in passing—with a lovely young woman on his arm.

Afterward, Darlene was giddy. "Wasn't that great?"

"Perfect," Bow answered.

The following Saturday was the opening of youth deer hunting season. This was an orientation into a different sphere of adulthood, like a Bar Mitzvah or initiation into the Ku Klux Klan. In this, adolescents learned the value of blasting the shit out of things. This is what shotguns and rifles are for, except in the military, prison guards, and under certain—though oft dubious—circumstances, the police.

Blasting things is an American rite of passage, a seduction into our latent desires for purposeless destruction. This has little to do with the right to bear arms, defending oneself, or putting meat on the table. One gets a gun, one can't wait to use it. Blasting the shit out of things is as fundamentally intrinsic as suckling or getting an erection. In fact, adolescent boys are known to commonly get an erection by blasting the shit out of things.

This is where gun control advocates failed. We love wanton, senseless carnage. We either try suppression, and avoid guns altogether, or we succumb to acceptance, and blast the fuck away. Nothing else brings such a kick to our adrenal glands. Nothing gives us a greater sense of American unity. Nothing has a higher purpose than *kaboom!*

We blast animals under the pretense that this sanctifies the act and is something more than unadulterated bloodletting.

Adults couldn't legally blast until late October. They would enjoy this hunt vicariously through their progeny, salivating at the very least, cheating if possible.

On a crisp Indian Summer day, a young hunter or huntress, dressed fashionably in camouflage, would oil up the rifle, insert a raft of mini-missiles, and head to the woods with Daddy, Grandpa, brothers-cousins-uncles, et al—and even Mama on rare occasions.

Areas are baited, prime spots are located, and then the hunters, guides, and coaches hide and wait until some unsuspecting deer wanders by and blast the shit out away.

The bait used is doe-in-rut scent. No one seems to wonder how this is obtained. Do people sneak up behind a female deer with a sex toy and fondle its hiney, or show it Bullwinkle porn?

Then how is this invisible bouquet captured? Is the air about a doe's ass sucked up by a vacuum, captured in a balloon, compressed into a cylinder?

What process converts this into an oily liquid? Maybe perspiration is thus imbued (after all, the process has to make the doe a little tense). Maybe the essence is simply tapped directly from the source like sap from a tree.

"What do you do for a living?" one might ask in passing.

"I get female deer horny and collect the run-off in a bucket."

If this primal urge has not yet blossomed or abates—should the newly-indoctrinated hunter balk, freeze, miss the shot, or abandon the hunt for a video game—the errant youth would be chided or smacked down—or at least lectured about how the Constitution insists we blast the shit out of things for the good of the country.

Before the day is out, however, he or she would revel in blasting the shit out of things for its own sake, because this is part of a communal heritage, or else be dubbed unpatriotic—or worse, a liberal.

Saturday was swamped at Jimmy's with all manner of neo-blasters. If good luck had prevailed, the kid had already bagged a deer and had the thing sprawled in the back of the truck. Time for an early, celebratory lunch, showing pictures of the kill, usually with the acne-prone huntsman kneeling beside or standing over the poor animal, who invariably has its tongue protruding.

If the youth, and his or her party, wanted to get a later start—though this meant more parental beer consumption and less blasting—they would load up on barbecue beforehand or take some to go.

With blasting the shit out of things and potential erections as exceptions, nothing co-functions with guns as perfectly as beer. Beer illuminates the true way, heightens the awareness of prey, and elevates the sight and smell of blood. Add this to the normal Saturday gorgers and there was a line waiting for a table all day.

Of course deer were not immediately at hand. They did not swim in the river or even vacation there. In this part of South Carolina one could be in the boonies in twenty minutes, ready to unleash. Jimmy's had a reputation spread from blaster lips to blaster lips. The diner was as much a part of the initiation tradition as alcohol, butchery, and whispered talk of women's privates.

The Pope was quick but could have used six hands. Debbie stepped in to turn the ribs and aerate the pulled pork, and Bow stepped in to do prep, making salads and pulling rolls out of the warmer. As long as they had a supply of clean dishes, the dirties could wait.

Occasionally, Abe would stick his head in, chomp his cigar, and take a good look around. Presumably, this was to see if anyone was idle, ill, absent, or dead. He would then withdraw and the swinging door would sway to a close without a word being spoken. By day's end, all parties were satisfied to some degree or another.

The night was breezy and people were laughing and talking loudly as they exited the office across the parking lot—happy to be liberated from the late shift providing customer service to the mal- and misinformed. Near the Hardees across the way, two pickup trucks honked in succession in the vehicular version of "Psst!" and "Oh, hey!"

Bow wore a long-sleeved shirt. The Pope wore his customary white T-shirt—the same one he had worn beneath his apron at work. Bow teased his decaf coffee and the Pope slurped his mud as if the day were beginning instead of at its end.

"How can you drink that stuff and still sleep?" Bow asked.

"I don't sleep much," the Pope answered. "But caffeine doesn't affect me that way. I suppose you know many over-the-counter sleep aids contain caffeine."

"Huh," Bow replied. He was in a rare contemplative mood, evil held at bay and lesser demons inviting more genteel and philosophical discourse. "Can I ask you something?"

"No."

"Are you happy?"

"Ah. A new definition for the word no. And no, I am not happy."

"I used to believe I was...before, you know, but now I believe I just didn't want to think about it."

"I know the feeling. Like now, for instance."

He was not intimidated nor shaken by the Pope's tone. He knew it to be pyrite. Oh, the Pope could be easily agitated when he was overly tired but the fire was *ignus patuus.*

"Can I ask you another thing?"

"No."

"Why don't you do something else?"

"You mean why do I have a different definition of the word no, or do I crave upward mobility?"

"You could do a lot more than this."

"So could you."

"I intend to."

"Maybe I do, too. Just waiting for the right moment."

"How long have you been doing this?"

"Seven, eight years."

"And the right moment hasn't come?"

"I...am...very...de-lib-er-ate..."

He let it drop. Whatever connection he had made had come unplugged.

"Darlene said something strange the other day."

"And this surprises you?"

"She said something about my coming out project."

The Pope beamed. "I had her elbow deep in shit."

"Why?"

"I told you. She needs to make a commitment to herself. That was a start. Doing something she absolutely would not do otherwise."

"I don't have to do anything like that, do I?" He instantly regretted speaking. His mouth hung open as if he might suck the words back in.

The Pope cocked his head. "Do you want to live?"

"Of course. I don't think I ever really wanted to die."

"Well, I wouldn't know. Seemed you were trying harder to die."

"I know what it looked like. I'm just saying I don't know what good making a big deal out of it would do."

"Maybe nothing. But if you make a pledge to yourself and mark it, you may be more apt to honor it."

"We'll see," he said tentatively.

"Excellent," the Pope replied. "Tell me. Have you ever been funny?"

A few nights later, Bow was sitting on the sofa listening to *Toys in the Attic* by Aerosmith. All the lights were off except for a desk lamp perched on the counter. The relative darkness still suited and soothed him. This had become his ritual to unwind. Eyes closed, motionless shadows without and blissful noise within, he did not notice when the Pope sat down in a chair at the dinette table.

When he finally opened his eyes, he saw the Pope shifting in the seat, trying various positions on his lumbar area. He would settle for a moment, then move again. He turned off the music.

"Back ache?"

The Pope grunted. "Just can't get situated."

"Want me to get you some Tylenol?"

The Pope shoved a couple of throw pillows behind him, sat back, and remained still. "No. I'm good."

Bow had spent four months with this man and still stepped lightly. "Want to talk?"

The Pope looked at him, though not in pique as much as amusement. "No. Just a little off, I guess."

"Sorry."

The Pope nodded painfully. "I hate it when I let myself get out of sorts."

"You can't control everything."

"Well, I can do better than this."

Bow was at a loss but was left uncertain. He understand pride. He understood self-discipline. He even understood intransigency. None of these fixed a backache.

The Pope bent to remove his shoes, his grimace fixed, his grunt echoing throughout the space. "You had me fooled."

"How so?"

"The music. I had you weighed as a country music fan."

"Some of the new country is okay. I grew up on the old stuff. My old man loved George Jones. Couldn't stand it. I can download some country if you'd like."

The Pope soured. "God no."

"Oh. Thought that's where you heading."

"Not I. I hate that shit."

"Oh," he said, confused.

The Pope remained in one position for only a few seconds. He adjusted himself intuitively without impeding his train of thought.

"Your so-called New Country is just a way for people with bad adenoids to pretend to be rock stars."

Bow recognized the tone, the temper, the acceleration of words and the escalating volume.

"And what is it with awards shows. There is some interminable country music award show every fucking week. It's like, 'You heard Doodad Jenkins latest song, 'I'm Just a Has-been Now That She's Become a Lesbian'? No? It's a champ. We should have an awards show for it.' I can't fucking take it."

Bow stifled a snicker. "I see."

"And the hats. Always, those fucking cowboy hats. Indoors, too. 'Yeah, I know it's impolite to wear my hat indoors but it's my signature.' Shit the fucking bed, it's everybody in the goddam room's signature. Hell, I bet very few of those clodhoppers has ever been on a horse. They're wannabes. Well, I've got news for those yahoos."

"What?"

"You can't ride the horse, you don't wear the hat."

Darlene rescued him. No sooner had she entered and looked when she said, "Oh, shit. You've got one of your backaches, don't you?"

The Pope closed his eyes and swatted the air as if waving her away.

Darlene kept her gaze on The Pope, but said, "C'mon, Bow. Let's go for a walk."

Bow had finally gotten relaxed and didn't want to move. Once outside he faced Darlene. "What's up?"

She spoke softly, though no one inside or out could have heard her in full voice. "The Pope gets these awful backaches. And he hates anybody to see him like that."

"You mean hurting?"

"Yeah."

"Vulnerable," he added.

"That, too."

They didn't move far. Bow led her to the old Adirondack chairs and sat down. Darlene hovered near the Pope's chair as if afraid to move.

"Go ahead," Bow said. "He won't care."

Even then Darlene lowered herself in slow-motion and sat so gingerly she hardly touched the cushions.

He reached a hand and patted her arm. "You ran yourself ragged today. You're entitled."

She eased herself snug. "The throne. I'll be damned. If you hear him coming tell me quick."

"It won't matter."

Her hips sagged but her upper body was still frozen in position, clinging to the arms of the chair as if for support. "Made good money today, though."

"Great."

"Almost three hundred bucks."

"You earned it."

She raised her legs to admire her feet, tapping her toes together. In her new white shoes, she looked like Dirk Nowitzki from the ankle down. "Yup. I did."

"You investing any money?"

She made a face. "You sound like him now." She pointed her head toward the trailer.

"Sorry. Didn't mean to."

She yawned. "Most of anything left over I give to Mama for Junie."

"I wasn't being critical. I just meant it's always good to have a rainy day fund."

"I know. Every time I get ahead something happens. The car dies or the baby has to go to the doctor or it gets too hot in the apartment and I turn the AC down and run up the electric."

"Tell you what. If you decide you want to save a little, give it to me. I'll put it away for you. That way you won't have it and won't even miss it."

Her face went blank, pondering this. "What if I want it?"

"I'll give it you."

"That wouldn't work."

"Why not?"

"The only way it would work is if you told me no."

"With your own money?"

"Yep."

"Okay. You decide to do it, I'll save it for you and won't let you have it."

"But what if I really, really need it?"

"I'll give it to you."

"Nope. You'll still have to tell me no."

"You'll want it eventually."

"Yeah. Not until it's grown some, though."

"How much is that?"

"Don't know yet."

"Okay. I'll keep it for you and tell you no until it's grown enough."

Satisfied, she said, "Thanks, Bow. You're such a good friend."

The next day Darlene gave him a twenty. He got an extra zippered bank bag from Abe and put it in the bottom of the narrow drawer he used for his socks and underwear.

Twelve

The pursuit of personal power is as dynamic as the will to survive, the sex drive, or bagging the last cookie in the jar. In theory, personal power is the acquisition, retention, and utilization of any means to enhance the components of life.

Personal power is generated by demonstrative advantage. This could be as simple as persistence—

A forlorn lothario with acne conglobata strikes out with every woman he meets, until he becomes a pen pal to a woman in prison named Beulah, recently approved for conjugal visits.

Or resourcefulness—he lands at a competition for seeing-eye dogs (and their masters).

Or determination—he finally has his face sandblasted smooth and takes dancing lessons.

Most personal power comes from exceeding a set standard—the fastest one wins. How this is accomplished, however, frequently relies upon having an edge.

Edges often rise unbidden, and may have little to do with merit or traits associated with personal power obtained by conventional means.

Rich Uncle Ed names his favorite nephew sole beneficiary just before he succumbs to a high blood pressure-induced stroke at Wong Li's Friendly Massage Emporium and Karate Academy.

A lowly intern fresh out of college gains access to the secret corporate minutes of a major tech company and makes out like Warren Buffett on insider trading.

Edges, as any other ego-driven pursuit, may also be pernicious.

A dark horse emerges from nowhere to win the grand slam of ladies' tennis and gets beaucoup endorsements until it's discovered she has faked her DNA test, and is in truth named Buster, wears falsies, and tapes down a dingy and a set of nuggets.

Personal power is also protection against potential hardship, or at least the lessening of its impact. Strength of every sort begets endurance, and also awareness of, and access to, remedies not always gleaned by all.

Acumen is alacrity.

Lastly is the realization that what is defined as personal power by most is a condition most frequently reserved for the habitually successful, regardless of how it came about, and those less frequently so are left with small, common victories. There is no momentum, and should some veiled opportunity present itself, is likely to go unnoticed because rarity obscures vison.

Rarest of all are those who neither explore, pursue, or otherwise endeavor to obtain any kind of personal power. Rising indisputably distinct, may simply be ignored, shrugged away like the sound of traffic, familiar but pointless to engage.

These indifferent souls are ignorant only in the most literal sense, purposely disregarding whims and longing, perhaps bruised by discouragement, yet still gloriously *alive* in some alternate state of grace.

Bow saw a red Corvette in the parking lot after hours. This was an older Corvette, a classic, late fifties or early sixties. Bow knew a collector's item when he saw one. He had seen the car before, occasionally at the Sunday gatherings, with a tall, refined-looking man about his age. One of those too sound in presence to be one of the Pope's beneficiaries but casually attended nonetheless.

He retreated to the shadows. The Pope exited the trailer carrying a small satchel, and after a certain amount of jockeying around, wedged himself into the passenger's seat. Bow remained cloaked until the car pulled away.

Darlene joined him. He stuck a hand out and absently patted her back. She waggled with pleasure and he focused elsewhere.

"I know that look. You off daydreaming?" she asked.

"Just thinking."

"I'm scared to ask what."

"Nothing, really. You have any idea where he goes at night?"

"The Pope?"

"Yeah."

"Nope. I do know he has a lot of dealings outside this place."

"But you don't know what."

"No idea."

"Maybe he's got a girlfriend."

Darlene shook her head. "He told me once he don't need that no more."

"Why would he tell you that?"

"Because I asked him."

His eyes widened. "Why would you ask him that?"

Darlene acquired a look of reticence and chagrin. "I tried to fix him up once."

"What?"

"Waitress we had before poor Mickey. She was kind of floozy."

"So why would you try to set them up?"

She shrugged. "I figured he had—needs—you know, and she would have been ready to rock and roll."

His lips popped sideways. "Wish I'd been here to see that."

"Yeah, it was weird," she said self-consciously. "He was nice about it, though. Thanked me but said not to do it ever again."

"What happened to the woman?"

"Went home with a customer one night and never came back."

Abe came out with two tied trash bags and flopped them into the dumpster. He glanced at them briefly and offered only a hawking sound as he returned inside.

"Abe's an odd guy," Bow opined.

"He's just quiet," Darlene answered. "He's got a good heart. He just doesn't like to-do about anything. The Pope really runs the show."

"He could probably make some money with his sauce."

She nodded. "I know. I told him the same thing."

"What did he say?"

"He was done, whatever that means. Said he was already done and didn't want no more flights of fancy."

"Huh."

His runs had become far more intense and he stretched the course to just over a mile there and back. He was not a gifted runner, though even with his twice-a-day cigarette habit he breathed easier, more rhythmically, never desperate for air at a normal pace.

Six in the morning and still dark. The sun had not appeared but in the distance above the river a horizontal band of gray lightened, expanding by the moment. *Life in the Fast Lane* by the Eagles assaulted his ears. Instead of jogging his way up to speed and distance, he ran at half-speed from the outset. If he had to slow down, he would walk until his thumping heart subsided and regular breathing returned. Then he would start running again.

From a distance, or the perspective of a stranger, he seemed normal, if overly quiet and reserved—a benefit as he was infrequently observed by anyone other than the staff, and then only from the periphery, and usually transient.

Dreaded images did not imprint as often or as powerfully, but he didn't trust the pause or believe this was anything more than a pause. There had been insufficient time to suffer all the smart barbs of exile, too soon to be absolved or even granted a reprieve, especially with so much turbulence swirling about him.

At times, he would still provoke himself to recall the experiences that had so enfeebled him. Above the music, he welcomed such ghoulish accomplishment. No matter the infrequency, he still viewed every recollection with hundred year-old eyes.

He did not believe in his own value with great conviction, but in the dewy haze of dawn, his heart pounding, his lungs heaving, he relished being. This was not an epiphany. This was not a bolt of understanding. This was a common sense conclusion far less optimistic than pragmatic.

He existed in the flesh. What to do? At the turn, he opted to move west along a side street a few blocks, and return to the trailer on the sidewalk past the old homes and buildings. He felt powerful and agile.

Across the way and down two blocks he saw the upper floors of the hospital. The hospital was four floors in a single building. The place exuded the confidence of having a major health institution, the Medical University of South Carolina, a couple of hours away in Charleston. No heart transplants here. No experimental therapy. No new treatments yet to be Googled.

He ran past the street parallel to the medical center and briefly looked in that direction from force of habit. There he saw something in the parking lot across the street from the main entrance. The red Corvette. He stopped momentarily. So, the out-of-place man from the gatherings could have been a doctor, an administrator, or the guy who hosed bird shit off the brightly-lit Welcome sign.

Overriding his aversion to the unfamiliar, he dashed across the street and trotted down to the entrance. He had already recovered his breath when he reached the main desk, occupied by a large, robust lady with black hair cut so short the bob resembled a yarmulke. He approached slowly, silently, and spoke so softly as to dare being heard.

"Excuse me. So sorry to interrupt."

The lady looked up, placed a sheaf of papers on the desk, and eyed him with something like carnality. "Yes. How may I help you?"

"The old red Corvette across the street. Do you know whose car that is?"

"Dr. Bennett's. He won't sell it, though. You don't know how many people have asked."

"Not that. I was just curious. I thought I saw an old friend of mine with him. A biggish guy, big head, short hair—I think he's a cook somewhere."

"The Pope," she said. "Yes, he's a volunteer." She paused. "He's here but I don't think it would be appropriate to interrupt him."

"Oh no. I wouldn't think of it. Perhaps I could leave him a note..."

"That would be all right, I think. Leave it at the fourth floor desk."

Part of the fourth floor was the cancer ward. Savagely strange how there is the same proportion of these patients no matter the local population. The nurse at the desk had her back to him, and he stepped down the hall, moving quickly, purposefully, yet still soundless. Most of the doors were closed, and not quite time for a shift change. He heard a television in one room, a woman talking in another, and weeping in a third, but nothing he recognized.

Down the opposite hallway the floor swept into a turn, revealing another handful of doors. The sign overhead was jarring—Hospice. Bow moved slowly past each door. At the third on the left he heard a familiar voice, though far more tender than his experience. He slid along the wall until he could peer into the room without being seen.

The patient was unconscious in the bed, tethered to IVs, and the painfully slow, monotonous beep of the monitors.

The Pope's back was to the door. He spoke as if the patient was wide awake and alert. He opened a book on his lap.

"We begin something new today. Dickens. Good choice. 'Whether I shall turn out to be the hero of my own life, or whether that station will be held by anybody else, these pages must show.'"

Bow was more curious than inspirited at first, spending a moment to plot the scene, wondering if this was routine or happenstance. As he listened and the Pope continued to intone, so lightly as to be an idyll, motes of understanding gathered and his heart floated achingly upward.

Mercy spoken to the deaf is yet mercy, and all mercy is immortal. Would that someone had spoken so to him.

The Pope stood in his customary place on the stump. The crowd, now bearing sweatshirts and jeans, gathered beneath a temperate sun and among wisps of steam rising from coffee cups.

"I guess everyone knows it's football season. Yes, that great American tradition that mangles the young and sends the older but unwiser into rheumatoid arthritis and premature dementia.

"Football has been inserted into every facet of our lives. Don't you just love a good football metaphor? 'There is no I in team'. Of course there is no I in bone damage or encephalopathy, either."

Scattered laughter came so predictably as if a laugh track.

"Life," he continued, "is like a football game. Sometimes you block for whoever has the ball, sometimes you chase whoever has the ball, and sometimes you sit on the bench. Every so often, you might even get to carry the ball.

"Most of us are bench-sitters. There is no shame in this. We are normal, average, like the buttload of others we encounter every day.

"By the way, did you know that a butt is an actual unit of liquid measurement? It's true. A buttload of wine is a hundred and twenty-six gallons. I'm guessing a shitload would be more."

Darlene's laugh was a mishmash of hungry goat and asthmatic jackass.

"In football, the game is measured in yards. You advance a few yards. Sometimes you lose a few yards, always seeking the goal. If you are nothing but a spectator, you still participate, because you can feel the energy, the ferocity. You're afraid to even go to the can because you might miss something.

"But what happens when you strive for that goal, using every ounce of strength you possess, doing all the work to be faster and stronger, and never quite reach that line? What happens to your soul if you do everything the right way and are still denied?

"In 1907, a young man took the small inheritance he had gotten when his father died and moved to Vienna, Austria. An artist, he applied to the Vienna Academy of Fine Arts, certain he would be accepted. He wasn't. His drawings were deemed unsatisfactory.

"In his youth, he had shown a rare talent for drawing. In high school, he had struggled, and was bored, but was sure he could get that fire back with a little encouragement. He made an appointment with the school to find out why he was rejected and was told he lacked ample skill to draw people. He was told, however, to try architecture because he did have a good sense of building structure. He could draw many of the noteworthy buildings in the area from memory.

"During this time, his mother was dying of breast cancer, so he returned home. She had been operated on but that hadn't worked. As he thought about his future, he knew he couldn't get into architecture school without a high school diploma. So he decided to brush up his work, especially sketches of people, and re-apply to the Academy the next year.

"But when he returned to Vienna in 1908, his money was gone. He was essentially homeless, and even shared a room at a poor men's home. He begged for money. When the time came to reapply to the Academy, he wasn't even allowed to take the formal test. His sketches were judged as very poor.

"Some of you may know this story or parts of it. This was Adolph Hitler. And as a poor, bitter man in Vienna, he formulated his ideology. First, he blamed his failure to be admitted to art school on a Jewish administrator. He blamed his mother's death on a Jewish doctor. He became something of a survivalist, with a kill-or-be-killed mentality.

"Now we all know Hitler was nuts. We all know he was a sociopath. But what would have happened if he'd been accepted to art school? Perhaps we would not have known him at all. He did manage to sell a few pictures of Vienna landmarks he copied from photographs. So maybe he would have ended up an obscure, hysterical creature who drew greeting cards or something, you get my point.

"Instead, we know what happened.

"So, consider this. An art critic led to the Holocaust. Someone given the authority of artistic life and death over young people had determined this man didn't belong, and thus began a drive to the goal line that left six million Jews massacred, and over fifty million people dead. "Now, I know you think I'm being overly dramatic. I probably am. But each of us has been denied in some way—most, many times. We do not always get to choose who has authority over us but we also know that good marionettes become martinets when they are allowed to make important decisions that affect other people.

"Had the eighteen-year-old Hitler been accepted to art school, odds are he wouldn't have been a better person. He was a damaged, paranoid little man. But who are the people who were accepted that year? How many of them do we know by name? How is one person designated for nurture, and another not?

"He would have been in his mid-twenties before he finished school. By the time he realized he might fail as a commercial artist, he may have avoided service in World War One. He probably would not have gotten involved with Vienna's Social Party, nor absorbed the anti-Semitism of the Austrian press.

"Instead of art, he learned about intimidation and fear. Instead of art, he learned to organize rallies and manipulate the masses. At the very least, he probably wouldn't have returned as the conqueror of Austria in 1938. He would have stalled on the fifty-yard line.

"We have become increasingly aware of the damage sad little rejected people can do.

"The Holocaust is as scary as it gets. Happy Halloween."

At Bow's suggestion, Darlene brought Junior to Port Royal for Halloween trick-or-treating. Halloween fell on a Thursday and nine was too late to begin, so she arranged to leave at seven and Bow arranged to come in early the following morning to finish clean-up. Only a handful of neighborhoods kept porch lights burning.

Most celebrants gathered in groups these days. Kids were urged to congregate at the mall where each store distributed candy and coupons, or in church basements where no mischief could be done. Some churches gathered the children to warn of the damnation honoring such a holiday insured.

They dressed the little boy in a devil's costume and hit about forty or fifty houses. Bow hadn't spent a Halloween with a child in twenty years. He could not remember spending much one-on-one time with his granddaughter in her short life. He remembered several occasions when she would crawl into his lap, sucking an inverted thumb as the sandman came. These were times when everyone was about but busy elsewhere and the stillness between grandfather and granddaughter respected.

Junior giggled and had a wonderful time for his first full-fledged Halloween. "Trick-or-treat" became a mantra he had not known before, and he wore it out. From the time they ushered him from one house to another, he repeated the phrase at least twenty times. Eventually this evolved into "Treat Gimme, treat gimme". Bow was repaid in mini-Snickers and Kit Kats.

They arrived back in Estill at nine thirty. They left with Grandma's admonition "He'll get sick from all this junk" swimming overhead. Darlene tossed the keys to Bow and asked him to drive home. He hadn't been behind the wheel of a car in all this time but thought it might be relaxing.

Darlene was quiet, and if not morose, then glum.

"That was fun," Bow offered

"Yeah, it was. Thanks."

"I know you miss him."

She faced forward and groaned. "I couldn't take care of him. Even with all the money in the world."

"Why do you think that?"

She did not answer for a minute. "He wears me out."

"He's a toddler full of energy."

Several moments later Bow heard a distinctive sigh and knew something was wrong. "What is it?"

She rooted around in her purse and withdrew a wadded, a-b-u tissue. She unfolded it and honked. Then she refolded it, finding the only square inch mucous-free and wiped her upper lip.

"I can't say it out loud," she said. This set her off on a whimpering jag, another treasure hunt into her purse, another previously-used tissue, and another blow and wipe.

"Tell me, Darlene."

She shook her head and tooted like a muted cornet.

"Okay, then," he replied.

Darlene trembled. "I can't take being around him for very long," she blurted, then snorted back the tears.

He did not fully understand her despair or consider this so tragic. "You lose patience. So what?"

Darlene wailed then, wailed as if Abe had sold out to some vegans. "You don't get it. After an hour or two I'm done. I can't take it. I don't have the gumption to give him any attention. I can't take the stress. My own son, and I can only be around him a little bit before I start losing it."

He spoke softly, unsure what to do. "All mothers are like that in the beginning."

"But ain't that supposed to come natural?"

"Who says? Did you nurse him, cuddle him?"

She sounded like a bassoon with a busted reed. "O' course."

"Did you hold him when he cried?"

"Yes."

"Longer than a couple of hours?"

"He was just a baby."

"And now he's different. He's a growing little boy. And you aren't there to see it. You don't know what he needs and what he doesn't need. You don't know how to mother him anymore because you haven't had the chance. You can't do it in a couple of hours every week."

She looked at him then, her lips still aquiver. "You think?"

"Yes. You were fine when we were out with him. It's only when he got tired and fussy on the trip home and you couldn't get him still."

"But I feel so bad about it."

"I know. And maybe you'll have to learn to be more tolerant. But not being able to cope all the time doesn't mean you don't love him."

"No. I do love him. I know that."

"Then don't worry about it so much."

Darlene slowly breathed her way into clarity. They drove on, through the murky ribbon before them. Toward home. Toward the river that led to the immeasurable sea.

The air smelled of ozone and the river was preternaturally calm. A fishing boat chugged past just above idling speed and Bow and the Pope listened until it passed.

"What's with you and the Hitler story," Bow said.

"It was a dramatization of possible outcomes when we screw people over, or allow people to be screwed over right in front of us."

"Yeah, but that's pretty extreme, don't you think?"

"The repercussions were extreme." He paused. "You don't know this, but I give the same speech every year."

"Why?"

The Pope ignored the question. "You want to talk about Eddie Lee?"

"Nope."

"Can you tell me why?"

"No," he said tersely. "I just don't want to talk about it."

The Pope leaned back in the old chair. "Okay. No problem."

"I'm doing okay without it. I hope I never have to say his name again. I would love to never hear it again."

"Fine. I won't push you."

"Will you promise not to bring it up again?"

"No."

"Why not?"

"If I knew that I would know why I keep bringing it up."

Bow scowled. An unfamiliar odor floated above the incoming tide, an earthy smell, empty of whole water, like freshly turned dirt in a soft rain—as if a hundred ancient tombs had been opened all at once.

"You've been around Darlene too long," Bow said.

"Now you know where she gets it from."

Again they ceded themselves to idleness. After a time, the Pope spoke, and in that plaintive voice he rarely used.

"My old man," the Pope said.

"Sorry?"

"My father. He died on November third, not so many years ago."

Bow nodded, not looking at him. "Oh. I'm sorry."

"He made it to eighty."

"That's good."

"He was German. Born in 1927. And he knew Hitler."

"I guess everyone knew Hitler then."

"This was different. My father lived in Germany. He was Mischling, Second Degree."

"I don't know what that means."

"It means he was one-quarter Jewish. His grandmother. That meant he had limited rights. That meant suspicion. He joined the Hitler Youth in 1942. By then there were eight million kids. He did everything asked of him—and more. And never complained or brought attention to himself. This kept the party away from his family. He was even in the corps of future officers of the Wehrmacht Infantry. By the time he was sixteen he could drive a tank, and out shoot most of the men in the regular army. He also spied on Bible studies and churches, to make sure the love of Jesus wasn't interfering with the final solution.

"Until D-Day, the war was still in doubt. Hitler could have withdrawn from Russia and still kept a tidy piece of Europe. In the final days of the war, my father defended Berlin. An eighteen-year-old kid. On his own. After Hitler put a bullet in his brain and the rest had fled, my father was a guerilla fighter, unattached to any unit, still a member of the Hitler Youth, moving from building to building, popping off Russians.

"He was captured, questioned, and miraculously, sent home. He never got over how kind the Russians were to him. Even as they raped the city, they let him go. Of course, home wasn't there any longer. His parents were dead. He emigrated to the U.S. He met a German woman, another refugee. He was already past forty when I was born."

The Pope stood up and twisted from the waist. Then he bowed his back. Then bent down as far as he could, all of which resembled an exercise class at a fat farm.

"He hated Hitler. He hated the Nazis. Everything he did was to keep the heat off his family. The building they lived in was destroyed by friendly fire in the chaos. In the end, it was all for naught. He didn't even tell people he was German. He told them he was Dutch. He and my mother became Americans. But he didn't want people to know anything about his life. Not even me. My mother told me the story after I was grown."

"I'll bet it was a shock."

The Pope sat again.

"It's ancient history. Some of this shit still bugs the hell out of me."

"Sometimes we are injured by things that happened long before we were born."

The Pope looked at him suddenly and gave him time to continue.

Bow waited, measuring his words. "This is nothing compared to what happened to your family, but when I was about sixteen I was helping my mother clean out the attic. We lived in this huge old house with a full attic. Some of the boxes were so rotten the stuff in them was scattered all over the floor. She was throwing stuff away and putting other stuff in new boxes, re-labeling them and trying to keep it organized.

"I found a bunch of envelopes with a rubber band around them. The name on them was Ramona Lessing. My mother's name was Ramona, but her maiden name was Tucker. I asked her who Ramona Lessing was. She turned red. I knew she was going to tell me it was nothing, get me to drop it, but I wouldn't let it go. Finally, she said it was her.

"She had sneaked away when she was seventeen and got married. They kept it a secret. She lived at home and he lived at home. Every few days they would meet somewhere. In those days it was hard for her to get out. Old South rules and all that. He would write her letters and give them to her to read while they were apart. Later, when the truth came out my grandfather—who was a real ball-buster—made sure they got an annulment. Then he ran the poor guy out of town."

"Do you know who he was?"

"No. Not really. Mom never heard from him again, or so she said, and even if he'd tried, my grandfather would've been all over it. So I didn't ask anything else about him. And I'm sure what my grandfather did was right in the long run. My mother was just a love-struck kid.

"But it did make me wonder. Maybe she was never able to love like that again. Maybe having this guy she loved torn away from her like that ruined her in some ways."

"May be," the Pope said. He breathed aloud, as if a last gasp. "Every family has secrets better left alone."

Thirteen

Adult hunting season kicked in, allowing all the dads, uncles, grandpas, brothers and cousins, to blast the shit out of things on their own, most of the time leaving the neophytes home. Jimmy's was awash in so much camouflage clothing the white supremacists were indistinguishable from the Jaycees.

Much of the blasting had become redundant anyway. There was such an overpopulation of deer there were better than even odds of hitting one with a car. Many deer foraged so near to civilization they lost their reticence around humans. Men of adequate stealth could get close enough to hit them with a rock

On Saturday night, a couple of hours from closing, there had just been a mass exodus but over half the tables were still occupied.

The Pope called out. "Bow! Bow!"

Bow was jamming to *Sunshine of Your Love*, by Cream, and didn't hear. The Pope arced a wooden spoon in his direction, bouncing off the back splash and into the rinse sink. Bow jumped with a start, then sneered for a second, but pulled the plugs from his ears and looked.

"Bob needs help bussing a few tables. Can you help him catch up?"

"Sure," Bow answered. He quartered his phone, grabbed an empty cart, and pushed through the swinging doors into the dining room. He greeted Bob and began clearing the nearest table.

He heard laughter. Silly, put-on laughter. Nothing unusual except overly loud with an Elmer Fudd quality. And...he had heard it before. He looked over his shoulder without turning around and saw three men sitting at a center table. They were dressed post-hunt, like apprentice lumberjacks in plaid shirts, khakis, and ankle boots.

They were attorneys and Bow knew them all from home, though they had never opposed each other in court. One was a divorce lawyer, one did real estate contracts, wills, and probate, and the other lived off his inheritance, sitting in a lavish office yakking on the phone all day.

Rarely did any of them represent a criminal defendant unless some kid with a rich daddy faced a misdemeanor. Then Bow would get the call, be a sport, and drop the charge to "suspicion of", and a modest fine. Every lawyer in the district knew Bow as a reasonable man and had his number on speed dial.

Bow's reaction was swift and telling. He ducked his head beneath his shoulders, keeping his back to their table even when impractical. Once the cart was loaded and the surface wiped, he pushed the cart into the kitchen at one-half Mach, tore off his hairnet, tossed it behind a faucet, and loped through the outer screen door, all in a single motion.

"Bow!" the Pope called after him. "Bow! What the hell..."

The Pope wiped his hands on a cloth and followed after him. He charged through the door but did not see him. He was just about to call out when he heard panting. There was Bow leaning against the back wall in the dark, his head hanging, hyperventilating.

"What's going on?" the Pope demanded.

Bow did not move a micrometer, but puffed and heaved and spoke in a low, breathy voice. "I can't help right now. I just can't."

The Pope's demeanor changed, not the gamut, not to sympathy, but to a realization. "Christ. You saw somebody you know, didn't you?"

Bow could only answer with a nod as he convulsed, tears coming in spasms he could no longer contain.

Something stirred in the Pope. Irritation, agitation, antipathy—all to mask feelings of helplessness and futility.

"Come back in when you can," he mumbled.

Bow finished his shift without a word and without moving from his area. Nor did he listen to the music that had enlivened him. He heard only his own disconsolate thoughts, and the echoes of so many familiar voices in accusation and condemnation, and the brand of ill-judgment wielded by those who had been granted by familiarity tacit permission to strike and wound.

The lesions reopened and tore as deeply as they had in the beginning. He was snatched to the awareness of loss not to be reclaimed or overcome except in cosmetic measure. After his shift he went straight to the trailer. He had spoken only to Bob. He had pulled him aside and whispered an apology for leaving him in the lurch. Bob merely watched him sad-eyed.

He unfolded his bed and lay in the darkness.

When the door to the trailer opened, he turned to face the wall. He had changed out of his clothes and lay atop the blanket in his underwear. He heard a click and the lamp on the front counter burned but he and the Pope were veiled in dusk. Bow was motionless, hoping to be ignored. He had curbed the tears but the grief remained and enveloped him.

This, the Pope ignored, though he did move to the rear bedroom. He changed into a clean pair of hospital pants and T-shirt.

"I know you weren't expecting that." His tone was impassive, his voice flat as he pulled on his clothes.

Bow did not reply. He remained inert, feigning sleep.

"I have to go out. You want to get anything off your chest, now's the time."

Again, Bow remained immobile, grateful that the Pope would leave him to his solitude.

"Okay then. Suit yourself."

As the Pope gathered his things in an old canvas bag, he stopped near the doorway. "I know this hurts. I know how you would be ashamed to be seen like this. But you've made a lot of headway. Don't waste it on people who never cared about you in the first place."

"I can't do this right now."

"Fine," the Pope said.

"Fine," Bow mimicked him.

The Pope turned brusquely, but at the door he paused.

"You know all this could have been avoided." There was both a plaintive and critical element in his voice.

"Go. Away. Please."

The Pope marched two steps back into the room, his irritation showing as his oversized clothes rustled when he stopped. He spoke sharply, a thin blade, and not as banter.

"All you had to do was apologize. All that kid wanted was for you to say you fucked up. And he would've gone away. And it would have been over. Do you know how many people would trade their souls for something that simple? There are people who say I'm sorry a thousand times and it's never enough. So grow the fuck up! Stop being so pathetic."

Bow turned over and looked. The earth trembled but the breach was slow to unplug. Tears flooded and he fought them with rancor. "You don't know what you're talking about."

The Pope's tone eased but his words did not. "I saw you on the news. Standing there with your stiff upper lip declaring to the world that shit happens and them's the breaks."

"It wasn't like that. Not at all."

"How was it?"

"Insane. I didn't know what to say."

"No. You knew. You just couldn't bring yourself to do it."

Then he swiveled and left.

Bow stood on shale. As the chasm opened beneath him, the unbearable air bursting through every layer of resistance, tears fell again. For a time, he couldn't breathe, was afraid to breathe for fear of collapse. The hubris of tears.

He rued his self-deception. He had been safe in hiding but now cowered. The ghosts of Eddie Lee and his granddaughter hid dormant, ready to nudge him off his precarious perch and into the churning throng.

He wept, sharper even than when the cuts were fresh and new. He wept for his own foolishness, and at the absurdity of his aspirations these months, and for the time spent in retreat and delusion. He wept great gouts of regret, scraping his interior walls to a raw and bloody pulp, wishing he could simply dematerialize.

The Pope quietly reentered the trailer. He appeared more exasperated than repentant. He huffed as if extinguishing a candle. "I was too harsh. I realize that. I didn't think..."

Bow calmed himself, breathing more regularly, tears staunched to a trickle, though this was a façade, an evasion. He was suspended in place, where constraint and urgency were intertwined, and whichever end unknotted first held sway.

He spoke softly, achingly. "I saw the police report after—it—happened, you know, and found out he still had his arm wrapped around her when he shot himself. Somehow he held on even when he fell. Almost like he was cradling her on the ground. Like they had fallen asleep in that position. Like he cared—"

Bow then turned again toward the wall. Quiet returned and the muted light yielded to black, and after a few moments the door opened and closed. He squeezed his eyes tight and submitted himself to obscurity and the vanity of a sleepless night.

Later, how much later he did not know, the door opened slowly again as if someone was trying to enter quietly, though it squeaked regardless. The same voice so unskilled at whispering, whispered, You okay, Bow?"

He didn't respond. He had exhausted all tears and would not allow a repeat.

"I knew they was jerks," she said. "Hogged the table for like an hour-and-a-half. They were shit-assed rude. Kept asking for coffee refills like I had nobody else to see to and then left me a five-dollar tip on a forty-dollar tab."

He did not move but cleared his throat. "Sounds like them."

He finally looked when he heard the swishing of clothes. Darlene pulled her dress over her head and tossed it on the table. She removed her bra, unbinding her bosom into graceful lobes.

"Darlene—?"

"I'm gonna love you a little Bow."

"You...what?"

"It's mine to give."

"You don't have to—."

"Shhh, now. It's all I got. Just let it be."

She stepped free of her underwear. She knelt beside him on the floor. She kissed his cheek and stroked his hair. Again she whispered, easier now with her lips so near.

"Tonight ain't your doing. It's hard enough to take the part that is without having anything else piled on. It's gonna be okay, Bow. I promise."

He reached and took her hand. She drew his to her lips. She continued to feather kisses and moved her other hand downward. She stroked and kneaded until he was ready, so tenderly, so dexterously, as if she could feel his every pleasure or pain.

Then she sat atop him. She needed no foreplay. She did not even bend to kiss him. She held his hands in hers near the union between them, and rocked, again delicately and with such a conservation of motion she seemed clairvoyant.

Bow did not move, but in the quiet dim, pieces of his battered soul crawled upward like wisps of smoke. There was no lust. There was no desperation. Whatever needs existed were not of the flesh. He was caressed slowly, leisurely, with only the slightest hint of pressure. He did not boil nor lock with anticipation.

The coupling was a dreamy crescendo, a gradual ascension that liberated every manner of helplessness, as if walking through rain, wind and storm, then suddenly arriving in afternoon sunlight, the burden of coarse and saturated clothes falling away piece-by-sodden-piece.

Darlene seemed to feel everything, her eyes closed, content to render her part without translation, without a word or sound, with no seasoning except benevolence. At times she would draw his hands and place them on her breasts, but did not impede the pulse they shared. She 28seemed to know, without question or response, the accomplishment of virtue, of shared atonement. She was not lost to the sensation, but hers was refined by generosity.

No insistence or necessity or cloying hunger intruded, only the palpation of the divine cosmos seamlessly connecting.

Both dreamed. Like dreams of all sympathy present in a darkening cloak. He dreamt of solace. She dreamt of affection. So attuned was she, she felt the faint, initial quiver at his root. She sought to release the gathering fever as he tensed beneath her. Neither burst nor pushed through the confines. Each slid through gauzy curtains into the outer room.

Tremor upon tremor quaked, these, too, clasped and did not clash against each other. Vibrations melded and they rode the bending wave until it slowly played itself out. Darlene disengaged and lay beside him. They held each other in silence except for the sound of shuffling covers. Once secured, they lay peacefully.

"You think you can sleep now?" she asked.

"Don't know. Maybe."

Darlene stroked the back of his head and hummed *The Itsy Bitsy Spider*. Never before had the ditty been so angelic.

This small world wept. The rain fell for three days and scrubbed the oaks clean of dead and dying leaves. Autumn was still warmer than Bow had experienced in North Carolina. There, proximity to the hills thinned the air and the cold hung trapped between the peaks. Here, the ambient heat blanketed the land and sea, even when northern winds prevailed, especially as the day drew on.

The rain was brisk. Brisk and relentless—an ugly gray rain. The rain fell in visible lines, unaffected by wind. Drops were linked, separated by the unmeasurable and undetectable. Bow woke depressed to the tintinnabulation on the trailer's shell, but did not accept this as providence, nor even requital. Better to be melancholy on a rainy day.

Eventually, the sun shone again. Bow and the Pope had not sat out for a while. The seats were soaked and matted with wet leaves. The Pope brought a blanket to cover the wet surfaces. Bow simply flipped the cushions and covered his seat with a towel.

They had not spoken any more of the incident with the hunters and Bow was content to let the episode fade. He had not been discovered. He had not been viewed with contempt. Neither had he been viewed with pity, gratefully, for this he could not bear. The incident would not have mattered at all except for what the men would have reported when they returned home, the hum of villainous gossip delighting all who heard, and, of course, where he was and what he was doing. Poor man, how far he has fallen.

If things had changed with Darlene, these were kept in the separate compartments of separate hearts. They did not talk more, or linger more around each other, though this was difficult to assess because they spent a lot of time together anyway. They did not show any more outward affection for each other and their night of intimacy had not been discussed or repeated.

Still, each smile, each gravitation of eyes-to-eyes, held a greater warmth. Perhaps it was exactly as Darlene had described—an act of charity.

Neither was Bow so foolish to think the Pope did not know what had transpired, but he had shown no inclination to talk about it—another form of relief. Even now, he smoked his British ciggie and looked out across a waterway he could not possibly see. With the rain had come caliginous nights. .

The Pope coughed. "You know what they say is the reason for smoking?"

"Not nursing enough?"

"No. It's our way of controlling fire, which has been passed down for hundreds of thousands of years."

"No kidding."

The Pope took a mighty draw. "That and to prove the old maxim."

"Which is—?"

The Pope blew out a nebula of smoke. "People suck."

Bow laughed. He needed to laugh. The conversation waned. The moon was shaded by quick clouds, the shape changing every few seconds. Naked, it was a three-quarter moon. Cloaked, it was at times a crescent, a half, or an amorphous ass with a crooked crack. There was no magic in it. Neither was there doom. There was a quality of sameness, a demonstration of the dependable.

The Pope looked at Bow. "Can we talk about Eddie Lee?"

Bow met his gaze. "I thought we did that already."

"Well.... this is just my curiosity."

"Then no."

"Okay," The Pope said agreeably.

Bow surveyed the blinking red light of a jet passing overhead. He wondered where the passengers were going. He wondered how many had been inspired to travel by affirmation and how many by adversity. "What do you want to know?"

"His lawyer must have been a real yutz."

He was relieved. Something docile and within his faculty—oil to rusty gears. "No, he was good in the beginning. Made all the right points. But afterward he ran through appeals like he was on the clock. He wanted out. He never really looked into anything. The grounds for his appeals were all pat without anything new. Like bad instructions to the jury. Not granting a change of venue. That kind of stuff. He should have saved one appeal, at least, until he found something—and, of course, there was something to find."

"And everyone moved on."

"Yep."

"Even you."

"Even me. It was a big case. Didn't have a lot of homicides. But I wanted to get back to the routine stuff. Easy stuff."

"And you never thought anything was out-of-whack?"

"I really didn't. I thought it was a loser-on-loser crime and needed to be flushed."

"I can see that."

"Yeah?"

"Sure. I think you were right about that in the beginning."

"Maybe."

"Just had the wrong loser."

Bow wondered if he, too, had been sleepwalking, not only this case but his entire life. Had he ever chosen to do anything primarily for his own good? Had he ever been willing to do anything contradictory to the assumption of others who claimed to know him, care about him?

"Well, I know I'll never forget it."

"No. It defined you. Still does."

"Yeah, but that's what I'm trying to do now. Undefine myself."

"Find out what you'll be when you grow up?"

"Something like that. It's easy to procrastinate when the down feelings come."

"I always thought procrastinate was a one-word oxymoron. It should be anticrastinate."

Bow lit a cigarette. "You may be onto something."

The Pope narrowed his gaze. "Well, if you want to be a mensch and do your coming out project, that could help."

An apprehensive twist of the lips. "I don't see how."

"You will know you are capable of being alive."

"I know that already. Why does it matter to you?"

"Darlene."

He reacted, but the binding and unbinding happened so quickly the exchange was eye-quick and spontaneous, and he held his suspicion. "Darlene will be fine."

The Pope slowly turned his coffee mug in his palm and scanned the trees, as if he could count them all even in obscurity. "I want her to have a win."

Then the night claimed them again.

Fourteen

The end of November was approaching, eight months since the tragedy, five since his banishment. Bow still grieved. How could he not? Of course he had more energy. Of course he was able to function at a higher level. So much of the foul clutter was still embedded and he was ever aware. If there were a thousand pieces to be processed, he had only managed about seven hundred. High percentages usually meant success but percentages do not matter when every shard is honed to a keen edge. Some of these he thought to have been ground into slivers kept resurrecting themselves.

More mundane things also gnawed at him. He had made no contact to say he was okay. His daughter would want to know. No matter the gulf between them she would not wish him dead. He had thought about emailing or texting, but always managed to convince himself otherwise. He had not sought anyone to tend to his business. There was his father's house and other assets. He had not hired anyone to be his advocate in the divorce. Hell, he could already be divorced and poorer for it. He had done nothing to settle the lingering grim of his former self. Nor would he do so today.

He didn't mislead himself about his part in the affliction that led to his demise, though he wished every part to be reconsidered by others in a kinder light. He also realized he would have done what he had done regardless. He may have taken a few days to scrutinize more details about the case, but nothing would have changed. He would have still failed, and he would have still been ensnared in the same dick-grabbing paroxysm of mindless terror.

Yet...had he reviewed the security tapes himself, or reviewed the information from Duke Law expeditiously, he would have acted differently. He was absolutely certain. He would have taken charge and steered the process toward a more affirming solution. He would have made the appeal himself. He would have given Eddie Lee the check himself and sent him on his way. He would have sculpted his words and actions more carefully, regretful but not contrite. He would have avoided being ambushed.

This was all useless, of course, a nod to guilty pride. He had never been one to brood over fine points or second-guess himself. As much as he sifted through the slag to placate the gods of sanity, the shit kept churning. At times, his best hope was to simply endure until he found the first calm place just above the cusp of death, and take refuge there.

His recovery had taken quantum strides in every direction. As he had grown stronger, he had thwarted more and retained less, chipping at each part until, incinerated, ashy bits would flit away. He had never expected that every such effort drew him nearer to the world that had forsaken him. He had neither the will nor desire to retrace those steps—abject memory upon abject memory. He just wanted to believe in the potential possibility for peace.

Above all things that served him well was the sweat. This was not a physical purgative, nor was it metaphysical in the sense that there was universal forgiveness available through toil. The omnipresent perspiration was an indicator, a green traffic arrow toward an unknown future, now not so intimidating.

In many ways he was becoming a human being, even in areas previously lacking that had nothing to do with Eddie Lee.

Bow had raised his daily run to five miles and had broken forty-five minutes, though with such short strides he resembled some little yapper dog that took ten steps per linear foot. The mornings could dawn in the upper forties so he had switched to a sweat suit. He had begun to run without music and he missed it. The music made him less aware of his sore knees and lagging breath, but he wanted fewer distractions as he reached for the far shore. Moping had replaced desolation. He could still smell the pile of shit. He just no longer wallowed in it.

When he ran without music he was more attentive to the materiality of his surroundings. Even at an early hour the color of bustle infected his senses. Fishing boats and cruisers moved all along the river. To the north the drawbridge was up to let a three-mast sailer through. Dry leaves and sticks crackled underfoot. Even the old homes of sighs and whispers, reminiscing and mourning, had activity all around them, especially on the city street beyond.

A street sweeper hummed as its large broom whisked up the dirt. Commuters dotted the city streets. The bark on the pine trees resembled shingles, overlapping with rough connections, the tree bare where one or part of one had peeled away. Standing water in the bottoms of small, earthen basins had dried up, leaving a shiny brown pattern like a mosaic, or a puzzle with many identically-hued pieces. Hidden birds made odd sounds he had never heard before.

He also talked to himself. If this was a compulsion too odd to broadcast, at least it resulted in more constructive thoughts. "Yeah. You can do five miles without stopping. You couldn't do that before. You have people who care about you. And, you are safe, safe, safe."

Bow had learned to blow smoke rings. This was an arcane talent, a pre-1962-cigarettes-cause-cancer bit of voodoo, usually to impress kids. No one knows how many men came to a tubercular end from decades of nursing a tobacco tube, seduced by a father or uncle who could blow smoke rings. He was working at making a smaller ring sail through a larger one but hadn't made it work yet. He didn't get much practice from a couple of smokes a day

He could have used a blanket sitting out in the dark. He had gone from profuse sweating in the kitchen to a light airiness outside but at least wore a jacket.

The Pope appeared to be asleep in his chair. Bow didn't want to disturb him but sitting out had been his idea. Fifty-odd degrees is cold when you are out in it, especially if not suitably dressed. The Pope didn't seem to mind.

"Let me ask you something, How did these Sunday things get started?"

Only the Pope's lips moved. "I'm very religious."

"I thought you said you didn't believe God does anything."

"Ah. My religion is barbecue."

"I'm serious."

"So am I. The saving power of my barbecue has been spread far and wide."

"Then why bother with the sermons? Why not just eat?"

"Maybe I like to talk."

"Sometimes I think what you say is over the heads of those people. Sometimes it's over mine."

The Pope opened his eyes. He lit a smoke. Then he blew three smoke rings, each smaller than the one before. The second gently sailed through the first. The third through the second and the first.

Bow watched as the rings slowed and spread apart into thin, translucent trails. "Showoff."

The Pope popped two large rings and blew a stream through both of them, like an arrow, and the rings stayed intact before passively dissipating.

"Most of those people have had things dumbed-down for them their entire lives. They have been taught to accept. Taught not to look. Taught about a GQ Jesus who wants them to believe whatever they are told. Taught that the Bible says Republicans are good and others are evil, and that if Jesus were here today, he would bomb family planning clinics, murder gay people, and preach about how the devil seduced pacifists—that if you don't do as I say, you will perish, because I say so. People believe in signs of the Apocalypse but don't believe we're toxifying the planet."

"What if they're just—you know—simple."

The Pope eyed him acutely. "That's presumptuous."

"No. I don't mean simple-minded. Most people operate on one level at a time. Even smart ones. They don't—multi-task—in their heads."

"An astute observation."

"You've rubbed off on me."

"I hope it's not contagious."

"You could get your point across in other ways."

"That would defeat the purpose."

"What purpose?"

"Enjoying talking. If I weren't the least bit articulate, I wouldn't enjoy it so much."

"You are one strange guy."

"Ouch," the Pope said facetiously. "Besides, they already decide those things for themselves. They know they have to listen to me blather on before they can eat. Kind of like marriage."

"I always went to church, but I was never that gung ho about organized religion."

"Oh. You like disorganized religion? You must be Catholic."

"Funny." He lit up.

The Pope sighed a long stream of smoke. "Do you believe in grace?"

"I guess so, yeah."

"Grace is supposed to be a catalyst for change. It isn't some inert gas hovering around your head. You have to take it in, embrace it, let it reform you. Otherwise it's useless."

"What's your point?"

"The so-called Evangelicals and Trumpites showed how dogma is the enemy of grace and nobody got it. If you are unaffected by grace, how can you claim to be a redeemed person?"

Bow smoked and considered. "I still wish I had more faith."

"I know. But I'll tell you something about faith. Everyone wants to believe in something they think will help them without working for it or getting their hands dirty. Grace is what gives you the kick in the ass to do those things."

"Maybe. I guess I meant having some kind of spiritual connection."

"That's what grace does. Faith is easier if you think about it. You are connected to whatever you believe."

"What do you mean?"

"If you believe in a rock, worship the rock, pray to the rock, the rock will serve you whether it actually does anything or not."

Bow nodded absently, desiring to relax more than focus. Then he blew a smoke ring that wavered as it faded like an off-kilter tire. He hurriedly blew a smaller ring through it before the first completely disappeared.

"Success!" he cried.

The Pope then blew four smoke rings, the last no bigger than his pursed lips. All shot through the center of the one before.

"God has spoken," he said.

Bow had finished his station shutdown in record time. He stood outside in the nippy air, waving to each of his co-workers as they left for home. A different car—an old beater desperately needing to be shot and buried—shook as it idled in the parking lot, waiting for the Pope. What foray into beneficence was on tonight's agenda? If the Pope persisted, Port Royal might become Paradise.

Darlene came out and checked to make sure the back door was locked. She looked at Bow and smiled as she approached.

"Hey, hey, sugar britches," she said cheerily.

He stood in the darkest spot near the parking lot, beyond the outer edge of the street lights. Darlene was backlit, an aura surrounding her head, her irises agleam with pin dots. They had not talked about the night of the meltdown and both seemed to understand there wasn't a need.

"What's up with you?" he asked.

“I’m slap wore out,” she said. “I can’t hardly stand up.”

“Why don’t you go home and take a hot bath?”

She did not answer directly. “So how are you doing? Really.”

“Good. I feel good.”

“You think?”

“Like a mama’s boy at Christmas.’

“No more bad dreams?”

“Oh sure. Not as many. Maybe I’m just a weenie.”

"No. You’re a good guy who got whacked big-time.”

“Who gives a Nancy Nuthummer about that?”

Darlene cackled. “Me, for one.”

“Thanks. I’m really okay. Not totally. But okay.”

“Oh,” she said.

Bow thought he heard disappointment in her voice. “You don’t believe me?”

“I do,” she said, drawing out the words. “Just checking.”

“No I am. Promise.”

“Well, you know, I just wanted to be absolutely, positively sure, just in case.”

“In case of what?

“In case you needed a little more... comforting.”

“Oh. You mean...”

“Yeah.”

“Are you serious?”

“I wouldn’t be doing my job as your sponsor if I didn’t make really-really, beyond a doubt, no maybes, swear-to-Jesus sure.”

Bow felt a rare expansion in his chest, and also in his pants—the last of these more obvious. This wasn't simply sexual gratification. This was a return to a more humane contact with life, a sympathetic respite from the whole sordid mess.

But a boner was a boner.

"You know," he began, "I do feel a little down in the dumps."

A few nights later Bow and the Pope sat at the dinette table in the trailer. Bow unfolded a piece of paper from his pocket and smoothed the wrinkles with his palm. He was stalling.

"Go ahead," the Pope said.

Bow spoke warily, monotonously, a mortician delivering a eulogy. "You ever been on a highway and a semi tries to pass another semi in front of you and then there's a hill and you're just stuck there while the guy takes fifteen minutes to get around? Doesn't that just chap your ass?"

He saw no expression on the Pope's face. He continued. "How about trying to pass a truck only to find somebody cruising the passing lane. And he's going exactly the same speed. You're stuck there mile after mile. And he ain't moving. So you get on his bumper and flash your lights and he still won't budge. Then you see the back one of those funny little hats. Then you see he's from New York—"

"Okay," The Pope said bluntly. "I see we have work to do."

"Not funny?" Bow asked.

"Not just the material. Physical expressions and vocal dynamics are important."

Bow grimaced. "I have to know what to say before I can practice how to say it."

"You want to quit?"

"Maybe I should do something else."

"You've spoken in public lots of times. You understand tone and what to stress."

"I would never go over-the-top in court."

"I'll bet you gave it the old Baptist hoodoo at times."

"We're Methodist," he said.

The Pope stood up. "See? That's what I'm talking about. That was almost funny."

Bow shook his paper "What about this stuff?"

The Pope made a face. "Need to find different subject matter."

"Okay. What should I do?"

Again, the Pope thought, his face morphing into solution. "Potty humor is always good."

Every night for several weeks after Jimmy's closed, Bow could be seen pacing a line between the trailer and the far street light in the parking lot, a distance of about ninety feet. Every so often he would stop and glance at the pages in his hand, bringing them closer to his eyes if need be.

Occasionally, he would gesture, as if conducting an orchestra only to have a bee land on his baton and remain attached no matter how hard he shook. Words were too muffled to identify but were repeated several times with various parts emphasized.

Darlene stood beside her car and watched with fondness. The Pope stood near the back door or the diner.

"Think he can do it?" she asked.

"God only knows," the Pope replied.

The older of the two Holiday Inns was closer to town than the Interstate. Locals who had never stayed there, or had stayed there less than an hour or two at a time, still frequented the restaurant and lounge. The best seafood around drew people in and was a faintly lit oasis. Friday and Saturday night karaoke also drew a crowd. People love to sing when they're a yard past drunk and Port Royal was no exception.

Sunday was open mike night. The space was narrow and had a stage at one end barely big enough for the microphone and a single step in every direction. The room maxed out at ninety with twenty-five tables. Open mike night was only for the sufficiently blitzed. The amusement was rarely amusing, but people still showed. The booze was cheaper and everything seemed better as the evening progressed. This was a no cover charge, come-as-you-are party, and after a few belts optimism got a miraculous boost.

Darlene and the Pope sat near the back so they wouldn't be a distraction. Darlene ordered a mai tai and the Pope ordered ginger ale.

Bow was in the men's room upchucking for the third time. He was dressed like a dude ranch cowboy—western shirt with faux-pearl buttons, bolo tie, straight-leg jeans, and a pair of boots he'd gotten at a thrift store. He hoped the previous owner hadn't been afflicted with some virulent form of foot fungus.

In honor of the Pope, he also wore a cowboy hat. He had been careful not to get expungement on his outfit, but the rank odor permeated the room and probably stuck to his clothes like milk a week past expiration.

Darlene looked on with unmistakable pride as if witnessing her child's first recital. The Pope looked on with silent delight.

When the emcee took the stage everyone applauded, though primed to boo and jeer at the first opportunity.

"Tonight we welcome a newcomer. Please make him feel at home. Ladies and gentlemen, Santee Slim!"

Darlene whooped. Bow walked onto the stage and stood there awkwardly until the sound subsided. His hands were twitching, his legs too far apart, and he had a serious squint that made him look like a character in a Manga film.

He used a different voice. Not a radically different voice but slower than usual with a broader drawl.

"Anybody needs to go to the bathroom, now's the time."

A few chuckles rose and fell—then silence.

"I'm sure most of you have fought the war of the toilet seat, right? 'Don't leave the seat up! Put the seat down!' My ex-wife woke me up once from a dead sleep just to whine, 'You left the seat up! You have to put it down!'"

Bow held his index finger above his groin and wagged it. "So I did what she said. I put the lid down...Then I pissed all over it...Wrote my name...did the sign of the cross...played tic-tac-toe......I was working on the preamble to the Constitution when I ran out of pee."

Gusts of laughter spun throughout the room, birthing a smidge more confidence.

"Any of you men ever have to pee when you're on the town? Not easy, right? Especially these days of gender identity. You never know if the guy you're standing next to just got out of prison and is looking for a date or some wiener jockey is celebrating his coming out...

Someone in the back hacked caustically and the people around him chirped.

"...You ever wonder why people call it the *bath* room? I mean, nobody ever goes in at halftime, fills up the sink, takes off his clothes, and squeezes in...Or dips a hankie and scrubs his pits.

More snickers than laughs but the energy had begun to build.

"Some call it the *lavatory*, like people are in there conducting soap experiments... 'Well, Dr. Sphincter, what do you think?' 'Lathers up good but still smells like a cow pasture'. "

Airborne laughter spread like a wave and he was off again.

"The most common name is *rest* room. You work in a public place and people come up to you and say, 'Where's the rest room?' Makes you want to wait a couple minutes, run in there, catch them with their pants down, and pound like hell on the wall of the stall. 'You're not resting! You're not even laving!'"

Giggles and guffaws rang out, and the same guy had a coughing fit.

"Know what I really hate? You go into the men's room to take a nice, leisurely wizz. You're feeling good, you know. Just get an easy flow going. Suddenly there's this horribly pungent, nauseating smell, and you realize there's a guy in the stall with Crohn's Disease who has just downed a Roman candle burrito at El Saguaro's Taco Shoppe because his kids dared him to. And you flash back to a time when you were a kid and the toilet backed up, and there was your old man plunging the hell out of everything with water overflowing onto the floor like Niagara Falls. And...it...just...s -t-i-n-k-s....so damn bad."

Bow gestured and paused a few beats, gathering himself.

"That's why I think they should change all the public toilets from Men's and Ladies' rooms to Number One and Number Two rooms. Nobody would have to change anything but the signs—maybe add a few stalls.

"All the Number Ones would use the Men's room since it has both pissoirs and toi-lettes. There would still be plenty of privacy. The men would only be seen from the back and women would have the stalls.

"Imagine the pithy exchanges... 'How's it hangin', dude?' 'Just dandy, ma'am. I'm guessin' you went heavy on the sweet tea.'"

"Then of course, the former Ladies' Room would be the Number Two room, as it only has stalls. Not only would there be complete privacy, but no one but the inflicted would be subjected to each other's...emissions—and of course, the accompanying turbulence."

A few howls echoed again.

"In my more fanciful musings, I imagine this concept spreading far and wide, maybe even with an announcer, like that guy who calls the Kentucky Derby...."

He cupped his hands around his mouth.

"In Stall Number One! We have Rosa 'Caca' Ramos. Rosa was just released from the hospital after an accidental Milk of Magnesia overdose from a bowling night bender of Jalapeno and Pimento nachos. She was recently spotted in Frank's Fine Fish eating a sardine and anchovy sub with a Mountain Dew-prune juice chaser." Bow made a long, wet flatulent sound. "Yes. Thank you, Rosa. Ladies and gentlemen, stall Number One!'"

Everyone applauded.

"In Stall Number Two! We have Alvin 'The Honker' Lavoie, down from Ontario in his 1997 Winnebago Adventurer, with his lovely wife, Iris. Alvin has had to crap since Atlanta, when they stopped at Cracker Barrel for their all-you-can eat cheese grits and sausage breakfast buffet. Alvin did pull over north of Augusta, but no sooner had he begun to squeeze than

Iris banged on the door to the thunder box with the admonition 'Make sure you light a match!'

"Poor Alvin endured poopus interruptus, and has been sitting on piles for over three hundred miles. Not to mention that during the last leg he downed an entire party-sized bag of peanut M & M's while listening to his wife recite the entire Visitor's Guide to Monck's Corner."

Bow made a series of hard, painful straining sounds. "Thank you, Alvin, for that wonderful rendition of Mendelsohn's Concrete Dookie Serenade. And we all know you sneaked a Dr. Bovine's cattle enema in there with you, uh huh. Watch out contestants. This could get ugly."

The roar rose and lingered and Bow stifled his own laughter.

"And finally...In Stall Number Three! We have Lily 'The Tuba' Ackerson. Lily popped her lap band last month when she binged on neverending chili night at Big Ed's House of Salmonella. Lily is scheduled for a colonoscopy tomorrow but couldn't resist the cauliflower dip at her book club. Eight beano tablets subdued the thunder-from-down-under around the ladies but then she panicked and chugged a Metamucil smoothie just to be on the safe side. She's been holding it for forty-five minutes, and if that rumble is any indication, she's ready to let 'er rip! Watch out, folks, she's armed. Get ready to duck!"

"Dear God! She jumped the gun!

"And...They're off!'"

That was all he had. Bow thanked the audience and stepped back. The small crowd exploded and Darlene leapt to her feet. The Pope clapped the way one does at an opera, but a grand smile also sparkled. Bow soaked it all in like early morning sunlight and basked in the sound for a few moments before he doffed his hat, waved, and left the stage.

On the drive home Darlene was ecstatic.

"You did it! You were so good. I can't believe it!"

Bow was wired with excitement. "Yeah, I think I pulled it off. I was just trying to remember everything."

Darlene reached and shook his arm. "I am so proud of you, Bow."

"Thanks. It feels great."

"If they could see you now, huh?"

Darkness crept in but he muscled it aside. This was *his* moment. Still, he answered quietly. "Yeah. If they could see me now."

Fifteen

The penis is a marvelous implement with myriad functions. Although it is used most often as the conduit through which urine is eliminated in the male, perhaps its greatest distinction is as the channel through which sperm is propelled into the uterus in search of an egg. First one there, jackpot.

Evolution does have a sense of humor. If the process were indeed designed for simplicity and ease, most penises would be better aligned with the ovaries so the sprinters would not have so far to travel, relatively speaking.

For the donor, the utter delight in participating serves as a powerful enticement to continue. Hurtling potential sons and daughters into the void really, really, really feels dandy.

Vital to a thorough understanding of the male's role in reproduction is the acknowledgement and acceptance of the original intention regarding sperm expulsion—i.e., the quicker the better. There are several logical reasons for this.

First, the *fire when ready* condition is natural. The human male did not invent the immediate physical response to this stimulus any more than he invented the pain reaction when he accidentally sits on his testicles. He did, perhaps invent the phrase *let's do it again*, as a result of this function. Otherwise—

The male of yore—way, way back yore—was prompted and expected to fertilize multiple partners. This served to enhance the gene pool and to keep the males close at hand, as they did not know whose offspring was whose until the similarity in habits such as belching, grunting, and breaking wind were revealed.

Also, the antediluvian male, until fairly recent history, was unaware of any female pleasure center. Females themselves were unfamiliar with their own buzz buttons until horseback riding came along. Later, the male was enlightened, but, as in all evolutionary matters, this was woefully slow.

Finally, the male, having such ponderous and contrary information, was baffled. In his mighty effort to reconcile this nature versus nurture hypothesis, he appeared less than empathetic. However, as he matured and responded to this information with appreciation and commitment—as his emotional and even spiritual growth demanded—he assumed his role as the primary purveyor of female satisfaction, fear of implied deprivation notwithstanding.

Unfortunately, some males are yet remiss in the Tao of female satisfaction , concurrent with the advent of alcohol and team sports. This dilemma has not been completely resolved. The male, as a heretofore-necessary partner in the reproductive process, may discover himself unnecessary in this function, as women learn to harvest his seed by alternate means.

Once proven superfluous, he may then become reliant upon himself, or else some substitute, to open the gate and let the stallions run free—and cop that fire-in-the-hole tingle.

Therefore, it is logical, and in his own best interests, to become more attentive to partner satisfaction before he unlimbers the member lest he be impelled into a quasi-permanent liaison with a latex gal named Trixie, who is wholly unconcerned about how trigger-happy he is.

The fold-down bed was barely wide enough for the two of them.

"Who gives a Waldo Wedgieburger about that?" Darlene offered.

This time there was more urgency, fueled by giddy eagerness, and the joyful residue of Bow's graduation. He took full advantage to explore every perfect part of her, or at least to her knees. Darlene sighed with his caresses. The sounds she made were refined, even delicate. He discovered a sweet spot on her neck with the stiff odor of waning perfume, and an acidic taste, but kept his lips there and kissed as softly as he was able.

A half hour of slow smoldering. Then, coalescence. A steady rhythm, *con abbandono.* Whenever he felt that electric urge to ejaculate, he decelerated until the compulsion passed, and began again.

Finally, Darlene grunted low and shuddered, granting Bow license to release. He felt it deep in his bowels with the twist of a knot.

They lay there silently, wrapped in each other's arms. Bow had never held anyone in such a way. He had never been given license. With Marie, it had always been a casual pat and a trip to the bathroom to wash herself. He didn't know what any of this meant. He didn't want to think about it. He had no history with these neo-revelatory incursions.

"Bow?" she said, more than a whisper, less than full voice.

"Yeah?"

"Have you ever wanted to be someone else?"

What an odd question, though he did not puzzle long. "You mean like a football player or something?"

"Or just different."

"No. Not really."

"Were you happy before?"

He thought again, still not moving. "I was content. I was settled into a life I was comfortable in."

"Do you miss it?"

Again he thought, muddled now though not punitive. "I miss my daughter."

"Yeah. I get that."

He pondered then and snatched a mote long-abandoned. "Once. In college. I was different."

"What was it?"

"I saw smart kids who couldn't afford tuition or books. With loan programs and grants, I thought that anyone who could get in could go to school. I thought between the school and the government there was always a way."

He craved a cigarette but didn't want to move. Her breasts pressed warm against his chest and her nest tickled his package. "I knew kids who worked two jobs just to keep up. Maybe they could have gotten loans but didn't know if they could ever pay them back, or were too scared to run up such a big tab. Whatever, many of them struggled, or didn't finish."

"What did you do?"

"I started a program with the school where people could donate extra scholarship money and put it in a pool to help those people. You stop applying for scholarships when you've got enough to pay tuition, books, and expenses. I got people to keep applying. I also got kids who didn't need financial help to apply for scholarships just to contribute to the pot. I even got the school to subsidize certain required courses to make them cheaper."

"God, that's wonderful."

"Well, it wasn't much. Maybe a couple hundred bucks a semester. There were hundreds of kids who needed help."

"A couple hundred bucks is a couple hundred bucks."

"I suppose."

"What happened?"

An interior door slammed shut. Memories were sealed behind it. He opened the door just enough to peer in. "I was under a lot of stress. I had to bear down and work harder to make sure I got into law school. My father reminded me of this a lot."

"Your father made you stop what you were doing?"

"I guess so. Yeah. And, sad to say, I never once looked over my shoulder."

"You could've been like the Pope."

"No. This was only the one thing."

"But it could've led to other things. You would've been good."

Bow considered if the *good* she referred to was the action or himself. Yes, he could have been good, more than decent, more than common. "I still couldn't be anything like the Pope," he said finally.

"Why not?"

"I could never make barbecue sauce that good."

Darlene snickered and moved her lips to his. She massaged him between the legs. Bow thought this was hopeless. He hadn't managed a double-header in thirty years, since his first encounters with Marie, but he enjoyed the kiss.

Darlene held her lips against his ear. "Nobody has ever been so tender with me before."

His pecker saluted like Veterans Day. He eased atop her and they quickly became reacquainted.

The black night had settled in but the Pope decided he and Bow should take a walk. The temperature had not reached sixty that day and was falling as light faded. They enjoyed the new night, knowing such times would be infrequent as winter settled in, however mild. This wasn't Key West and it wasn't southern California.

The Pope felt cooped up easily, perhaps because of his limited movement at the grills. There was no one else to spot him.

They walked leisurely toward the old ports. Once, massive ships had anchored there as goods from the north were unloaded. Charleston and Savannah had become far more practical for the modern container carriers than tiny Port Royal with its narrow egress.

Vestiges of the former anchorage were still evident in the deep-water moors and massive alleys created by buoys. With a bit of local knowledge and a penchant for imagination, one could envision clipper ships laden with fabric from England and Europe.

Neither of them had dressed warmly enough. Undone by overconfidence. Signs of the season were prevalent, however. The hardwoods were bare, their leaves bedded at their roots, brown and withered now. The gray limbs of the dogwoods were twisted into the claws of old crones. The wild azaleas were dead vines. Even the evergreens were not ever green. Needles had fallen, and many more still in place were brown with hunger, making the trees look sickly.

The Pope flexed his hands and closed them several times. "I'm concerned," he said. His tone was confessional, not adversarial.

"About what?"

"You and Darlene."

"Oh," Bow said.

"I'm sure you have thought about this and think you understand how it's going to work, but it won't happen that way."

"I think we've got a handle on it."

"Maybe. For now. But it's gone too far."

"We've got it covered."

The Pope wasn't satisfied. "I would hate to think you were using her."

Bow blushed immediately, not in embarrassment but in annoyance. "You underestimate her and we shouldn't have this conversation."

"I understand. Under normal circumstances I wouldn't care. These aren't normal circumstances."

"It isn't what you think."

The Pope hiked up his pants. "Any time someone says that, it's usually close to what the other is thinking."

"I'm not using her."

"Maybe not by your definition, but you may have forgotten how gullible she is."

Bow had become stiff and his lips were white. "I don't think this is any of your business, but she initiated the contact."

"I know she started it. That's no excuse. When this ends in catastrophe, who's going to clean up after? Not you."

"What makes you think it's going to be a catastrophe?"

"You're kidding. You know no good can come from this."

"I'm not sure that's true. Good has already come from it."

"Come on, Bow. She's not going to be in your life. You'll be on your own doing whatever you'll be doing and she'll be history."

He ingested this. He enjoyed her immensely but knew little of how serious her connection was. No matter the satisfaction, he did not want to be cruel. If he left with no intention for further contact—or infrequent contact—this would prove cold if not callous.

"So you think I should put a stop to it now."

The Pope stared at him for a moment, his expression as inscrutable as ever. "You've accepted the reality and she hasn't. She may be dreaming of a day when you come home to her." He paused. "Fair or not, whoever knows more in a sticky situation has the responsibility."

Bow didn't believe Darlene was that fragile, or that she envisioned a future together, but the prospect was sobering. He couldn't be the cause of more grief. Better to rip the scab now before it scarred.

"You can shit a white horse for all I care!"

This was not the beginning, of course. The beginning had been much more civil, if confounding. Bow and Darlene sat on opposite sides of the dinette table in the trailer. Bow dreaded the hour and was also heavyhearted. In all his years, he had never had such a conversation.

Darlene was counting her tips. She stopped and started twice. Bow waited with

strained patience, looking for an opening. Finally, she wrapped the roll of bills with a rubber band and jabbed it into her purse.

"You should break those up," he offered.

"Why?"

"Because if something happens you'll lose it all. If they're separate you wouldn't."

"What could happen?"

"I don't know. A pick-pocket maybe."

She snickered. "It'd take fifteen seconds for anybody who sticks his hand in there to find it. Hell, sometimes I even have to root around to find it."

"What if he just grabbed your purse and ran?"

"Then it wouldn't matter how they was wrapped 'cause he'd have the whole thing."

So much for an opening gambit. "I guess you're right." He began again. "Listen. I'm worried."

"About my money? That's sweet."

"No." He breathed aloud. "About us."

She had been alerted by the sigh. "Okay," she said cautiously.

He fidgeted like a kid. "I don't think we should sleep together anymore."

She showed no emotion, but her eyebrows formed a V. "Why is that?"

"You know. Someday I'll probably leave here."

"Yeah. So?"

"Well. I just don't see a future for us."

"Who gives a Larry Longjohnson about that?"

"I do."

"Well, don't. I know there ain't no future for us."

He was caught off guard. "Huh?"

"I know you aren't going to be a dishwasher forever. You're too smart for that. I know you'll heal up enough to start over. And I won't be going with you."

"What if we get attached to each other? Wouldn't that make it worse?"

"I'm already attached to you. You're my responsibility, remember—"

"I thought that was over now."

"—and even if you weren't, I would still be fond of you."

"And you don't think sex is different?"

"Maybe. Just because we do it don't mean we're joined at the hip."

"No pun intended."

"Huh?"

He wagged his head. "I'm just not sure any good will come from it."

"I like the poke," she said. "Don't it make you feel good?"

"Of course."

"Then how else are we going to get the poke?"

"We won't."

"But every time we do it, it'll get better."

"Life doesn't work that way."

She scowled. "You say. I don't."

His eyes wandered. "I just think we should cool it."

She rose in a stew. "Do what you want, then. You can shit a white horse for all I care!"

Later, in the diner, she watched him at a distance of her own design, her aspect a recognition of the end.

Khrystile didn't show for work one day, and despite every effort to track her down, no one could—even the Pope. He had checked her apartment, the hospital, and with law enforcement. No luck. She had fled with her new paramour and the Pope was noticeably wounded for several days—and crabby besides.

As Bow opined, "The mark of the grouch is six-six-six, plus tip ." No one knew what the Hell he was talking about.

Her replacement was Ruby, a mildly-challenged forty-year-old who had spent her entire adult life working for a federally-funded contract company that stuffed envelopes, counted screws and put them into small plastic bags for do-it-yourself furniture kits, and other simple tasks.

She had lived long enough to have been called *retarded*, transitioning to *slow*, to *mentally impaired*, to *handicapped*, to *challenged*. Her mother had just passed and her social worker found a place for her in a group home but thought Ruby was ready to join the outside workforce and live more independently.

She wore her dark hair in a short flip, which did not help her appear more intelligent, and had a round, pleasant face with no trace of Downs. She did waddle when she walked, stiff-legged, side-to-side like a windup penguin.

She had learned to swear without inhibition, probably without comprehension. She may have heard so much of the argot she didn't recognize a difference. She placed no more stress on the curse words than she did with other adjectives. Most people would eventually recognize a disability but she was still warned to mind her language within earshot of customers.

Every time she agreed with the same phrase, "Okie-fenokie."

She could write, though illegibly, and as this was all part of some grand social experiment, the government provided her a simple, hand-held computer tablet that had every menu item in large letters. Debbie was given a small printer and put a hard copy of all Ruby's orders on a tack board near the Pope's grill with the others.

In spite of obvious deficiencies Ruby was remarkably quick, knew how to add multiple quantities on any item, and was able to deliver special instructions verbally.

"Old lady with the pink hair don't want too much fuckin' sauce on her samwich."

Darlene gave her an offhand warning. "Now, Ruby."

"Oops. Forgot which ones not to say."

"Well, you gotta remember."

"Okie-Fenokie."

She was brought to work and retrieved by a social services van, was always on time, and did not complain. She did not talk much beyond what the job required. She seemed to struggle with co-worker names, so she called everyone *Bud,* even the women. So with every future admonition, which occurred daily, she would declare, "Okie-Fenokie, Bud."

For whatever reason, she took to Bob, and during idle times would follow him around as he bussed and cleaned tables, carrying on a one-sided conversation. His was the only name she remembered. If Bob minded, he didn't say, and was able to ignore her.

"You like trucks, Bob? I like trucks. Someday I'm gonna have a big red truck with a horn that plays Dixie and one of them little trees hangin' from the mirror. I know I can learn to drive it, too. Anybody can learn to drive a truck, right? Christ-a-mighty, I got a fuckin' customer."

Bow simmered, surprised by how long the irritation stayed glued. How noble was noble? What if the Pope had simply been wrong and separating himself from Darlene was purposeless? He was also bewildered. Among the legion of doubts that had appeared, and now nested—came a disturbing uncertainty.

Maybe he had underestimated his affection for her. This was not merely sex. After all he was fifty. The fire still burned but only on those spare occasions when the candle was lit. Perhaps this was nothing more than the tangibility of her and her generous heart.

He missed her.

He also found it more difficult to see her than he realized. They spent no face time together. Bow could spend the entire shift facing the back wall. In such close proximity, however, they could not avoid each other. She smiled and waved every time their eyes met. She showed no sign of disappointment or anguish. She was still Darlene, there at the edge of his air space.

As the days progressed, some of his discomfort passed or else melded into the obdurate melancholy now customary. Thinner and more bland than before, it was still a potential force—and a warning. In those darkly translucent nights when his guts were full of worms, he would muster a resistance born of such frequent infections.

When he could find no diversion, or had no energy to create one, he sat motionless and gazed into the abyss, knowing, at least, that he had moved farther away from it, though not far enough. This didn't cheer him or evoke more confidence, but it did name him a survivor even if what torment remained was excruciatingly slow to fade.

Then, of course, there were always new torments.

Far easier now to find respite, yet still a battle.

This mid-autumn day was blustery. The Pope sat in his lumpy throne. His only concession to the weather was a long-sleeved T-shirt. Bow didn't want to take any chances. He'd bought a nice zip-up coat and a toboggan cap, thermal socks and a pair of long-johns. He was prepared for Alaska, so nothing on the coast of South Carolina would take him by surprise.

The Pope had uploaded music on his phone and sat with ear buds attached. Bow expected him to be listening to something classical but he heard *Gimme Three Steps* by Lynyrd Skynard.

Maybe he had contributed something after all.

The Pope turned off the music and scrutinized him for a minute. "You cold?"

Bow shrugged. "Not really. And I don't want to be."

"I like the cold."

"You originally from up north?"

"Yeah, somewhere."

Bow rubbed his hands together. "Darlene say anything to you?"

The Pope nodded. "She asked me if I had anything to do with what you told her. More precisely, she said, 'You stuck your big fat nose into my goddam business, didn't you?'"

"Sounds about right. What did you say?"

"I contended that my nose is not fat."

"After that."

"I said what in good conscience I had to say. I lied and said I didn't know what she was talking about."

"Well, it's done. Not happy about it, but it's over."

"I know. As you said, it's done."

"Yeah."

The Pope brightly sat up. "Hear about Ruby's new adventure?"

"I don't think so."

"She walks up to Abe and says, 'Jesus Christ, Abe, change the goddam station! Okie-Fenokie, Bud?'"

Bow chuckled half-heartedly. The Pope added a dead-on imitation of Darlene's accent. "Now Ruby. From now on don't say anything to anyone except 'May I please take your order?' and 'thank you'".

"You think she'll stick?"

"Who knows? She's not stupid. She came up to the counter today and shouted, 'Dude wants to know we got mountain oysters'."

"Someone shining her on."

"Yeah. Didn't think she knew what they are."

"What did you do?"

"I had a bucket of those little meat balls I use in soups and smoothed a couple down and covered them with chicken gravy. Put them on his plate."

"Seriously."

"She comes back later with a big old grin on her face and says, 'Dude didn't eat the oysters. Wanted to know what they were from. Told him they was goat balls. Too little for bull, too big for pig, Bud'."

Bow then laughed without effort. "That's perfect."

Sixteen

A rare wind came. Coastal areas are accustomed to hurricanes, if not accustomed, then not surprised by a tropical storm. Their infrequency, coupled with the odds of a storm crashing into any specific space, made the gamble worthwhile. Hurricane season was over. In cooler weather, low pressure systems are coiled tighter than a python, and the jet stream moves hundreds of miles in a single day. Add this to the warm water of the Atlantic south of Bermuda and into the Caribbean, and there is wicked chemistry—with the potential for destruction on a massive scale, and the temperament of a horny bear.

This was no hurricane. Little rain fell at all. This was a mighty gale that covered four hundred square miles. Winds blew steadily at fifty miles-per-hour with gusts up to eighty. Everything had to be tied down or hidden inside thick walls.

The trailer was already anchored in concrete. The Adirondack chairs were too large to move indoors so they lashed them to a tree with bungee cords, their cushions stored elsewhere.

The Pope lamented that his chair would never sit right again. Bow thought the wind would snatch them up and batter them into kindling but kept this to himself. This was the first time he had ever seen the Pope close to anything like panic. How the mighty cherish their seats endowed by divine right.

Business went on. People still clamored for pork fat, perhaps even more now that the end was near. By midday anything not secured and weighing less than a hundred pounds was so much shrapnel.

A newspaper vending machine crashed through the front window of City Hall. A bicycle made a Wicked Witch arc over two city streets and ended up on the steeple of the Church of God. The resultant sermon must have been illuminating.

Interior/exterior pressures were unbalanced and windows shattered in symphony, a freakish concert of cymbals and drums. Many boats were damaged, even under cover. One sank when a shovel from God knows where flew from the sky and speared the hull.

No one was killed. Most injuries were caused by carelessness. A large branch shot through a bathroom window causing the owner to later seek treatment for spastic colon.

Coincidentally, perhaps curiously, the measurement used for wind speed is called the Beaufort scale. The wind did not howl, but whistled, at times tauntingly, at others, angrily. The tone never changed, though the volume rose and fell with the intensity of the blow.

The unpredictable surges scared everyone the most. These came with no warning, surfing the heavy air, lambasting everything, scouring walls, hurling limbs, felling trees outright—shrieking as though too long ignored. When a gust drove against the windows of the diner, flexing the inflexible and rattling doors, everyone retreated.

Except Bob, who calmly wiped tables and swept beneath them.

By mid-afternoon only four tables were occupied. The place suddenly went dark. This time no flicker or swell of machines returning to life followed. Dark as space. Darlene grabbed a flashlight and carryout boxes. She scooped up the remainders of meals, and helped the handful of customers out the door. Then she locked it. Abe watched in dismay how six checks were abandoned and would not be paid.

Everyone gathered near the large window and watched, even the Pope. The kitchen area was blackest of all. Each time the brute reared, they all instinctively recoiled. No one talked. Just oohs, aahs, and whoas. During the next swell—a sudden rush like a swing of the bat—Darlene clutched Bow's hand. He let it be.

Beyond terrified, Mickey was as wired as a ferret, having just had a hormone treatment. He rubbed his beard until the skin beneath glistened with oil. He chewed on his pen until it split.

Ruby watched without expression but rocked from one foot to the other every few seconds. Abe did not move from his counter stool but also searched the sky for either relief or warning.

"I know a good ghost story," the Pope said with a wink.

"Screw that," Darlene returned. "We need something hopeful. Bow? You have to know a good story."

All eyes slid in unison toward the dishwasher. The interior was hushed and still. "Well, maybe I know one or two." He stopped, seeking some evasive tale until his lips moved with satisfaction.

"Some of you may remember 2011 in North Carolina. There were tornado clusters everywhere. Over thirty spotted in one day alone. And after a few days of this, we had a lull, only to be hammered again later. It was awful.

"One day a tornado jumped from the east a hundred and fifty miles to a little place in Bertie County. Bertie is rural and sparsely populated. Sixty-seven homes were destroyed, thirty-seven of them mobile homes.

"When the twister came over the hills, everyone ran for cover. There weren't many options. Most found the nearest brick house and got in."

"Just like the Three Pigs," Ruby said.

"Exactly," Bow replied. "Well, one older couple who lived in a mobile home were in a bind. The wife was in bed with pneumonia, so weak she could barely move. And her husband wouldn't leave her. She begged him to go, saying if anything happened to him she would never get over it. But the old man stayed.

"The storm began to blow just like this one except in a tight spiral, round and round. Pretty soon it closed in on them. The husband peeked out a window and watched as the wind ripped the roof off the brick house down the road with nearly a dozen people cowering inside. Then it came right at them."

He stopped to breathe and everyone leaned toward him in anticipation.

"The tornado flew right over top of them, ripping the trailer to shreds. The trailer literally exploded and the last thing the old man did was to fling his body across his wife's as a shield, and hang on to the headboard with all his might.

"He remembered the whole world flying past him, and then he must have passed out. When he woke, and this was sometime later, the only thing left of their home was the little patio. Pieces of everything else were strewn around the yard.

"He heard a moan. Quickly, he stood up. His wife lay there without a scratch. The bed was in the same exact place as before, only now outside. They were safe."

"Wow," Darlene said. The rest made oohing sounds. "She was spared by a real miracle."

"She died the next day," Bow said after a moment. "The pneumonia killed her."

Everyone groaned and Darlene hit Bow on the shoulder with her fist. They all split up and moved elsewhere. The wind was dying.

Ruby looked at Bow confused, her head slightly cocked to one side like a puppy. "I don't fuckin' get it, Bud."

Bow was propped up on the sofa. He listened to the receding blow. After two hours without power, Abe let everyone go. Ten minutes later, the power was back on. The Pope was gone. He had made sure everything in the freezer was okay. Cleanup would have to wait until the next morning but there was not much else to tend to.

The first thing the Pope did when the storm subsided was to find the old Adirondack chairs. They had survived intact, though now hung from the straps two feet off the ground like sides of meat. Tomorrow the cushions would be replaced and they would be back in business.

His thoughts were a billion miles away, a stream of consciousness so useless these would be among the first to go should the old gray hard drive need more space. They were meaningless for several reasons.

First, they were unsuitable for a mature man. Secondly, they represented the exhumation of a settled issue. Finally, they disturbed the delicate balance between his id and its lid.

An example— 'Darlene's nipples look like bullets when she's aroused'— 'rubbing against her snatch is like wearing a cashmere jock strap'— 'she can squeeze her cooter muscles like your fat aunt's hug—and it's won-der-ful'.

The trailer door inched open. He looked up. Not afraid, but creeped out. He watched the door without blinking. Must've just been air pressure. Then he saw a wad of dark hair before anything else. Darlene poked her head inside as if it were a disembodied member from some micro-budget horror flick. She smiled abashedly. Her shoulders followed, then arms snaking in mid-air.

"I ain't armed," she said.

He perked up instantly, but he revealed nothing, except he discreetly covered his lingering stiffy with a pillow. "Come on in."

Darlene slow-stepped down the aisle and sat at his feet. "I've missed you."

"Me, too."

"I know the Pope put you up to it. He's got it all figured out there'll be too much achin' for a breakin' down the road if we keep bumpin' and humpin'"."

"He's probably right."

"Well, nobody wants to live knowing that hurt's coming."

"There's no way we could avoid it that I can see."

Darlene frowned. "We ain't babies. I think we can handle it."

"Maybe. Why risk it?"

Darlene assembled her thoughts, her eyes skyward as she did. "Okay. Say we keep on ropin' the cowgirl. How bad's it gonna hurt when we say adios, on a scale of one to ten? A Eight?"

Bow sought her eyes. Avoiding heartbreak hadn't been for her benefit alone. "Nine."

"Okay. Even knowing what's coming, how much good would there be between now and then?"

"Knowing what's coming? Maybe a five."

"Not seven?"

"Leave it at five."

"That leaves us four in the hole. Okay?"

"Okay."

"Now. Let's say we stay like we were in the beginning and cut out the four-legged tap dancin'. How bad's it gonna hurt anyway because we've been friends, too?"

He smiled shortly, quickly, like a tic. "Six."

"So worst case, being belly-bumpers leaves us four in the hole but only being buddies leaves us six in the hole."

"I'm not sure that's how it works."

"Well, any way you look at it if we keep on makin' jello we're still two to the good."

Bow surrendered. He had known he would the moment he saw her at the door. If she hadn't made the overture he would have in the next few days, Pope or not, his latent meanderings aside.

"Maybe so."

"Then why beat this horse instead of riding it?"

He motioned to her and she slid into him—resting her head beneath his chin, wiggling into the perfect position like an old dog. He knew she was up to something by the near-silent pop of saliva as the corners of her mouth spread outward. She pulled the pillow away, and placed a hand loosely over his crotch.

"Anytime you're ready," she said.

The Pope was nursing a small but nagging cold. The day was gray and when the wind came up everyone shied a little. Even so, proprieties must be maintained and free food trumped all but the most persistent caution.

"Never trust anyone who says, 'nobody's perfect'," he began. "It's a lame alibi for people too lazy to find a decent solution. Of course nobody's perfect, but that's a pitiful excuse for fuckups that someone should see coming.

"During the winter of 1620, the Mayflower docked and the pilgrims found an abandoned village. It was a sizeable area. Corn had been planted, the land was already tilled, and there was a fresh water stream nearby. They couldn't believe their good fortune. They sang praises to the Almighty for such a gift.

"But the reason the village had been abandoned was that the Wampanoag tribe had contracted a horrible disease. Leptospirosis, which comes, oddly enough, from the urine of the black rat. Ninety-percent of all the Wampanoag had been infected."

"Incidentally, most Native Americans celebrated a kind of Thanksgiving long before the English. They celebrated the harvest and benevolent spirits, but the Macy's parade was invented by white people.

Sparse snickers arose and fell.

"Now. The black rat is not indigenous to those parts. It had stowed away on previous European ships. The plague that nearly destroyed the tribe came from explorers and settlers. So what had been deemed Providence by white people was actually the result of pestilence— ignorant, clueless pestilence.

"It's important to remember that one man's gratitude is another man's misfortune. Maybe we don't feel we have a lot to be thankful for. Nobody should have to paint a happy face on things just because people who have it better think we should. Sure, we all have things to be grateful for: our lives, our relative freedom, the people we care about. Maybe we even try to get more out of things, to captain our own ships to fairer waters, so to speak.

"Maybe the best we can do is to not to make things worse for anyone else in the process. No matter how much misfortune we encounter, don't create misfortune for anyone else. If that's the best you can do, so be it. You're ahead on that big karmic scoreboard in the sky.

"Have a happy Thanksgiving."

Mickey was late so Bow helped Darlene wrap silverware sets. He arrived fighting the histrionic wave again, and one look at the others sent him bawling as if he'd had the most beautiful baloney pony on layaway and someone bought it out from under him. He flew into the rest room.

Darlene's eyes widened sorrowfully. "Pitiful. Just pitiful."

"I thought he just had a hormone treatment."

"Still gets him worked up. It must be hard not knowing when you'll get the next one."

"I'd give him some of mine if I could."

"Newp," Darlene said. "You're gonna need all of yours."

Bow was changing out the rinse water, bopping to Alice Cooper's *Billion Dollar Babies*. He caught the aroma of attar, like the smell of a week-old rose bouquet. A tap came on his shoulder. He started a bit, turned off the music and looked.

He had seen her before at the gatherings. She was one of the meager and looked like a biker chick past her expiration date. She was poorly thin with sleeves of tats shoulder to wrist. She had stringy blonde hair, bleached to oblivion and as stiff as straw, held together with so much spray her coif looked like a hat. She wore a five-dollar ring on every finger and big loops hung from her earlobes. She wore purple eye shadow so dark her lids looked bruised, and foundation so thick it resembled spackling over a stuccoed wall.

She stuck out her hand. “Cyndee.”

He shook her hand. “Bow.”

She nervously wiggled her fingers, her nails like lavender stilettoes sharp enough to gouge flesh.

“Can I talk to you for a minute? In private.”

He gestured to the back door. He led her to a vent spewing out warm air. A roar like a car wash but manageable. He decided not to smoke but offered her one before putting the pack away.

“I never smoked, thank God. Except some crack. Didn’t have a problem giving that up once I found smack. Got off the needle only to get hooked on booze. Now I’m off the booze and drink ten cokes a day. Ain’t that a helluva tune?”

“Everyone needs something,” he said.

“Yeah. I reckon.” She studied him. He didn’t know what to make of it. He waited her out.

“You’re the lawyer who sent that boy to prison, aren’t you?”

The air eked out of him but he didn't pale. "Maybe someday I'll be known for something more than that, but yeah, I'm the guy."

"But you're a lawyer, right?"

"Not at the moment."

"Look. I wasn't slammin' ya or anything. I need some advice and don't know where to turn."

He wished himself far away, more than across the room—in another country. "What kind of advice?"

She moved a step closer as if two feet mattered were there eavesdroppers. "My kid's in jail. He's only nineteen. He ain't a great kid, but I wasn't a great mom, either. He's guilty of something, but not what he's in jail for."

"What's he in jail for?"

"Possession with intent to distribute weed."

"What's his sentence?"

"Thirty months."

The sentence wasn't harsh, even with recent liberalities toward marijuana. He still wanted to be elsewhere but gears clicked into motion. Rusty and ill-used but able to turn. He looked at the woman, biting her lower lip, her eyes twitching in their sockets as they silently pleaded. He had seen the same look a hundred times before from the other side of the courtroom, and felt the scant rise of mental activity. Such was a feeling nonetheless.

"Tell me about it."

"God, I need a belt of something."

He took her hands in his. "No. Just tell me what happened."

She hawed for a time to corner her thoughts, but began speaking before finishing. "He ain't no dealer. He was just doing a favor for a friend, or a friend of a friend. This other little prick got busted, see. And the narcs said they could work something out if he gave them his dealer. Well, the shitass, Lonnie, didn't have a dealer. He scrounged, see, and would buy a matchbox's worth from anybody who was holding. But he didn't want to do a long one in jail. So he called Boyd—my son. Asked him if he could get him a quarter. Boyd didn't know what was what. A quarter pound is a goodly amount. But he wanted to be righteous, you know? So he called around and found somebody holding a pound and the dude said sure. So Boyd takes this little twerp to the guy and they do the deal. An hour later, the cops show up at my door."

"Couldn't he have given up the guy who had the pound?" He was thinking like a prosecutor and saw the pain in the woman's face.

"Maybe he shoulda. But he didn't. His lawyer told him to plead guilty and he'd get a break. He got two-and-a-half years, out in two maybe."

He wasn't ready to be lawyer. Not at this time, not with this case, and not for the defense. The deal had been a set-up, legal, but still a set-up. Nothing had been gained. No bigger fish, no up-the-ladder, no conspiracy. The chain of evil-doers remained intact and untouched. Thus was justice.

"Public defender?"

"Yeah. I got no money for an appeal."

"Okay. Tell you what. I'm not sure there are any grounds for a good appeal. And I can't get directly involved. But if you can get me the file I'll take a look at it. If I find anything, maybe there's something we can do. I honestly don't think I will, but I'll give it my best shot. I promise."

"Thanks," she said. She still trembled. "Jesus, I could use a little taste."

Later that night Bow was lying back with the tiny TV balanced on a tray upon his chest, a foot away from his eyes, while the Pope prepared to leave.

"What's on?" the Pope asked.

"A Beatle tribute band on PBS. They're not bad, except the station breaks in after every third song to beg for money. It's either that or a Dawson's Creek rerun."

"Yikes."

"At least." He turned the TV off and set it aside. "You send Cyndee to me?" It was an innocent question.

"No. I told her to leave it alone. I told her you were in the same shape she was. Not entirely true, but I didn't want to get you involved. She needs something to hold onto. This isn't it. She needs to focus on something else. But, this is what she has."

"I'll look at the case. I couldn't give her much hope, either, but I gave her my word."

"That's nice of you." The Pope paused, his hand on the door. "Case or no case, she's not strong enough yet to get completely straight. A grain of salt."

Bow went blank but nodded. Sometimes there isn't enough sunlight in the world to warm all the cold hiding places. "Can't hurt."

A few nights later, the Pope entered the trailer and found Bow sitting in a dining chair, his stocking feet propped up on the edge of the dinette table. He had his reading glasses perched on his nose and a pencil between his teeth. He had received the package from Cyndee and was reading the trial transcript. He flipped a page.

"Anything to it?" The Pope went into the bathroom and could be heard washing his face through the open door.

"Not much. The fact that he was just brokering the deal to help somebody out doesn't matter. Kid didn't even take a cut."

"That should account for something," the Pope ventured.

"Maybe. But the cops knew he wasn't a dealer. Just needed to get a bigger fish on paper."

"So that's it."

Bow lowered his feet to the floor. "Well, there are a couple of things in the initial interrogation that show the intent to entrap. Question is, so what? Who cares about entrapping a drug dealer? That's what you're supposed to do. Only thing I can see is to try and prove the kid's not a drug dealer."

"But he made the connection."

"Yeah, but he never actually possessed the dope or the money. He transported the buyer. And the guy who had the dope wasn't charged. Lonnie didn't know him and Boyd wouldn't give him up. Cops didn't even pursue that angle."

"And the world keeps spinning 'round."

"Yeah, they nailed who they thought was the easiest mark. On the books that's a double."

"What else?"

"This Lonnie bozo picked Boyd because he knew Boyd couldn't hurt him. Listen to this. Original interrogation. Question: 'Who do you buy drugs from?' Answer: 'Lots of people. I only get enough for a few joints at a time. Guys don't even miss it, and I still have to cough up twenty bucks. It's a rip-off.' Question: 'You never buy more?' Answer: 'I ain't made of money. You know how much an ounce goes for?' Question: 'If you had enough money to buy an ounce, who would you buy it from?' Answer: 'I don't know. Never done it.' Question: 'I get that. But if you could, who?' Answer: 'Probably Boyd.' Question: 'He's a dealer?' Answer: 'No. But he's always holding, and I know he wouldn't stick it to me.' Question: 'You think he could get you more than an ounce?' Answer: 'Maybe. He knows a lot of people.'

"Poor sap," the Pope said.

Bow put the papers on the table and rubbed the bridge of his nose. "Not only that, but they specified the amount. Four ounces. Just to make sure it was enough for a distribution bust."

"Is that an angle?"

"Might be. This kid admitted Boyd wasn't a dealer in interrogation. And as far as we know, Boyd didn't gain anything."

"Tainted evidence?"

"No. Not specifically." He stopped for a moment and blew fog on his glasses, wiping the lenses on his shirt. "I remember a case once. This concierge in some glitzy hotel was known to provide male guests with a phone number should they ask where to find some 'companionship'. So they sent a cop in undercover, got the phone number, and then busted him. The lawyer for the concierge got the case tossed."

"Because he didn't take money?"

"No. He did take money. Because he acted like the Yellow Pages. He used information known to others but maybe not to out-of-towners. The money he got wasn't an issue because he got tipped for things anyway. And he didn't solicit. He just provided information."

"Even though it was illegal."

"The phone number was a private number but attached to an escort service. A registered business."

"Yeah, but Boyd did more than supply information. And selling weed isn't a legitimate business."

"I know. It's a stretch. But if I can prove the dingus targeted him strictly because he knew information, then the most he could have been busted for is conspiracy."

The Pope reappeared. He had shaved again and now wiped his face with a towel. He looked toward the table with a wry grin. "Jeez, Bow, you really are a lawyer."

"Yeah," Bow answered. "Used to be."

Bow wrote an appeal quoting case law. The Pope started a collection to pay the filing fees. Whether the court would take the appeal seriously, everyone would have to wait. If Bow were pressed to elaborate, he would have said only that it felt okay to goose the old noggin again.

Darlene was missing throughout. She and Bow had hardly uttered a whole sentence to each other. On Friday, Bow invited her to join him after work.

"Thought you'd come by before now," Bow said.

Darlene peeled off her coat. She pried off her shoes with her toes and sat on the sofa and stretched her legs. "I know you've been busy."

He sat beside her. "A fool's errand."

"So how'd it go?"

He smiled to himself. "It felt a little strange to get into that stuff again."

"You've done it before."

"Never tried to get a dope dealer out of jail before."

"But you haven't lost anything. In your head, I mean."

"Well, you and I both know it'll never be the same."

She looked into him, as if seeing something deeper and more substantial than a plain T-shirt and khakis, and hair in dire need of a trim.

"But that's the real you, isn't it? That's the real Bowman."

He looked into the window at his own dark reflection and saw a glimpse of what she had seen. He wore a clever disguise, but in the wavering depths lay someone he recognized, though he took little comfort in it.

"I don't know what's out there. You know that."

"But you could do it now."

He stood restlessly, went the refrigerator and got a glass of milk. "I don't know. Maybe. Probably not completely. Not like it was."

She made that short, sigh-sound of resignation, a single, sharp breath and counterfeit smile. She reached for him and they held each other. She closed her eyes, knowing he was ready to move on whether he admitted it or not. "Okay."

His eyes slid shut as well, a different perspective, a separate horizon. He still had doubts. He still wanted to hide. Could he actually be Bowman again? He wrestled with inadequacy, prone to submission, recognized the absence of some more persuasive catalyst, because, in no small part, he clutched her then because he yet needed her.

The appellate judge did not overturn the conviction, nor did he order a new trial. What he did do was provide an opinion that suggested another appeals judge might order a new trial. He agreed the police had *created* a dealer instead of exposing one. He also found it disturbing the defendant had never owned the drugs in question, nor the money, and that the informant admitted he had approached the defendant only because he was potentially less hostile, and knew beforehand he would not have such a quantity without collusion.

The prosecutor took note and the parties agreed to reduce the felony conviction for intent to distribute to a conspiracy charge, and reduce the sentence to six months. Since Boyd had already served over four months, he would be out in less than two.

Cyndee was elated, but when expressing her gratitude in hugs and kisses, the pungent echo of lingering alcohol bloomed from her lips. Worry had been her salvation, the impetus for reflection, or what passed for reflection. Now the world was rosier again, and so was she.

Seventeen

Bow had known he would be alone Thanksgiving Day and had done his best to prepare himself. Darlene had her mother and son, and the Pope had many invitations. In conversation with himself, he decided the most assuasive way to pass the day was to follow his normal routine, with perhaps minor variations.

He went for his run. Days were still growing shorter and dawn bled into being. The tall pines guarded the outer gates. The ancient oaks defended the path on both sides. Occasionally a muffled sound would float through the canopy from afar. Mostly, it was quiet. Port Royal was still asleep this early on Thanksgiving Day.

The sound of his breath joined that of his footfalls, but these brought an odd intimacy and unique comfort. These times were his and his alone, symbols of strength and stamina, and the fortitude through which he had spared his life.

He hated his separation from his family on such a day, but should every unsentimental fact be told, he had been an outsider even then. His wife and daughter would administer every activity while he would sit and watch football, or anything else that might keep his son-in-law from beginning a conversation. Of course when his granddaughter had come along, she had served as a wonderful embellishment. His granddaughter...

He shaved, showered, and changed into casual clothes. He went into the diner and made a small pot of coffee. He sat in the booth farthest from the windows along a wall. He wanted to make sure anyone who drove up—and invariably some boob would— might see the empty parking lot and the place locked up tighter than a nun's boudoir, then turn around and move the Hell away instead of tapping on the glass and asking him the dumbest of dumb questions.

The Thursday *Observer* weighed over five pounds, most of which were ads for Black Friday, the Bubonic Plague of consumerism. Even so, he took his time, sipping then rewarming his coffee, reading every story, then perusing every ad to see what all the brouhaha was about.

Just before noon he walked south to the cypress marsh park near Battery Creek. He hadn't been in the park proper, and decided to do the mile-and-a-half loop. The boardwalk was sufficiently elevated in places to discourage snakes from sunning and scaring the tourists. Now they hibernated and Bow didn't worry.

He wore his lined jacket and a worn and fading *Gamecock* ball cap. The cap had been left behind and Bow had grabbed it out of lost-and-found, naturally checking for buglets, laundering and fumigating before placing the lid anywhere near his head.

As the aroma of anticipation kept the rest of the town stuck in place within leaping distance of the dinner table, if not there already, the park was completely vacant. At first glance, the park looked like those sterile green spaces at rest stops. As he moved inward, the time before people revealed itself.

Down a shaded corridor to the first expanse stood the cypress marsh. Cypresses are ancient inhabitants of wetlands, unique in that some of their roots extend above the water's surface to breathe the salty air. At one time every gaudy tourist trap in the southeast was filled with cypress clocks, lamps from cypress knees, and cypress souvenir plaques offering rib-ticklers like *I speak Southern, y'all.* The grove also held a few scattered aster and myrtle trees but they looked out of place in standing water.

These watersheds cling to rain, eventually settling. The silt is its own ecosystem. He saw a large egret walking on stilted legs, snapping up bugs with its pointed beak while searching for a juicy fish. The nostrils of an alligator lolling in the weak sun slid across the surface of the water, scanning for a snack. Wading birds were unmoved, knowing a single flap of wings would take them out of danger. Sometimes they were careless, and a gator got a feather sandwich. There was a certain symmetry to the chain of life as bugs dined large on dead alligators.

A large duck pond appeared from the next length of wooden path. There were no ducks. Perhaps Port Royal was not south enough for the winter, though a large snapping turtle watched over the pond from an exposed arm of a felled tree.

A cacophony of unidentified and unmelodic sounds of ticks and scratches filled the swamp. A fish rolled beneath the surface in disapproval. One entire side of the pond was covered with lily pads so thick a weightless creature could move from one side to the other without getting wet. The omnipresent gray moss hung uninvited from large and small limbs, inhaling nourishment from the air.

Placards were posted every so often illustrating local flora. Besides the pervasive cordgrass, goldenrod and firewheel grew there, both looking otherworldly. A flat bridge crossed the next section only a few feet above a stagnant sliver of water. The wetlands functioned as a filter, trapping much of the muck and scree so clearer water seeped into the river.

In some places the machinations of human hands were obvious, with pipes and hoses and well-crafted ingresses with picnic tables and trash bins. Bow didn't care. Never one to fully appreciate nature, and with too short an attention span to absorb scenery for its own sake, he felt the docile presence of wonder warmly spread from belly-to-chest. Even when the park encountered city streets within eyeshot, they slipped unnoticed into the background.

This was primordial Earth, the land unshaken by all things unnatural. A rowdy fight between two gators did not trouble it as much as human chatter. This land was not meant for apperceptive life. Our most noble deeds did not move it. Our deceits did not reach it. Our strife went unrecognized.

Yet somehow, reassurance rose invisibly like timeworn air. She was the mother from whom all life emerged, in its earliest, sludgy form. She knew us. She knew from whence we appeared, knew our potential, and was saddened by what we became. Her benevolence was inherent in her form, shallow waters and soggy land, and beds of tall grasses beneath the arms of wise old trees providing sufficient shelter from the storms of human minds—human hands.

His comfort rose not from the marsh's call but from its impassivity. Courage grew not from largesse but endurance. He derived a poor and pathetic *joie de vivre*, not from history, but from its timeless serenity.

He made a double ham and cheese sandwich for dinner. He buttered the bread and baked the sandwich open-faced. He added lettuce, tomato, and light mustard, and closed it. He found potato salad in the big refrigerator. In honor of Thanksgiving, he drank cranberry juice mixed with lemon-lime soda. He sneaked a piece of blueberry pie, nuked it, and piled high vanilla ice cream. He cleaned up after himself and made sure everything was exactly as it had been before.

This was the best Thanksgiving he'd had in memory.

He spent much of the afternoon snoozing. He could sleep for a week straight and still not catch up. Darlene had come earlier in the evening and now lay comatose, whistling softly through her nose. Her leg twitched slightly as if dreaming of chasing rabbits.

Later that night, approaching midnight, he could not sleep. He rose and pulled on pants, shirt, jacket, and slipped into his warm moccasins.

He found a half-pack of the Pope's smokes. He took a couple and stuck them in his shirt pocket. He snatched a small handful of kitchen matches. Then he went outside, closing the door slowly to make as little noise as possible.

He stood back behind the trailer and lit up, securely hidden from all view. The trailer was just an outline in the dark and could have been anything from an outbuilding to a mirage.

Suddenly antsy, he tried to harness his disquiet but failed. Where was he again? Of course, the asylum amid the other escapees. Yet here he was among them, caring for them, in debt to them. This was what troubled him. He had crossed the desert feeble and parched and had been given a can of diet root beer to quench his thirst. Nothing was ever enough.

He felt guilty about such comparisons, and shallow, being critical of such plebian care or the simple fact he considered everything so rough-cut, or that their kindest, sincerest efforts were found in any way lacking.

Who else would have tended to him at all? Gratitude is a bloodless companion when more is necessary. In his sanest moments, he knew he was ready for something more compelling, more widely stimulating, more satisfying.

He also knew he was being a dick and he was a wreck about that, too, though did little to unwind the coil.

In thirty minutes he had smoked both cigarettes. Smoking stimulated residual angst even more. He did not lament his state as a shattered man and a dishwasher as much as he did raising a cigarette to his lips and sucking tobacco smoke into his lungs, a habit long despised as a weakness of the *undesirables.*

A newer SUV pulled into the parking lot and stopped short of the end. The Pope exited the vehicle, waved to the driver, and ambled toward the trailer. He had a sweater slung over one arm. As Bow stepped once into the lean shadows, the Pope started, stopped with recognition, then moved into the trailer without a word. In a few moments he returned with a couple of military surplus-type blankets and tossed one to Bow.

"Let's sit out for a bit."

"It's too cold," Bow protested.

"Can't help that."

Bow cocooned himself in the blanket. The air was not bitterly cold, of course, but every time the wind breathed a raw bite followed like pins in the flesh. When the air was calm, the cold felt good upon his face.

The Pope sat as he always did, rustling himself into position. He spoke dryly. "I thought we had an agreement about Darlene."

Bow was in no mood. "We're okay."

"No," the Pope said simply.

Eyebrows creased. "No? What do you mean *no*?"

The big man's voice acquired a sting. "I've known her a lot longer than you have. And I'm telling you no matter what you think or what she thinks, she won't be able to handle it all. She's just a big kid."

"I think you've lost touch. She knows what she's doing."

The Pope lit a smoke, his hands trembling noticeably. He exhaled in exasperation. "I have tried to reason with you about this because I thought you were smart enough to know these things but if you don't stop it, I will."

Bow huffed. "Be my guest. She is the one who came back. She's the one who pushed."

"Dammit, Bow. I'm only telling you what you should already know. She has these romantic thoughts about how life ought to be and she is incapable of creating any part of it."

"I know you're protective of her. But maybe you ought to cut the cord."

"You don't know what you're talking about."

"I know this is between Darlene and me."

The Pope adamantly shook his head. "It isn't."

"Look. I know you are top dog around here and like being the Pope and whatever else goes with it, but this is none of your business!"

"Bastard," he grunted.

"What?"

"You heard me."

The clash began in earnest, like middle-school boys facing off.

"You're a bastard and a prick."

"And you're a self-righteous son-of-a-bitch."

"Ungrateful, self-satisfied asshole."

"Dick."

"I'm warning you. Leave this alone."

"Why the hell does it even matter to you?"

"Because she's my family!"

All fell still. Something bearded and unworldly was involved here. Worst of all, and frightfully so, Bow looked deep. The Pope appeared stricken.

"She's the only family I've got," he whispered.

Bow paused, unsure, but compelled by a nascent sense of conviction.

"We're all family here."

The voice remained subdued, though his body remained bound and rigid. "No. Not the same." He took a couple of smoke-free breaths. "Look. I was completely shut down when I came here. I wasn't capable of much of anything. We took to each other right away. Goofy kid cared about me. Gave me a cause. Accepted my advice even when she was far healthier upstairs than I was."

"I know the feeling."

"I can never forget that. It is something sacred to me."

"I understand."

"Yes. The despair, the feeling of being completely alone, of course. But you had love. Not perfect, maybe, but you had love up until the very end. You probably still do. I didn't. I'm not sure I ever really did."

"You've been loved, I'm sure."

"Not in a very, very long time." He stopped again and slowly turned his head a few times to loosen his neck. "I was married and had a seven-year-old daughter. At times I think my daughter was the only person who'd ever really loved me. My wife and I had an intellectual connection. A love of science fiction and a healthy agnosticism. But never a real passion for each other."

The wind died and the sounds ceased as if what were to follow would illuminate everything within sight and magnify everything within reach.

"When my business failed, I realized something. Horribly savage, but weighty. My wife had grown up. I hadn't. I enjoyed running my little shop, telling stories about writers, sharing trivia about certain books, playing with tobacco. Being a professor of useless trivia. Now all that was gone and I didn't have a clue about the rest of my life."

In the parking lot, a dead leaf skipped over the asphalt from lume to gloom, as if watching for evil spirits before dancing to safety.

"What happened?"

"She met someone *responsible*, ambitious in his own way, without dreams or pretensions. A CPA. She got a divorce. They married and moved to Colorado, taking my daughter with them. I know, I could've made more effort, been more assertive, but I didn't do any of that. I was hurting so much I figured we would all be better off if I went ahead and let go. Instead of fighting. Maybe my daughter would remember me but someone else would raise her. And whatever reasons she believed for me not being around would be okay. Because the reasons wouldn't have anything to do with me, and because I wouldn't be around to tell her otherwise. That was over fifteen years ago."

He stopped, unmoving, seeming uninvolved, lifeless.

"I've had no contact with her since. I was too fucking damaged to do anything. And by the time I could have or *should* have done something, years had passed. And I still did nothing. Maybe you're right. Maybe I am too involved around here. It isn't anything I wanted. I tried to help one person down on his luck and two more appeared. The same as I tried to help you. I know what it is to lose. I know what it is to want. I know what it is to find life as a…casualty."

He cleared his throat so the ragged congestion cast by sorrow would not reveal itself. He spat into the grass.

"As smart as I am and as level-headed as I can be, I was consumed by a single thought. My little girl was stolen from me."

"But Darlene loved you."

"Yes, she did."

Bow consumed this, and as he did, admittedly stumbling along, the strand that possessed the most clarity separated from the rest just enough for affinity to scale the steps of his awareness, sluggish and ungainly as it was.

He had been rescued when it most made a difference and when no one else made any effort to simply recognize his personhood. He would not be so dismissive again, even if unspoken and rattling like loose pebbles inside his own head.

He listened to the air for affirmation but heard nothing, and was still satisfied. The truth burned as an ember not so easily doused.

"Yeah, she's got me good, too. I'm not sure I could let her go."

This is the hour, and you've got the power, Lord

"Jesus Christ, Abe!"

Just before opening one morning, Mickey made another mad dash for the bathroom. The hormones—or shortage thereof—had erupted again. Ruby watched after him, her mouth open in misingestion. When Mickey exited, tucking his shirttail into his pants, Ruby toddled toward him a few steps.

"Are you a boy or a girl?" she asked.

"Ruby!" Darlene leapt in. "That's not polite."

Mickey waved her off and spoke calmly. "Well, Ruby, I'm a boy. But I don't have all my boy parts yet so I guess you could say I'm still in between."

"You mean you ain't got no doolie?"

"No."

"How come?"

"I wasn't born with one. Hopefully soon I'll go to the doctor and take care of that."

"What? They gonna glue it on?"

"Not exactly, but I think you get the idea."

Ruby's top lip shot up to just beneath her nostrils. "Fuck that, Bud."

They were spared nothing the day after the holiday. People pushed through the door in quick rotation the minute the diner opened, as if White Rabbit-late. Some had already raided the stores, as puffy-eyed and droopy as basset hounds. Some of these were satisfied to have risen early enough (or not gone to bed at all) to claim that *while supplies last* special item, ignoring that they would never use it, or use it sparingly, or use it stubbornly to justify the expense. One doesn't tamper with bargains, or the esoterica of its Zen.

Some looked as defeated as the Chicago Cubs, not finding exactly what they were seeking, or not seeing anything that provided the tingle they desired. These would plunder for the next three weeks before settling on gift cards.

Some had the *I-ate-the-last-brownie* dispositions, knowing they had purchased, or would soon purchase, everything they wanted off the Internet, most of which could be wrapped as well.

The entire weekend was insane. They ran out of ribs. The truck had delivered the day before Thanksgiving but the Pope had under-purchased. They offered barbecued chicken at half price instead. Anyone who had dined there before knew the meat was just the platform for the sauce anyway.

Dollars flowed like...dollars. Better than Labor Day. Mickey was nearly finished with his hormone treatments and paid for the remainder in advance. He soon sported a goatee.

Ruby was able to buy a small TV for her room, even though she was reported three times for referring to her customers as peckerheads loud enough to be overheard.

Darlene made almost eight hundred dollars in tips over the weekend, and gave Bow fifty dollars to save. Bow, Debbie, and Bob got fifty-dollar kickbacks.

Bow bought an entire carton of cigarettes for him and the Pope to share, with only about a pack-and-a-half destined for his own brachia. He would be way ahead in the bummage department. No one knew if the Pope earned anything extra or not. In fact, no one knew if he even got paid.

There was a satisfied collapse after Sunday closing. In a few days everything December represented—the holidays, the crummier bowl games like Paducah U vs. Watercress College, and the last autumn month in Port Royal—though winter for everyone northward—would be carried in on the wings of fallen angels.

For now, everyone in the Jimmy's sphere was appeased. Shit may run downhill but who really knows from whence fortune cometh, good or ill. There could be a natural disaster or a fire or an outbreak of food poisoning that would force the diner to close, leaving them all unemployed, no matter how far-fetched.

Maybe they could each throw in a few bucks, buy lottery tickets like those office pools who seem to win with some regularity, and make their fortunes.

Wouldn't Mickey be a wooly booger then?

Again, Bow accompanied Darlene on faith. They pulled into a triple storefront and parked. The middle shop was *Hair Today Gone Tomorrow.*

"No, Darlene. I don't want to cut my hair just yet."

Darlene made a noise low in her throat like an attack dog. "You ain't. This is just a styling."

Bow cautiously followed her in. There were nearly a dozen stations, all abristle with activity. The salon smelled of ammonia and burning hair—and the formaldehyde odor of hairspray. He shuffled his way to the third station like a chastised child. There, a middle-aged woman no more than four-feet-ten, her hair short and gray with pink streaks, and so thin she could hide behind a telephone pole, reached and hugged Darlene.

"This is Patti," she said. "Patti, Bow Carter."

Patti smiled with painfully white teeth, and moved in to hug him too. Her head rested on his sternum. She stepped back and surveyed the terrain, cupping her chin with the fingers of her right hand.

"What are we doing?" she mused.

"He likes the length. Just make it...neater."

Patti ushered Bow into the chair and draped a barber cloth around him, clasping it at the neck to prevent hair from slipping in, though some always found a way.

He took a good long look at himself in the mirror. His face had always been too round, and chin-to-throat too shallow. Now his cheeks were taut with no loose flaps, and the space beneath his chin looked deeper.

"Color?" Patti pondered aloud.

"No," he said quickly.

"Well, it's not thick enough in the back to cut it straight across. I'll have to layer it to give it body."

"What's that mean?" he said anxiously.

Darlene patted his shoulder.

"It means I have to feather the hair at different lengths or it will stay shitty like it is now."

"So you'll cut it."

"A little of it. Don't worry, hon. I can fix anything."

He watched in the mirror as she snipped. Comb and scissors flashed. Fingers moved too quickly to follow, working as if by their own will. The entire time Darlene and Patti talked and laughed and complained, and made odd noises without drawing breath. In six or seven minutes, it was over.

Patti squirted a glob of foam into her palm and reached for Bow's head.

"No!" he said sharply. Everyone not under a dryer looked at him.

"It's just a little styling mousse," Patti explained.

"No," he said more calmly. "Leave it dry."

Darlene and Patti frowned at each other as if he were a toddler who just soiled his pants.

"Okay," Patti added, "but you need a decent shampoo and some light conditioner or it'll frizz and you'll look like Shakira."

"Who?"

Darlene interjected. "Fix us up on the shampoo."

She paid and they left.

She spoke as if to a baby. "Now was that so bad?"

He patted every inch of his hair as if looking for lost keys. Actually, everything felt pretty good. The ends were even and the loss of length was unnoticeable. He ignored her even after they got into the car. He continued to look himself over in the mirror.

"Oh, you're Be-you-ti-ful," she said.

Then he smiled and flipped up the visor.

Eighteen

Cold weather tiptoed in— highs in the fifties with lows dipping into the thirties. What's tepid to a bobcat will freeze the nads off a tomcat.

Life modulated as the season altered everything in its path. Everyone switched to warmer clothing full-time, except the Pope, who wore short-sleeved shirts except when he was outside for any length of time.

The gatherings were often cancelled. Bow asked the Pope how everyone knew when the gathering had been cancelled, and he mystically replied , "People aren't so stupid as to stand around in the cold, ribs or not."

He was still able to run most mornings, but was finished before he completely warmed up. The closer he and Darlene became, physically and emotionally, the more he obsessed about his future. He did not have a map nor a step-by-step plan to whatever he would become, but he could not shed the thought.

Perhaps now that his mind was no longer as cluttered, this empty space longed to be occupied so the *unclean* would not return. He had befriended fear and worried that fear had become docile, yet lurking, latent, poised. The urge toward progress was doubtlessly nudging him along, even when he was unaware. No matter the temperature or the mood of the day, he accepted as necessity what he could not ignore. He would have to make some decisions soon.

He still proceeded with caution. Naturally, he realized he would not foolishly forfeit his education and experience. He simply did not know where to begin.

He had not investigated opportunities nearby. He enjoyed these small spaces and living near the water. Maybe Charleston, with its ancient streets and arcane history. In a town that size he could prosper and still remain anonymous.

He could never be in the public eye again. Recognition would be a distraction in any venue. Maybe he could do research for a large firm, or practice corporate law, or be an institutional attorney who sat in an office all day and never saw daylight firsthand.

Perhaps he could be the head dishwasher at some *café haute de gamme.*

Bow was working at the sink with steam rising from dangerously hot water and lost in *Silver Dollar Forger* by Nazareth, when Darlene tapped him on the shoulder. He flinched. He couldn't help it.

"Kid out there wants to see you."

The lines between his eyes creased deep. "Who?"

Darlene was in a hurry. "I don't know. Some young guy."

He dried his hands. "Okay. Send him around back."

The young man was in his early twenties, a Kid Rock redneck with long, greasy hair, a thin scraggly mustache and chin music. Bow had not seen him at the gatherings and was suspicious.

He hated being out in the cold.. His only other option was the trailer, which he would not do, or a car, which he did not have. He already had his arms crossed and his hands clutching his biceps. This was a bit of chutzpah but the point was made.

"I'm Billy Bangs," the kid said. "I won't bother you but a minute."

Bow immediately catalogued his name for Darlene. "What can I do for you?"

"You helped Boyd. He's a friend of mine. I'm in a jam and have to go to traffic court Thursday."

Bow repeated his litany. "I'm not a practicing attorney."

"I know. Boyd's mama told me you weren't in the business no more." He kicked at a rock and missed. "Here's the deal. I've had two DUIs but nothing in over three years. I've pulled my shit together. I finally got a decent job. I haul logs from the woods to the mill. They know all about my past, but give me a chance anyway. So I started even."

Despite himself, Bow was curious. "What happened?"

"I swerved to miss a deer and hit a tree. In my own car, not the company truck. But the cop still gave me a reckless driving citation. Maybe 'cause he saw my record. Maybe he thinks I'm Dale, Jr. Anyway, he don't believe me about the deer. If I get hit with reckless driving, I'll lose my insurance. Even if I don't, my job's on the line."

"Any witnesses?"

"Just the doe. They're as thick as squirrels around here. Everybody knows that."

He really wanted no part of this. His adrenalin elevated as it had before, as did his pulse. "Tell you what. I'll write a statement for you. You can give it to the judge and read it into the record. Maybe it'll help. It's all I can do."

Billy grabbed a frozen hand with both of his and shook. "Thanks. I really 'preciate it."

Bow called to him from the door. "Come by tomorrow. I'll have it ready."

Billy struggled with the reading but not nearly as much as he would have had he not rehearsed at least a dozen times, or if Bow hadn't simplified the legalese.

"If it please your honor. I realize my previous convictions may create doubt as to the va-lid-i-ty of my story. But what I told the officer is the whole truth. The record already shows that I hadn't been drinking. And I would like to state for the record that I have been gainfully employed as a driver this past year without incident. I cannot prove I was trying to avoid a deer, though I feel this should be reasonable to everyone. Nor do I deny the facts of the accident. But as a professional driver, I don't see how I could be expected to maintain complete control of my vehicle under such circumstances.

Had I been headed north, I would have been able to avoid hitting a tree because the woods on that side are set back from the road. Maybe I would've gotten my car stuck, but no one would have gotten involved in any legal capacity. But since I was going south, and the tree line only fifty feet from the edge of the road, I would not have been able to avoid hitting a tree under any circumstances at legal speed. I respectfully ask the court to dismiss the reckless driving portion of the citation in the interest of fairness, and so this incident will not be on my record, published, or reported to my employer."

The next day Billy stopped by with a bottle of Crown Royal and thanked Bow with childlike zeal. Bow was gratified, if not more than a little pleased with himself. Later, Abe spotted the bottle on the counter and eyed it the way a shark eyes a mullet, salivating all over his cigar stub. Bow gave it to him, a grand gesture, even if Abe did not seem grateful, though he did seem a little more spry after that.

Ruby dashed in like a Ritalin junkie, her eyes agleam, and her coiffure sashaying against her head. No one knew what was going on—if she was on a new medication, or thought she was late, or had a pickle in her panties, and no one wanted to know. Darlene and Mickey were content to ride out the storm, deaf, dumb, and blind, until Ruby aimed point-blank at Bob. Bob did what he always did, continued his work without attention or comment.

"Bob. Bob. I'll bet you don't think I've ever had sex, do you? Most people don't. But I have. Me and this guy who used to put labels on these coupon things to send to people to save money, even though it was a waste of time 'cause most people just throw them in the trash without looking at them, used to hide in the closet where they kept paper towels and toilet paper, and oh I forgot, a stinky old mop, and do it. We had to do it standing up 'cause the floor was nasty, so maybe that don't count as much as laying down, but we did. Every week or so. It would've been more except he was kinda—you know—touched. So I had to get him going or else he'd just stop, and that made me mad. But I've done it. Believe me?"

Bob flicked his eyes to her and back, the look in them like a cornered mouse.

"Ruby!" Darlene called. Ruby didn't respond at first. "Ru—by!" Ruby finally turned. "Come on. It's time to open."

Ruby reluctantly shuffled over, her face downcast. As Darlene moved away Ruby's head snapped up as if on a spring. "I know you've done it standing up," she said to Darlene.

Darlene shot eye-darts in her direction. "Mind your manners."

"Okie-fenokie. Yep," Ruby said as she ambled off. "You long-leggy ones like to do it standing up."

As Christmas drew nearer, Bow became sulkier. This was in small increments, not noticeable from day-to-day, but as the decorations went up, and reminders of the season were blasted from all quarters at all hours and in every direction, the accumulation took its toll, and was apparent from one week to the next. He became morosely quiet and avoided conversation with everyone. The Pope was still gone most of the time—this was his busy season, too—allowing Bow his disconnection.

Even Darlene gave him space. She worried, naturally, but he revealed nothing of substance. Also, she loved Christmas. She was a Christmas Eve kid, waiting in unfeigned anticipation for the bewitchment to follow. She was also a relatively new Santa, and even her mother, in caustic predictability, could not spoil the season for her.

She stayed with Bow that Sunday night. These nights were wonderful, sleep-late-the-next-morning nights, though sleeping in for him was seven fifteen. Whatever else harassed him, neither his desire nor his performance suffered.

They took a day trip to Savannah on a bright, crisp morning. The day was unusually balmy, sweater weather. Savannah is the oldest city in Georgia and also a port. As people become increasingly removed from junior high history, many forget Georgia was one of the original thirteen colonies.

This was long before the advent of mullets and moon pies, though there was a precedent for marriage to first cousins, and that had come from royalty.

Like Charleston, Old Savannah has two hundred year-old buildings with wrought iron balustrades and fenced-in gardens. Savannah was a planned city, and over twenty squares remain, nearly all with a statue of some luminary in stolid pose. Trolleys shuttle tourists every twenty minutes on cobblestone streets. Homes narrow and tall sit on plots of land no wider than a driveway. Tales of pirates and privateers abound.

Savannah rests beneath a canopy of emerald trees, and newer hotels are designed to blend in with the ancient architecture, though automatic doors and plaster cornices are a dead giveaway. River Street follows the broad Savannah River the length of the town. Old cotton warehouses have been converted into shops and boutiques, and unintentional kitsch. Massive ships and tankers are idle at port. A thousand places can be found to eat—from bare bulb dining to crystal chandeliers—and none of them are bad.

Some parts of Savannah resemble New Orleans without the bebop.

They strolled through a square decorated for Christmas, walking from sun to shade, limb-to-limb. Bow had barely said a word, though he was not dour or pouty.

"Don't be bummed," she said softly.

"Not bummed. Thinking, mostly."

"Another holiday among strangers."

He patted the small of her back. "Not strangers anymore."

"You know I'm here."

"I know. It's comforting. Besides, I can see you."

"Just because you're all grown up don't mean I can't smack you if you need it."

"I'll try to be a good boy."

"It's going to be okay. I know it."

"You're always good company."

"Am I?"

"I never want you to be down on my account."

"Who gives a Vicky Dickdodger about that?"

"Well, I don't want you to feel diminished by transient, yet intransigent, circumstance, or by dint of specific aeromnous-nous," he said wryly.

"Yeah," she said seriously, "me neither."

A week later the Pope shook Bow's shoulder, and not at all gently. Bow turned over reluctantly.

"What's wrong?" he asked.

The Pope looked agitated, but his voice was gentle. "Let's talk a little."

This was outré bizarre. The Pope had never done this. He was the bollard to which everyone else was attached. He needed nothing—left nothing unsolved or unreconciled. Now it was after three a.m. and something was akilter. Bow sat up and pushed back his hair.

"Shoot," he said, stifling a yawn.

"Outside," the Pope said.

"Now? It's so cold."

"In the diner then."

"We'll have to leave the lights off."

"What, you want us to play hide-and-seek?"

"No. Keep people from banging on the window to see if we're open."

The Pope chuckled. It sounded like the bawl of a buffalo calf.

They stayed in the kitchen, the warmest spot in the building, anyway. The Pope put on a pot to make tea. Bow had never heard the kitchen so quiet. The overhead lights were harsh and unyielding but there were no others to use. The fluorescent bulbs hummed as the lights popped on. Bow glanced over at his station. It seemed unfamiliar to him for some reason, though he made a mental note to scrub the drying rack before using it again.

The Pope brought two steaming mugs and they sat at one of the work tables. Bow cupped his hands around his drink. The porcelain was warm but not boiling hot. Enough for heat to spread from his fingers and get the blood moving quicker.

"What is this?"

"Try a sip."

Suspicious, he collected a few droplets on his tongue. It was sweet and flavorful. "Good."

"It's the same recipe as my sweet tea. Extra honey and a pinch of cocoa."

He took a healthy drink. Then he stopped. "Crap. It's got caffeine in it, doesn't it?"

"Decaf," the Pope said.

He kept drinking, warming his insides. He killed the rest and rose to get a refill. "Really?"

"Of course not," the Pope said. "You ever tasted decaf tea?"

Bow set the pot down with a thud as if it had grown thorns. "Why didn't you tell me?"

"You wouldn't have tried it otherwise. Tell me the truth. Don't you feel all warm and tingly now?"

"God," he groaned. "You are so full of crap."

"Ain't I though?"

"Well, you don't seem depressed."

"Getting a rise out of you makes my heart sing."

"Yeah, yeah."

The Pope reached and clinked his mug against Bow's empty cup, while Bow sulked, or made a show of sulking.

"To Bow. The guy who gets up in the middle of the night to sit with a friend."

"Don't have a choice. Got nowhere else to sleep."

"There's that."

Bow got a glass of water. "What's got you down?"

"What makes you think I'm down?"

"You wouldn't wake me up for small talk."

"How do you know I didn't need your help to find a left-handed spatula?"

"We already have one." He sipped his water. "You wouldn't turn to me unless you didn't have a choice."

The Pope looked at him. In the light, neither of them had an advantage. "Why do you say that?"

"Because I'm the screwed up one."

"Not so much now, I think."

The words provided a swell of wherewithal, no longer so obsolete, his sanity unquestioned. "So tell me. Quick before I have to pee."

"Okay. I'm just feeling... restless."

"Why is that?"

"Don't know. Exactly."

"You do know. More than I do anyway."

The Pope got a refill. Now they stood facing each other. Bow leaned against the table and the Pope leaned against the counter. The Pope was himself again, showing nothing. His face was expressionless, his true substance hidden somewhere inaccessible. Perhaps he was assembling the perfect, noncommittal words. Maybe he was rethinking his decision to confide. Confession was as foreign to him as the samba, yoga, or the World Cup..

"It's Christmas," he said finally.

"What about it?"

"I hate it."

"That's it?" Bow thought he was joking.

The Pope folded his arms across his chest. "I'm serious. I know it sounds bizarre. How can anyone hate Christmas? I *really* hate it. It's torture for me to get through it."

"The holidays make a lot of people feel lonely and isolated."

"It makes me want to shoot everybody."

"You're kidding, of course."

"Not by much."

"Why? Nobody really *hates* Christmas."

"There it is."

"What is it? The commercialization and all that?"

"It's not a real thing, for one. Christmas was already phony before it became so commercial. That's just the corporate monolith exploiting the phoniness."

"Why do you say it's not real?"

"Its sole purpose is to engender feelings that don't really exist past the age of six."

"That's what it's for. It's the sentiment more than anything else. Except for the Jesus part. Is that why you think it's phony?"

"Couldn't care less. It's artificial."

"So what if it is?"

The Pope's voice lost its sting. "Darlene says Christmas spirit is people's way of forgetting what assholes they really are."

"Sounds like her. Except for the 'who gives a hicky dicky' or whatever."

The smile in the Pope's voice rang true. "The bard of Beaufort."

Bow sat again. The night was empty and the emptiness could be felt through the walls. He had come to better understand the night. He did not embrace it but had made peace with it on its own terms.

"Why can't you just ignore it then?"

The Pope sighed and shook his head. "I can't."

"Why not?"

"Because that's when so many people seem to need me. They want to be whole for just one day and they believe I can help them do it."

"And you can't do it and that makes things worse?"

"No. Because I *can* do it and it makes *me* feel worse. I feel like a hypocrite. I feel like I'm part of the con."

"If it really bothers you that much, why put yourself through it?"

"I still want to do what I do. Without Christmas. I wish I could feel differently. I don't want to be the guy who slips and tells the kiddies there's no Santa Claus."

"Have you ever thought of going to church or something? Try to get into it more?"

The Pope's eyes widened. "Good God! That really would do me in. Everyone mooning over a baby Jesus like he's a puppy got caught in the rain. I'd set the manger on fire and end up in jail."

"The music can be very inspiring and uplifting."

The Pope ignored him, and shifted into another gear.

"People don't know what the fuck they're singing about. They might as well sing about Baby Batman. It's a ridiculous use of music."

"Well, it's real to a lot of people. Me, for one."

"It's horseshit. First of all, if it were really about Jesus then not an extra dollar would be spent until all the needy were provided for. Secondly, it's not his birthday. Nothing described in any of the events would have happened in December. Early Christians glommed onto the pagan solstice festivals. Thirdly, people don't really change because of it. They pretend for a little while, then stop pretending. It's like having your bowels clogged up. Just because you have a good dump doesn't mean it'll never happen again."

"Graphic."

"And another thing. I can't stand the people who aren't a part of it but cash in because so many other people are saps."

"Like who?"

"Jews for one. Hindus, Muslims, Buddhists. Milking the market."

Bow looked at him skeptically. "How—by doing their jobs?"

"Forget that. Forget about the card companies, the toy makers, the hokey commercials. Forget about the maudlin TV shows. Did you know a Jew wrote *White Christmas?* Irving Berlin. And what could be phonier than Barbra Streisand singing *O Little Town of Bethlehem*. Good God! It would be like us singing Hanukkah songs."

"I've never heard one."

"That's not the point."

"Abe's Jewish. Listens to Christian music all day long."

The Pope continued, his words punctuated by jabs of giggles. "You know why he plays that station?"

"Why?"

"He thinks everyone who lives here is a Christian and listens to that kind of music. He doesn't know Jesus from Whoopi Goldberg."

The tension snapped like a Jenny Craiger in an Oreo truck. They hee-hawed like a pair of teenage boys having a farting contest. One would subside, and by the time he ebbed, the other would start up again .

The Pope had moved past his discontent. All he had needed was freeform malice.

"I can just see Abe singing along to *We Wish You a Merry Christmas*," Bow said.

"Beats trying to come up with a Hanukkah song," the Pope retorted.

No one expected snow and they were not disappointed. The coast of South Carolina saw snow about as often as it saw a Democrat win an election. The jet stream twitched, however, and an icy, forty-five-degree drizzle fell in a thin veil. Steady, but sparse. The only way to get drenched was to stand still for a minute. People moved in awkward scurries as if to dodge alternating drops.

A couple of days were scant and silent. The weather subdued everyone. Only the irritating clink of china and silverware, the low murmur of patrons' voices, and the radio—the station had switched to all Christmas tunes for the duration—were consistent, and consistently cheerless.

The whole staff bumbled around like novices in a monastery. Bow, alone, with earplugs shoved deep, noticed no difference. Music made the gray tolerable. The sun would come again in due course.

Darlene groused under her breath.

"This ain't Christmas. This is Old Testament crap."

A rare sunny day brought highs in the sixties and the gathering was open for business. Christmas had come early for the Pope. He was again able to pontificate, releasing disquiet in his own peculiar way, while others relied upon sex, booze, reefer, or barbecue—sometimes in combination.

"Many of the world's ills, or the vast majority of them, exist and fester for one simple reason: Lies. Think about it. What cannot be restored or enhanced by honesty if done with a caring or penitent heart.

"Now I know sometimes we hedge to spare someone's feelings. I know small lies do a small amount of damage. But mostly, lies are told for the sake of the liar. We all lie. We can't seem to help ourselves.

"Politicians and writers do it for a living."

Everyone laughed. The mood was ripe for festivity.

"Myths are lies, but mostly, they're little white lies because we know they're just stories written to entertain us, maybe with a lesson attached. Not only that, we need them. They are part of a cultural heritage we pass along to the next generation.

"I'm not going to spoil things by saying Christmas is a myth. But you have to admit we haven't got a handle of who's really the boss, Jesus or Santa Claus."

Once again, Darlene set the tone, snorting as if choking on a bone.

“In Iceland—yeah, I know, anything about Iceland is bound to be weird. In Iceland, they have the Yule Cat. The Yule Cat is a very large beast that prowls the land at Christmas eating people who don’t have new Christmas duds. Sheep ranchers used the story as an incentive for their workers to finish processing the autumn wool in time for the holiday. The ones who took part in the work would be rewarded with new clothes, but those who did not would get nothing and become Christmas dinner for this ginormous cat.

“Funny they haven’t made one of those cartoons about it to show every year.

Cheer rolled through the parking lot into the street.

“The first recorded Christmas wasn’t celebrated until three hundred years after the fact. The earliest story about Jesus in the Bible is in the book of Mark, and even that was written several decades afterward. Mark doesn’t cover the birth of Jesus. He starts with the Baptism when Jesus was about thirty years old. Another guy named Luke comes along and reads Mark and says, ‘well, the son of God needs a bit more pizzazz, don’t you think?’ Enter the Immaculate Conception, the angels in the manger, and three wise guys from somewhere else following a star to where this kid is’. Probably singing carols as they rode merrily along.”

He stopped to draw breath. Everyone was smiling as if bewitched but few knew what the Hell he was talking about. No matter, he was on a roll.

“By the way, *Jingle Bells* is not really a Christmas song. It was written about Thanksgiving. My guess is a song about the wholesale spread of disease to the native tribes and usurping an entire population wouldn’t be catchy enough. Besides, we don’t sing Thanksgiving carols, anyway.

"Like I said. I'm not trying to spoil anything for you. Everybody has a right to feel good at least once a year and December 25th is as good a time as any.

"I hope you find some shiny new clothes under the tree. At least you won't get eaten.

"Merry Christmas."

Nineteen

Jimmy's normally closed at six on Christmas Eve, but this year Christmas was on Monday, so they closed for Christmas Eve and Christmas. They closed at six on Saturday, the 23rd, creating a nice holiday weekend.

As in years past, Jimmy's opted for a secret Santa so people wouldn't feel obligated to buy for everyone. Frankly, no one wanted to buy for everyone. No one wanted to buy for anyone.

Even the party was lackluster, since Abe insisted on having the soiree in the diner after Saturday close, more like detention than a celebration. There were only seven of them and they spent ten hours a day together as it was. No spouses or significant others were present. No one was sure anyone had a significant other except maybe Bob, and Bob wasn't talking.

Still, everyone put forth the effort to make things festive. The Pope broke the rules by giving everyone a five-dollar gift card, except Abe, who was favored with a pair of expensive cigars. He almost smiled.

Darlene wore a Santa cap and distributed the gifts with a flourish as each name was called. Bob trailed each gift to its recipient with a large trash bag. Bow made a cider punch with apple juice and cinnamon. He told everyone it was spiked to loosen reality's grip, though it wasn't. Ruby seemed bewildered. This was so much like her everyday demeanor no one noticed. Debbie was quiet, disinclined to insert her teeth, and Mickey was so placid Darlene wondered if he hadn't taken an early dose of Nyquil and mistimed the kick-in.

Abe had moved away from the counter for the party but only to give everyone an envelope before he vanished. Bow's held two hundred dollars in cash. He had saved nearly three thousand dollars, more than he had saved when he earned ten times as much. He had moved his stash to a baggie in the freezer. He wasn't worried about theft. He kept a written clue in his wallet should he forget where he put it that read *cold hard cash.*

Bob got Ruby a battery-operated toy red truck. She was as excited as a kid, though her approach was a bit scary. She put the car on the floor and chased after it like a four-year-old, until it hit something solid and flipped over, its wheels spinning in its death throes like an unlucky turtle. With a weird eye and dark face, she kept running it into the wall at full speed, before picking it up and doing it again. Everyone hoped she never got her license.

Darlene got Bob a Spanish-English dictionary. She explained it to him, speaking as if to a half-deaf ninny. "This is Spanish," she said, pointing, "and across is what it means in English. See? *maldicion* means *dammit* in English. That's a good one to know." Bob nodded his thank you, then resumed cleaning up.

Bow found a used book store and bought the Pope a dozen sci-fi paperbacks. The Pope was gracious, stating he only had five of them already.

Ruby got Bow a bright yellow T-shirt with a map of Thailand embossed on the front and the caption *Come to Thailand and Phuket.*

Debbie got Mickey a new multi-bladed razor with a battery in the handle, enabling the whole thing to vibrate. Optional usages were implied should the transition to manhood fall through.

Mickey got Darlene some pale green nail polish. Her feet would look like she'd been stomping toads.

The Pope got Debbie an extra-extra-extra-large tube of Orajel.

By seven-thirty the goodwill had run its course. They would see each other Tuesday and resume the relative complacency that had served them so well.

Darlene was going to spend Christmas with her mother and boy, but spent Saturday night and Christmas Eve Day with Bow. She packed an overnight bag and moved into the trailer after the party.

Christmas Eve was another sunny, windless day, and good to be outside.

"Let's drive over to Hilton Head and walk along the beach," she said.

The causeway traveled over cord grass and salt marshes onto the Island. Hilton Head was a different animal from the rest of coastal Carolina. More an adult-oriented enclave—no rides, no games, no henna tattoos, no convex-bellied couples from West Virginia.

As a barrier island, Hilton Head had once been home to the Geechi Gullahs, the blue-gummed blacks who had maintained their African culture for four hundred years. Now Hilton Head was a hideout for people of means, primarily non-Africans, to escape those without means, including Africans.

Still, the incurious sea was there, irrespective of everyone. The sun clothed and the sand parted with every step along the shore, though it may have suffered mightily beneath Darlene's barkers. Her footsteps looked like the Manhattan skyline after the apocalypse.

It was mid-tide, the sand more expansive and steeper into the surf. The wet thunder rolled relentless in its inimitable sojourn in and back. A surprising number of people were out and about, though a path near the top of the sand was clear of traffic.

They had not walked far when Bow stopped, turned, and kissed her without hunger, long, deep, and lingering.

Darlene held his elbows when they broke. “What was that for?”

“I feel good.”

“Yeah?

“Yeah. I really do.”

“I’ll be damned.”

He smiled and kissed her again.

They continued to stroll, the vast Atlantic to the east. The sun hung winter-low, as if it would move horizontally across the sky. Darlene clasped his hand. He stroked the back of her hand with his thumb. Emptiness was a misnamed concept anyway. Something always remained within, if only haze. They walked shoulder-to-shoulder, accepting the gift of tranquility.

Later, at the trailer, they sat beside the tiny ceramic tree on the counter and exchanged presents. He lit a stubby holiday candle. She gushed over the necklace and earrings. She put them on immediately and looked in the mirror.

“They’re beautiful, Bow.”

“Don’t get too carried away. The stones aren’t real.”

“Who gives a Penny Poonpacker about that?” She handed him her gift.

He opened it slowly. It was a small computer tablet. “Wow.”

“You’ll have internet access now. If you tilt it just right you can pick up the Wi-Fi from the Hampton Inn down the block. The password is prhotel.” She took a breath and looked at him guiltily. “Used to date one of the guys in maintenance down there.”

"It's wonderful. Now I can keep up with the real world. Thank you."

"Well, I know this Christmas can't be easy for you."

He shook his head. "Not going there. This is the only Christmas I have. No sad talk."

Silence engulfed the trailer for several moments until the candle crackled. They looked at each other, realizing neither had much else to say. The moment was neither awkward nor revelatory, except for the simple fact they were comfortable together in the quiet.

She lay back and put a canoe on his thigh. He massaged her foot, mindful of her second toe, which stood at attention like an ICBM.

She closed her eyes and nestled her head into a cushion. "That feels good."

He took the practice seriously, kneading the ball of her foot with his thumbs. "You spend too much time on your feet."

"So do you."

"I have padding. You have to run all over the place."

"Knew that when I signed on. Ooh. There. Ooooh, that's it."

He was working where the toes joined the foot. "Any money in foot massaging?"

"Don't know. But you could make a fortune."

Again they became quiet. Again they did so with no static in the air.

"Bow?"

"Yeah."

"You ever have one of those TV kind of Christmases for real?"

He slowed the massage as he thought. "When I was little, we would go to my grandparents' on Christmas Eve. I had a few cousins I grew up with. Aunts and uncles. We would sleep on little pallets made of blankets in the living room by the tree while the grownups talked at the kitchen table. Guess that's as close as I got."

"What about when your girl was little?"

He waited for the twinge, now rising as a pinch, dully, not piercing. He pictured his granddaughter's face for a moment but allowed the vision to cycle through.

"Not really. I mean, it was fun to watch her open her presents but it wasn't what you'd call warm and fuzzy."

"Why do you think that is?"

"I don't know. My wife isn't—wasn't—a warm and fuzzy person. Not sentimental at all. She liked organizing things. We always went to Christmas brunch at a neighbor's and everyone got wasted on Bloody Marys. Maybe it's because we only had the one child. I don't know. You?"

Darlene huffed through her nose. "God, no. Mama had to work half the time. I opened my presents and watched a parade on TV."

"Junior's getting to the age where you could have a special day."

"Yeah, maybe. But not with egg nog and a fireplace."

"He doesn't know that."

"I know. Just getting harder to fake it."

"Why do you have to fake it?"

"Not all of it." She pulled her foot away and propped the other one on his leg. "Too much pressure to make it magic."

He knew this was not about Christmas. Life is a duplicitous bastard, imbibing hope and pissing paradox. Only the guileless ever possess the unshakable faith to embrace a future and not be deadened by consequence.

They made love that night. They stripped off their clothes and drifted into bed. Darlene still wore her necklace and the candle still burned, casting their shadows on the curved walls.

They made love in every sense. They created something that had not existed before. They had bonded as friends and as lovers but now they became some new entity, some—thing. An obscure, near-invisible thing—an earthbound thing apart from all celestial mechanics—a thing unknown to anyone else—a thing that might not long survive, but a thing nonetheless.

No two had manifested love in a sweeter, purer, and truer sense, even if those at hand were oblivious to it.

Darlene showered soon after in preparation to go to her mother's. She had a few things in the bag for her son—an oversized stuffed tiger, a truck that made revving sounds when wheeled along the floor, a talking book about an absent-minded Raccoon named Clark, and some new clothes.

Beside her car, they parted with a hug. Darlene seemed adrift with apprehension.

"You going to be okay tomorrow?"

"I'll probably go into the diner and see if I can't find a ball game on my new tablet."

"You could still come with me."

"Family. You should be with family, mom and all."

Darlene nodded and positioned herself in the car. She smiled bravely and waved as she drove off.

Bow expected the gouge, the despair, easily scaling the weaker portions of unseasoned *noblesse*, seeping from the lower bowel, slithering unnoticed until too big to defy. This didn't come. He made some cocoa and put on some Christmas music. He swore to himself that he would not think of his daughter, and immediately thought of nothing else. She had been a permanent piece of his life's puzzle. She was now the *only* permanent piece, his single legacy, five hours and ten million miles away.

He fell asleep without intending to fall asleep, a gift granted by the spirit of Christmas.

He woke early. What to do on Christmas Day? He started his tablet. He entered the Wi-Fi password and smiled to himself when it worked. Now he could add cable thief to his resume. What could anyone expect from a lowly dishwasher? He scanned the headlines. He preferred the feel of newspaper but this was quick and easy.

He spent most of the morning hanging ten on the worldwide web. By noon his head was crammed with so much pointless information, he wondered if any brainpower had leaked out in the interim. He went inside the diner and reheated a few strips of turkey and mashed potatoes. He toasted a couple of rolls and added cucumber slices doused with honey mustard. He put it all in a to-go box and ate in the trailer.

He dozed off soon afterward. At some time during his siesta he retrieved an army blanket from the pile. He did not remember anything else.

Now, he returned his attention to the old footlocker at the foot of the Pope's bed. The padlock still sealed its contents.

Everyone had secrets. Everyone was entitled to them. Everyone was under lock and key in some fashion.

Darlene returned at five. He threw off the blanket and met her at the door. She had pieces of pumpkin and pecan pies mounded beneath aluminum foil.

"Didn't expect to see you so soon."

Darlene sighed as she entered the trailer. "I know. You aren't going to make me feel guilty, are you?"

"About what?"

She put the plate in the refrigerator. "About bailing on my kid before the end of the day."

"No."

She sat in a chair across from him. "Well, I wanted to get back here."

"The diner?" he teased.

"Mr. Funny."

"So how's the boy?"

She smiled. "He loved everything. He went nuts over that ball you gave him. Once he knew it made that clackety-clack sound whenever it rolled, he wouldn't stop. Screamed like a skinned cat when Mama took it away from him."

His eyes glinted over the rim of his cup. "That's from me to you."

"What is?"

"The ball."

"I don't get it."

"It makes noise. And your mother..."

Darlene's mouth flung open wide. "You sneak. You got him something that makes noise just to get on her nerves."

"Yep. Guilty, guilty, guilty."

She got off the chair and slid beside him. "You are so bad." She put her head on his shoulder and held his arm. "You know, this sucks as a couch."

"Not much good as a bed, either."

"Oh, I don't know. Got just the right amount of bounce."

"Not too comfortable for sleeping."

"Who gives a Willy Woodbanger about sleeping?"

They were slammed the day after Christmas, especially at lunch when local workers reclaimed their routines, or needed a sweet cholesterol injection to stymie the credit-card-over- the-limit blues. The three o'clock lull was the first time anyone had a break.

Bow walked the lot to where the gathering was held, just to limber up. He told himself he was doing okay. He had a credit card, a cell phone, a tablet, and a six-inch ponytail. Once again he had become a man of standing.

He enjoyed the first rush of cool air after the heat of the kitchen and managed a few more minutes without a jacket. The routine of work still placated him. Not particularly noteworthy, but he had consumed the value of repetition, especially when its elements were so basic. Most of the time his mind idled in neutral. He wondered if he had simply become callous in his detachment. He held firm the perception of the world as tolerable, and everyone in it as the first layer of many. With only a couple of exceptions, he didn't feel the urge to look much deeper.

The pulse of days never stopped. Time sped and slowed with the unforeseen, but was never at a standstill. In these minute variations, Bow found more than sufficient cause to endure.

Mickey was almost always in a good mood. He had thick stubble on his cheeks, fur beneath his nose and on his chin, and ape-hairy arms. He had at last completed his hormone treatments. Maintenance doses were far less expensive. Now, he only needed a cannon to be a complete man.

The radio stopped working and Abe finally spoke. “Darlene!”

She quick-stepped to the counter and turned the dial in slow motion until praises to the Almighty floated in the air.

“You musta slid the knob a bit. And change the goddam station!”

In an effort to keep Ruby away from Bob she was told he had a virus. He could still do his job, but it was very contagious. The first day, whenever he would come to bus a table nearby, Ruby would move to the adjacent booth or table, and cupping her mouth with her hands, whispered to the customers, “Don’t let him spit on you. He’s got the AIDS.”

By the next day, Bob was cured. Ruby was still told to stay away from him. She pouted a while, and would unleash a rueful moan every time he walked by, but she didn’t accost him again.

Twenty

The Pope prepared over eighty pounds of ribs. New Year's Eve would bring in the pre-party partiers.

The diner was to close at six, as every other Sunday, and the crew was in high anticipation they would close early, as revelers moved from cholesterol to alcohol. This was not to be. No one seemed in a hurry and people were still arriving at fifteen before six. Abe locked the doors at six, and a few who came a minute or two afterward were perturbed to be locked out.

Darlene made an announcement to the twenty or so diners who remained that the restaurant would close at six-thirty ready or not.

"That's when the both hands are on the six, dickwads," Ruby echoed.

At six twenty-five several groups still hadn't budged. Darlene and Mickey made the rounds with Styrofoam boxes to pack the leftovers and shoo people away.

A couple of men who were likely a pair got snippy with Darlene, and she apologized by saying, "It's New Year's Eve, Princess. Ain't you got nowhere else to go?"

The Pope had prepared wings, dip, salsa, and chips for the workers to take home. This was a wonderful gesture, though Abe looked through every box and did the math in his head.

Everyone had plans for the evening that did not include any of their co-workers, except Bow and Darlene.

Ruby approached one and all, looking for something to latch onto, but all fled, raising a finger in a 'hold that thought' mode even with her in mid-sentence, never intending to return. When she would approach one all others would scatter in a kind of full-body keep away.

Debbie stepped up and invited Ruby to come with her. Then Ruby discovered Debbie intended to spend some of the evening in church, and demurred with,

"Church on a fucking holiday? No thanks, Bud."

Bow and Darlene had long, sometimes irritable, discussions about what to do that night. Bow wanted to party a little, to be among the commotion. He was ready for noise, and the thrashing of a nameless crowd. A bit of cabin fever had set in, confined to small spaces in the kitchen and the Airstream.

Darlene was ready for quiet, a respite from the hectic pace of the diner. She wanted to see a movie, maybe go to Krispy Kreme and watch them make donuts.

They compromised by deciding to stay in with the option of going to Beaufort before midnight and watch the fireworks, maybe taking some fresh donuts with them.

What, if anything, the New Year represented to Bow, he kept to himself, and did not embrace the passing of the year, nor number the days, nor agonize over the unyielding progression of time.

This had been the worst year of his life and he simply didn't want to look upon its end as anything other than an unceremonious turn of the page. There was enough drama in the world without his participation.

Darlene had a bottle of Brut champagne. She had put a lot of thought into it and was pleased with herself. Both changed into T-shirts and comfy pants, and popped the cork. They sat leisurely at the dinette table in the low light. In fact, the only light burning was the overhead light in the rear that glowed faintly over the Pope's bed.

Darlene lit a candle and put it on the table between them. She pulled out a couple of short-stemmed wine glasses and poured both half-full. They clinked and sipped.

"You want music?" Bow asked.

"Got anything nice and pretty?"

He had a CD player in his little clock-radio. He popped in an old James Taylor record.

The guitar sang low and the voice brought serenity, then settled into the background. They both fell asleep before midnight.

Sometime during the night Bow roused to a foggy half-sleep with Darlene twirling his hair with her fingers.

Welcome to another lap around the sun. Let us finish mending. Let us make it through with as few complications as possible, and with only the most common of misfortunes.

The Pope handed Bow a business card. It read 'R J Haywood, Esq.'

Bow frowned. "What's this?"

"He wants to meet you. It's not what you think."

"Usually that means it's close to what I'm thinking," he said smugly.

"Doesn't matter. It's none of those things."

R. J. Haywood's office was on the third floor of the Bank of America building in a wing where six or seven tenants shared a receptionist. These were one-horse tradespeople who either didn't have the gusto to be part of a larger outfit, or such a spirit of independence this was not desired. Probably eighty-twenty in favor of the latter.

Bow walked past two different financial planners, a CPA, and a one-man logistics company. All the offices were tiny, without waiting rooms, and each pair of eyes peered out as Bow passed, sizing up the prospects.

Haywood's door was closed. Bow rapped politely and was greeted by, "Come in," in a refined drawl.

He entered. There was barely enough room for the desk and a couple of client chairs. Part of this was due to Haywood's bulk. He was of indeterminate age as the overabundance of collagen smoothed his features. He could've been thirty, he could've been forty-five. Behind him an open door revealed a row of file cabinets in what was once a closet.

He was a defense lawyer, or said unkindly, ambulance chaser, slip-and-fall avenger, health hazard vindicator, advocate of the little man for forty percent a pop. He rarely went to court. A couple of phone calls and he could squeeze, ten, sometimes twelve thousand dollars out of an insurance company.

He rose and offered his hand. "Bowman Carter. This is a pleasure."

Bow shook his hand and sat where indicated. He could not shake an unpleasant vibe, though Haywood seemed genuinely jovial. He still did not trust him. All lawyers conducted themselves with artifice.

"What can I do for you?" Bow asked.

Haywood simply watched him with a tight-lipped smile. "I know you don't want to discuss the past. But I know your reputation."

"Which one?"

"Yeah, I know everything blew up on you. But you're a good lawyer."

"I'm not looking to practice law."

Haywood grinned larger. "I know that, too." He paused, as if deliberately, and lowered his chair to sit erect. "I'm a former 'client' of the Pope. About two years ago I entered into an unwise relationship with a woman I was representing in a divorce. We were taking her old man to the cleaners and playing hide-the-salami on the side. I'm accustomed to angry women. Part of the attraction. All that pent-up passion. When it was over, I thought she'd just go away. She didn't. I was afraid to get a restraining order because—"

Bow should have been appalled but wasn't. "It would bring unwanted attention."

Haywood leaned back again. "Exactly." He drew out the word—egg-zact-ly. "I've eaten more than my share at Jimmy's, as you can probably tell, and an acquaintance of mine told me about the Pope—about being proficient at extricating people from...delicate situations. He advised me to be blunt. Confront the woman about another adulterous affair her husband didn't know about, and which had continued throughout our...association. How he knew about this, I have no idea. Maybe he was bluffing. I was about to poop my pants. She goes to the South Carolina bar and I've got a ton of explaining to do and would probably be censured."

"And she folded."

"Like a Dollar Tree card table."

"The guy really does know everything."

"At the very least. I was a regular at his Sunday meetings for a long time."

"Haven't seen you there."

"The Presbyterians took me back about a year ago. Tithing will do that. Anyway, I'm trying to do some good. Don't get me wrong. I still make most of my money haggling with insurance companies. But…things come my way and I want to see them through. And I could use some help."

"I'm not sure what I could do."

Haywood rested on his elbows for emphasis. "Here's what I'm thinking. Say I have a case that isn't going to make any money for anybody. Maybe you could help me with research or write a motion. I'll pay you, of course, though it couldn't be much. You would simply consult. And no crap cases, I promise."

"I'll need to think about it."

Haywood nodded. "Tell you what. Next time I get something like that, I'll bring it you. You can pass or you can accept. Fair enough?"

Despite his uneasiness, the sturdy sense he was in the wrong place, a switch flipped *on.* He tried to ignore it, convince himself it was just his imagination, but there it was, aloft and aglow. "Okay," he said finally. "But don't bank on it."

Bow entered the trailer and found the Pope lying in bed on top of the covers. Two cords from separate heating pads snaked from the wall and disappeared beneath his lower back. He held a paperback from Harlan Ellison in one giant paw.

He emptied his pockets on the counter. "I'm thinking I should come at you with a big stick."

The Pope peered over his book. "You can always walk away. I made sure that was the deal."

"What about not getting me involved in the first place?"

"I thought you might get into it, on a casual basis. Was I wrong?"

"I'm not sure I'll ever be a lawyer again, a trial lawyer, anyway."

"You keep saying that. But you *are* a lawyer, trial or not."

“Maybe I’m not sure I want to be.”

“Then don’t. Look. What if you’d been a mechanic? Somebody’s got car trouble and not a pot to piss in. What would be the harm in mentioning you?”

“If I’d been a mechanic I wouldn’t be here.”

“Don’t be obtuse. It might make you feel better doing another good deed.”

“Yeah, yeah,” he muttered.

“Are you telling me it wouldn’t?”

“What?”

“Make you feel better.”

“I don’t know. Maybe that’s not the point.”

“Suit yourself. But sometimes feeling better is all we have to shoot for.” The Pope went back to his book. “You tell Darlene you love her?”

“No. God. Why would you ask that?”

“She’s floating around like a fairy princess.”

“We’re in a good place right now.”

“I know. I do the laundry around here. I see the sheets.”

Bow’s phone rarely rang. Darlene usually texted. He occasionally made inquiries about movie times and such. Now it hummed and startled him. It was Lawyer Haywood.

“Got one for you.”

Bow was sitting in the diner, empty except for the tinny sounds of the Pope in the kitchen prepping for the lunch crowd. He sat in a booth and watched the people who worked in the office building down the block trudge from their cars to the doors. How the mighty had fallen.

They displayed neither sorrow nor grief. Theirs was an acute dissatisfaction, a sullen catatonia. Dejection shown like a runny nose, united in wordlessly pleading for the roof to fall in.

Inertia was enfeebling. This, he understood all too well..

He was reading a two day-old *USA Today* left by a guest of one of the nearby hotels. He didn't mind stale news. In fact, he found it liberating. By now the dramas and celebrations described had been partially resolved, efforts made to fix or unfix, and required little reflection on his part. The sports scores were fairly fresh, as he rarely watched or listened to a game, and the fluff was comically timeless, as most of the contents proved trivial to any person brighter than a birthday cake.

He folded the paper "Shoot."

"Got a kid busted for shoplifting."

"Nothing remarkable about that."

"No, but it's getting out-of-hand quick."

"Go."

"Import from Bosnia or somewhere. Fifteen. Her parents don't speak English. Probably too dumb to learn. Store Manager is being a hard-ass. Had her arrested. Wants her pound of flesh. Kid's still in jail. I'm going to post her bail this morning."

"What did she steal?"

"Art supplies."

"You're kidding."

"No. That's the thing. She's got a school project and her parents wouldn't cough up the cash. Probably thought it was frivolous or needed the money for cigarettes. All those gypsy types smoke like it's the Rapture."

"Doesn't the school make provisions for things like that?"

"If they do, she didn't know about it. Free lunches, of course. So, what do you think?"

"I'm still waiting."

"For what?"

"The punchline. It's a misdemeanor beef. She could plead guilty, pay the fine, live with the embarrassment. Couple hundred bucks. That it? You need help to raise the money?"

"Not just. Look, she's a sweet girl. Petrified. She knows she's going to take a lot of shit in school. It's this...woman at the store. Wants to make a point. Wants to make sure everybody knows how hard her job is with all these immigrants coming over here, working cheap, stealing our stuff."

"Are they illegal?"

"No. Been here over a decade. Refugees. Blame the mackerel snappers. Catholic Social Services are the bleeding hearts to end all bleeding hearts."

"I get it."

"So..."

"All the manager can do is sign the complaint. Court isn't going to make this into anything it isn't."

"She wants to shame the kid. And she wants everyone to know it. She's going to the local paper and telling anyone who will listen what a travesty it is to have *these* people over here. And there are plenty of ears."

"That's not all of it, is it?"

Silence fell, accented by heavy breathing. "You remember that kid from last year and all the bullying hubbub?"

"I wasn't here last year."

“Oh. Yeah. That’s right. Kid gets teased at school because she doesn’t fit in and tries to off herself. Hangs herself in the closet. Only the apartment is a million years old and the rod breaks.”

“She lives.”

“Yeah. Her family practically shuns her. And everybody treats her like a leper. School ignores her. She’s on her own.”

“Okay.”

“This is her.”

Bow promised to think on it and get back to him that day, as time was critical. At least the girl would be out of jail and home. Her parents would probably curse her in some guttural language or plead with her to behave herself—how could they save face in this great country with all her mischief? —but he doubted they had even fixed the closet rod yet.

He stepped through the swinging doors to the kitchen. The Pope was reassembling the grill after cleaning.

“You know any soft touches at the paper?” he asked.

The Pope didn’t ask why. “One,” he answered. “Frankie Martinez. Covers sports, though. Knows everything you’d ever want to know about high school football around here.”

“He owe you a favor?”

“No. Not really.”

“Okay.”

“Sorry.”

“No prob.”

Bow sat down. His coffee was cold. He slid it aside, thinking, trying to push random thoughts into a straight line like misbehaving children. He was shoulder deep in water, getting ready to take a step over his head. He should care, help the girl. He didn't really feel the grip but he knew the difference. What he didn't know was how to convey feelings he didn't have.

Frankie Martinez was in and took the call. The only accent he had was soft Southern, smoothed by time and education.

"What are you, second generation?" Bow asked.

Martinez chuckled. "Third. And Cuban, not Mexican. Grandfather made cigars in Tampa."

"Coronas?"

"No. Presidentes. Big, stinky ones."

"Where did you study journalism?"

"Nowhere. I played baseball. Class of ninety-six. People not from around here are completely unaware of how good the baseball is in South Carolina. Even at Clemson. What can I do for you, Mr.—?"

"Carter." Bow spent a final few seconds wrangling his thoughts. "I need a sympathetic ear."

"Your boy is a football prodigy but doesn't get enough playing time."

"Not exactly." He paused again. When he resumed, he was mindful to be concise, and without exaggeration or hyperbole. Straight. He was in court again. "I need three minutes to tell you a story."

"Only three?"

"If you do not care about the story, you will at least know it will be over soon."

"Ah. Please. Proceed."

"A family immigrates here about ten years ago due to an unstable local environment. They bring with them a five-year-old daughter. The mother and father don't care to assimilate beyond what is necessary. The daughter is quick, learns English, begins school, and becomes the only means through which her parents communicate. Naturally, she doesn't fit in."

"Naturally. And because her parents have no ambition to be fully integrate they remain poor."

"Probably. As the girl grows she does the best she can but has far too much responsibility to flourish and is too young to escape."

"And, if she comes from a male-dominated culture, probably wouldn't escape if she could."

"She enters high school and is even more out-of-place than before. Now, her peers are bigger, more confident, well attuned to all aspects of their own subcultures, cliques, social media, and the like. She becomes the source of ridicule."

"Snarky."

"At least. Her parents do not understand her tears. She isn't hurt. She has no bruises. So they prod her into being tougher."

"She must man up."

"Grow a pair, yes. So to speak. She doesn't know how, of course, so everything gets worse. One night she tries to hang herself but fails."

A pause came on the line. "I remember such a tale."

"As an astute journalist, you would."

"Has she finally succeeded?"

"No. She was arrested for shoplifting. Not clothes. Not make up. Art supplies for a school project she cannot afford and doesn't know how to obtain."

"Her parents will struggle to overcome the shame of this."

"And, to exacerbate the situation—"

"Good word. Solid. Did you study journalism?"

"Not even close. But, the manager of the store believes this was not only malicious, but proof positive that our current immigration policies are to blame, and wants to bring this issue to light in the brightest possible sense."

Martinez didn't respond. After a moment he said, "Sorry. I've been taking notes and wanted to make sure I could read my own writing. Sorry, Mr.—?"

"Carter."

"Yeah. Sorry. Are you a subscriber to this newspaper?"

"No."

"Too bad. We need to bolster circulation. Nonetheless, please obtain tomorrow's issue. You will see an article there."

"Really?"

"Yes. I also write so-called human interest articles from time-to-time under a nom de plume."

"That isn't Spanish."

"My Spanish is terrible. Such a small newspaper, many of us take on other functions. I am expected to empty my own trash can and clean up after myself, if you can believe that. I will also forward the article to other outlets. Perhaps one of the local television stations might find it interesting. Also, is the establishment victimized by this incident independent or part of a chain?"

"It's the Bargain Attic. I don't really know."

"Aha. Part of a chain. Maybe someone in their PR department would also be interested. I will make sure they are aware of the article."

"Thank you. I truly appreciate it."

"Mr. Carter. May I ask what your interest is in this matter?"

"I...need to do this."

"I see. Too bad you don't have a son in high school who is a supremely talented football player and is also a remarkable cellist. It would be good for business."

The next morning the article appeared. The gist of it was not the failure of the school nor the insensitivity of the average mid-teenager. The crux was about how well-intentioned agencies and groups bring people into this country, help them find minimum wage jobs, give them pep talks for six months, then abandon them to the elements—a situation in which some do not have the proper covering.

'The girl is not strictly a victim of poverty or bullying. The girl is a victim of neglect. The girl is confined to a closet with a broken rod and expected not to blink in the light of day...'

The local NBC affiliate picked up the story and did an interview with Lawyer Haywood. The *Savannah Morning News* also did a story, stating that calls to the corporate offices of Bargain Attic were not returned.

Within a week the matter was settled thusly; the charges were dropped and the girl did not have to pay restitution as she had not succeeded in obtaining the items. The school issued another statement that any bullying would not be tolerated. Also, they vowed to make certain all students had access to any and all required supplies. The girl's parents would shriek at her until all the shame had been expunged but she would not have a record.

She would still be alone, unfriended. She would probably survive but as an isolated figure ignored even by her own ilk who had come too far in their own circles to risk scrutiny.

Perhaps the girl might find escape in two-and-a-half more years with acceptance to some institution of higher learning far enough out of the reach of those who subscribe to the most heteromorphic form of love.

The requirements of the last of these was Bow's price. He had exacted from Lawyer Haywood a promise to check on the girl from time to time. Bow knew what it was like to be utterly alone and this girl didn't have a big-nosed, big-footed woman to press flesh with a couple of times a week, even if this had been desired.

Twenty-One

The river heeds nothing, but holds the wisdom of uncounted years in a safe and sacred place.

The river is deaf to all but remembers every note unfurled above or alongside, welcome to mingle in its depths. The river is alive as the algae in its far divots is alive, as the deer moss hidden beneath the rocks upon its shore is alive, as the grasses protruding from its immobile shallows are alive.

The river does not judge the foibles of men, nor praises his triumphs, nor mourn his tragedies. The river proceeds on its timeless course no matter who is present, or who is absent—who pays homage or curses the motion beneath, eager to grasp and hold without release.

The river is unmoved by invention, even when such affects its depth and breadth and motion. Should its passage end, its course rerouted or might subdued, the river would not respond, but would simply cease to be as all things ultimately cease to be. The river is unencumbered by cause or caring.

The words of men, however gracious, however poetic, mean nothing—are nothing. The river has no vanity nor requires validation.

The river is water, and only water, though water is the beginning of everything, the source of all creation.

The river accepts every leaf, branch, or twig—every bit of earth and soil above and beneath—every touch, human or otherwise, with no complaint. The river suffers every violation unaltered, and every consequence is met with stoic unconcern.

Conditions may change, or be changed, but its purpose never wavers.

The river simply flows, unwary, free in its station, even as inspiration for delight or lamentation from the souls of all attending creatures.

The river is an accident of nature, a ditch where water ran as the great seas subsided, now capturing the rain and drainage of other waters, the means through which water passes into the sea, and where the retreat of the sea snakes its way back.

The river's journey is ever outward.

Always.

This is its immutable purpose and its legacy. The river serves the rising tide inward, the ebb tide out, and is as predictable as the revolution of the earth.

The true sanctity of the river lies in its fidelity. The river never fails in its purpose, a testament to consistency, the unchanging water of life.

This has engendered the faith of men, so they may yet continue to dream.

January is real winter, by far the coldest month, blue balls weather if one is not sufficiently clad. February is fickle, certainly not spring but warmth will no longer turn to ice at first blanch.

Bow missed the raw heat of the sun. The land still slept and the half-lit days could provoke jerks and shivers. Now, highlights of an ascending day were present. Pre-dawn mornings were the coldest part of the day.

He expanded his route through and around a public golf course, adding an extra mile. Occasionally he would spot a few hard-core duffers out flailing the sticks. The course was flat and sandy, dotted with the remains of pine woods.

He ran silent as his breath fogged the air in tempo.

Thoughts seeped into consciousness from a cluster rife with activity . Some pooled and some dribbled away. More dripped into untended layers. These were simple concerns, yet affected by a now-covert trauma.

Here he ran, stirring as he filled a mental shovel, spilling as much as he discarded, often hurling a near-empty blade over his shoulder. Still, he was there, digging into the muck stroke-after-stroke. Lately, always the same.

He found dread in possibilities reborn and alive in renewal.

Sanity presented its own difficulties, honed by tragedy. How much easier it was to live in the cloister of unreason and inconsequence, where he could consume whatever mental opiates he needed to prime a vacuum into tolerability. Not so much now.

The carnival life had saved him but static outweighed despair. He made no claim to bravery, boldness or certitude. What he was and what he should be rang in his ears. Risk was a luxury for the self-assured. He was not made for luxury.

He ran harder, pushing his body where his mind would not follow, where exhaustion became a surrogate determination.

Life was propelling him forward like the daredevil shot from the cannon, when all he really wanted was to be the cotton candy man.

A rare February night near sixty degrees, sleeves, perhaps, and little more beyond the norm. Any respite from the cold built false optimism, especially when the wind came off the water.

Bow and the Pope did not talk as much and were not required to talk at all. Whatever the Pope might unveil, the stringent lessons of survival were no longer necessary. Some may follow, but none so urgent.

Bow had nothing to ask, little more to say, less he wanted to hear. He, too, lounged in the stillness, enjoying occasional banter, leaving wounds to prickles, prickles to trifling itch, itch to mindless scratch.

They enjoyed the time in transition, as if time no longer mattered.

"I'm pretty sure Bob is illegal," the Pope said..

"You said that before. But you hired him. Didn't you look into it?"

"Hell, I'm not sure he was even applying for a job. He showed up one day and I had him bus tables. He never said a word. Never asked about pay, never asked for a day off, never seemed worried about *immigracion.* He's probably illegal. Got the look."

"The look? That's so racist."

"No. Hearing the name Tayquon and know he's black with an unimaginative mama, is racist."

"Like a Chinese fiddle player."

"A drunk Injun."

"What about Mexican women and hotel rooms?"

"Asians and left turn signals."

"Holy-roller preachers, fried chicken, and fat...ness."

"That's not a real word."

"Could be."

"Nugatory is a real word."

"No kidding. What does it mean?"

"What does it sound like?"

"Nothing good."

"Close. It means useless—without value."

"As in we are sitting here nugatory."

"Nugatorily."

"Is that a real word?"

"It is now."

They volleyed on for a minute. "Nice night," Bow offered.

"Christ. You aren't stooping to the weather, are you?"

"Music, then."

"What period?"

"Sixties. What genre?"

"Blues."

"I don't know blues from the sixties."

The Pope looked in disbelief, nearly all of it pretense. "Eric Clapton? John Mayall? Early Allmans. Janis fucking Joplin?"

"I never liked Joplin," he said. "Too shrill for me. I like the softer stuff."

"Dylan, people like that?"

"Yeah."

"Joni Mitchell?"

"Not too."

"That's a sign of sexism, you know."

"Not liking Joni Mitchell?"

"No. Listening to a man whine into a mike but not a woman."

"That's just a matter of taste. I'm not a sexist."

"No?"

"No."

The Pope shoved his butt deeper into the chair. "Good. That speaks well of you."

Darlene was frazzled and Bow watched her with growing concern. Wracking his brain, but finding no worthwhile solution, he asked her out on a date.

"What kind of date?"

"A man-woman date. You know, dinner and whatever. Maybe stay in a hotel. Call in an early Valentine's Day date. I know you've been working too hard."

"Like a pity date."

"No. A nice date. Call it an appreciation date."

"You mean like a real date?"

"We've been on dates before."

"Not dress up dates."

"What's wrong with a little romance?"

"If you're not spoofing me, I'd love it."

"Why would I spoof you?"

Darlene eyed him skeptically. "We usually get right to the poke."

"I enjoy your company even without...that."

"Me, too. Just we never do it."

"Maybe it's time we did."

"That's really sweet."

"I'm glad you think so.."

Her eyes moved northeast in unison, reaching for a thought. "We're still gonna get around to the poke, right?"

“Oh, yeah.”

Bow bought a navy sports coat and a royal blue mock turtleneck shirt. Darlene wore a black dress with a plunging neckline. Bits of lace from her bra peeked out above the V. She had her hair done, the back tucked into a tight bun still reeking of spray and wore her Christmas necklace and earrings.

Jack’s was a steakhouse in Beaufort in what had once been a house with a back porch facing the promenade that lined a canal to the river. During the winter, the river was visible with a view of the bridge to Cat Island, but the reeds and marsh grasses had already thickened to the point where only faint glimpses of light shone like fireflies in the distance.

They had promised each other they wouldn’t talk about the diner or anything else of daily familiarity.

“I got new socks,” Bow said.

“I got black panties,” Darlene replied.

They were served their salads, crisp green with a tart vinaigrette. They had ordered wine but neither liked the flavor much.

“So how is the dream quest going?” Bow asked.

“Thought that was on the no-talk list.”

“Doesn’t really have anything to do with work.”

She forked a cherry tomato into her mouth and bit down. “All I ever really wanted was a good job and a decent guy.”

“You’re smarter than that.”

She put her fork down and wiped her mouth. “Listen, Bow. Being with you is great. But don’t make me more than what I am.”

He knew she was overly tired. “What do you think you are?”

She stabbed at a stray black olive. "I'm a small-time girl with a small-time life just trying to get by."

He studied her. She was a rough-hewn, overgrown kid playing dress up that fit worse than a hat a couple sizes too small. What greater fortune was there to be unlocked if out of reach, hiding too far ahead, too wily to catch.

He also knew she had a quality that far outweighed her limitations. He simply had no way to help her.

"I think you're selling yourself short."

"You're the dearest man. You think I don't know every time you touch me it ain't just belly-rubbin'?"

The promenade was a broad walkway of old brick and mortar bending along the canal. Lit with old-fashioned black streetlamps, small trees perfectly trimmed and identically spaced were encircled by pavement, like soldiers at parade rest.

Bow extended an elbow as they ambled and Darlene took it. The lights on the water danced and moved as they moved and he sank deeply into the depths. He really never wanted to leave. Maybe he could just hang out his shingle and hope for the best, doing little bits of business that came along.

"Enjoy your fish?"

"I did," she said quietly. "Thanks."

"I didn't do anything."

"Yeah. You did. You wanted to make a nice date for us, and you did."

"That's what people do on dates. What's bothering you?"

Darlene moved closer, hip-to-hip, draping her arm around his waist. "Sometimes I get stuff all piled up inside and squashed down and I don't have nobody to talk to. Well, the Pope, of course, but I mean somebody to take my side."

"You can always come to me. You know that, right?"

Darlene became coldly diffident inside a moment. "That's the problem."

"What is?"

She wagged her head and blew like a balky horse. "Damn you, Bow Carter," she said finally.

He stopped. "What did I do?"

"You made me need you."

They checked into the Hampton Inn. There were not any grand hotels unless you went to Hilton Head or Savannah. The room had a king-sized bed.

Darlene said, "We won't know what to do with all that room."

They fell asleep watching an overblown adventure movie.

Sometime in the deepest part of the night, when the dark shrugs into its thickest coat, they turned to each other simultaneously and fell together, as if responding to the same voiceless beckoning, and hungrily made love.

False spring was common in those environs, the temperature stretching into the seventies, a harbinger of what was to come, but a temporary respite before cold rain and vaporous breath resumed.

The Pope was in his element, taking full advantage of the lull, preaching the gospel of seasoned treacle and pork sacrifice.

"Did you know there is a difference between an idiot and a moron? An idiot has the mental capacity of someone three years old and younger, and a moron has the mental capacity of someone between seven and twelve. God only knows who made that distinction, probably a moron.

Laughter came easily now in the wink of the sun.

"We think we know something and have it in a nice, neat little box, and then we realize we don't know shit. Take love for instance. Everybody thinks they know what love is, what it's supposed to feel like, how we're supposed to behave. I don't know about you but I haven't got a clue."

The women laughed louder than the men, perhaps illustrating his point.

"In ancient Rome, priests would gather in the sacred cave where Romulus and Remus were nurtured by a she-wolf. They sacrificed a goat for fertility and a dog for purity. How they came to believe those animals would do the trick is unknown. Probably due to bad wine.

"Then they would turn the goat's hide into strips and dip them in blood and march up and down the streets of the city slapping women with the bloody strips of hide. The women didn't seem to mind because many believed this would make them fertile for the coming year.

"Later, the young maidens would put their names in a big urn and the single men would each draw a name. They would spend the next year getting acquainted, so to speak, and thus invented the key party.

The crowd applauded, as sun worshippers primed for abandon.

"Naturally, Christians eventually commandeered the festival, as they are wont to do, and turned it into a day of love. This happens the middle of every February. Now the greeting card companies and the florists keep it going.

"But no matter what, remember this. Love anyway. Even if you are an idiot or a moron. After all, what better way is there to be in love than be stupid about it.

"Happy Valentine's Day."

Out-of-the-blue, Bob started whistling. He whistled the entire shift. No one minded. In fact, he was something of an artiste—clear and clean with no swish of air diluting the sound. At times, Darlene or Mickey would recognize the song and hum along. Bob would smile in affirmation. The place was happier—not Snow White happy—but the day seemed brighter and the air seemed fresher, and the waitresses moved with more pep-in-the-step.

Abe ignored all this, except once, in a nanosecond, and so quickly that anyone who noticed would doubt her senses, Darlene swore she saw him bop his head once to *It's So Easy* by Linda Ronstadt.

Ruby recognized a couple of the songs. Either they had played the radio at the center where she worked or she had listened a lot on her own time, but when she knew a song she teetered side-to-side the way Ray Charles did at the keyboards.

Unfortunately, Ruby could not whistle or hum. So she sang. Rarely did she find the right note, so when she sang it was severely off key and flat, birthing a jarring, grating sound—like the trash compactor on a garbage truck. After an hour, Darlene could take no more. She told Bob to stop whistling. He complied.

Ruby continued, however, grinding through her entire repertoire until the end of the day, sometimes singing the same tune two or three times in succession.

"Jesus Christ, Abe. Turn the goddam music up!"

Twenty-Two

March was designed as a preview of spring but by mid-month spring arose full-fledged. By month's end, the afternoons could already be sordid in the invisible miasma of enveloping damp, though not yet hour-by-hour, or even day-long.

Bow still had his Monday morning routine of reading the Sunday paper, even with his tablet. The world was easier to stomach in black-and-white. Not so loud. No competing voices clamoring for attention. Quiet no matter the punctuation.

He saw the picture in the Metro section. At first it didn't register. There it was. A four-color image—perfectly styled dark hair, a carefully constructed smile. A dark green suit and a small, gold crucifix around the neck. And the headline—

Political Newcomer to Seek District Seat

Elise Harris, his former assistant—now acting District Attorney. He saw the Judge's oily hand in this—running her for Congress. His stomach burned. His betrayal was complete. He read on. Her platform contained little of substance just the way the public liked it. A return to family values. North Carolina values. Lower tax rates, less government, less government spending, a strong defense. I'm on your side...for now.

As betrayals go, this was a survivable one. Like taking your dream girl to the prom only to discover she was there primarily to show all the studs what they were missing. Elise would have an uphill battle anyway with so many hipsters in the western counties. Pity that the bucketheads who supported her were in the minority, albeit vocal. This was a throwaway seat to gerrymandering to keep the lefties from bitching. She would lose. Big.

The shovel-to-the-head part of the betrayal was about six paragraphs in.

When asked about the Eddie Lee Edwards debacle when she was an assistant to former District Attorney, Bowman Carter, Ms. Harris said, "It was a tragedy for everyone. I did my best to bring what I felt were certain—inconsistencies—to light, but was ignored.

Bow merely sat there, the sun having lost its luster, his coffee having grown too bitter to swallow, the air inside too stale to breathe. This was an out-of-body experience, a deadening to all feeling so he would not grab a knife and slit his throat.

Eventually, he talked to himself, as he had throughout his recovery.

You knew something like this would happen. You're really okay.

Even so, gloom set in. Too many burs and pricklies to avoid. As he rose to his feet and tossed the paper in the trash—even the Parade—the last thing he whispered to himself was,

Well, what did you expect?

One night just before closing, Darlene turtle-necked her head through the service window.

"Bow!"

There was no reply. Bow had the buds in his ears and swayed slightly as he washed the deep pans.

Darlene shouted, "Bow—man...!" in a loud, sing-song voice.

Finally, he turned, though more to peruse the state of the dirty pan inventory than respond to the call. He saw Darlene waving, turned off the water, dried his hands, and shut down the music.

"There's somebody here to see you!"

Bow grimaced, afraid someone else had come for legal advice when he was kaput from thigh to sole. He entered the dining area and saw a man sitting at a booth, his hands clasped on the table, his chin resting upon steepled fingers. The man acknowledged him with a sharp uptilt of his head. Bow approached cautiously, not recognizing him.

"Frankie Martinez," he said, extending his hand.

Relieved, Bow smiled and shook but did not introduce himself.

Martinez was tall and slight, nearly bald at the scalp but with thin hair resting on his collar. He had unnaturally long fingers like a basketballer a foot taller, flesh so tanned it looked like leather, and wire-rimmed glasses with lenses so small they barely covered his eyes. Bow glanced back toward the kitchen and then sat down.

"I didn't know who you were," Frankie said, "and didn't know how to find you."

"How did you find me?" Bow asked.

Deep dimples appeared when he smiled. "The Pope. He knows everybody and can find just about anybody, but lo and behold, you were already here."

"Yeah, he's everywhere."

"Like rednecks."

All the lights were suddenly extinguished except for a single row above the table. The Pope appeared in the doorway long enough to say, "Lock it up when you're finished."

"Sure," Bow replied.

He and Martinez surveyed each other for a moment. "Arthur Bowman Carter," he said finally.

Doubt appeared like blush on a virgin. "One and the same."

"Sorry. Your buddy Haywood likes to brag."

"What can I tell you, he's a lawyer."

"Couldn't figure why someone not really involved would call about the girl. I was curious. Hey. Please don't be concerned. I'm not going to ambush you. I just wanted to chat."

He nodded, fearing the worst. "About?"

Martinez raised a shoulder. "Would the meaning of life sound contrived?"

He didn't respond to the attempt at levity, though his posture unhitched a bit.

"Maybe I shouldn't have come. But you have to know, there's a story here."

"It's been told," he said.

"Not from your point-of-view."

"I don't have a point-of-view."

"From a different perspective then."

He adamantly shook his head. "Doesn't matter. I failed and it cost me everything. Cost other people, too."

"I know. But you have to admit there's more. I mean, you're here in Port Royal, working at a diner for what, minimum wage?"

"I needed to regroup."

"I know. Odd way to do it."

"It's where I landed."

Martinez sighed, knowing this would go no farther. "If you ever decide to speak out, please let me know. You would be treated with respect."

Bow nodded.

"That's not the only reason I came. I wanted to thank you for the story. Got a lot of mileage out of it. Anything to keep from covering high school basketball."

His face brightened a bit. "Thank you. She's got a chance to be okay now from what I've heard."

"Good. Good." He flicked the handle of his mug with a finger and took a brief hiatus. "How you got from there to here...," Martinez wondered aloud.

"Not anything I planned."

Martinez rose to leave. "Helluva story." At the door he extended his hand again. Bow shook it and walked him out.

"If you had to do it all over again—"

Bow breathed painfully. "Not sure anything would've changed."

Martinez appeared puzzled. "Knowing what you know now?"

"Oh. I would have ditched law school, taken up the guitar, and started a band."

The man was a walking stereotype. Red face, short haircut, rough hands, jeans, work boots, and a checked shirt. He wore a bright yellow-orange vest with wide reflective stripes that looked like part of a Ronald McDonald costume. A hard hat rested on the table to the side.

He was one of those people at road construction sites who held traffic in one direction so those in the opposite direction could take a turn. He decided who would go when. He wielded a pole with *stop* on one side and *slow* on the other like the staff of Moses.

His voice was loud with an affected drawl. The accent was real, in desperate need of polish.

"I want a cheeseburger all-the-way except onions. Hash browns instead of fries, and coffee."

"What do you want on your cheeseburger?" Ruby asked innocently.

He flashed a hard look at her. "I said all-the-way."

"Lettuce, tomato, pickles? Mustard, ketchup or mayonnaise?"

"Do you not know what all-the-way means?"

"Yes. And I ain't that kinda girl...most of the time."

"What? You some kind of retard?"

Without missing a beat, Ruby drove the heel of her hand against his forehead. "No. I ain't."

The man leapt to his feet. "Jesus Christ! I'm going to have you busted for that!" He fled the diner.

"What about your fucking cheeseburger, Bud?" she called after him.

Gloria Smock was too tall with a sharp, pointy nose and a crest of reddish hair pulled back into a knot. She wore thick glasses which made her appear to be looking through deep water, and all-in-all looked like an angry chicken. She was the director of the program from which Ruby had boomeranged, and was grossly apologetic the experiment hadn't worked out longer than it had. They would all miss Ruby, except perhaps Bob.

She had another suggestion, and also another candidate she was certain could manage the job without disunity. He was bright and articulate, mildly autistic—about the thirty yard-line— with a side of Asperger's syndrome. He was *extremely* high-functioning and anxious to connect with the real world.

He was hired on a trial basis. Gloria mentioned the only irregularities affixed to his condition were he did not like to touch people, which could be a benefit, as Darlene was known to pat a shoulder occasionally with the words, "Thanks, hon," which some found irksome. He did not smile much or laugh at all, which, if construed as disinterest or haughtiness, could be a three-legged horse but was not a deal-breaker, at least at the outset.

His name was William. Not Will, Bill, Billy, or Willy. William. Call him by any other name and he would correct you with a too-loud "It's William!" He was young, in his early twenties, trim and smart and tidy. He kept his short hair combed, his shirt tucked into his trousers, and his shoes impeccably shined.

His reserve was interpreted by most customers as professionalism. He always used the terms "sir" and "ma'am," never screwed up an order, had obsessively meticulous penmanship, and did not dilly-dally. He did not interact much with other staff members, which was appreciated more than he could possibly know.

The first couple of weeks went smoothly, and when Gloria next inquired, the Pope gave William due approval. However...one thing not mentioned was that not only did William never touch anyone, he scorned being touched as well. In fact, any physical contact, even accidentally, could produce the most calamitous results.

On a Friday night, when everyone was in full and constant motion and Jimmy's was overflowing with at least four groups continuously waiting for a table, William had served an older couple—a really *old* couple—who had been impressed with his mature manner and diligence. Besides leaving a twenty-five percent tip, the gentleman patted William on the back as he departed.

William immediately dropped his tray, spun, and flew across the room, his arms drawn to his chest, his hands flapping synchronously like a Pixar pigeon, and screaming like a twelve-year-old at a Taylor Swift concert.

The noise was loud and piercing, reminiscent of an old air raid siren except a full octave higher, and for a far longer duration than most people could hold their breaths. Once he reached the opposite corner, he stuck his nose in the seam, banged his head, and unleashed the same shrill wail, growing louder if such was even possible.

Everyone was more than alarmed. Every customer immediately dashed to the exit door, elbowing each other for leeway, leaving behind half-consumed food and drink, not to mention their tabs. The whole joint was soon cleared except for employees, all of whom (except the Pope) stood and stared, remaining cautiously at a distance.

Gloria was called. She got William calmed and quiet and whisked him away with little more than a sorrowful look of apology. She never called again.

That was that, except as the pair of them reached the door, Darlene called out, "Bye Billy", which set him off again.

Jimmy's was short-handed two full weeks before a replacement was hired. Bow was pulling double duty but the tips were decent. He still did not enjoy mingling with customers, but was courteous and efficient, if not overly jocular.

Even Abe was called to duty, though his approach was to stand at a table, pad in hand and cigar stump in teeth, and mutter "What's your pleasure?" Some patrons didn't realize they were expected to order until Abe gave them the squinty stink-eye.

The Pope hired a college kid named Marvelette who would only be there through the spring and summer. "Your mother must have been a big Motown fan," the Pope said. She responded with a puzzled smile.

She was lanky with skin albinism pale, a russet colored mini-fro up top. She resembled a Q-tip used on an ear infection. She had a friendly face and a warm demeanor, and learned the drill quickly.

Every time Bow moved within her line-of-sight she gawked in his direction. Bow could feel her gaze like a gnat fizzing around his head. He would look and she would smile, and he would quickly divert his attention elsewhere. After a couple of weeks of this, she followed him back to his station.

He was sitting on a case of orange juice yet to be put away, sucking on sweet tea in an enormous giveaway plastic cup advertising a movie that had come out three years before and had bombed. Most of the image had been scratched away. Bow frowned when he saw her. She smiled apologetically and kept her distance.

"Don't mean to trespass into your deal here," she said.

"It's okay," he replied, but still eyed her suspiciously.

"Man, how I would love to pick your brain."

He focused warily. "I'm sorry?"

"I'm a law student at SC in Columbia. Third year this fall."

"Oh."

"Yeah, I know who you are," she said, contrite.

"If you don't mind, please keep that to yourself. Everyone who works here knows, of course, but it's not for general public consumption."

She backhanded an invisible fly. "I understand. You have the right to hide out somewhere."

Bow grunted low in his throat. "I'm not hiding out. I'm just ...taking a break."

"Hey, I get it. So am I. The stress was getting to me." Again she fell silent and studiously looked at nothing, as if gathering her thoughts. "Would you consider it?" she asked finally.

"What?"

"Having a few conversations with me about the law."

He didn't hesitate. "No."

The Pope had splurged on a newer phone. Bow could hear Creedence and John Fogerty's voice float past the earbuds. He handed the Pope a fresh coffee and sat down. The phone was turned off, leaving them only with the gentle hum of life around them. The night produced perfect conditions—sixty-five degrees, faintest trace of a breeze, no bugs yet—a Tinkerbell night.

The Pope seemed mellow, or else solving some far-flung issue in his head. He sat slumped in his chair, his legs splayed and crossed at the ankle.

"CCR," Bow said. "Need to add a couple of those tunes."

"People used to think they were southern, but they were from San Francisco."

Bow was drinking water over ice. He twirled the liquid in his glass. "Maybe they were from southern San Francisco."

"Could be."

The back cushion of the Pope's Adirondack chair was hemorrhaging foam. "You should get new cushions," Bow suggested.

"These will do," the Pope replied.

"I never really liked a lot of southern rock," Bow mused aloud. "Then again, I never really thought of myself as a southerner."

More hillbilly than redneck?"

"What's the difference?"

"Rednecks believe wrestling is real and stock car racing is fixed. Hillbillies don't know the difference."

"Well I know better. They're both real."

The Pope idly lapped his lips with a finger. "Good man."

"Sad about Ruby," Bow said.

"Yeah. But it was inevitable."

"You think so?"

The Pope nodded and blew smoke through his nostrils like a cartoon bull. "Dreamers don't belong."

"She was a dreamer?"

"Yeah. She wanted something out of reach."

"Maybe so. Sometimes that's okay."

The Pope shook his head. "If life has taught me anything, it's that there's a huge difference between wanting more and wanting the impossible."

Bow bit down on a piece of melting ice. "I can't believe that. Dreamers created everything good we have."

"That's a lovely thought. You should use that in a calendar."

The Pope began speaking even before he ascended the stump.

"As you are aware, the vernal equinox has come. Equinox meaning the same duration of night as day. This is reasonably accurate, if not precise. The earth tilts, see, so the lengths of daylight and darkness are never exact. But you get the idea.

"This invariably brings us to Easter, because if you didn't know, Easter is determined by the vernal equinox. Also, the full moon. I've always felt Easter was a kind of ignominious holiday, not because of Jesus, who obviously suffered, but because of his ardent, though severely misinformed, followers.

"Easter is always determined as the first Sunday after the first full moon after the vernal equinox. So Easter changes every year. Odd, don't you think? How do you explain in all sincerity that Jesus was reborn on March 26th this year and April 4th next year and was March 31st last year?

"A moveable feast of crucifixion and resurrection.

No one knew whether to laugh or remain silent.

"To confuse the issue even more, you have the third day scenario. I never quite got a handle on that, either. Was the poor guy resurrected on the third day or after three days? I mean, any dolt can calculate that if the crucifixion were on Friday afternoon, then three days later would be Monday afternoon, not Sunday.

"Of course ever since Martin Luther King Day the Republicans have been tres sensitive about too many Monday holidays, so it's just as well, I suppose, that it's celebrated on Sunday. Besides, everyone is already dressed in spanking new ensembles and ready to go."

Snickers moved in a wave, spread through the assembled.

"We also know that Easter is another holiday commandeered by Christians. The pagans celebrated the coming season and rebirth, a time of planting and making sure all our reproductive parts were in working order.

The Pope paused and the people fell silent, unsure if he was finished.

"My interpretation of Easter, which is only vaguely relative to the divine, is not that Jesus is God's Dumbledore and can do almost anything, nor even that life is eternal, which makes the Baptists happy, but that death is the end of all pain."

Silence fell so heavily only the traffic on the far street could be heard.

"We end up hosed off and spruced up, and we hurt no more. To cease hurting is the true peace. To be aware of this is true salvation.

"I have a feeling that if Jesus could have seen how everything turned out, he would have stayed dead.

"Happy season of fertility."

Twenty-Three

Are all recollections truly beneficial, definable, calculable? If we were to separate the uplifting from the destructive, the illuminating from the obsidian, would we find we must suffer one for the sake of the other?

How are these opposites to be measured, much less balanced? Are the dearest and mild ever enough to diffuse the terrible, or are we cursed to recall every sordid grain?

These thoughts, these—reminders—exist to dredge and bring to the surface all we have refused to confront. As our dreams are often wishes for the future, memories recreate the past.

As much or as little we seek to summon times done and completed, some rise untoward from the depths. Those lovely may remain close to the surface for a time, as we relive and relish some mote of gladness. Those cruel and callous images from when we were the most desperate may hide and reappear no matter how often displayed, no matter how strongly we believe they have been adequately subdued, and when we are least prepared.

Even the strongest revelations of beneficence can do little to allay the coercion of the smallest remembered ordeals—the storm that overwhelms the sun.

If indeed these can never truly be tamed or subverted by force, then they can only be withstood. They will never disappear. Eventually they will sleep or lie dormant until some new crisis begs for companionship.

Is life then a state of worry and constant fear? Is the presence of dark angels, even in long repose, enough to restrain every single state and quantity of good?

There are also delights in the world that can be witnessed, if not created, touched, if not held, inhaled, if not digested, and treasured, if not amassed.

These may not always be enough, but they may always be found.

The rain was more than a spring mist or even an April shower. These were ceilings of water pressing down so frequently as to be indistinguishable, and so thick as to be inescapable. Standing water soaked shoes through to the socks and on to bare ankles. Business was off but some of this was because of spring break.

A couple of hours before nightfall the sun popped free and gave the world a good wipe down, and patted the surfaces dry. Azaleas had bloomed. What had been brown became green. What had stayed green became greener.

Bow stared at his tablet and yawned. The occasional nightmare rebounded every few weeks.

Always in vivid color, always shocking, red and black and brazen, like a modern art painting.

These he did not remember—or few details. He knew when he woke what had happened, feeling jumbled and tangled, the dismal sound of small pieces of metal clanging around in his head.

Perhaps it would be better to remember every frame of torment than to feel the same pain in mere echoes. His worst fear was that the same dream would recur until at the height of its ruinous intentions, would reveal itself in every specific terror, and destroy so much of what had been hard fought to gain.

He put away his tablet.

No one here would recognize the day, if any had ever known. Many weeks from spring into summer had passed before Port Royal. Only a handful would remember without coaxing—not the incident but the exact day. Those who did would stand at the gravesite and curse every rotten part of Arthur Bowman Carter.

He wished he could be among them. Not as a forgiven, restored person, but as a member of those who knew firsthand the lingering power of casualty. Even despised, belonging to those few was preferable to separation on this day.

This was a pitiless anniversary. One year ago, all matter in their universe had changed with utter permanence. His wife, his daughter, his son-in-law had borne the brunt of despair, just as he had borne the brunt of dishonor and disaffection.

He had not even been given leave to collapse then. He was to be rendered imperceptible, damned to nonexistence. He was not to be part of their grief and especially not a part of their rare smiles of healing these many months—nor of any future. He was to be seen by them as bereft of life as Eddie Lee.

For to them, he and Eddie Lee were the same. Twin sons of affliction. Purveyors of death.

He was again grateful for work. He could do his job on auto-pilot. Peril lay in unchaining his mind. He had thought to confide in Darlene but stating his true thoughts was dangerous, and would only confuse and upset her. She was capable of understanding the raw meaning of his injury—a festival of wrath and regret—but perhaps not the entire depth of his suffering. A great wound could be watched until it healed—or whatever part was capable of healing—but not appropriated.

He could confide in the Pope but there were no words he wished to hear in response, especially if he knew what they would be before they were uttered. No words would matter, anyway.

His music helped. Guitar rock from a time when he was untouched by grief. This was a guilty pleasure as a young man, with a college roommate who listened to an obscure radio station at all hours. He had said the music helped put him to sleep, a freakish thing since most of the music was frantic and loud. Bow had listened until he crashed himself, learning the hooks and patterns by osmosis as he slept, the way some try to learn a new language.

He had not been pacified by the noise. Nor was this a recollection of happier, simpler times. He worked harder in college than he had as an attorney. The music was a pleasure unshared, forsaken when the real world brought a career, a home, marriage, and the unvarying tones of security.

Now the music was his and his alone, a peripheral part of his identity among those he had come to know so recently. No one he had cared about—those who shared the passion of loss—would have recognized any of this.

So he listened, as he always did. He struggled without relief or complaint. He drew tears and fought them back undiscovered. He died and buried himself countless times unnoticed. He trembled imperceptibly and suffered the whole of his own damnation masked as a normal day's work.

After two days the reminders of this most stubborn torment gradually drifted back into hibernation. Within a week Bow returned to those more sufferable troubles.

During a break Bow leaned again the rear wall breathing air too soon to be insoluble. He looked up to see Marvelette approaching, feeling irked and put upon. "I told you I can't help you."

She cocked her head agreeably. "I just wanted to get some air."

He looked away, listening to see if she moved. She was probably a great kid. She just misplaced her curiosity. Eventually, he spoke—and in a kinder fashion than before. "I really don't think I could be of much help to you."

She pounced. "Are you kidding? Your conviction rate was outta hand."

He inhaled with sudden pride. "Most of my cases were penny ante stuff. And I pled out a lot."

"So what? You were at what, ninety-something percent? I have no idea what I'm going to do. I like the idea of defense, but a part of me wants to put the bad guys away."

He relived the satisfaction. "Yeah, it's a good feeling."

"So...would you? Just talk. You'll see I won't be a nuisance."

He searched for an escape but found none. "Okay," he said. "We'll give it a shot."

He sat with Marvelette at a booth an hour before opening. The Pope and Debbie made purposeful ruckus in the back. Bow had water and Marvelette drank skim milk. If she were any leaner she wouldn't be able to stand without holding onto something but looked fit enough to qualify as a lifeform.

"We spend weeks studying case law, knowing the whys and wherefores, and the whole time everyone is really thinking about ways around them."

"That's the law. Everyone is in it to win."

"I guess. I just haven't really fallen in love with anything."

"Maybe you won't. I never did."

"That's depressing. Sorry."

"No matter how big your white horse is, it's still an occupation."

"But not just."

"You could say that about anything. Washing dishes."

"Something else I don't get. Some people treat the law like it's some kind of religion, even though at the same time they're trying to figure out how to break the commandments."

"That's because you have to know the law, chapter and verse, whether you agree with it or not. You can be clever enough to cross-examine someone. You can bring down the house with your summation. But there is always going to be a time when you need case law, and you need to get it right. That's the law's sacred testament. People can and will interpret it differently, but everyone has to use it."

"Was it your calling?"

"No. That's way too virtuous for me."

"So it was just a job for you."

He took a drink of water. "No. It was more than that. I mean, I was pointed in that direction my whole life, but once I got into it, it was more than a job."

Her eyes sparkled. "Somewhere between a job and a religion."

"Yeah. I guess I was a doubter aware of the possibilities."

"Always as a prosecutor?"

"It's easier than defense. As a prosecutor you just have to tell a story backed by facts. In defense you have to create a different story and make it plausible."

She paused momentarily "Does that apply to the Edwards case?"

She had caught him off guard and he coiled to strike. "See, this is why I didn't want to get into this."

"I...Sorry."

He gave her a no-harm look "If you want my input, you'll never mention that again."

He looked toward the kitchen doors as if a summons would come at any second. "Time to go to work," he said.

Bow and Marvelette continued to meet a couple of mornings a week. She always had a list of questions and Bow always had answers. He felt functional in a divergent way, mainly in the utility of and connection to his temporarily abandoned marbles, milky and obscure from neglect and ill use. She always left their encounters with a sense of achievement, and he always left their encounters with a sense of achievement and a low-grade headache.

She was recovering from burnout, though was obviously still enamored. He envied her.

Alone, he thought of her passion. Having no direction was not the same as being lost. He had the feeling she would succeed no matter where she landed.

Had he ever dared to peek beyond the frail but stubborn walls of his experience into the aspect of any greater aspiration? He had inherited the law. He was the oldest son, next in the line of succession. Yet for the first time in forever, he missed his work.

Riding the winds of newly unearthed self-possession, Bow approached the Pope after work. "I want to buy a car."

The Pope showed no enthusiasm or concern. "You got a budget?"

"Two thousand, tops. Hopefully less. I know it'll be a bucket but I want to be able to come and go a little more."

The tumblers were already moving in the Pope's head. "Give me a couple of days. Let me see what I can come up with."

Bow borrowed Mickey's car, a fifteen year-old Lincoln with uneven paint on the doors. Darlene would have been happy to take him but he didn't want an audience, or a coach.

The man lived near the outskirts of Bluffton on a couple of acres. In the rear, an old barn in peeling red paint had been converted into a garage. The door stood open revealing an oily floor and shelves packed with tools.

He was tall with a thick waist. Strong the way men who had worked with their bodies were strong. His hands were hard with hairline cracks all through his palms. He had worked in textile mills most of his adult life until the mill closed down. Now he bought old junkers and reclaimed them.

He had gray hair cut into a flat top and all his teeth. They shook hands. "Lonnie Pruitt."

"Bow Carter."

He stood aside to let Bow have a better look. It was a 2006 Ford Taurus in what had once been tungsten gray. The paint was faded in large blots and wide slashes. Bow looked inside. Upholstery in three shades. Discolorations on the fabric and vinyl. Cassette player—do they still even make cassettes? An odor like sweat and pine cleaner. It was a dog. It was perfect.

"Six cylinder. High miles, but I did a partial rebuild on the engine. Replaced some parts but most I was able to do with a little tinkering here and there. Should be right unless you're gonna be on the road a lot."

"Nah. Just around here."

"The last fella owned it was some kind of salesman. Put fifty thousand miles a year on it. Easy highway miles, though. I honor a year partial warranty. Anything in the guts breaks, I fix it."

"You were recommended by someone I trust."

He flashed his teeth. "The Pope?"

"Yeah."

"When my wife was in hospice he came and sat with us. She was out of it, but him and me talked about fishing. He didn't know much but didn't put on any airs about it."

"Sorry," Bow said.

"It's over. Three years now."

"So, how much?"

"I got eight hundred in it. Going to ask fifteen. For you I'll do thirteen hundred."

Bow was going to test drive it but the deal was done. He would have to buy insurance and a tag. He reached for the door handle to open it when a brief flash of light grazed his eyes.

Off to one side in the barn the sun ricocheted off a small disk. He looked in that direction, and his feet followed a few steps.

Lonnie walked past him inside. The chrome was the back of a mirror and had caught the light. A tarp covered the rest.

"Wanna see?"

"Sure," Bow said.

Lonnie whipped off the tarp in one go, the way a matador twirls his cape. It was a motorcycle, black and chrome and nothing else. Dings in the gas tank. Rust on the handlebars. One foot peg missing half the rubber sleeve. Evil. Wonderful. Bow could say nothing.

"Eighty-two Honda seven-fifty. Great old bike. Honda really knew what they were doing in them days. Harley hadn't got their stuff back together yet."

Bow approached the bike like the last, hidden package behind the Christmas tree. He touched the seat. It had been repaired with tape, but was smooth and neat.

"How much for the bike?"

"You ever owned a motorcycle?" (He pronounced it motor-sickle.)

"No. But I've always wanted one."

"It ain't hard, but it ain't easy neither. Clutch on the left hand, gas on the right. Shifter down at the left foot. Two brakes—right foot and right hand. You don't use that one except in an emergency. That's for the front wheel and will send you flyin' if you ain't careful. Cars won't watch out for you and you gotta watch for grit in the curves or else you'll slide the hide right off of you."

Bow hadn't moved his eyes from the machine. "I've ridden before, just never owned one. Went to Atlanta once with a friend when I was a kid. He had three or four bikes."

"Well, then you know what you're in for. Get wet in the rain. Freeze in the winter. Bugs all the time."

"How much?"

"I gotta get a full grand on this, being a classic. I had to practically rebuild the whole thing and put it back together."

"Fine. I'll take it."

"You need to ride it first."

"I will. But I want it."

"Fine by me. I'll even throw in an old helmet."

Bow became a biker in a lightweight sort of way. Seven hundred fifty cc's produced plenty of horsepower. He bought a leather jacket, a pair of boots, and several pairs of the thickest jeans he could find. For a while he cut short his morning runs and when the sun had been up an hour it was warm enough to ride. The helmet was a royal blue metal flake that sparkled with each angle to the sun. The noise was a throaty amalgam of roar and erosive sputter. For the first few days he revved the engine at every red light just to listen.

For a good ride, he would leave town, justifiably paranoid about drivers the entire way. He sought out backroads and ancient trails. The land was mainly flat and he craved to cruise up mountain roads but that would have to wait. The whole state of North Carolina gave him the willies. He searched out different routes every day until he had a dozen or so were mapped in his head. More with combinations of these.

He had never been much for fantasies. He always wanted to be cognizant of his mind's every track, beeline and wriggle, apogee and nadir. Regardless of the outcome or lack of control, he needed to be conscious of every step. The concrete had always been necessary for his equilibrium.

Now, he flew.

He did not imagine himself as a bird, surveying a diminished world. Nor did he envision himself afloat, gliding upon unfamiliar currents. He flew as a creature of the wind, sailing through its veiled walls, down its ghostly corridors, at times into brightness as a companion to el sol. He reveled in the sun the most—the gloss of radiant light, the palpability of all-encompassing brilliance.

Even at risk, he was not afraid, for the lighted sky demonstrated its value each passing moment. The exposed world whispered life, and not just a reclaimed life, but a life beyond—a life unexplored. A new measure of being.

This was life as it should be. Life as it never was. This was a life of motion—not in haste, but smooth and methodical. He had learned and he had digested this: he was no longer Arthur Bowman Carter, the third. When he first lost himself, forfeiting all sanity, pummeled into submission, he had not considered who might reappear. He had not considered reappearing at all. Scarred, yes. Alone, yes. Fearful, yes.

He would not have conceived, and certainly not believed, that a man of decent substance would slip free of the bonds of ill-restraint and become something beyond recovered—something new and wholly original. A re-formed man. What remained of the anterior man had transmogrified. Even the bits that had scattered were accepted, if not embraced, for these bore significant importance in the shaping.

Loss had become liberation. Doubt had become revelation. Malediction had become redemption. Death had become motion.

Bow knew Darlene was upset he spent so much time with Marvelette, but she didn't bring it up. He looked at her into an all-seeing mirror. Every nuance, every slight movement of lid and eye. Every tic of the lips that would seem imaginary otherwise. Every quiver of muscle from the jawline to the ear. He knew what an aching heart looked like. He intimately knew every detail.

On a warm Sunday morning he took her for a ride on his motorcycle. He gave her the helmet and did without, except for goggles. Her head so encased made her features even more pronounced. She looked like a goblin with decent orthodontia.

Darlene was noticeably anxious. "If we get killed on this thing I'll be pissed."

"Just hold on."

Bow proceeded with some measure of doubt. He wondered if his enthusiasm could be shared, or if not shared, then appreciated. He was uneasy about anything that might exaggerate their differences.

He took the old highway toward Savannah, then cut north onto a two-lane blacktop. This road was more open, though virtually flat without rolls or dips. Both sides were lined with farms—soybeans, corn, tobacco. They passed through a pecan grove, each tree uniform and creating an archway overhead. Darlene spoke, but her words were carried away. She pulled herself closer to his back and wrapped her arms more tightly about him. Her warmth passed through both jackets.

They cruised easily, passing few cars, seeing scant signs of life. He was airborne again, afloat upon the sky, a breath inside a sea of air. He moved in a straight line, dipping a wing only to negotiate a curve, slightly buffeted at times, unencumbered always. He was a maverick, a beast without herd or flock, a lone sailor awash in a boundless sea.

He pulled into Jimmy's parking lot and coasted to a space behind the trailer. He held Darlene's arm as she dismounted and stood on shaky legs. He helped her with her chin strap and freed her from the helmet. He was jacked in all ways.

"You enjoy?" he asked.

"I like to froze to death."

Bow realized he could no more dispense this magic than convey it, though he found himself markedly liberated.

"It was nice to have you along," he said simply.

"Always nice to be had," she answered.

Twenty-Four

Bow and Darlene sat at a table enjoying mini-brunch before eleven. Darlene had toast with strawberry preserves and milk. Bow had a cup of chicken noodle soup. He rarely ate breakfast food. Too sweet and too greasy.

Darlene listened patiently while Bow regaled her with a few of the innumerable virtues of life on two wheels. She let him ramble because she had never seen him so animated, and believed this was a portent of better things.

Mickey entered snuffling again and as red-eyed as an asthmatic. He passed the table without looking in their direction. He was quivering forcefully, and breathed through his mouth as if winded. He was in a sorrier state than Bow had ever seen, as if *RuPaul's Drag Race* had just been cancelled.

Darlene gulped the last of her milk and looked sad-eyed toward the bathroom door. "Somebody's got to figure a way to get that boy a dick."

"I think it's worse than that," Bow said.

Mickey came out. If there was any improvement in his mood, he didn't show it. Again, he ignored them.

Darlene called out. "Mickey! What's wrong?"

Mickey turned and opened his mouth but nothing came out. Inside a nano his visage decayed again, this time into a full-blown convulsion. Devoting all his air to blubbering, he sputtered the words.

"My—lawyer—quit. Don't—know—what—to do."

"Hire another one," Darlene suggested.

"Can't—afford—it." Then the wave swelled and crashed again and he moved through the swinging doors to stow his purse.

"What's the lawyer for?" he asked.

"You know. Mickey was fired over this sex-change thing and he was suing the school board and the school."

Bow looked off. His flight response was cocked and ready. No one could expect him to get involved. This would take far more than a phone call or a wordy brief.

Darlene noticed his reluctance but plunged anyway. "Somebody's got to do something," she suggested.

"Not me," he said flatly. "Maybe the Pope knows somebody."

"What about that lawyer friend of his. He owes you one, right?"

"He's not that kind of lawyer. Don't think he's up to it."

"Who gives a Benny Bonewaggler about that?"

"If she's got a case, she needs a bulldog."

Bow soon discovered the situation was more acute than he realized. An appointment to depose the principal of the school was two days hence. Reluctantly...no, more than reluctantly—squeamishly, anxiously, and grudgingly, Bow contacted Lawyer Haywood to step in. He, too, protested, as he was hesitant to enter a fray so late in the process, but more, to engage an adversary sure to lead to a courtroom. Time and money. And wading in deep water.

Bow agreed to be there and serve as co-counsellor. The change in representation was approved by all. The school, as personified, knew the original representative had abandoned a doomed proposition and grew all-the-more confident in its position.

The day before the deposition, Bow brought Haywood a sheaf of papers.

"What's this?"

"Questions for the depo. In order. And then potential responses to their answers."

"Jesus Hallelujah."

"Not a big deal. Their answers are going to be fairly predictable. I don't want to open my mouth unless I have to."

They had agreed to meet in the school board attorney's office. He was an avuncular man, fiftyish, with triple chins that draped over his collar like some unnamed blob in a Mexican horror movie. He was visibly self-assured and grinned like a gator.

The principal was a thin, washed-out man, who nervously brushed the few remaining hairs he had with his fingers. He was only in his forties but bore the denouement of spending so much time with teenagers.

Bow and Haywood sat down opposite the enemy across a four-foot width of conference table. It gleamed in the fluorescent light. The only witness other than the four was a stenographer, a no-nonsense type who did not smile even when smiled upon.

The lawyer's name was Bartle. The principal's name was Mullen. The stenographer did not introduce herself and ignored everyone. If Bartle recognized Bow, he said nothing, nor was there even a mote of suspicion when Haywood introduced Bow as Mr. Arthur.

Bartle spoke first. It was his pony and he wanted to make sure a sense of decorum was maintained throughout the process. His voice was surprisingly high-pitched, though monotonous. "I want us to agree on some ground rules. I want to avoid any hostility or direct accusations. I want us all to behave like professionals and maintain common courtesy."

"No problem," Haywood answered, and they began.

Haywood drew a breath and then stepped in—on tiptoes.

"Regarding Ms. Williams. For the record, please tell me why she was terminated?"

"Poor work performance," Mullen said.

"Can you be more specific?"

"Her work was unsatisfactory."

"How so?"

"It did not meet our standards."

Haywood blew impatiently. "In what ways?"

"In several ways. You have the file."

"Do you plan to be this uncooperative all day?"

Bartle interjected. "South Carolina is a right-to-work state. Any employee can be terminated at will."

"That didn't answer my question."

"It will have to suffice."

Haywood looked down at his notes, flustered, shuffling them with quivering fingers. He was outmatched. He raised his eyes to an unoccupied point near the door, caught in aphasia. He didn't say anything.

Bartle curled his lips into a half-sneer.. "Is that all, Mr. Haywood?"

Haywood didn't respond. Bow wanted to slide under the table until everyone else left. Instead, a familiar voice rose from nowhere

"Any objections if I continue?" All eyes slid toward Bow. What the hell had he done?

"Are you familiar with the procedure? Mr. Mullen is a busy man. As are we all."

"Yes," Bow answered. "I have been admitted to the North Carolina and South Carolina bar. And I don't think this will take more than a few minutes."

Bartle sighed deeply. "Very well. Continue."

Bow eyed Mullen directly, speaking in colorless form.

"To finish up the last question, Ms. Williams was under contract, wasn't she?"

"Yes, but we still had grounds to terminate."

"Well, that's what we're asking the court to determine, isn't it?"

Mullen didn't answer and Bow proceeded.

"In reviewing Ms. Williams' record, the performance review leading to her termination is the first such blemish. Is that correct?"

"I'm not sure," Mullen said, as instructed.

"So you are not familiar with her record then.""Of course—"

"Is it the first blemish in a six-year career or isn't it?"

Mullen reddened. Bartle interceded. "We will stipulate that there was no previous disciplinary action."

Bow nodded. "She taught health but she was hired primarily as the girls' basketball coach, correct?"

"Yes."

"In the last six years her record was one-eleven and thirty-three, correct?"

Again Mullen stuttered. "I don't know."

Again Bartle stepped in. "Stipulated pending further review."

"That's over a seventy-seven percent success rate."

"I suppose."

"Do you know how many middle schools of similar size there are in this state?"

"I'm not sure."

"Two hundred twenty. Do you know how many girls' basketball teams have a higher success rate?"

"No."

"Sorry, I couldn't hear you."

"No."

"Six. Only six out of two hundred schools have a better record over the same period."

"I don't see the relevance."

Bow gasped in faux disbelief. "You have a teacher with an unblemished record, who has never even been late, and a proven record of being one of the best coaches in this state, who was unceremoniously fired after an alleged single incident. Correct?"

"I, uh..."

"Please move on," Bartle interjected.

Bow complied. "Please state specific details of her termination."

"There were complaints."

"From whom?"

"Students. Parents."

"Such as?"

"Discomfort with Ms. Williams'...health...issues."

"How many?"

"I don't know. I'll have to look."

"Does four sound reasonable?"

"Okay."

"So four parents complained."

"I'll have to check."

"And how many students?"

"Many," Mullen said certainly.

"How many who were in her health class or on the basketball team?"

"I'll have to look."

"One," Bow asserted.

"No, I think it's more than that. You also have to consider the morale of the entire student population, and her co-workers."

Bow nodded and paused. "Do you know how many coaches in the same position are men?"

"I don't think that's relevant," Bartle added.

"Over seventy-five percent. Three-quarters."

"I still don't see the relevance," Bartle repeated.

"Was the individual who replaced her as coach a man or a woman?"

Mullen stuttered. "I really don't know."

"A man. I checked." Bow took a breath. "What if job security was her primary focus?"

"How so?"

"She knew men were preferred in these positions. Perhaps she thought the best way to keep her job was to become a man."

Mullen snorted. "That's preposterous."

"How do you know?"

Bartle had heard enough. He pointed a stiff finger at the transcriptionist, but kept his eyes locked on Bow. "Off the record. Mr. Arthur, no matter how clever your argument is, she is not going to get her job back, or any job in the public school system. Nothing you say can compel them to do that."

Bow organized his notes and spoke softly, yet gave each word equal weight. "She won't have to work. She'll be able to retire."

Bartle smugly pursed his lips. "My, aren't you confident. This is still South Carolina, my friend."

Bow's eyes lit for a moment. "Not anymore."

"I beg your pardon?"

"We're going federal now. Title seven. Gender bias. Hostile work environment because of gender. Pesky federal law. A couple of uptight parents and one bratty kid and you roll over because you think it's easy. You know full well why you canned her. You'll get the amended complaint tomorrow. Federal court is Atlanta, by the way, not good ol' boys from the Lowcountry. I'm anxious to see what the district's insurance provider has to say. There will be an investigation soon, I expect. Shouldn't take too long. Then we'll see where we are."

Bartle darkened and Mullen looked as if someone had plucked his nose hair.

On the way out Haywood was self-conscious, apologetic. "Great job. Sorry I couldn't get it done. Don't do many depositions."

"Don't worry about it."

That's how they parted.

The next morning, Bow got a call shortly after nine o'clock. It was Haywood.

"Just heard from Bartle. They're offering Seventy-five K. I think we should hold out for more."

Alone, Bow managed a knowing smile. My how the conceit of modern man affects all memory. He considered for a moment to ask Haywood the state of his underwear the previous day.

"No. Accept the deal. That's enough."

There was a long hesitation, the ensuing remarks certain to be questionable. "Uh, what percentage do I get?"

"This was supposed to be a favor."

"I know. But we won."

Bow thought for a second. "Okay. You keep the five."

"Yeah, that seems fair enough for an accommodation."

The air went dead for a moment, followed by a sigh. "We're done," Bow said calmly.

There was more silence on the line. Finally... "Okay. I get that."

Bow gave Mickey the news and had to wait a full minute for the bawling to stop. "It's not as much as it sounds. But it's enough for you to finish your treatment and maybe a year to get back on your feet. Eventually, you're going to have to work somewhere. Probably away from here."

Mickey honked into a tissue. "I know. I've been thinking about California. I'm a good coach."

Bow smiled at him. "At the very least."

They did not throw Mickey a bon voyage party but everyone wished him well and every future success. As Bow and Darlene stood in the parking lot, Mickey snotting up like a troll as he climbed into his old car, Darlene waved and shouted—

"Hey Mick! You got the cash now so treat yourself to a big ol' dong!"

Mickey's replacement was a short, round black lady who looked like a bowling ball with Mr. Potato Head limbs. Her name was Levetra and she had been a waitress for a long time but was looking for a change of venue. Some place where servers weren't crawling all over each other.

The Pope introduced her to Darlene, as the de facto commander of the wait staff. Darlene looked her over as if she might sniff her at any moment.

"Were you born a woman?" she asked brusquely.

Levetra was obviously taken aback, but answered. "Yes, I was."

"And do you intend to stay a woman?"

Again, the look of sheer puzzlement.

"Yes. Yes, I do."

Darlene's smile stretched from east-to-west and she extended her hand. "Welcome to Jimmy's!"

Bow wanted to do something to make Darlene feel more appreciated but everything he suggested was rejected.

"Just spending down time with you is special enough," she said, with a chortled nod to the pun.

They drove to the high school and walked the track instead. The scenery might have been dull and repetitive but they would know exactly how far they had gone. There was no one else in sight.

Bow drifted away. Darlene noticed, afraid there were sore spots still to be exposed.

Instead, he said, "The Pope's home a lot these days."

"We can go to my apartment."

"That's not what I mean. He just lies in bed and reads with pillows and heating pads under his back. He needs to go to a chiropractor."

"He's got a doctor. I've seen the pill bottles."

"He hangs out with a doctor. The guy who drives the convertible."

"Well, he's stubborn as shit about stuff. Gotta do things his own way."

"Should I say something?"

"Like what?"

"I don't know. Like maybe he ought to get checked out from top-to-bottom."

"You want to be buried or cremated?"

"We've been able to talk about things lately," he said defensively, though quietly.

"About his business?" she asked in disbelief.

"Some."

"Huh. Well, I still wouldn't say anything right away. These things pass. Maybe he's just waiting it out."

"Yeah, okay."

"Want to go to my apartment?"

"I don't know. I haven't had all my shots."

She karate-chopped his arm at the bicep.

They strolled, silent for a few minutes. He instinctively slid his arm around her waist and she squeezed against him.

"Why are you still here" she asked thoughtfully.

He'd been somewhere else entirely. "Do what?"

"I know you're ready. You've been ready. You could have hit the highway months ago."

"I'm in no hurry."

"But you're ready. Past ready."

"I don't know what I'd do yet. You trying to run me off?"

Darlene smiled but was stone serious. "I know it's not me."

He thought he had the answer pat but stopped short. "I think about you all the time."

She tried to meet his eyes but he was looking straight ahead. "Not enough, though, is it?"

He turned to her. "You trying to get me riled just for the hell of it?"

She shook her head. The moment floated lightly to a soft landing. Then she laughed under her breath, a harsh laugh, however soft, an animated villain laugh.

"What is it?" he asked.

She scoured the horizon, still caught in bitter amusement. "All along I've had my head set to be hurt and mad. I thought that was the best way. There would come a time when you would leave and if I was mad enough, I'd be ready for it. That's shot to hell."

"You want me to make you mad?" Again, his attempt at levity failed.

"You couldn't if you tried. Not no more."

He should have panicked. He should have run and hid. He should have pretended to pass out and feign amnesia when he came to. He couldn't. Not now, maybe not ever.

"I would never just up and vanish. Can we not worry about this now?"

She conceded, if only to staunch the blood-letting before she embarrassed herself and put him on the spot. "Okie-fenokie, Bud."

Ashes of an old fire still smoldered but did not flare to life. If he had become a better man, he couldn't say—maybe not even think it. Maybe he had become someone unrecognizable to his former self. Maybe he had stumbled onto some elevated road, bright and sunlit and yielding to every step.

"Besides," he offered, "we still have business to attend to."

Darlene smiled genuinely, mischievously. "Bumpin' and a humpin'."

"Pokin' and a strokin'."

"Amen, brother."

Twenty-Five

For a man closer to retirement age than early adulthood, Bow had had relatively few close relationships. After he passed the bar and began his career, he had not sought any. He had not turned any away, either, but no matter—none had come knocking.

What he had were acquaintances. Those who wanted to be on his good side, either from church (because God expected this of all his children at least one day a week), or in the workplace—other attorneys, court employees, his small staff, even the Judge.

He seldom needed a favor. He seldom needed companionship from anyone. He would laugh and joke with a trio of men during a round of golf but nothing more was necessary. He and his wife would host occasionally, but, again, this was optional, at least from his point-of-view. He had many opportunities through service clubs to interact with men of similar mind. This, too, became superfluous. He was known by everyone in the area. How had a deeper form of familiarity become so unimportant?

Physics.

How much energy would be required to create and maintain a genuine friendship when the odds of success were already long?

Was this merely another dim view of humankind through a lens ground by years of dealing with so many malefactors? Was this a way of avoiding the discomfort of outreach? Was this the desire to keep those intimate parts of himself hidden, with no desire to speak of them or bear the reactions from another? Was this simply a matter of mistrust?

He had come to believe that authentic friendship is about loyalty, and loyalty is at a premium in the legal profession. The sooner this proposition is made sacrosanct, the easier it is to cope, since all such revelations are as painful as they are confounding. Fortunately, what he learned from betrayal was a recent exercise and not one of long experience.

So many vibrant feelings eagerly exhibited were as thin as December ice, that *reaching out* carried expectations in folded hands—that compassion was limited to the more cursory nicks and bruises and not the deep, penetrating gouges. Such thin benevolence is transient and lacking stamina.

Perhaps a poorly defined part of his attitude lay in the competitive nature of law school, which he had avoided, or his profession, where he was so often petitioned (and these were obvious performances), to compromise. In his favor, these had not made him harder and more cynical. He simply acquiesced to the basic nature of things and the most prudent response was to remain aloof and disconnected.

In subjective physics there is only effort and prospect, and for the latently sensitive, the forlorn acceptance of the restrictive constitution evident in hearts and minds.

Were these few souls at Jimmy's his friends? Darlene, of course, but this was a thorny rose yet to be resolved. Was the Pope? Not by appearances. The Pope was too quick to criticize.

Though together throughout the long days he had still been a man alone.

From a brighter day and more benign vision, he recognized the gilt edge of simple decency. He had been given a job to keep himself busy. He had been given a secure place to live. He had been nudged toward the center and away from the steep and rocky rims. He had not been asked nor expected to conform.

They had not cast him aside.

More than anything else, he had been gifted loyalty and everything necessary to heal, and as such, was divinely perfect.

The Pope, Darlene, and to some extent everyone at Jimmy's, were his only true friends. He could rely on them without fear. They had asked nothing of him and had given him life in return.

Bow dressed in blue jeans, a pullover shirt, his navy sport coat, and blue running shoes. The Pope pulled up in a bright yellow pickup truck. He dressed as he always did except for a Velvet Underground T-shirt.

The truck was immaculate.

"Whose is this?" Bow asked.

"Abe's. His way of fitting in."

"With a Japanese truck the color of mustard."

"Misguided a bit, isn't he?"

This junket had been the Pope's idea and Bow was looking forward to it. An Aerosmith cover band was playing Sunday night at a club in Savannah.

Fifty years ago the building had been the best, latest, never-to-be surpassed supermarket. Fifty thousand square feet. Certain to put the corner grocer out of business. Until the Super Store came along with over a hundred thousand shiny square feet of vittles and accessories, and put this supermarket out of business.

The building had gone through many incarnations. This was a desirable location with plenty of parking. Now it was a nightclub called the Restless

Spirit. Painted black with white angels displaying a painful howl, the club hid in the dark. Parking was free and lit like the day.

Inside, the place was massive. Hundreds of people mingled and the place still wasn't crowded. Along the left wall were games, from pinball machines, miniature bowling and basketball, Skeeball, and the entire history of video games. Bow had stopped gaming at Space Invaders and didn't recognize many others. Beyond these were two dozen pool tables.

Along the right wall were two long bars, separated by an aisle where the bathrooms and snack bar were. In the center were at least a hundred tables. Waitresses in black trousers, shirts, and shoes, and a bowler hat with a pair of devil horns, scurried in all directions.

Bow and the Pope took a smaller table. At the far end was the stage, and in front of the stage was a large open area which served as a dance floor, mosh pit, or octagon, depending on the *musique du jour.*

"Are you planning to get drunk?" the Pope asked.

"No."

"Good. Because I intend to."

Bow ordered his light beer and the Pope ordered a shot of Jack Daniels with a Seven-Up chaser. He inhaled the shot. He took his time with the soda. Once it was gone, the set-up was repeated.

The cover band called themselves Arrowhead. None of its members remotely resembled their counterparts. The lead singer looked like one of the Van Zant brothers. The music was spot on, however, note, chord and tone. The vocals were not quite there. The singer hit all the notes but didn't have the same elfin qualities as Steven Tyler. Of course, part of this could've been Bow's prejudice, as he expected this singer to leap into *Free Bird* any second.

The band was loud, the crowd was jumping. The evening was a blast.

The Pope draped his arm around Bow's shoulder as they ambled across the parking lot. The shot/chaser maneuver had been repeated six times but the Pope wasn't sloppy drunk. After two hours of head-bopping and fist-pumping, the curious pair had become aligned in something other than trauma.

Bow's ears rang and he was half-deaf, but he didn't care. He had downed three beers himself but rationed over three hours, and was not impaired in any way. More placid than potted. Okay to drive. They walked to the truck like conjoined twins.

At the outskirts of town, when the streetlights yielded to empty space, Bow relaxed.

"Decent renditions," Bow said.

"That singer," the Pope grunted. "That dude was no lady."

"Well, you can't have everything."

"No. I guess not."

"Aerosmith circa 1981," Bow offered, after a moment.

"Sorry, I don't know the significance."

"That's when they all became full-time test pilots for pharmaceuticals."

"Everybody needs something to fall back on."

"Yep. But before they imploded... I loved all that stuff from the seventies."

"You were born with a rock-and-roll heart."

"Fuckin' right I was."

"And the body of a librarian."

"Maybe. But a hip librarian."

"That's my goal in life. To be hip," the Pope said.

"Yeah? You might have to settle for being the Pope."

"I'm hip to that."

The conversation lagged but the mood did not change. Both wore goofy grins that required no explanation, just as the silence required no attention.

After a few moments, the Pope belched, fuming the cab with the gooey odor of semi-processed whiskey.

"You like golf?" the Pope asked. He slurred the word a bit. It sounded like *gullff*.

"To watch or to play?"

"Watch."

"It's nice for background noise for a Sunday nap. Not lately though. Why? You like to watch it?"

The Pope exaggerated a brisk shake of the head. "Nope. Too spoiled."

"Yeah? How so?"

"Everybody has to stand around in total silence when they're taking a shot like it's a requiem mass or something. Bunch of sissies."

"Well, they need to concentrate."

The Pope blew a long raspberry that echoed. "Basketball players have to concentrate, too. When they're shooting free throws, I mean. But you got a couple thousand people looking them right in the face waving their arms and screaming for them to miss it."

"People are closer in golf."

"That's a sorry excuse (shurry exskoosh). Know what I think?"

"I'm sure you'll tell me."

"Make the golf spectators stand back about twenty yards or so. Then they get to wave their arms and shout 'miss it' to their hearts' content. We'd see about it, then.'

He seemed placated. Bow held a chuckle. "Sounds like a great idea."

Ahead Bow saw something at the far reaches of the headlights and slowed down. Something was bouncing on the road. Debris, maybe, though it remained in one place.

"You see that?"

The Pope squinted. "Some smartass put a fish out there."

They heard the sound at the same time. The Pope rolled down his window a few inches. A horrible howl echoed, an alarm with a perforated speaker. A coyote cub with tonsillitis.

"Good lord. What is that?" Bow said.

The Pope waved him forward.

Bow stopped about twenty feet short. The lights caught a flopping animal but no other details. The sound was constant. He put on the flashers. There was no traffic.

The Pope moved first. He walked to within a few feet and peered down. "It's a cat."

"What?"

"A cat. Its hips and legs have been mangled. Probably hit by a car. Trying to drag itself with only its front legs."

"Stuck to the road?"

"Maybe. Weak, too, I'd guess. We need to do something."

"Like what?" Bow asked.

"Put it out of its misery."

"Oh," Bow said. "Maybe I can find a big stick and whack it."

The Pope stared at him. “That’s harsh.”

He pondered. “How about I just line up the tires and run over it again.”

“Jesus, man. That’s too cruel.”

He was exasperated. “You got any ideas?”

The Pope shook his head. “See what Abe’s got in the back of the truck.”

Bow walked back and looked in the truck bed. His face grew evil in the red of the taillights. He could make out a few items, made easier because they were all garden supplies. “He’s got a couple bags of mulch. A bag of fertilizer. A new hose. Some loose cardboard. And a hoe-thing.”

“Who you callin’ a ho’?”

“Funny. It’s like a hoe except it has prongs instead of a blade, like a mini-pitchfork. That would do the job.”

“Boy, you are one sadistic bastard.”

“It would be quick and easy,” Bow protested.

“No. Gotta think of something humane.”

The hose was a loose fit to say the least, but it worked. Bow stuck it up the tailpipe about two feet. They scooped the cat up with a piece of cardboard. The pitiful thing yowled in such desolation they both shivered. The Pope gently laid the cardboard on the passenger seat. He took the hose and put the free end inside, then closed the window until it held the hose in place.

Crude, but it would have to do. He watched the carbon monoxide smoke drift into the cab compartment with a look of satisfaction. Then, they both stood back. Way back.

“I can’t believe we’re gassing a cat,” Bow said.

“In Abe’s truck,” the Pope replied.

“You don’t think there will be enough left over to hurt him?”

“I hope not. We’ve got to drive it home.”

Afterward, they kept the windows rolled all the way down and the fan on high. Even so, they stuck their heads as far out of the windows as they could. Two old dogs. The only thing missing were lolling tongues.

"You realize we left that thing in the front yard of a church," Bow said.

The Pope seemed pleased with himself. "Perfect place for it."

If the Pope was hurting, he revealed nothing. Except in private. He didn't shudder, grimace, or slow down at work, and probably showed no signs on his extraneous rounds.

Bow had even begun to search for causes of and remedies for aching backs. The results were incoherent. Backaches had too many causes, and he feared if he extended a hand in that direction, he might pull back a nub. He even thought about a gift certificate for a session with a masseuse but that was too transparent.

Perhaps the symptoms might be short-lived, because at the next gathering the Pope was full of vim and vinegar, and hopped onto the stump like a game show host, sans applause.

"Originally, it was called Decoration Day. After the Civil War, towns all over the South would venture into the churchyards and family plots to decorate the graves of those who died in the military, most in war time. May 30th was chosen because it wasn't the date of any particular battle or noteworthy event. The men who died were honored.

"Even then those poor mothers knew what we all know now. War is fought by poor men to protect the interests of rich men. Most of the Confederate soldiers didn't own slaves. The moneyed elite needed to preserve their way of doing business. And, as now, they needed to find a way to incite everyone so men would fight—as if they, too, had something at stake. They call it patriotism. What it is, is exploitation.

"Some of you may have seen action. So I know you'll understand when I say that wars make life cheap. If life were a truly equitable enterprise, they'd make the leaders fight it out. That would put a stop to it.

"Well..."

"Later, Decoration Day became Memorial Day, practiced by nearly everyone, until over a hundred years later—in 1971—Nixon finally made it official, as he was also astute in the cause-and-effect aspects of turning poor boys into so much lifeless pulp, and a willing purveyor of human wreckage.

"The last president to see combat was the elder Bush. It probably won't happen again, not because we've gotten smarter about war, but because we keep electing chicken shit guys who would rather live vicariously through the seemingly endless supply of the needy young.

"God help us."

"Anyway, Nixon made it official. Eventually, Memorial Day became one of those asinine revolving Monday holidays, instead of May 30th.

"I like to keep things simple. Memorial Day is the unofficial but well-intended beginning of summer. And that's okay by me. So whatever it means to you, have a nice summer."

Even with the relative passivity of the coastal winter, much was left to be reclaimed in the ensuing weeks. People returned to the exterior light as if they were snowbound Dakotans. Everyone soaked up vitamin D from the sun, drained those few gray months, until around mid-June when all were chased inside to air-conditioned comfort.

Bow was not so finicky. Sure, the air now blew like an oven on his motorcycle jaunts through the Lowcountry but he relished them nonetheless. He was a creature of exploration now, unafraid of any woodland trail or clay path. He could dodge raccoons and outrun dogs as well as any man on two legs and two wheels. He was also extremely careful. He still wore his jeans, boots, and jacket regardless of clime. He wore a coating of sweat like the oil of the catechumens, and the resultant scent like vestments.

He spent a few hours every week discussing the law with Marvelette. He got to know Levetra, and discovered she sang in the church choir every Sunday, and could shoot pool like Eddie Felson—often on tiptoe with her belly pushed flat against the rail, since she was so short and round. If she ever lost her balance, the kinetic energy would've sent her hurling backward all the way across the street.

He and Darlene did more than chase the rabbit. They talked more, though as yet not so much more to matter. The Pope was in good spirits. No one ever knew what thought or felt, or even if he was a battery-operated android with a prop cigar. Bow had seen him every day for a year and had never seen him actually smoke.

Bow cut back to a firm two cigarettes a day—at break and before bed—like clockwork. He and the Pope still enjoyed sitting out in their old, faded chairs in the cover of night even when the air became as thick as fog.

This is how they had begun. Most of their conversations were casual now. Few had any more import than chitchat. A lot of the time they spoke not at all.

Bow convinced the Pope to put an air conditioner in the window high upon the back wall of the kitchen. This had been tried and failed once before—not enough horsepower. The circulating fan could at least push cooler air around now.

Hot air rose as cold air fell, shuffled about by the fan, and cooled a single ten square-foot space between the main grill and the sink where no one ever was. Standing square beneath it was the only way to get the full effect. However, the ambient temperature of the kitchen did cool to around ninety degrees.

The Pope gathered everyone one Tuesday morning and posed them outside near the Jimmy's sign for a picture. The Pope, Bow, Debbie, Darlene, Marvelette, Levetra and Bob, all with unnatural smiles, except Bob, who smiled as easily as most did not. Abe took the picture—maybe several, no one knew at the time—then unceremoniously went inside to his stool.

The Pope gave everyone copies and Bow had the better of the two printed, framed, and displayed upon the ledge above the sinks. Seven souls who would not know each other in any different life, and who would probably run and hide if they ever crossed paths in the real world.

Occasionally life vomits and everything is better for it.

One morning Bow woke with a sense of purpose and made an insane decision. Well, perhaps not insane, but well off the pavement. This thought rose from some uncharted region where every purpose was subject to fine-edged inspection, followed by acute suspicion, ending with abject dismissal.

This was not the case, however. He did not cower or spurn the idea, though neither did he embrace it. If there was any motive at all, perhaps the desire to hear it all spread and exposed, from subjective onset to subjective end made the most sense. Maybe the end had not yet appeared in full amplitude. Regardless, he believed he was prepared for this dubious excursion should the required assurances be met.

He called Martinez on a Friday morning.

"How do you usually spend your Monday mornings?" Bow asked.

"Recovering from an orgy of athletic competition," he answered. "Which translates to as little as I can get away with."

"Would you like to have coffee Monday, say about eight-thirty or nine, unless that's too early?"

Martinez answered with a hint of curiosity in his voice. "No, eight-thirty would be fine. Where?"

"Here. Jimmy's, if that's okay."

"Won't you be closed?"

"That's the idea."

Monday morning at eight twenty-five Martinez saw Bow through the window and gently rapped on the door to get his attention. Bow let him in and they sat at one of the far booths. The table was already decked with mugs, coffee—regular and decaf—and an assortment of embellishments.

Martinez drank his coffee black with two sugars. "If it's too strong I add hot water," he remarked. "This is perfect."

Bow had already prepared his concoction and reheated it.

"Why is diner coffee always better?" Martinez asked. "Better grade?"

"No, we use the cheapest stuff we can get. Probably because we scrub the urns after every batch and don't let the coffee sit long enough to get bitter. 'Course we go through it pretty fast."

"So. Any specific reason you called this meeting?"

Bow deadpanned. “I’ve been playing a lot of badminton and am thinking about turning pro.”

Martinez nodded affirmatively. “Have to move to Thailand for that.”

“I’ve already got the shirt.”

Martinez poured a tad more to warm his coffee. “Eddie Lee?” This was said kindly, with no trace of accusation.

Bow began hesitantly. “In a way. I’ve never tried to articulate any of this. I may not be able to. I want to see if I can. And there are conditions.”

“Sure,” Martinez said agreeably.

“No publication until I tell you. Not right away.”

“You leaving?”

“I don’t have a specific plan, but probably. I’ve got to make some decisions about the next step—where do I go from here? What do I do?”

“I understand.” He pulled a small voice recorder from his pocket and discreetly placed it on the table. He put it off to the side where it wouldn’t be in the way.

Bow saw it and froze for a moment but soon faced forward again. “Where to start.”

“Doesn’t matter. Wherever you want.”

He took a breath and a beat. “There is so much. I thought I had a slam-dunk. I really did coast. In hindsight I should have pushed the cops more. It was all too neat and tidy. I’m not sure Eddie Lee even knew the hamper was there.”

“Were there any fingerprints on the knife?”

“Not on the handle. Nowhere.”

“A frame.”

“A little one, yeah, but I should’ve seen it.” He sniffed back the beginnings of a summer cold. “But the biggest thing is that disc from Duke. I meant what I said back then. I never saw it.”

“You think you were set up?”

“Oh no. Not deliberately. I think the package was set aside and forgotten until all hell broke loose. I think my assistant didn’t do her job. I didn’t get any of the follow-up calls, either. I did get a voicemail from up there mentioning the *package* but ignored it. I didn’t know what package he was talking about and thought it was a mistake—or there was something on its way.”

“So that part of it was just sloppiness.”

“More or less, yeah. A lot of that is on me. I’d begun to campaign. I let it ride.”

He felt a measure of disgrace evaporate every time he spoke. Seeming so long ago and not, the recollection had become dark and fetid, noxious and lethal—ingrained in every cell in his body and everything he touched, covering more area by spreading itself so thinly.

He was by no means free, though as more dross escaped, the greater his relief. No hold was so great that it could not be pried or chipped or swept clear, and if moored so securely it would not yield to force, it lifted cleanly, crest to root, through longing.

Martinez quietly said, “She won her primary.”

At first Bow did not make the connection. “When was it?”

“Last week. Next will be the general election.”

“What a farce,” he said bitterly. “She won’t get in. She’s a sacrificial lamb.”

"Why do you care?" he asked. He continued before Bow could respond. "She ran over your toes with a tank. Now she's taking your spot?"

"I don't care about the politics any more. I didn't care even when I was stupid."

"You cared about something."

He calmed himself. "I did a good job."

Martinez waited before continuing. "What else?"

Bow fell silent. Wisely, Martinez let him steep until he came around on his own. Finally, he raised his eyes and in them were the ills of several lifetimes, and more than he could bear.

"I didn't know what happened to Eddie Lee in prison," he said softly. "Prison isn't the school dance. It isn't supposed to be. But he couldn't take it. He never came around. It killed him."

"But some of that is his own fault. You didn't create his personality, or how he looked at things. You didn't teach him right and wrong. That part of it is on him."

"Maybe," he said. "But he shouldn't have been there in the first place, at least not for murder. And when he got out...I had no idea how damaged he was. And look what it cost me—all of us. He was shady, okay, but he wasn't a killer when he went in. That's what happens when a big part of you dies. The part left behind wants to kill."

Martinez allowed Bow to sort all the pieces. Then he spoke gently, as if to a child.

"Your daughter moved away."

His brows lowered and his eyes narrowed. This was an intrusion. He didn't respond angrily, however. "You've done your homework."

"I didn't involve anyone else," he said in defense. "Most of it I found on the internet. I didn't even have to ask anyone questions."

Bow slowly nodded. He wasn't sure what any of this meant. "You know anything else?"

"Not really. Her husband got a job in Charlotte. Whether he got transferred or they moved on their own, I don't know. Like I said, I didn't talk to anybody about it. Didn't feel I had the right."

"You're a reporter. You don't need the right."

"Well, I didn't want to poop in the shower. I'm weird that way."

"I believe you. Want some more coffee?"

The ultimate irony, (*le pisser deluxe*) about inescapable and insistent momentum—especially after facing oblivion, then realizing a reformation rising from misfortune, dragging its putrid trail behind it—is the new heart must seek well-being in people, places, and conditions far removed from those key to recovery, just as those who sponsored or shared the initial wounds. When everything broken knits and heals, the outwardly familiar is yet changed.

The transitional—like the old--must also be stripped and buried in order for any new endeavor to root and thrive. Nothing of any past substance may intrude into accomplishment or the impenetrable darkness recently eschewed can rise again. Though a mended leg may be more fit, treading much the same as before, its owner's instinct will be to shun anything perceived as akin to the source of injury, even in healing.

Sadly, perhaps cruelly so, the healer is yet a reminder of the affliction.

No one of prior familiarity can play a part in this affirmation, except for the motivation they have already provided, and the recognition of and enduring dedication to their heartfelt contributions.

Any parting of the ways with those who gave solace with no expectation of recompense, can be particularly heartrending. Yet despite all selfless nobility, those who bind the wounds as their primary function can rarely assume any other role once done. The passion of understanding cannot be maintained, though affection may remain. As outcomes move from shadow, the same treatments are no longer effective. Every ending—no matter how afflictive it is in its own right; and certainly regrettable—is still a necessary ending.

This new heart, or at least that part of the inner self named the heart, may intermittently grieve the loss of what was for a time. The initial trauma, with all its trial and tragedy, has faded. The ruin, whether slight or excruciating, had waned like the settling sun, fever and blister settling into dusk.

The nostalgic awareness of transformation may be of benefit but cannot be revisited. Regardless of benefit—and the definite potential of new vitality, however long it takes—there is such longing in any growing distance from the awful familiar that the infection can seem more painful than the original blows.

Of course there is a sensible, common optimism made easy. What is current, having been the thrust of a new foundation, a novel competence, and the means to persist and expand, as it is well-grounded and unblemished, must continue without the harassment of the past, as well as the hands of endearment and respite, and must also serve to dissuade any retreat.

This is the only true rebirth.

Bow began to search for employment away from Port Royal.

This particular Monday had a promising beginning. Bow craved a fat chicken sandwich, and during his run he listed the ingredients in his head. As his mind meandered, he looked toward the river. Suddenly a strip of orange light gleamed through the trees. He stopped and moved to get a better view. He had seen sunrises before on his runs and greeted them with more satisfaction in their consistency than appreciation for their elegance.

Now he looked with eyes wide open. A bank of white clouds hovered above the horizon, and beneath them, heaven had gone blue and orange. The blue was so soft it blanched at its edges, and the orange was a liquid version of autumn leaves. The sun had not yet appeared but had announced its coming with temperate grandeur. This is the world dreamt of—the world without privation. He lingered until the brash orb stuck its crown above the skyline, and off he went again.

As he cooled down, breathing more evenly and walking the area between the trailer and the parking lot, he felt the buzz in his pocket and retrieved his phone. He had a message, odd so early in the day. Probably a sales pitch or misdial.

Darlene. Hysterical. Shrieking as if the whole earth was deaf and asleep. "Junior's hurt, Bow. It's bad. We're taking him to the hospital now!"

The call had come thirty minutes before. They would be at the hospital by now. He changed into jeans and a shirt without showering, and rocketed his motorcycle across the parking lot.

Junior had been excessively fussy that morning. He rubbed his ears, probably an infection, and whined non-stop. Darlene's mother had grown accustomed to every mood and every change of mood, but on this morning she was recovering from a night of too much beer and not enough food (or will). After retrieving the juice carton from the refrigerator, this accented by a particularly shrill wail from the boy, she slammed the refrigerator door closed in exasperation.

She hadn't realized Junior was so close with his arm in the way. The door snapped the bones like twigs. She heard the sharp sound and the scream, and was sick to her stomach.

They were nowhere to be found when Bow reached the emergency room. Junior had been admitted. Bow made his way to the children's ward and found the room. He slowed and moved quietly to the open doorway. A nurse was preparing to leave. He saw Darlene rocking the boy. Both sets of eyes were closed and he followed the nurse outside.

"How is he?" he whispered.

"He'll be fine," she said calmly. "It was a clean break. Easy to set. Should be as good as new. He had a little bump on his head, too, and the doctor wanted to keep him for a night just to be on the safe side."

"Thanks," he said as she moved away. He returned to the room and stood outside the doorway. He did not feel misplaced but did not want to disturb them. Junior slept on his mother's chest, his small arm in a cast, the opposing thumb in his mouth. The chair rocked gently, though Darlene seemed to sleep as well. He remained silent, and if she was aware of his presence, she did not respond.

They were alone in the room. Grandma wasn't there. He decided to leave them in peace. Perhaps he could write a note and leave it at the desk. Before he turned, Darlene sighed. She did not open her eyes or make any other sound. And as he waited, he watched.

She did not seem fractious or panicked. She did not seem weary or threadbare. She did not even seem to be relieved. She appeared purposeful. Perhaps there was no inherent prowess to motherhood. At that moment, however, Darlene embodied that and more.

This may not have been her *dream*, as she had described—her touchstone to satisfaction and accomplishment. This may not have been an aha moment where every errant fraction moved to form a whole. This was not emblematic of every ambition she had carried within but not expressed.

Maybe it was a reckoning—a better state of personhood. A revelation of goodness. An untaken road to meaning and the onset of a love she had craved but had never imagined.

He left silently, leaving them to the unfamiliar aspects of profound bliss.

Twenty-Six

When the heart ceases to beat, regardless of the cause, and remains dormant until all electrical impulses end, and the blood stops flowing, and no attempt at resuscitation is made, or is made and fails, we are clinically dead. Our bodies have succumbed to ischemic injury. Within a minute—less actually—the brain also fails and all tissue loses function in preparation to decay. The brain, that extraordinary globe of thought and thoughtlessness, has one final illusion to perform. There is a mighty surge of impulses—like some mental orgasm—where the mind is hyper-focused and inordinately sharp.

This action, lasting mere moments, renders all things sublime. Every imagined person or place or event seen or dreamt of comes into view with absolute clarity and every memory is fresh and unencumbered—even those of chaos and calamity.

One final valedictory accomplishment before the last tone of humanity is ended.

No matter the elements of faith or superstition, or cultural conviction or expectation, no one truly knows the aftermath. Thus, the advent of faith, superstition, familial influence, and impulse. Any or all of these may be true. At the very least they provide comfort when the weight of mortality becomes unbearable.

Few seek to hasten the end. Even those tormented by illness, hunger, loneliness, homelessness, and the lack of resources, seek solace in death east of the last resort. They stubbornly cling to this world without any prospects for betterment or even conciliation.

Many claim to know all the reasons we can not, will not, or do not view our own termination kindly. We have family and friends who love us and are loved by us, who inspire and share gladness.

The everyday business of life leaves us breathless to persevere; to enjoy our surroundings, to benefit from knowledge, and even tolerate those trials that might test us or make us stronger.

We do not wish to abandon any of these experiences. We wish to continue, to persist, to inhale life in any state—to clench the binds with desperate strength.

All estimable moments are sufficient to cling to the continuation of flesh-and-bone. Yet perhaps we overlook the greatest (and simplest) motivation of all.

We simply do not want to miss anything.

No matter its effect on us, we look forward to the events every new day brings. If these are hostile, we may shrink, but if these must rise in order for more fruitful hours to appear, we do all we can to withstand and overcome. We delight in the prospect of new, unexpected circumstances, cower from every perceived threat and reproach.

Because we are yet alive.

Enshrouded in pall, cowed by circumstance, tempered by moments when the common becomes grand and the grand becomes glorious, nothing else matters.

We don't want to miss a single moment, or occasion, or experience, or breath.

Bow was as neurotically protective as a new father. The Pope was amused but chose to give him every consideration.

"You've ridden before," he said for the third time.

"I had a bike years ago. An old, fat guy's bike. A Goldwing."

"Watch the throttle. It sticks if you try to punch it."

"No problem."

"And don't speed shift. The clutch won't take it."

"Just looking forward to a nice little cruise," the Pope said. The helmet was too small but going bareheaded did not bother him. He started the cycle and let it idle.

As Bow raised another issue, the Pope revved the engine, drowning him out. He waited and tried to make his point again. The engine revved again. He raised his hand, an emphatic finger pointing skyward and tried to shout above the noise. The Pope leaned on the throttle.

Finally, he conceded and waved him off. The Pope clicked into first and moved away—speed shifting through the first three gears across the parking lot.

Bow closed his eyes and bared his teeth. The Pope pulled into the street. He listened until he could no longer hear the roar. Probably, long after.

Daylight was fresh. Bow went for his run. Traffic was light, commuters hunched over their breakfasts, tourists still abed.

The Pope hit old U.S. 21, the road to the barrier islands,. He was not much of an explorer. In all the years he'd lived in Port Royal, he'd never owned a car, nor had he ventured farther than fifty miles in any direction. He was unconcerned about getting lost. He had been there before.

Every two-lane road in this part of the state looked alike. Unless a change of color or texture in the asphalt, not much variation existed. Dirt was red-brown. Trees were mostly conifers. No one sought to change anything.

He was content to cruise. He cut through the sea of air with a look of satisfaction, if not overt pleasure.

He didn't think of anything specific. He spent most of his energy thinking about the world as it was. He was not a half-empty—half-full person. What he enjoyed filled a shot glass. What he disliked but tolerated filled a gallon jug. What he hated filled the ocean. At times it was all he could do to open his eyes.

He hadn't ridden in over twenty years. The thrum of the engine and the wheels on the road did not spawn memories as much as the feeling of absolute aloneness. This is what he craved, though at times could also be found in glass, jug, and ocean. Regardless, he had grown weary of grief long ago.

A man may have to smile to be content but not to function at his highest mental capacity.

As he neared St. Helena Island he saw a trio of sweetgum trees. Sweetgum lumber is reddish and prized for plywood. These did not blend with the pines and palmettos. They stood before and apart. Sweetgum leaves have five points and seed pods everywhere. The pods were round and covered with spikes, like blowfish spawn. Each pod contained as many as fifty winged seeds which would flit away as the pods fell to the ground and opened. The locals called them monkey balls.

The trees were in full canopy and overlapping. The trunks of each were so close together they appeared conjoined. An adult could not squeeze between them. They commandeered at least sixteen hundred square feet and looked like the friendly green hydra in a fairy tale.

Once in the confines of the island proper, he slowed as he passed the old oak tree spanning the road where the legendary End Light orb was said to dwell, eerily hovering in the dark, some restive spirit haunting the space—a lorn lover, a forgotten soldier or harried slave. No matter, the sun bushed brightly now, the ghost at rest.

He parked near the path and walked to the shore, the sand wet on his shoes, the slope shallow at low tide. He and his wife had found this place years ago on a rare vacation to Hilton Head when they had been at peace together. She had just been promoted. He had just started the old shop. She had chosen this time to tell him he was going to be a father.

He had returned to this place upon first landing nearly a decade before. He had thought then to walk into the depths and drown himself. Now, he simply watched the immortal sea.

This had been an idle Monday. Burning charcoal colored the air. Some son-of-the-Confederacy had come home late from work only to have Ma'am inform him she had promised young Beau and Belle homegrown hot dogs. Bratwurst was for Yankees.

Bow carried two large glasses of sweet tea over ice, a thin wedge of lemon floating at the top. A hummingbird tapped the feeder they had installed at the corner of the trailer. A stray cat mewled as it crossed the empty parking lot. Bow looked to make sure the dumpster lid was closed. He put the glasses on the erstwhile table between the Adirondack chairs and looked about.

He found him beyond the brush, standing on a flat rise overlooking the river. He approached the ledge and looked outward. The river glittered in the last remnants of the day, clasping its hand over the corporeal. There were indistinguishable noises heard, seagulls diving as wraiths and the bay beyond shimmering as a withering mirage.

When he looked aside, the Pope wore a mask he did not recognize, nor could he describe. Had he been compelled, he would have said it was a look of longing, but for what, he could not say. What the Pope ever saw was impossible to gauge and he did not pursue it.

"Got tea back at the chairs," he offered.

The Pope did not speak nor look nor move except for the unmeditated blinking of his eyelids, and then, infrequently. Finally, he said, (in a voice so slight it did not disrupt the air),

"Do you know how old this river is?"

Bow remained patient, though perplexed. "No."

"The water has been here a hundred and fifty million years. It became the river about twelve thousand years ago during the last ice age."

He waited, expecting more to come. "Long time."

"Can you imagine what the world will be like in twelve thousand years?"

"I can't imagine what it will be like next week," he said in jest. The joke floated away in a hush.

"We are lent to time. A few, brief seconds. That's all there really is."

"Yeah?"

This time the quiet was not so serene, but hungry, waiting to be filled. After a few seconds, he glanced again at his friend. The Pope remained motionless except that his lower lip trembled slightly—undiscoverable unless focused upon in doubt.

Bow looked away to check his imagination, but knew what he had seen was real. With one final glance he saw a stray tear flicker on the big man's cheek.

He once more looked straight ahead, though now bereft, incapable of comprehending the moment, as a child might. He became afraid, but of exactly what, he could not say. He could not question nor could he speak, and time lingered in benign fret.

Finally, the Pope retrieved a handkerchief from his pocket and discreetly wiped his face. He returned to the same precise position as before.

"I guess I'm just tired," he said simply.

The Pope laid the spread then left. He didn't appear until everyone had eaten. He was clear-eyed and his Neanderthal head was rock-solid. He spoke kindly in rimless tones and without any hint of discomfort. If anything was amiss, no one noticed, except he seemed world-weary. Nothing a couple days off wouldn't cure.

His voice was gentler than usual, musical, though *andante* rather than *allegro*. People suspected he had a sore throat, maybe a touch of hay fever.

"I have come to believe that time is an abstract concept. It only exists as a point of reference. It has no other function. Hours, minutes. Months and years. Decades and centuries. These simply measure the distance between daylight and darkness on a continuous basis.

"It takes photons eight minutes to reach from the sun to earth but a million years for them to wriggle to the surface. We bathe in ancient light

"Yet because we change as we grow older, and our lives are temporary, we are always aware of time. We may be grateful for it, we may hate it, we may wonder why time seems to pass us by even as we are in the midst of it. We may fear it, knowing we cannot outlive it.

"But also remember this. If we believe in time, then we know shouldn't waste any of it. Because in our world, the time we have is all there is."

"This is why we hope, and hopefully, we prepare ourselves to take advantage of the good when it comes. Hope also gives us the strength to bear any disappointment, even if it becomes obvious our hope is an illusion, or so far from us we will never reach it.

"False hope is only false when we stop, or move on, or leave this world. As long as we can function no hope is truly vain. We hope for a lot, and when we get little, we despair. We hope for a little, and when we get nothing, we despair.

"All I know is that without hope, we insure our own failure.

"When we hope, we must also act to discover its tangibility. We must make a promise to ourselves to seek out possibility and embrace it. We must think about more than just surviving, but of carving out a better life for ourselves. We must make ourselves ready. And when we move beyond the boundaries set for us, we must cross over them so softly no one takes notice.

"Sometimes hope is the only optimism we can muster.

"We are all capable of more. Whatever your demons. Whatever your addiction—even an addiction to misery itself—whatever has always held you fast to the same footprints—you are capable.

"So be ready. Even if you retreat, be strong enough to move forward again. Be more. Work harder to be more. Find something worth the effort to be more. Then stick your toes in the water and never look back."

"Never stop hoping. Never stop moving forward. Never stop trying.

"Live."

Then he gingerly stepped down, and without another word, walked slowly toward the trailer, entered, and closed the door behind him.

Confusion colored the air until Darlene called everyone to help with cleanup and bustle slowly wriggled its way in.

A week later, the Pope took to his bed. He never complained and he never explained. After the first dozen queries of "Are you okay?", and the same glaring response, Bow stopped asking.

One morning the Pope didn't get out of bed at all. Abe was in a panic, or at least a panic for Abe. He bit a deep crease in his cigar. He would go into the kitchen and point at Bow. Debbie would get his attention. He would look and Abe would simply move his eyes to the back door, his way of asking him to check on the Pope.

He had done this a half-dozen times and it wasn't even the supper hour. Afterward, he stopped trying to listen to music. He just listened for Debbie's yell.

The Pope must have foreseen his illness. He had prepared a hundred pounds of ribs, thirty pounds of brisket, sixty pounds of pulled pork, fifty pounds of barbecued chicken, and ten gallons of sauce. All Debbie had to do was pull what she needed from the refrigerator, warm on low, and slather on the sauce over a half hour or so.

The Pope did not leave the trailer or get out of bed as far as anyone knew for the next three days. Everyone was worried.

The next night Bow woke to an eerie silence. Some part of his subconscious knew something was amiss, the way someone who sleep near railroad tracks will wake when a scheduled train runs late. The Pope's bed was empty and he wasn't in the bathroom. Bow stepped out into the calm night. He heard a crash coming from the kitchen inside. He ran through the back door.

The Pope leaned hard against a prep table, both hands keeping him upright. A half dozen deep pans were scattered on the floor. Bow went to him quickly, and as the Pope vehemently told him to stop, Bow picked up the pans and stacked them on the table.

"What's going on with you?" he asked, his voice sharp, more fearful than angry.

"Almost out of everything," the Pope said. He was winded, struggling for breath.

"Tell me," he urged.

The Pope said nothing as he continued to prop up on his hands, his head bowed. His arms were shaking as if under a tremendous weight.

"I'm calling an ambulance."

"No, wait," the Pope said, grimacing.

"You're in bad shape."

The Pope breathed in through his nose and out through his mouth, steadying himself. "I know what it is. Just leave it alone."

"What is it?"

He faced him fiercely. "Mind your own fucking business!"

Bow didn't back down. "Tell me what's wrong."

The Pope huffed and puffed again and lowered his voice. "Please, Bow. Just let it go—for now."

"Will you at least let me help?"

"Done. You can help me into bed."

The Pope dosed himself with a handful of pills and was still asleep at eleven the next morning when the diner opened. Bow explained to all it was just a bug and chased them away. He went outside with Darlene during a break and huffed a cigarette as if facing a firing squad.

"Something's bad wrong, ain't it?" she asked.

"Yeah. I think so. But he doesn't want to talk or see a doctor."

"What do you think it is?"

He shook his head and lit another smoke in a single motion. "Ruptured disk, maybe. I don't know."

"Wonder why he won't go to the doctor?"

He was afraid to answer. Maybe seeing a doctor wouldn't matter. He made a feeble effort to smile.

"You know how stubborn he is."

An answer, but not *the* answer.

A couple of nights later, Bow was awakened again. This time an empty voice whispered his name. He sat up and turned on the bedside lamp. The light was spectral and spread throughout the space without illuminating anything.

The Pope was in bed, motionless. His eyes were closed and he was obviously fighting against pain. He was clammy and gray, and his voice did not carry much beyond the bed.

"My wallet," he said.

Bow retrieved the wallet from the dresser and handed it to him. He stiffly opened it and pulled out a business card. "Call him."

The card was for a Dr. Chris Bennett. The Corvette man. Written on the back in ink was a cell number. Bow stepped away and punched in the number. The doctor answered on the fourth ring. He, too, spoke in the faded breath of recent waking. "Yes?"

"Dr. Bennett? This is Bowman Carter. You don't know me, but—"

"I'll be right there." Then they were disconnected.

Bow went outside. He was working on his cigarette allotment for three days hence. The convertible pulled up. Dr. Bennett got out, his hair disheveled as if he had driven with the top down. He hadn't. He wore a pullover shirt, shorts, and running shoes. He carried a bag, nodded politely as he passed, and went into the trailer without a word.

Bow paced and smoked. He went inside the diner and filled a plastic glass with ice and soda then returned to his post. No sounds penetrated the trailer walls. Silent as if buried underground. At three a.m. the night was graveyard quiet.

After forty-five minutes Dr. Bennett stepped outside. His face revealed nothing. He greeted Bow with the same practiced smile as before. He tossed his bag in the passenger's seat of his car and returned, nodding at the cigarette.

"Got any more of those?" he asked.

Bow tilted the pack and shook until a filtered end was exposed. The doctor took it delicately between his lips and leaned in for a light.

"He said for me to talk to you."

"Okay," he said hesitantly.

The doctor took a deep drag. "Several of us work the ER on a rotating basis. A few years ago I was on call. It was near the end of the shift so I knew if I didn't get a call soon, I was home free. No call-in that night. I had a couple glasses of wine. Half-hour later, I got called in. On the way,

I swerved to miss a stupid possum and ran into a ditch." He took another puff and exhaled before continuing.

"I wasn't drunk but I was a bit buzzed. I was worried somebody might smell it on me, or mistake being banged up for being impaired. Didn't want to risk it. Didn't want to have to take a field sobriety test. Cops think anything is hinky, they charge you first and figure the rest out later. Every arrest is publicly listed, guilty or not. Could've finished me. I would have ended up giving hernia exams to Nicaraguan soccer players."

He looked toward the trailer.

"He showed just as the cops came. How, I don't know. He talked to the cops. I have no idea what he said, but the next thing I know the police called the hospital, explained I had wrecked in my haste to respond to duty, and to get someone else to work the shift. Funny how such a little detail can fuck up a life."

Bow did not have to imagine to understand. "Yeah." He waited. "What's wrong with him?"

The doctor tossed the cigarette toward the dumpster and missed badly. He walked over and stepped on it far longer than necessary. He gazed at the trailer door. "He has final stage prostate cancer."

"Jesus."

"He's known about it for a long time. Eight, ten years, maybe. Before he came here."

"You're kidding. Treatment didn't work?"

The doctor looked at him solemnly. "He refused treatment."

"What?"

"He has small cell carcinoma—neuroendocrine cancer. The protocol is surgery, radiation, and chemo. The surgery would have been brutal.

Prostate gone, may have even been castrated, gutting him from butt to belly-button. Then get fried with thirty doses or so while taking chemo the same time. Even after all that there are no guarantees of any improvement. So, he walked away. It's a slow-growing cancer most of the time. He'd probably had it before it was diagnosed and didn't know it. A dozen years relatively functional is a long lifespan for no treatment. Too late now."

Bow was incredulous. "Nothing at all?"

"No. Once the cancer starts spreading it accelerates. All I can do is treat the pain."

He had fallen off the ladder. Decisions lead to consequences and some consequences lead to waste, and waste inevitably darkens life. But to forego any chance for a longer life? How could he have done this? He knew but didn't like it. The Pope had chosen to live and die on his own terms.

"What do I do now?"

"He won't recover enough this time to resume his life. He doesn't want anyone else to know. You'll have to cover for him."

"How am I supposed to do that?"

"Say he's got a mild form of meningitis—not contagious, but he'll need to rest a couple of weeks, and he can do that here. No visitors, just to be on the safe side, unless he asks."

"And after a couple of weeks?"

The doctor wore the eyes of an old man who had seen far too much of the world's backside. "By then it won't matter."

Bow found lying to be easy, even to Darlene. Make an illness sound horrible—though potentially recoverable—and everyone is eager to believe.

The Pope gave Bow his sauce recipe. He made more sauce. Not perfectly but acceptably. Debbie had seen the Pope dry rub the meat often enough to wing it. None of the customers complained. Bob pitched in with the dishes and everyone was eager to help, except Abe, who listened to Bow's updates and groaned as if a meteor was headed for Earth.

During this time Bow and the Pope were in near-constant communication but exchanged nothing critical. Sometimes the Pope would ask for a soda. Sometimes for a bowl of cereal. Sometimes water for pain meds. Sometimes to make sure he didn't fall down in the shower. Much of the time they talked about the barbecue sauce.

Bow was grilled daily. Did he measure every single ingredient? Did he add them in the proper sequence? Nothing about the mortality of men.

Late that Wednesday night, Dr. Bennett appeared without being called. The Pope had drugged himself into a deep sleep, his breathing raspy but regular. Bow stepped out as the doctor entered.

Ten minutes later the doctor exited and stretched. "Did you know the word pandiculation means the act of stretching?"

"No, but I have a friend at the newspaper I'm going to try it out on."

"He told me to tell you to stir the sauce before letting it sit."

Bow flashed a weak smile. "I already have."

"Mélange means mixture. Another good word. Bum another smoke?"

He retrieved a pair and both lit up.

"I work a lot of crossword puzzles," the doctor added. He took a long drag. "Won't be long now."

He bit his lower lip hard enough to hurt. "How long?"

"Tonight? Tomorrow? Not long."

"I need to call Darlene and a few of the others."

"He won't want to see them."

He rubbed his forehead and stepped away. "Doesn't matter."

Darlene arrived and leaned into his arms. She sniffled but didn't cry. Neither did she let go. The rest of the staff came at intervals, were told the truth, and stood by at a distance. Abe came long enough to put a *Closed until Further Notice* sign on the door, then left. No one knew how to contact Bob but he made his way there anyway. He prayed silently and crossed himself every few minutes as if to make sure God was constantly aware of the situation.

Bow made coffee and propped open the back door to the diner so people could come and go as needed.

Around midnight a couple from the gathering showed up. Shortly thereafter, more from the gathering appeared. Somehow word was spreading but no one asked how. People showed up Bow didn't recognize. A police officer, a nurse still dressed in scrubs, the low and bedraggled, and people of obvious influence.

Darlene knew a few and whispered details of whatever catastrophe had brought them to the Pope originally. By two a.m. over sixty people huddled in small groups in the parking lot. Occasionally there would be laughter, as someone described an anecdote that hadn't been as funny at the time. Even then, they were respectful. Many were silent.

Dawn broke slowly that morning, enveloping the horizon from end to end before rising, as if the heavens knew the significance of the day. The doctor entered the trailer every twenty minutes or so and all conversation stopped, waiting until he exited, shaking his head as a signal to resume whatever they were doing.

A little after seven the doctor emerged again and whispered to Bow. "He wants to talk to you."

Bow hesitated, rattled, and looked helplessly at Darlene, who smiled through her tears and nodded encouragement. He went in.

The back of the trailer was eerie, the mound in the bed covered by a blanket up to his chin, his chest rising and falling in slow cadence.

He sat in a chair at his bedside. The Pope opened his eyes and looked at him without turning his head. "What horseshit, huh?"

Bow smoothed the blanket where there were no wrinkles. "Yeah, it sucks. Any pain?"

The Pope shook his head. "Got more Oxycodone in me than Black Sabbath."

"Good."

"Really didn't want you to get involved in all this but Abe is going to need a lot of help."

"No problem."

"Everything else is set. I've got a will. I don't own anything but it covers all the details."

"What about the trailer?"

"Abe owns the trailer. Part of my deal."

"Okay."

Bow looked through the walls to the brightening day, though the area about him remained in shadow. "Thank you for saving my life."

"Thank Darlene. This was her idea."

"No. It was always you."

The Pope tried to shift his hips but didn't have the strength. "You know I used to weigh three hundred and fifty pounds? Now I'm down below two hundred. Couldn't keep clothes the right size for long. Finally said screw it. Wore what I had." He slowly closed his eyes and opened them again, as if trying to focus. "Eight years ago I did exactly what you were trying to do. I gave it all up and came here to die. Didn't know it would take this long."

Bow swallowed hard to stifle the emotion, a part of which was irritation. "You could have lived."

The Pope slurred his words. "Statistically, not much," he said in his own inimitable way. "Besides, we both know better. I told you before some people just don't belong in this world. That's the difference between you and me."

Bow sharply wagged his head. "No, no, no, no."

"Listen to me. It's okay. Really. I've been prepared for this."

"Bullshit."

"Truth."

Bow wept. He maintained control of every sense and feeling, but he wept nonetheless, large globules blurring his vision before cascading.

The Pope began again. "You are not like me. You know what it's like to live without questioning your entire existence. You'll get all that back."

"I don't want to go back."

"I'm talking about who you are. You don't have far to go now."

"I don't know what that means."

"It means you are not a failure. Never have been. Never will be. This wasn't an end for you. Just a temporary obstacle. You just didn't see it. I had no future. Not really. I did what I could with the time I had."

"I'm not doing all that great now."

"Maybe not. But you will." He unleashed a dry cough that shook the bed. "I need a favor. I need you to hold things together here for a while. Let everything settle again before you do anything"

"Okay."

The Pope forced a vacant smile. "You wouldn't bullshit a man on his deathbed would you?"

He matched the smile. "I might."

"Good. I knew I could count on you."

The tears flowed more quickly and he couldn't stop them. Death may serve some carnal purpose but in the corporeal now, served no one. The Pope reached a hand from beneath the covers and gripped him at the wrist. Bow placed his free hand atop the others and squeezed.

The Pope labored for a breath before continuing.

"I know you don't believe me, but I'm ready. Things just didn't work out for me. I've spent the past ten years trying to understand why. You know what I learned?"

"No," he whispered.

"There are only two ways to make it in this world. You're either lucky or can accept failure with a smile. Neither applies to me."

All he could believe was the waste of noble virtue. "Would it matter if I think you're wrong?"

"It does. But don't obsess about it. Don't be angry about it, either. We're as different as piss and lemonade, you and me. I had nowhere else to go. There wasn't much more I could do."

He closed his eyes and for a second Bow thought he was gone. Then his eyelids flickered open a final time. "Besides, my life really ended on November eighth, nineteen eighty-three."

“That when you lost your business?”

“No. That’s the first time I heard Madonna refer to herself as an artist.”

Twenty-Seven

The Pope's given name was Ivan Snedeker and he was from a small town on the St. Croix River about a hundred miles from Eau Claire, Wisconsin. The St. Croix is a tributary of the Mississippi. Bow smiled knowingly when he learned the name. The Pope's father had given the Nazis a final *dans ton cul* by naming his son after the Russian who had let him go.

He was cremated privately, as per his wishes, and his ashes given to Darlene. She was to scatter them on the river. This was illegal but all she said was, "Who gives a Jenny Junkjacker about that?" She had lost her savior, mentor, and friend. She decided to hold a final gathering the following Sunday and scatter his ashes then.

Surprisingly, only Bow and Darlene were to be present at the reading of the will. Others were affected but not materially in the final record. Ivan—the Pope—bequeathed his remaining cash, two thousand dollars plus, to Darlene, for unforeseen expenses. His clothes, books, and all other personal items determined to have any value, were to be donated to the local homeless shelter, as once many years ago, he had used a bed there for a couple of weeks.

He also left the key to his dominion to Darlene—his sauce recipe. No one could make more sauce without her. She was humbled but didn't know what good it would do her. Bow knew otherwise.

To Bow he left the contents of his trunk with the following note: "You may not be able to do anything. But you can do more than I ever did." Bow's curiosity would now be satisfied, though he had lost the desire.

Darlene became the sauce progenitor, keeping the recipe close at hand until she had memorized it to the dram. Debbie could do everything else until a new cook was hired. Darlene asserted she should be paid a royalty for the sauce. Abe disagreed. She advised him to make his own fucking sauce. He offered her a hundred bucks a week off the books for preparing the sauce. She accepted.

She also asked the radio station to be changed, but was denied.

Darlene wanted to be present when the foot locker was opened but Bow put her off. She had seen him depressed, chewed up and regurgitated by anguish, as haunted as the gatekeeper of Hell itself, even irked and irritated. She had never seen him as dog-dejected as he was now. She stroked his arm and left him alone.

Bow tossed the lock on the bed and opened the lid.

Inside he found four packs of Dunhill cigarettes in a carton and he tossed those on the dinette table for eventual consumption. There was a cigar box with a dozen or so photographs. One was of Ivan standing outside the Pipe & Page. He had indeed been huge then, with a Humpty-Dumpty waist and belt sashed beneath his man-boobs. He had a full head of sandy hair, parted on the side, and that same smirk that said he knew too much for his own good.

There were several pictures of his daughter, none beyond the age of seven. Even then she was headed in his direction with chubby cheeks and a double chin. There were newspaper clippings from his wedding announcement, his daughter's birth announcement, his divorce, and the brief obits of both parents.

There was a small ad for a going-out-of-business sale. These were all in a tray. He removed the tray to get to the bottom.

Wrapped in a pillow case were four large binders, all filled beyond capacity. Each bore a title though no dates. Bow kept them in order until he realized the one on the bottom was the oldest. He opened the first.

A manuscript. He read the first few paragraphs. A novel. He quickly scanned all four. They were all manuscripts. He moved to the sofa to read on.

The four comprised a science-fiction series about life on a distant space station told from the perspective of the drudges—those who performed the menial tasks such as cleaning, minor repairs, fetching and delivering supplies, and the like. Even with the greatest technology ever

produced, shit jobs still had to be done.

The setting was not completely original and the story was short on plot. No phaser battles, wormholes, or eminent discoveries in deep space. Just the same types of people who run the world at various levels. The Pope's voice rang in his ears as members of the vanguard were subjected to the most exacting analysis by their subordinates, often, laugh-out-loud funny.

The characters were clever and cleverly constructed. Some were typical—even stereotypical. The loose-lipped who always gossiped. The oblivious leaders who couldn't get out of their own way. The plotters and back-stabbers looking to scale a few rungs, but who were often thwarted.

People on the make. The wise bartender, the reverend who drank too much, and a handful of earnest, untainted men and women who saw the good in everyone.

Many of these were also aliens.

A freighter pilot who was a swarthy red, almost black. The more he drank, the paler he became. A lady-for-hire who had the same features as a desirable humanoid woman but also had six breasts aligned the same way as most four-legged mammals, and was able to inflate them on demand for heightened pleasure.

A kid training to be a maintenance apprentice, barely three-feet tall and pinker than a rose, with spiky hair paler than his skin, and enlarged black eyes—and who made filthy puns in eighteen languages—only two of which were from Earth.

The story also told of how future technologies might rapidly evolve but people remained much the same. All creatures were grossly *human*—even when not—especially in their more suspect behaviors. Many were stronger, more intelligent, had greater intuitive abilities, or were more rational, but none were beyond being a source of humor. Everyone, from every habitable planet within reach, had evolved much the same. And there were no sentient species so alien as to be unrecognizable.

Bow spent two weeks reading all four books. They were delightful even to someone who was not a true sci-fi aficionado. All were well-written in simple language and all the characters were genuine. Riches were won and lost, hearts were filled and broken, sports still commanded attention, as did fun and games, and politics still ruined things.

And, as always, whimsically funny, the spirit of the Pope peering out from the pages.

Bow had absolutely no idea what to do with them.

The last gathering was to feed and scatter, both the ashes and the attendees afterward. This would be a genuine parting at least for a time. Darlene had organized the food and prodded Bow into a eulogy.

Far more people than usual showed, an indication of the Pope's prominence. Darlene fretted they might run out of food. As people moved down the buffet line, Bow was greeted by smiles and the speaking of his name. He did not know how everyone knew him but these were not false civilities, and certainly not indictments.

After everyone served themselves, they clustered in a loose arc around the stump and all eyes were upon him. He nervously stepped up and the whole area became so quiet a bunny fart could be heard.

"We all lost a great friend. Even more, we have all benefitted from his generosity in some way. He either got us out of a jam, or helped us over a hump, or helped us find a job, or a place to live. Why would he do this? I think it was simple. Because he could. He could, so he did. And that's what he wanted for us.

"In many ways, I never really understood him. But I would like to follow his example, though I will never be able to do everything he did. He had a sense about these things and the capacity to figure solutions. And that can never be replaced. If I have learned anything from him, it's that doing nothing accounts for a lot of misery in this world. And he did what he could to plug the holes before things got out-of-hand. He made us all believe a helping hand still existed.

"So many people out there who are completely unaware of him, and what he accomplished, are able to live their lives as part of an unfeeling world because he filled the gaps they ignored. They do not know how close they may have been to disaster because he stepped in when they did not. Maybe they need to know. Maybe it would have been better had their lives also exploded in some way, but it didn't really matter to him. He did what he did, anyway..

"Regardless, he helped those he saw close-up, and the people he saw the clearest were the people who needed him the most.

"The world might never change, even when the worst happens. Pain does not always create kindness in people. But we who loved him will miss him terribly. So let us pass it on in whatever way we can. That is the way we thank him. That is the only way he would want to be remembered."

They moved in twos and threes to the shelf above the river and fanned out. Darlene stepped forward carrying a large stainless steel milk pitcher in both hands, cradling it to her chest. She had borrowed it from the diner. She intended to wash and return it when she was done. Abe would never miss it in the interim.

Her eyes were bloodshot and her nose was running. She said nothing as she poured the ashes over the water. Some sailed and disappeared. Most fell straight down and floated on the surface until they mingled and swirled away.

Oh beautiful, for spacious skies, for amber waves of grain.

A beautiful tenor voice, so mellow and breathy it seemed to spring from the open air. Everyone looked around. It was Bob. His English was near-perfect with only a trace of accent.

For purple mountains majesty, above the fruited plain.

By this time everyone joined in, singing with eyes aloft as if God had delivered the song upon the wafting wind.

America, America, God shed his grace on thee

And crown thy good, with brotherhood

From sea to shining sea..."

As people departed, offering gentle good-byes, Bob gathered the trash and leftover food.

"You've been sandbagging us, haven't you, Bob?" Bow said.

The small man shrugged. "It seemed appropriate."

A few moments later Darlene pulled Bow to the side, clinging to the pitcher as if it was solid silver. She wore a strange little smile and her eyes were wide and manic, like someone who had had too little sleep and too much coffee. She spoke quietly so no one else could hear.

"Oh my God, Bow. You won't believe what I done."

He felt a familiar sense of dread. "What?"

"I put some of his ashes in the sauce."

His head pulled back involuntarily. "You did what?

"I know. I know."

"Why in God's name would you do that?"

"No idea. Just did it."

"Jesus, Darlene."

"Should I tell everybody?"

"Hell, no. Just pray no one ends up in the emergency room."

Abe allowed Bow to stay in the trailer. He had become the designated (but unpaid) kitchen organizer. Darlene kept making sauce but jabbered throughout the process, asking for this and that—getting in everyone's way, pushing and shoving and reaching, until everyone's patience had worn thin.

Bow kept the peace, organizing set-up, maintaining the flow, even telling Darlene to shut up when it became necessary, and, of course, keeping the dishes clean. Abe didn't even charge him rent.

He had come starkly awake in the small hours of night with a plan. Not much of a plan as plans go, but a plan. In fact, this was probably the worst possible plan he could have devised but the idea had come so boldly and clearly he wanted to see if he was nuts.

Of course, he also had no other ideas. The only thing he had going for him was a notoriety quickly fading from memory.

He got the contact numbers for the Managing Editors, or Senior Editors, or whoever made most of the decisions as to what got published, for sixteen companies. A few were imprints of other larger companies.

He called them all. He asked for these people by name. He got none of them. A few assistants would not even allow him to leave a voicemail. As for the dozen who did, he left an identical message.

"My name is Bowman Carter. I am the District Attorney from North Carolina who wrongly convicted Eddie Lee Edwards, and whose family he destroyed. I have a book I'd like you to read. Please call me if you're interested." He left his number.

Out of the twelve, five returned his call. Out of the five, four responded somewhat brusquely when they discovered the book was not about the trial or its aftermath. Only one, an imprint of an imprint of one of the publishing giants was willing to read the book. He packaged the first manuscript and sent it in. A month passed before he heard anything.

When the woman called she did not sound overly-enthusiastic. "I don't suppose you would even consider doing a book about your—situation. You wouldn't even have to write it. We could handle that for you."

"No. At least not now."

"Thought as much." She paused, as if for effect. "It's a decent piece. Funny," she said, with no levity in her voice. "You said you're willing to promote it."

"Yes."

"You know what will happen."

"Yes."

"Can you handle it?"

"Yes."

"Hopefully, you can manage to steer the conversation to the book. I'm not convinced. But if you are willing to put yourself out there and let people know who you are, and let me have the piece without an advance, I'll publish it."

The publisher changed the title. The Pope had titled the series *It's Not My Job*. This was changed to *The Sky Is Always Clear In Space.* Bow began his part on local radio and TV.

Naturally, what everyone expected to happen, happened. Every interview began with questions about the Eddie Lee case. Bow grew weary of the repetition early on but he plunged ahead admirably. The memories scraped scars that needed new stitches but he was soon able to respond by rote, and always answered in the third person.

In most cases, he was able to work back around to the book. He never referred to the Pope as the Pope, nor did he elaborate on their association. The Pope became Mr. Snedeker and their acquaintance was attributed to a friendship during Bow's ongoing healing process.

Also, and sadly still in most cases, the interviewer had not read the text, or if so, misunderstood the symbolism or context. Some of the questions and comments were so insipid they made it difficult for him to maintain.

"Where is the book's setting?"

"A space station."

"And where is that?"

"In space."

Sales were slow in the beginning. Bow asked Martinez to revise his article, leaning more toward his exodus and how he had spent the past year. Included was much about the Pope, concluding with the book.

Martinez agreed and the article was finally published. Whatever happened to that guy who...? Within two days the story was picked up by major newspapers in South Carolina, North Carolina, and Georgia. In two weeks the feel-good entertainment shows shared the story. Soon the story was on every wire service and every news organization of note—and on every major website.

Bow's tragedy had become a marketing success. The book made the bestseller lists. HIs travels expanded. The story became about the disgraced lawyer who sent an innocent man to prison, and how he was shunned, and how an unpublished writer named Ivan Snedeker helped him recover. This series of events took on a life of its own but the Pope's book was always the culmination, as if the book had helped Bow reclaim his sanity. He appeared on all the national talk shows.

Few of the hosts or hostesses were over thirty and had only cursory frames of reference for what was readable. Morning-after-agonizing-morning Bow patiently answered questions and listened to irrelevant observations without shooting anyone.

Once sales accelerated, the publisher did an excellent job of putting Bow and the book cover in the faces of more and more people with far more extensive exposure. Certain responses became so common Bow could have written them on his forehead.

"Why are you promoting this book?"

"Because the author is dead and he was my friend."

"Will there be more?"

"Uh, he's dead."

"Oh. Right."

Of course, in this case there were more. Three more actually, but Bow sat on this information.

On one particular day, Bow was to appear on the highest-rated morning show on commercial television. The primary host was a young woman who had been hired away from the morning show in Seattle, and who had become universally endearing because she snorted when she laughed—and she laughed a lot. The world's pain was nowhere to be found at seven a.m. She wore an ever-present smile as if her cheeks had been sewn to the nape of her neck. Her modified pixie haircut had become the current rage and she wore contacts so dark blue she seemed on the verge of mutating at any moment.

Predictably, and grievously so, she wanted to make her mark by going against the grain.

As Bow waited in the green room, he heard her shouting down the hall at someone to "fix the fucking lights so I don't look like a ghost, or you'll be looking for another job!" Finally, during a commercial, he was called. They were soon live.

"A couple of things about the book," she said, her teeth on solar flare.

"Sure," he replied. The lights and the hour made him squint, so he looked over her shoulder to make it appear as if they shared eye contact.

"I found the general behavior of the main characters a little bit...unrealistic."

"How so?"

"Well, they're supposed to be smart but they all act a little... goofy."

"That's the point. Just because people get smarter, and technology improves, doesn't mean we become more serious or more competent. People's foibles don't change much. Plus, it's satire."

"Yes, but some of the more—negative—aspects of these characters are worse than they are now."

"I think he's saying that if we don't become more caring now, we won't be any better then. It's not an automatic part of growth."

"I'm not sure I agree."

"I understand."

"Americans always step up when people are in need."

"In a crisis, yes. What he's saying is under normal circumstances, people tend not to act until something affects them personally."

"Well, I don't agree with that at all."

"That's okay. As I said, it's satire."

"Nearly everyone I know spends a lot of time with causes."

"Okay."

She looked to the audience. "I mean, we all pitch in to take care of the less fortunate, right?" The audience wildly applauded.

He waited until the applause died down. "You do Alzheimer's fund-raisers, don't you?"

She perked up. "Yes, I do."

"Your father has Alzheimer's, doesn't he?"

Her smile drooped from force of habit. "Yes. He does."

"Were you involved before he was diagnosed?"

Her eyes became as cold as agates. "Well, not as much as I am now."

"That's all he's saying."

After the segment, she shook his hand and whispered, "Don't expect to ever be on this show again."

He nodded, weary from lack-of-sleep and jet lag.

"Let's hope not."

As things turned out, this, too, became a boon. The interview went viral. Her show's competitors were gloating, praising her talent with perfect smiles but delighting in her discomfiture when the camera lights dimmed.

The sci-fi geeks got into the act based upon the more obvious aspects of the book. The film rights were sold and foreign language rights were obtained. Once at the top of the bestseller lists, the bandwagoners and the simply curious dived in.

By the end of the first year, the book had made the cover of *Time*—a lovely article about a major literary talent now gone from us, lost to the ages.

Bow hired an agent and met with the publisher, revealing the existence of three sequels. A dozen years passed before the money finally slowed to a trickle. After the success of the movie, everything the first book earned, and with the rights and advances for the next three books, Arthur Bowman Carter III, had become one of the uber-rich.

By the time the series was finished, more than a decade hence, those simple stories had sold nearly a hundred million copies, and had spawned four films and a television series.

In death, Ivan Snedeker had finally become what he should have been.

Bob was actually Valentin Romero. He had fled Argentina with his wife and son when its economy was near collapse. In Argentina he had been a mechanical engineer. He had been denied refugee status and ordered to leave when his visa expired. He hadn't left. He was smart enough to know an INS agent did not lurk behind every Anglo face, but had no other prospects.

Bow helped him obtain a work visa and a job as a maintenance man in a bagel plant, keeping the machinery in working condition and lovers of Polish doughnuts in fine fettle. Soon Valentin would secure a green card, and eventually his family would become Americans. The world would miss a great busboy.

Bow bought Jimmy's for Darlene. Abe sold on the condition he could remain as cashier though he did this without pay. He still wouldn't let Darlene pick the radio station even after she installed a new sound system. New servers and kitchen crew were hired. Levetra stayed on, as did Debbie, but Marvelette had returned to law school. Darlene always asked each potential employee if they intended to remain the gender they were, or if they swore without thinking, or if they went apeshit when touched, legal or not to do so.

Darlene was smart enough to learn. She hired kids to give out small samples of barbecue at the grocery stores, especially when the snow birds invaded and were flush. She advertised and ran specials—the most successful being Wednesday all-you-can-eat wings for five dollars. Every

Chubbo, Chubesse, and Chubling appeared and insured the diner lost money on Wednesdays but when people saw the line into the parking lot, they assumed something memorable was afoot.

In a few years Jimmy's was remodeled and enlarged, including patio dining, screened and bugless, and romantically illuminated. Also, central heat and air. She started a catering unit and soon had every carnivore in three counties overdosing on sweet meat.

She had even been approached about marketing the sauce to retailers.

Darlene had found her dream. If anyone could be said to have graduated, she had. She kept the name Jimmy's for good luck and Bow always had a table of his own, though he usually ate in the kitchen or got take-out.

She never took full custody of Junior but spent more-and-more time with him as he got older. She ran the diner with the same frenzied energy as Ahab employed on the Pequod. She bought a home. Bow helped her set up investment accounts. She shared the wealth. Though the gatherings ended, everyone who had known the Pope now knew Darlene as the facilitator—and anyone in need was directed to her.

Every year on the anniversary of that sad and sorry day, the gathering reconvened. The crowd now measured in the hundreds and became something of an underground festival—a paean to free and fragrant pork, and to the Pope by association.

The trailer was part of the diner purchase and Bow lived there while establishing his own enterprises. He and Darlene drifted apart fairly quickly. They never had a falling out but with him traveling so much in the beginning, and Darlene taking over the diner, and both busy with the legacy the Pope had endowed them, they made no heroic effort to maintain constant contact though they chatted or texted frequently.

Shortly after the initial wave of the first book's success, and after Darlene had taken command of the diner, she stuck her head in the door of the trailer.

"Busy?"

Bow was on his laptop working on figures. Large numbers are not a chore when they are yours.

"Hey. No, come in."

"I want to stay with you tonight. If that's okay."

Neither had been involved with anyone since the Pope died.

"That would be nice."

"I was hoping it would be."

He still slept on the foldout bed, leaving the Pope's area untouched. He patted the cushion beside him, beckoning her to sit. "Well, I thought you might have found a younger, more genteel man than myself, you being a maven now and all."

She sat. "I don't know what that means." She reached and held him close. "I wouldn't have the business if it wasn't for you."

"That was all the Pope's doing."

"Well, you didn't have to do anything with those books."

"How could I not?"

They became still, though not uncomfortably so.

"Bow. Do you still love me?"

He didn't know whether to run or fake amnesia. He gently caressed her hair. "I'm not sure we could ever really be together."

"That ain't what I asked."

"I have deep feelings for you. You kept me alive."

"Still ain't an answer. I know we probably wouldn't live together, or get married, or have kids, or any of that. I'm asking you a simple question."

"You think dating me for the next thirty years while I get old and you stay young would be enough for you? I don't think so."

"Stop changin' the goddam subject!"

He moved his fingers to her cheek. He studied every flaw in her misconfigured face. They were not difficult to see. "Yes," he said finally. "I still love you."

She peered into him as if the heavens had parted and granted her insight into all the treasured secrets of the universe. "I never want to be touched by another man but you."

Twenty-Eight

His fatal march to the sea had become an unexpected pilgrimage to stupefying success. The Pope had died exactly a year after Bow landed in Port Royal. Bow, on the other hand, had been remade. Just after signing the contract, vaguely optimistic, and before the publication of the first book and all that followed, he emailed his daughter. She emailed back immediately, providing her address in Charlotte and begging him to come for a visit.

The address was a twin home with tan siding and dark green shutters and door. Bow did a lap around the complex before parking. His hands were sweating and he felt ridiculous. He should have dressed for the occasion instead of jeans and sneakers. At least he wore a button-up shirt. He rang the bell and steeled himself for anything.

The first thing she said when she opened the door was, "Daddy, your hair!" He still had not cut it and a tail hung to his shoulder blades. She fell against him and wouldn't let go for a full minute. "I've been worried sick about you. I tried calling after I realized you were gone. You never answered your phone. Then it was cut off."

"I lost it," he answered, a reply that could address every question.

They sat facing each other on the sofa. She clung to his hand. The room was meticulous if a little sterile. Bow noticed the bump on her stomach and was surprised, but said nothing.

"We're still settling in," she said. "We want to move into another house with a yard in a few years."

"Good. Good."

Tears rose in her eyes but her demeanor never changed. "Can you tell me about it?"

"I will," he began. "But not right now. It's too long and I'm still trying to figure some of it out."

"And you're in Beaufort?"

"Port Royal, actually."

"You're going to stay there?"

"For the time being."

She squeezed his hand. "I never meant for this to happen. We were all in such pain. I still am."

"I know, Sweetie. I know."

She rubbed her stomach. "You're going to be a grandpa again. I'm four months along."

"Good," Bow said, but he could not hide his doubt.

"I know. Bringing another child into the world so soon. My therapist said she thought it was a good idea. That's not why I got pregnant again, of course. I'm ready to take care of someone again."

"I'm glad. You're a great mom."

"Daddy, we never meant for you to leave. Not really. We just needed some time, and then you were gone."

He stroked the back of her hand. "I know. So did I. But I was responsible. And you and your mom needed me out of the way to heal. And I wasn't strong enough to just sit tight until you were ready."

"We didn't mean to blame you. Everything was so out of control."

"You should have blamed me. I got it all wrong. And after that I was pretty far gone."

"None of that matters now."

"It does. It always will. I'm still trying to learn to live with it."

"I know. Her birthday was hard. Christmas was impossible. I took all her pictures down. I've put some back up, but not as many as I had."

"I just want to be part of your life."

"You will. You are."

"That's all I want."

She squeezed his hand again. "You talked to Mama?"

He shook his head. "Don't want to drag her into this."

"I know for a fact she'd like to see you."

"No," he said quickly. A cloud passed over his face. "I can't go back. To any of it."

She nodded. "I think I understand. Just think about it, okay?"

"Okay."

She reached to hug him again. "I need my daddy."

He closed his eyes, lost in consolation. "Thank you," he whispered.

"For what?"

"For taking me back."

After the book was released, Bow contacted a realtor to sell the old house. Union Hills hadn't changed. A single day could have passed instead of a year. Memories flooded his brain but nothing stuck. The town didn't care about the inefficacies of common men, their identities or even their presence. Perhaps people would have recognized him and whispered but he was not afraid. He just didn't belong there any longer.

The book's promotion, especially when the Martinez interview broke wide, had forced Elise Harris to answer unwanted questions, primarily about the Duke evidence. Bow was no longer powerless. She continued to claim that she had passed it along, but her hasty return into her stock campaign rhetoric aroused suspicion. Local media had asked him for interviews but he declined. No point in playing he said-she said when he had little to gain.

He went to see the Judge. The Judge eyed him suspiciously but greeted him warmly and had him sit in a guest chair across from the massive antique desk.

"Jesus, Bow. I wouldn't have recognized you if I passed you on the street. You gone native?"

"Wanted to keep things simple."

"You got your head on straight?"

"Yes. Still not done though."

The Judge sighed in commiseration, and Bow knew it was counterfeit. "I can imagine." He drummed his fingers on the arm of his chair. "So what can I do for you?"

"I see Elise is still in the congressional race."

He old lion scowled. "I heard about all the articles. I don't know why you would want to dredge all that up now."

Bow looked at him firmly. "I want it stopped."

The Judge was startled but tried to smile anyway. "Well...I understand how you feel, but I don't see you have much say in the matter."

He leaned forward and focused. The Judge saw an intensity he had never seen before. "She sold me out. I'm not saying she's responsible. *I* am responsible. But she let everything blow up in my face. And she lied about it. You have to know I wasn't stupid enough to blow off that stuff from Duke."

"Well, Bow, the whole district is behind her."

"I'm not having it."

The Judge tensed, both cheeks tightening inward. He eyed Bow meanly and spoke threateningly. "I don't know what you expect to gain, but you can't come in here and make foolish demands. Sounds like sour grapes."

He leaned even farther forward, his chin over the edge of the desk. "I'm telling you plain and simple. She sat on that package. You want to debate this in public, I'm ready."

"You can't prove anything. The public has a short memory."

"Yeah, well I know where all her boyfriends are. And they don't shake hands. Makes not one whit to me but I know this district. And the voters aren't going to like a candidate who has her own dick route, especially with three different guys."

The Judge raised his eyebrows at that.

"I'll give you a week. If she's still in the race, we'll go to war. Let it all turn to shit."

"Dammit, Bow, the election is two months away!"

"More than enough time to get someone else."

"What in-the-Hell has gotten into you?" the Judge demanded.

"You hung me out to dry, you son-of-a-bitch! After everything my father did for you. You're lucky I don't kick your ass."

"You're way out of line, boy."

Bow stood and rested his fist on the desk. "You fuck with me and I will light you up! I know where all the bones are."

"Get out of my office," the Judge sputtered.

Bow sat out where he and the Pope had talked on so many occasions—or where the Pope had talked and he had listened most of the time. The Pope's old Adirondack chair rested exactly as he'd left it. Bow had updated his chair with new, plumper cushions and matching ottoman. He sipped his flavored coffee and read the *Charlotte Observer*. He no longer used the diner for his Monday morning ritual. He had regular weekends off now. Weather permitting, he enjoyed hearing only the sounds of the woods and the river.

The front page of the Regions section had an article about Elise withdrawing from the congressional race and speculated on the reasons, none being even moderately close to accurate. The candidate herself had explained she had decided to stay on as interim district attorney until the seat officially came available next year and run in that election. No doubt she would win. The Judge had to offer her something.

The wind soughed and the river sang. The same sounds he had heard so many times. Now, these seemed somehow kinder, melting into the background like elevator music. Now, the ear was more finely attuned, composed in gratitude, a beneficiary of gifted forbearance.

A couple of years after the book buzz took on a life of its own, Bow purchased a small office building within walking distance of the diner. A subsidized health clinic already existed in town but moved to larger quarters, taking up the entire first floor, and at a cut-rate lease. He also made sure any budget deficit was covered, as every new administration seemed to take aim at the derelict.

He established free legal aid offices on most of the second floor, replete with two full-time attorneys, not counting himself, and two paralegals. One of the attorneys was Marvelette. She said she had never thought about being a bleeding heart before. Neither had he. Both were willing to learn.

Additionally, there was space for a full-time liaison to help anyone access all government or charitable programs available to them. Housing, employment, education, food, and grant opportunities were made available to every soul with limited resources thereabouts. There were separate agencies for these, of course, but here everything was under one roof—and much red tape was reduced to confetti with the concierge approach.

There were still people of want and need but everyone had a place to start and would never be without assistance if desired. Twice a year Bow took seasonal clothes in every size, and all genders, to the homeless shelter—enough to outfit over fifty people. If they ever ran short, he would make another run. Every employee of his and every employee of Darlene's met one Sunday a month to put together packets including socks, underwear, toiletries, and a couple of gift cards for food.

People who wanted to work were subsidized into de facto apprenticeships with companies willing to hire them afterward, or at least provide them with marketable experience.

Bow converted the third floor of the office building into a loft apartment. He would miss the trailer but Darlene needed a place for the new cook, who had recently been released from prison after doing twelve years for manslaughter and had learned to cook there. He didn't like to talk but was a good listener, which suited Darlene perfectly.

He kept in touch with his daughter but this was the only tie he kept to the old life. At times he still became depressed. Every so often he would still have nightmares of monsters with guns.

As years passed, and each book and movie was released, he was still invited to appear on talk shows and in bookstores, telling the Pope's story. Ivan Snedeker had become immortal.

He and Darlene adhered to a schedule. Every Wednesday and every Sunday night they would spend together. Even as she grew as a woman of means, she remained the child to his adult. Though no longer broken, the fiercest needs empty and toothless, they still clung to each other, laughed with each other, wanted each other. She remained blunt and straightforward and wonderfully off-center, and he continued to be its beneficiary.

Everything, one-step-at-a-time. Before, Bow had been a planner, just as all the other planners and executors who lived considerable parts of their lives in the future. Him, no longer. His days and weeks and years were met as they occurred, like all life, in small bites. Whatever came his way—chore or opportunity—he tackled step-by-step. Even Darlene's orgasms.

One-at-a-time.

As the Pope once famously observed, "Sometimes life gives us roses and sometimes it just wants to shove the bush up our asses."

Well, who really gives an Angus McBlowholer about that?

There was one journey left to take and it took a long time before he felt ready. Old wounds could be breached, and some, never fully closed, might gape open, chafe and blister. Even so, he looked forward to a nice spring road trip.

Four years after the tragedy, three after the Pope's demise, Bow began a pilgrimage. The success of the books was virtually assured. He was well into his new life, his *calling.*

He traveled to the small Wisconsin town on the St. Croix River where the Pope had lived. He walked the sidewalks of the compact downtown area. Most of the storefronts were new or redone. Gentrification had invaded, though the traffic was hardly bustling.

The narrow cubby that had once housed The Pipe & Page had been absorbed into the Family Dollar store next door. Everything it had ever been now unidentifiable. He did not know where the Pope had endured his day-to-day existence but the house wasn't so important. The Pope's real home was an old Airstream trailer a long way away.

An old-timer with a Panama hat sat on a bench in the shade of an awning and read the *Minneapolis Tribune*. He wore dark green work pants and shirt, and polished dress shoes, his legs crossed at the knee. Beside him on the bench was a tobacco pouch, the stem of a briarwood protruding.

"Excuse me, sir."

The old man looked his way.

"You remember when there was a tobacco store here?"

The man folded his paper neatly and uncrossed his legs. "Shakespeare's place?"

"No. Ivan Snedeker."

His eyes twinkled as he twisted to face Bow head on. “We all called him Shakespeare because he was always quoting some book or some such. Used to go in there all the time. All the old loafers did. He could blend some fine tobacco.”

“Sorry to say he passed some time ago.”

“I know that, Mr. Carter. I know why he left and I know he’s famous now for those books. And I know you’re the man behind it all.”

“No. Not behind it. I guess I’m just the custodian. He helped me when I was going through a really tough time. I was there at the end.”

“Heard you tell the story on TV. Stirred things up around here for a bit. Old Shakespeare. He was a great guy.”

“Yeah, he was. Been meaning to make this trip. Just getting around to it.”

“Well, there’s not much really. No sign saying he was from here or nothing like that. Nobody under forty would remember him anyway. Maybe someday.”

“It doesn’t matter. He was a different man when I knew him.”

“‘Spose he was. Didn’t have any close friends I know of. Never saw him after the store closed down. Nobody knew where he went, and nobody asked.”

Bow pulled the car key from his pocket. “Thanks for the info,” he said.

“Sure.” He snapped the paper and watched as Bow walked away. “Mr. Carter?”

He turned. “Call me Bow.”

The old man gestured to the seat beside him. “You want to hear about who he was?”

Bow smiled and approached. “I got nowhere else to be.”

He stood on a bluff high above the St. Croix. The ridge bore little resemblance to the river at Port Royal. The St. Croix meandered with sharp turns surrounded by verdant hills. Grasslands lined both sides, and small grassy islands lay scattered within. The river was rocky with white water in places. In some areas the bank was flush with the river.

There was commerce to be had—boat rentals, tours, slips with the toys of the moneyed. Here below the bluff was the river as the river, deceptively deep with desperate secrets beneath the current, too many to name. Bow tossed a rock from above and watched it fall safely short of the water. These were places the river owned and trespassers were unwelcome.

He wondered if the Pope had ever stood here, or in some similar place. He quickly realized how unworthy the thought was. The St. Croix was little more than an image from this vantage, empty of the sounds that had conducted the pair of them from one contemplation to another those many nights. The Pope would not have sought such a place as this, perhaps not even appreciated it.

The river in Port Royal held all their secrets in its cloudy depths, some sacred, none trivial. They had heard its song, its laughter, its genteel whispers. The river had accepted grief without judgment or provocation. The old stream was a holy place.

More importantly, the river south was where Ivan Snedeker settled to await the end of days, and where he drew his last breath. A pure and perfect sanctity had been established, now valuable beyond measure.

Few would know, and fewer still would remember, perhaps himself alone, where life's most reverent moments had fallen into solemn and divine obscurity.

For its part, the river had already forgotten.

The next morning, he drove southeast into the flat lands. The trip was six hundred miles and he made it the same day. He lost an hour with a dip south to avoid Chicago before heading east again. So much open space. Corn and soybeans, and a single plot of sunflowers. By late afternoon, he was there.

He was hesitant and on edge as he drove down the rutted dirt road. Small houses leaned against the wind and a couple of rusty mobile homes were scattered among fields of dust. This was the last of it, except in memory, and could not harm him, though he was still filled with dread.

He could have simply turned around and never have been missed.

The mother was not home. The girl answered the door. She was a young woman now, nearly grown. She looked malnourished, with thin, lifeless hair and red face, in gym shorts and a T-shirt and dirty bare feet. There was a stark intelligence in her eyes, however, and warmth in her cheeks.

She closed the door behind her and stepped out into the yard.

"Mr. Carter," she said politely, extending her hand.

"Bow," he replied, shaking it. "Where's your mom?"

"Working."

"Maybe I should come back later."

"Wouldn't make any difference," the girl said plainly. "She wouldn't know who you are or remember much of anything. And if you explained it to her, all she would do is ask for money."

"I could do that if it would help."

"I know. But she'd blow it inside a month and be right back where she started from."

"Maybe you can help me then."

"Of course." Then she walked toward the car.

He watched after her. "I take it we're going somewhere."

"You came to see him, didn't you?"

They spoke little except for the directions she provided. The place was beyond the outskirts of the small town in the country. The day was as drab as the landscape. In the distance the water tower and the light poles from the high school football stadium could be seen.

The site was much larger than he expected. Several hundred plots were spread over at least ten acres and beyond that a short rise hid at least a hundred more. The dead were stuck just as they had been in life.

The graves beyond the knoll were newer, all with inlaid stones flush to the ground. The girl led the way on the concrete walkway toward the hilltop.

He glanced side-to-side as they moved, seeking nothing in particular. He would not recognize anyone anyway. There was not a tree in sight, the ground clinging to the elements alone.

"We're trash," the girl said suddenly, and in a matter-of-fact tone.

He stopped cold, looking on in disbelief. "Why would you even think that?"

She shrugged her tiny shoulders. "We are. No point in pretending we aren't."

"I know that's not true," he said helplessly.

"Don't patronize me."

"I'm not. That's a decision you make for yourself. No one else can make it for you."

"Maybe. I was born trash. But if I can escape someday, maybe I will. I'm just saying you have more reason to be grieve than we ever did."

He felt a familiar twinge, as bearable as second nature. "None of it should have happened."

"Something would have happened to him sooner or later. He tried to be good to me, but that doesn't mean he was a good person."

"Who do you think he was?"

"He was a thief."

"He was also a brother and a son."

Again she hunched her shoulders. "He was trying to get free of this place and his life ever since he opened his eyes. He just didn't know he couldn't."

At the crest of the hill she turned and looked at him. Her face was full of tenderness and understanding far beyond her years. "You and me, we live with it every day. Everybody else has moved on and will hide it where they won't see it any more unless they dig. And nobody in his right mind will want to dig."

"How old are you?"

"Seventeen. Almost eighteen."

"You don't have a part in this at all. You don't have to live with it."

"Yes. I do."

"Why?"

"Because I loved him." Then she pointed down the path. "Fourth or fifth row. On the left. In a few."

Bow stepped lightly as if he might awaken the spirits who rested there. She did not follow. He found the grave easily and stood at its feet. He read the simple bronze plate, revealing only his name and the dates.

He gazed down for a long time. A replay of the events flashed in his mind as if hurled from the pistol that had rerouted the course of his life. The movement played out even as he prayed for quick passage.

The pain cut from within, as if a wide blade rested between his lungs and now sought the light of day. Long wounds erupted vertically and diagonally, until the tip pierced the last bit of flesh and everything in its track bled freely.

Tears pooled and threatened to flow.

"I'm sorry," he whispered. "I am so sorry."

Bow later discovered that Sharonia was a senior and an honor roll student, and had been accepted to Indiana State University but had not enrolled. He hired a local attorney and set up a scholarship fund for her on the condition she attend class and graduate. Her counselor would monitor her progress and see things along. Her education, at least, was secure. She could break away if she wanted. No one could ask for more. This was the least he could do.

Finally, and at long last, all the dead had been buried.

FINALE

What then is the true value of being? Is life a bounty unto itself? Does the existence of heart and breath imply the presence of a soul, even among the mindless, or wanting of all senses? What if not? Is completeness only an arbitrary measure influenced by life, but only for those who wrestle disaffection tooth and nail.

What of those who possess every sensation, every faculty, strive to use every facility, but who are vexed by environments they cannot flee—poverty of land, poverty of soul—the inescapable presence of want? Are these to prize their lives in reverence, even as time brings no relief, no remedy, perhaps not even a fleetly passing speck of empathy? Does a different, more inert, God hear their prayers? Can there be sufficient nobility in simple survival to be life?

Are those of malady and trial without amelioration and cannot possibly be enlivened without miracle, when miracles are happenstance, and perhaps one for many millions, also expected to revel in their misfortune as beneficiaries of divine impulse? Is salvation surely the capacity to withstand and endure regardless of experience?

Alive is alive and living is living?

Even among the hardy, want appears and transforms ripe into spoilage as surely as spoilage decays. For these, recollections of contentment must serve the good. If all recall ceases, yet the rest machines onward, these, too, are caught in the will of heaven, to bear until impending night.

The mortal are simply not allowed to imply their own destinies.

How is this just, much less perfect?

To exist is to seek all that is attainable, beginning with all things in close proximity, elements within reach, easy to grasp, and whose orbits do not deviate. In these are the roots of perception, the plausible means to progress into the further and higher. These reveal goodness, and the benefits of enjoying serenity, felicity, accord—to the lesser and flawed like desire, ardor, and aggression.

All, by design or serendipity, channel into love—endowing and accepting—regardless of any others. There is no greater footing, no matter how confounding in the time to come.

Even the freely obtained cannot always be held, and only superficially absorbed. Love may recede. Love may sour. Love may wound. Love may be undone.

Love also prevails and rises from unexpected places.

At the outset, whatever goodness is out of reach, is still approachable with patience and persistence. Some treasures are exaggerations of those at hand and more visible. Some possibilities are too sophisticated and remain untouched without greater understanding. Some truths are impossible to interpret without the full knowledge and retention of the lesser, more visible components.

Even the best at hand are not sufficient deterrents to ills and despair. The all-encompassing is too confusing, has too many parts—too many separate voices—and cannot be consumed or repaired by any singular effort. Deficient outcomes can be mitigated, but are apt to be survived more than overcome.

The universal basis for life and livingness provides a trio of media to animate and enhance. One cannot continue whole without the least of these attitudes brought into being.

First, all are granted the capacity to love. Whatever the extent, no matter the adversity or complication or misfortune. To be at all—even without becoming—is to hold fondness for something, no matter how much or how little. Unreasonable and beyond bounds, perhaps, the opportunity to rise remains.

Secondly, all possess the potential to be loved. No goodness can penetrate the walls of humanness without one being held in regard by another. Desired or not, accepted or not, transient or not, limbs will wither and breath will expire in such a hollow as to be unloved. There is no other device, no alternative means, to circumvent this requisite. To be valued by another in any part is the sole opposition to extinction.

Lastly, all should be inclined to love others not of blood or union. Anyone in need, excluding none, may so easily subscribe to their own deformity they may seem irredeemable. They no longer hold the reality of spirit, even as they think and feel, their lungs expand and their hearts palpitate. This is more than duty or requirement. The restoration of counterparts creates the atmosphere for amity, for mutual pleasure, for one to unexpectedly revive another.

Then, we are uplifted into life.

Life is all we have. No matter the distance from transcendent felicity, the moment-to-moment rendering of consciousness, the recognition of environmental tendencies, and the possibility of supernal movement, *life,* without exception, binds us all.

Despite whatever currents await us, set in motion before we existed, these things must be enough.

No awareness is perfect, but none more perfect than this.